Unmasking Mr Kipper

Unmasking Mr Kipper

CHRISTOPHER BERRY-DEE

SMITH GRYPHON
PUBLISHERS

DEDICATED TO
Tracey, Zoe-Jane and Sasha-Louise

First published in Great Britain in 1995 by
SMITH GRYPHON LIMITED
Swallow House, 11–21 Northdown Street
London N1 9BN

A CIP catalogue record for this book is available from the British Library

ISBN 1 85685 097 8

Typeset by Action Typesetting Limited, Gloucester
Printed in Great Britain by Butler & Tanner Ltd, Frome

Contents

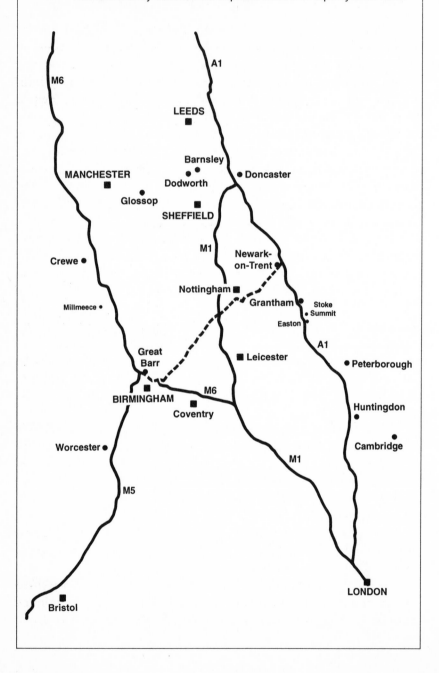

MICHAEL SAMS The key locations

----- The route taken by Sams to drive Stephanie Slater from captivity to her home

Acknowledgements

The study of violent crime – indeed, working with the killers of society's children on a first-hand basis – can be, at once, rewarding, exciting and distressing. But at the end of the road, the time comes to reflect on the journey and to remember all those individuals and organisations who, in their various capacities, helped to make the book possible and, hopefully, worthwhile.

First, I would like to thank solicitor David Payne who so honourably discharged his professional duties in defending the cryptic killer, Michael Benniman Sams. With his client's permission, David made available thousands of case papers and hundreds of scenes-of-crime photographs. Without his assistance, this book would have been a non-starter.

I would also like to thank Teena Sams, the wife of this errant offender. Teena supplied over 50 letters written by Sams from his prison cell, along with dozens of personal documents never before published. This cooperation has been extremely painful for her as she has had to relive almost every month of her marriage to a man who turned killer and kidnapper seemingly overnight.

Iris Walker, Sams' mother, allowed me access to other material, and it was through her help that I was able to visit Sams in Full Sutton prison. Her recollections of her son's formative years proved invaluable.

For information on the legal, medical and police aspects of Sams' heinous offences, one had only to turn to the case papers. The West Yorkshire and West Midlands police forces also helped both officially and otherwise where they could. Several names spring immediately to mind, yet I have honoured their requests not to be named in the text.

The Home Office provided much valued cooperation during the research, and responded quickly to any enquiry made, especially of the Prison Service and DOC1 Cleland House.

As always, I am indebted to Robin Odell who has co-written several books with me over the years. Without his continued support, this book would have been even more difficult to write.

For their personal support, perhaps now is the moment to thank all those who were patient enough to listen to my thoughts on Michael Sams during the last three years. The book would never have come about but for the love and encouragement given by my wife Tracey and my two daughters, Zoe-Jane and Sasha-Louise, who lost their father to his work for weeks on end.

Much gratitude goes to my parents, Patrick and May, and also to Bob Noyce whose analytical thoughts have gained me access to many a killer's dysfunctional brain.

Special thanks are extended to Frazer Ashford at Mainline Television, to Derek Block, and to my editor, Nancy Duin, who completely polished the final manuscript. Also to Robert Smith and Helen Armitage of Smith Gryphon, along with Professors David Canter and Elliott Leyton who support my research and writing about the criminal mind.

Finally I must not forget Michael Sams who, for all the wrong reasons, gave his permission for and cooperation to the project. He had much to say – unfortunately for him, almost every word is unprintable.

Introduction

On Monday, 28 July 1986, Suzy Lamplugh, a London estate agent, left her office in the Fulham Road to meet a client who had previously booked an appointment under the name of 'Mr Kipper'. A vivacious 25-year-old blonde, she took with her the keys to 37 Shorrolds Road where she was to meet the man at 12.45 pm. Despite a massive police investigation, she has not been seen since, and Suzy is now presumed dead. Murdered.

In June 1991, two more female estate agents narrowly escaped being kidnapped for ransom. Using exactly the same *modus operandi* as 'Mr Kipper', and selecting another house with vacant possession – 71 Westminster Street in Crewe – a mysterious 'Mr Lettin' tried, on different days, to lure both women to the property. On the first occasion, a local tradesman working nearby struck up a conversation with him and he left before the estate agent arrived. When 'Mr Lettin' tried again, for some reason he walked away as the woman approached him.

Two weeks later, a Leeds prostitute was attacked by a punter and only escaped with her life because she fought off her assailant. After throwing a brick at the windscreen of her client's car, she ran off into the night. Later she described the vehicle as a small orange car, and gave an excellent description of the man who, she said, had had an artificial leg. These details matched those of the man who tried to kidnap estate agents in Crewe.

On 9 July 1991, an attractive part-time prostitute was snatched from the seedy red-light district of Chapeltown, Leeds – the same spot where the earlier attack on the prostitute had occurred. Ten days later, Julie Anne Dart's naked body was found wrapped up in a sheet in a remote Lincolnshire field. She had been bludgeoned about the head, then strangled.

During the following weeks, her killer sent mocking, yet deadly serious letters to the police, demanding £140,000 in used notes or he would kill again. Then his game took another evil turn. He threatened to firebomb a department store, and made an attempt to derail an Intercity express train carrying hundreds of passengers. There was a homicidal maniac on the loose.

On the morning of Wednesday, 22 January 1992, a cold winter's day, estate agent Stephanie Slater was kidnapped after meeting 'Bob Southwall' outside a vacant house in a suburb of Birmingham. He went on to demand £175,000 for her safe release. The killer of Julie Dart had struck again.

Despite a police operation involving hundreds of officers from many police forces, the one-legged criminal escaped, on a moped with a box on the back stuffed with money, to disappear into thin air. Within hours, Stephanie, who had been held captive for eight days, was dropped off by her kidnapper just yards from her home. However, a neighbour spotted a little orange car and a dishevelled Stephanie talking to the driver.

The nation's police had few clues to the identity of the man they were hunting, so they turned to the public and a BBC programme, *Crimewatch UK*, in a last-ditch effort to orchestrate his arrest.

The day following the broadcast, Michael Benniman Sams was arrested at his workshop in Newark-on-Trent, and on 8 July 1993, the judge imposed life sentences for Julie's kidnap and murder and Stephanie's kidnap and unlawful imprisonment – four life sentences in all. He also handed down ten-year sentences, to run concurrently, for each of four blackmail charges. The murderer showed no flicker of emotion or remorse as he was escorted to the cells beneath Nottingham Crown Court.

I had developed a 'relationship' with Sams well before his trial and, after a year of frustrating negotiations with the killer and his solicitor, gained access to some 30,000 case papers. These included 400 police photographs, plans, medical and mental health records, and business papers, which covered Sams' crimes and history.

After meeting Michael Sams' mother and his wife Teena, I also took possession of the orange Metro car, the moped and Sams' camera, along with hundreds of photographs, a computer and virtually every official document concerning Sams, from birth certificate to last will and testament – passport, driving licence, academic records, running certificates. I studied them all carefully before meeting Michael Sams for two hours in Full Sutton prison.

No analysis of dreadful events such as these would be complete without examining the life and behaviour of the criminal responsible. Michael Sams is the principal character in this drama.

British society has chosen not to put these malefactors to death. If we are to spend hundreds of thousands of pounds of taxpayers' hard-earned cash accommodating this human scum – some of whom, claiming they are deprived, smash up prison property with regularity and assault hard-pressed prison officers – are we not entitled to ask for a little reward in return? For Michael Sams, like so many others of his killer breed, does have something to offer us all.

Unlike the American penal system, the Home Office will not permit easy access to these murderers for journalistic enquiry, and so the deviants sit in their cells, preserved like blowflies in amber. But if we could align their past antisocial conduct with their present thoughts – dysfunctional as they might be – society may just learn a little more about what makes evil tick. Armed with that knowledge, we might be better equipped to understand the behavioural patterns of other emerging killers, and apply that to prevention. It has to be better than murder, detection and imprisonment. The present system merely allows us to lock the stable door after the horse has bolted.

Over the years, I have worked closely with over 30 serial killers and other mass murderers. I have cooperated with American law enforcement agencies, the judiciary and all other crime-related professions. On a recent trip to the United States, where I work frequently with the most dangerous men and women alive (many on Death Row), two of the killers confessed to me previously unsolved homicides and rapes. As a result of these interviews, the police and states' attorneys are now clearing up these matters with the offenders' cooperation.

This book attempts to expose homicidal violence – indeed, the mind of a killer – far better than any words from Michael Sams himself. Society might never know the full extent of Sams' criminal activities; that information is locked away inside his head. However, this book rips away his everyday persona, his mask of sanity, and investigates whether, along with all his other crimes, he could be 'Mr Kipper': the kidnapper and killer of Suzy Lamplugh.

Christopher Berry-Dee
Hampshire
England

ONE

Michael Benniman Sams

Michael Benniman Sams entered this world at St John's Hospital, Fell Lane, Keighley, West Yorkshire, on 11 August 1941, born to Iris, a 25-year-old shopkeeper, and Ernest Edward Benniman Sams, a corporal in the 2nd Battalion, Duke of Wellington's Regiment. Another son, John, was born on 20 April 1945. This marriage ended in divorce in 1949, after which Iris married Sidney Walker. Michael was just nine years old, and it was his stepfather whom he came to call 'Dad'.

After demobilisation and the divorce from Iris, Ernest became a milkman. In 1962, he was employed as Post Office sorter before being promoted to postman. Shortly afterwards, he was caught in an ingenious fraud that enabled him to win bets on race after race at the horses. The scheme involved filling in betting slips with the known winner of each race, franking the envelope with the previous day's postmark (the franking machine being readily accessible in an unlocked cupboard at the post office) and then posting the bets. This gave the erroneous impression that the bets had been laid and posted before the race results were known. However, the odds of such continual good fortune were so enormous that a local bookmaker – suspicious of Ernest's run of good luck – called in the police. Mr Sams was arrested and sent to jail for six months. Young Michael not only came from a broken home, but his natural father was a fraudster.

Michael did well in school, showing a particular aptitude for the piano. In March 1951, he was awarded – 'With Merit' – the Trinity College of Music student's certificate in the 'First Steps Division'. In June of the same year, he gained a second-class certificate with 81 points at the Wharfedale Music Festival.

Michael also showed a keen interest in athletics. At the age of 11, he won second place at the Riddlesden Church of England School's annual sports day, held on 22 July 1952. That month also saw another music certificate drop through his letterbox. He had passed, with flying colours, the Trinity College of Music's student examination in the 'Preparatory Division'. Later in the year, he was also awarded the college's 'Theory of Music' certificate.

It seemed as if a month didn't pass without the boy winning something. June 1953 saw him proudly clutching the college's 'Junior Division' award; then he entered the Skipton and District Music Festival, gaining another certificate of merit. Iris and Sidney Walker being religious, Michael had to attend Sunday School, and while at the Keighley Methodist Circuit Youth Department, he sat for a lettering competition, attaining 55 marks and, of course, another diploma.

Apart from music and sport, Michael was particularly fascinated by the railway, and he took up train-spotting. For hours on end, he'd sit on grass-covered embankments and stone bridge parapets, watching the giants bellowing plumes of steam and smoke as they hurtled past him.

After passing the eleven-plus, Michael progressed to Keighley Technical School, where he gained 'O' levels in maths, chemistry and technical drawing. On 15 February 1958, when he was 16, he entered a cross-country race held by the Yorkshire Schools' Athletic Association at Shadwell, and gained third place in the inter-team event. Later that year, he passed 'O' levels in additional maths and physics.

From Keighley, he entered Kingston-upon-Hull Nautical College. In one year, he earned a certificate of great practical value, entitling the holder to present himself for examination as a second mate (or second hand on fishing vessels) after three-and-a-half years' instead of the obligatory four years' sea service. The nautical college also passed him in three further 'O' levels: mechanics, navigation and seamanship.

At the age of 19, Michael Sams joined the Merchant Navy. Photographed in his Clan Line dress uniform, he appears to have been a homespun young man, with a peak cap jauntily topping a high forehead that seems to indicate intelligence. For three years, he sailed the high seas, visiting most of the Mediterranean ports as well as Africa, India and Pakistan. Sams certainly had the ability to carve a successful career out of the merchant fleet, but secretly he pined for his native Yorkshire and the basic comforts to be found in Keighley. He resigned.

Immediately after leaving the Clan Line, he began working for Robert Clough, but stayed at the cotton mill for just a month before moving to Keighley Lifts, one of the largest and most established employers in the area. His mechanical skills and intelligence were soon recognised, and before much time had passed, he was charged with installing lift equipment across the country and overseas.

In 1962, the firm were contracted to install equipment at Sams' previous employers, Robert Clough. Fate now intervened. Sams was just 21 when he was introduced to employee Susan Little. Their romance blossomed over the following months, and they became engaged on her 19th birthday.

To many who knew her, Susan was the type of girl that every mother would want her son to marry. Pretty and neat, this was a quiet young woman from a respectable family. She and Sams were married at the parish church on 18 July 1964. For him, this was to be the first of three marriages made in Heaven that would end in Hell. And years later, Susan would be the woman who would send him to prison.

As a suitor with old-fashioned Christian values, Sams had lived apart from Susan during their courtship, at 24 Newlyn Road, Riddlesden. But now that the knot had been tied, the newlyweds purchased a home of their own, a recently built semi-detached house at 10 Providence Crescent, Oakworth. Sams continued working at Keighley Lifts until 6 May 1966, when he resigned to take up employment at Shorts (Lifts) Ltd.

His interest in athletics grew. During the next two years, he won many awards, and over the following decade, he was classed among Britain's top runners. He was certainly the most competitive member of the world-famous Bingley Harriers during that time, and on 30 April 1967, he completed the arduous annual Three Peaks race – rocketing over the summits of Ingleborough,

Pen-y-ghent, and Whernside in North Yorkshire, in 3 hours, 42 minutes, 8 seconds.

Over the years, Sams completed many a hard race in first-class time. For an individual of his stamina, intelligence and insatiable appetite for hard work, he would perhaps have been better suited to his younger brother John's choice of career – Her Majesty's Royal Marine Commandos.

In September 1968, the Samses' first child, Robert Edward, was born. Sams now claims that Susan behaved as if she were the first woman ever to bear a child, always needing to be the centre of attention. As for Sams himself, he not only had a mortgage and general bills to pay for, he also had a wife and child to support alone, for Susan had left her job at Robert Clough. With the bills mounting up, he started searching for a better-paid job, and in 1969, he joined Viewdell, a Bradford firm that installed warm-air central heating systems. Then, at the end of that year, Susan told him that she was pregnant again. Sams decided that, to survive, he would have to become self-employed, and he formed Axiom Heating Ltd, which he ran from a small office at home.

He then subcontracted his skills to Viewdell, whose offices were located in the middle of Bradford's notorious red-light district. When leaving their premises at night, he couldn't help but notice, even admire, the dozens of provocative, mini-skirted hookers, flaunting and selling their bodies. There is no doubt that Sams was aroused by these seemingly attractive women, for he would return many times to this form of low life – twice with the intention of abduction and homicide.

The workaholic pushed himself hard, but it was soon clear that he couldn't do everything himself. Susan helped with the paperwork to some extent, but if Sams wanted to expand his business, he would need a partner. He approached Keith Glennon, a former sales manager at Viewdell, who agreed to join Axiom Heating as co-director responsible for sales while Sams concentrated on installation and supplying parts. After a few months, they took offices in Manor Road, Bradford. Keith Glennon was to recall those early days when he was interviewed by the police many years later:

Michael was responsible for the company money and paperwork. He was a bright man technically – a very good fitter. But he was disinterested in the paperwork side, and somewhat neglected that aspect of the business. His spelling was very poor, as was his written grammar. Orally? He was fine.

Susan, too, later summed up Axiom Heating and her husband's commitment to it, in a written statement:

The company quickly became a very profitable enterprise, largely due to hard work. He would work long hours every day of the week; he was obsessed with success. He did dream of becoming a millionaire, but it was the thought of success that drove him on.

So Michael Sams was apparently able to apply the same competitive spirit and determination to his work as he had to sport and music. As the company expanded, the partners took on new staff in every department. Susan remembered many of these employees, but one particular name burns in her memory – that of Carl Metcalf, of Woodlands Drive, Howarth.

On 13 July 1970, the couple's second son was born, and they named him Charles. The Samses were now flush with money, so Susan went house-hunting for a more substantial property – more in keeping with their rise in society. They settled on a former nursing home called 'Oakfield' – a large detached residence in Low Spring Road, Thwaites Brow, Keighley. Within months, according to Sams, they started mixing with other fast-living people in the locality. He regarded them with derision, and later said that all and sundry – including the Samses – attended 'no-holds-barred parties where anything was acceptable, including wife-swapping'. But whether this is fact or simply a figment of Sams' twisted imagination, we may never know.

About nine months after setting up Axiom Heating, the two partners decided to expand into double glazing. Renting a small industrial unit at Acme Lane, Wisbey, they named this new venture Axiom Insulation Ltd, with both men enjoying the benefits of equal shares and stock to ensure fair play. The new enterprise started off well, so they employed a secretary, which released Sams to get on with what he was good at. Now he was earning *real* money.

On 30 April 1972, Sams entered the Three Peaks race for the

third and final time. In the first-class time of 3 hours, 23 minutes and 17 seconds, he finished in a blaze which he modestly attributed to a fast downhill run to the tape. And it seems almost as if, as he reached the end of the race, his life also began to take a downward turn.

In 1974, Sams fell ill, and it was thought that he had contracted meningitis. He was rushed to Airedale Hospital in Steeton, where extensive tests were carried out over two days. But it remained a mystery illness, which the medical staff could only ascribe vaguely to some form of viral infection.

Then, four weeks later, without explanation, Sams suddenly announced that he was going to sell his shares in both Axiom companies, to start something new. This decision came as a shock to his partner Keith and his wife Susan, for the two businesses were financial successes. Both tried to talk Sams out of this crazy idea, but his mind was made up. Nevertheless, the two partners went their respective ways on excellent terms.

Quite what compelled Sams to take this plunge into insecurity is uncertain – even he cannot adequately explain why. Perhaps it is worth noting that Viewdell, the firm that had used Sams as a subcontractor, went out of business at about that time. Sams might have been under the misguided impression that he could pick up all of Viewdell's former customers, giving him an excellent client base for a completely new central heating business. Later investigation into Sams' physical and mental states at the time would also give some clues to the reasons behind this drastic step.

Whatever the reason, Sams had learned few lessons from his previous work experience. While he did pick up a small number of Viewdell's clients, the question remains: why didn't he do this under the secure financial umbrella of Axiom Heating and Axiom Insulation? The break with Axiom proved to be the biggest business mistake of Sams' life. He threw away everything he had built up – and the Inland Revenue lost track of him for six years.

Sams' abandoning of this lucrative source of income also affected Susan. She had become accustomed to his mood swings, and she has since claimed that he had always had an 'obvious cruel streak'. 'This did not manifest itself often, but after the hospitalisation, it took him over completely,' she was to tell the police. She added that he became vicious and spiteful, but while she saw the change in him, others noticed nothing. In her statement to the police, she said: 'From that moment, partly due to the fact I had begun to grow up and become more assertive with Michael, and partly due to his mood changes, our marriage began to break up.'

To the few who knew the Sams family, Susan indeed changed, and it was rumoured that she had had what Sams would call a 'personal operation', the precise details of which are unknown. A close friend of Susan's in those days, Amy Rusby, explained: 'Young Susan went from Ugly Duckling to Beautiful White Swan overnight.' Gone were the frumpy clothes that Sams liked to see her in, and she took to wearing low-cut blouses and tight dresses. She became the life and soul of every party and, without doubt, one of the most attractive and vivacious women in the locality. In her own words, Susan had suddenly 'grown up' at the age of 31.

The time of recriminations had begun. Sams was now suffering all the problems inherent in starting a new business. As if playing a game of Snakes and Ladders, he'd climbed to the top, within a throw of wealth and happiness, but now he was back at square one, with only himself to blame. Susan, perhaps justifiably, was furious with her husband. After all, it was partly through her support that he had built up the Axiom businesses, and now she had to watch helplessly as their lives crumbled into ruins. And maybe she was justified, too, in seeking other interests. For years, she had been left alone with the children, never venturing out to live a life of her own; now, for a short while, she helped the Samaritans as a counsellor. As her love and concern for her husband gradually seeped away, Sams came to believe that she was rejecting him. He wasn't far wrong.

Today, when faced with accusations of neglecting his wife and sons, Sams defends himself rather pathetically by claiming that, during the summer holidays of 1975 and 1976, he spent a 'great deal of time' with his two boys. In a letter to his solicitor, David Payne, he wrote:

> I took them everywhere. To London a few times, the Tower of London, Natural History Museum, HMS Belfast, plus numerous other places they were interested in. We went to the Edinburgh Museum, various steam railways up and down the country. Sometimes by car, or sometimes by train.

The letter ends with a touch of bitterness:

> *On not one occasion did Susan go with us. This is easily born [sic]out by the fact that only the children appear on any photos. There was never a second adult to appear on them. In a way I suppose I was using the children as a substitute for my problems with Susan.*

In July 1976, the couple took their children on holiday to Morocco, in a last-ditch attempt to keep their marriage alive. While it was all laughter, ice creams and sunny days on the surface, the basic problems were not far beneath. At Pontin's M'Diq Holiday Camp, the two boys, following in their father's footsteps, won certificates in the sandcastle competition. Photographs show the two hot and happy children playing gleefully, while just yards away, up the beach, their parents are discussing what would prove to be an acrimonious divorce.

The family took a day trip to Gibraltar. Sams was keen to relive his early days with the Clan Line. First, he showed the boys the docks where his ship had tied up, then they rode the cable car to the top of the 'Rock'. Susan went off alone, shopping.

The boys then insisted on walking back down hundreds of steps to see Gibraltar's Barbary apes. Halfway down, Sams' right leg started to ache from an old running injury. He'd had problems with the knee in the past, but now the pain was excruciating. This was exacerbated when Sams had to hoist Charles on to his shoulders to carry him down the mountain. When they arrived back at M'Diq, Sams was in agony.

For the remainder of the holiday, the couple argued constantly when out of earshot of the children, who were having the time of their lives. During one heated exchange, Sams struck out at his wife, who promptly hit him back. There were long periods of sulking, when they refused even to acknowledge each other.

When the Samses returned to Keighley, the couple agreed on a trial separation. Susan would leave the marital home, taking the boys, and Michael would stay, running his new business from the third, now spare bedroom. On 20 August, Susan packed her bags and left.

During the following months, Sams saw his family frequently. Susan claims that his irrational behaviour continued almost unabated, but former friends say that the Samses were at each other's throats one moment, while pledging mutual undying love the next.

Nevertheless, now that she had time, alone, to reflect on life with her husband, and what a future with him held, Susan came to the conclusion that their marriage was dead in the water. With Sams' grudgingly offered financial support, she bought a house of her own in nearby Riddlesden, while he ended up in hospital for a minor operation on his right knee.

Some time after Susan had become pregnant for the second time, Sams had had a vasectomy. He has since claimed that he was 'cheated', for his wife left him after he had had the operation that destroyed any chance of him fathering children in another marriage.

No thorough investigation into the mind of a killer would be complete without studying the medical and psychiatric history of the offender, and we would do Michael Sams and ourselves a great disservice if an exception were made here.

The first document that I unearthed from his medical records (supplied as part of the trial papers to Sams' defence lawyer) confirms that, at the age of 35, Sams – suffering from depression – was pouring out his troubles to a Dr Egdell, a psychiatrist to whom he had been referred by his GP, Dr Pierce. Sams explained that he and Susan were separated but hoped for a reconciliation. In the same breath, he added that, a few days previously, Susan had told him that this was the furthest thing from her mind. He felt 'strangely relieved' about this.

No doubt lying back on the obligatory couch, Sams told the psychiatrist that he had suffered from attacks of depression, often becoming very moody. This substantiated what Susan had long been complaining about. Sams also mentioned severe frontal headaches, and that he'd had a vasectomy some four years earlier.

Looking through the family doctor's notes on his patient, Dr Egdell noticed that a consultant, a Mr Kavanagh, had X-rayed Michael's sinuses, the empty spaces in the bone on either side of his nose. These appeared not to be blocked, which was a healthy sign. But to be on the safe side, Dr Egdell decided to have them X-rayed again.

Following Sams' session with Dr Egdell, Dr Pierce had a talk with Susan about her estranged husband. He promised to look into Sams' viral infection, which could have been meningitis.

There is no reference in the medical notes to indicate that Sams received any psychiatric assistance or counselling other than that one interview with Dr Egdell. However, it is interesting to note that Sams had begun to suffer from acute headaches right after he was stricken with the viral infection, and then, four weeks later, he had packed in two profitable business ventures. Thereafter, he was the victim of sudden personality changes, when he would turn spiteful and vicious at the drop of a hat.

By now, Susan had found alternative male company, and Michael was not slow in following her example, chasing anything in a skirt. His ego had been damaged, and he needed to feel wanted again.

One of his customers phoned him from Leeds, asking if he would come and look at her central heating system. He would later write that he had 'fancied' her from the outset. Soon after this renewed encounter, they were having sex and Sams had fallen in love. But the woman was not all she seemed. She was a prostitute, and when Sams discovered the truth, he cut off all contact. The relationship had lasted only two months.

Through these stormy days, Michael paid maintenance to Susan. Then, in May 1977, they were divorced. A month later, Susan met hairdresser Alfonso Grillo, who was to become husband No. 2. Grillo rented premises in North Street, Keighley. To keep on good terms with his ex-wife in order to have access to his sons, Sams offered to renovate the salon at a reduced price. Afterwards, a bitter dispute ensued, and Sams stopped Susan's maintenance payments. However, he was soon hauled before the courts, and was jailed for seven days for contempt of court after he stuck up two fingers at the magistrate.

And contemptuous he certainly was. He had lost two thriving businesses; his lovely wife had fallen for a Latin lover; he was denied access to his children; and, to cap it all, he'd just spent a week locked up in the local police station. Feeling aggrieved, it was perhaps inevitable that he turned to his only friend – Carl Metcalf, formerly of Axiom Heating – for moral support.

Metcalf – whose name Susan was to remember so well – had known Sams since 1972, when he had worked for his company on a commission-on-sales basis. Those were the early days of double-glazing, which soon became popular with energy-conscious homeowners. Double-glazing salesmen were thick on the ground, but Carl was to lead the pack. With his good looks and smooth patter, he proved to be an excellent and persuasive salesman, equally able to sell spectacles to blind men and ice-makers to Eskimos.

Sams, the more introverted of the pair, was fascinated by Carl, but Carl did not share Sams' passion for the piano and running up and down mountains. Nevertheless, the two became close friends.

In 1976 – the date will become significant later – Sams had a discussion with his friend, during which he told him about a perfect plan to commit a kidnapping, only releasing the hostage after a substantial ransom had been paid. Carl, who thought Sams was simply indulging in fantasy, was quick to point out that everyone got caught trying to collect the cash. Sams had all the answers. As he outlined his scheme, it became more deadly with every twist and turn.

The plan entailed leaving a holdall containing a two-way radio in a left luggage locker at St Pancras station in London, which would be picked up by a courier on Sams' instructions. The courier would place the ransom money in the bag, then board a train bound north for Leeds. During the journey, Sams would make contact via the radio, and when the train reached a designated stretch of track, the courier would be ordered to throw the booty out of the fast-moving express – Sams had already chosen the drop-off point. He also knew, with his intimate knowledge of railways, that even if the courier pulled the communication cord, the driver would not be able to bring his locomotive to a standstill in under half a mile. By then, Sams would have picked up the money and got well clear of the area.

This intriguing plan appears to have been fatally flawed, for it relied in no small part on the efficiency of a two-way radio, which can be temperamental at the best of times. And success also depended on split-second timing: just a few seconds either way could mean the money missing the drop-off point and Michael Sams altogether.

Sams, however, was not to be put off by mere technicalities. He had already chosen his kidnap victim, he said. She was in her late teens or early 20s, recently married. Her father-in-law was supposedly a millionaire. Sams had already calculated that his divorce had cost him in excess of £30,000, with maintenance and other losses. He needed to recoup this, and there was no way he could do that by fixing customers' hot-and-cold water systems.

Carl later remembered Sams saying that they would take the woman to Oakfield and, removing her clothes, keep her captive in the cellar. Any ransom instructions would be prerecorded on a tape recorder. As a further precaution to prevent the victim's escape, the only door to the cellar would be reinforced with steel plate.

Shortly after Sams related his 'fantasy' to Carl, three men smashed their way into the home of newlywed Sheila Danby, daughter-in-law of a wealthy farmer and meat trader. The helpless and terrified woman was tied to her bed while the house was ransacked and valuables were stolen. The horrific experience shattered Sheila's life and she never recovered from it: a year later, she committed suicide.

Sams' early plan to commit a kidnapping came to light in 1992, after he had been arrested for the murder of Julie Dart and the kidnapping of Stephanie Slater. It was then that Carl Metcalf remembered the conversation with Sams and told the police about it. They, in turn, recalled the Sheila Danby case. No one was ever arrested or convicted for this earlier robbery, or is likely to be. However, it is curious that Sams' intended victim was, according to Metcalf, living in Riddlesden, and Sheila Danby resided in the same village ...

So it can be seen that, by 1976, Michael Sams was taking an unhealthy interest in serious crime. This interest could only have been heightened by the fact that, on 14 June of the same year, the trial of a kidnapper and multiple killer began. His name was Donald Neilson, dubbed by the media 'The Black Panther'.

Neilson was convicted of wounding and shooting to death a number of postmasters during a spree of armed robberies. He then went on to kidnap and murder 27-year-old heiress, Lesley Whittle. This killing, which must rank as one of the most brutal in British criminal history, came about as the result of a bungled ransom bid that went tragically wrong. After abducting Lesley from her bed at night, Neilson kept her – naked, tied up and with a wire noose round her neck – deep in a vertical drainage shaft at Bathpool Park, near Kidsgrove in Staffordshire. The kidnapper's plans went awry after a passing police car drove into the park. In a moment of sheer anger and frustration, Neilson kicked Lesley from the steel platform on which she had been standing, and she died with the steel wire noose deeply embedded in her neck.

Sams avidly followed every aspect of this shocking case as it unfolded in the press, and today, one can make close comparisons between the two men's crimes. This is all the more disturbing when one considers that kidnaps linked with homicides are extremely rare events in European countries, with the sole exception of Italy. Sams openly admired Neilson, to the extent of copying the Black Panther's *modus operandi*. Both men kidnapped young women with the intention of making ransom demands for their safe release. Neilson stripped Lesley Whittle, and Sams told Carl Metcalf he'd remove his victim's clothes, too – indeed, he later stripped Julie Dart. Neilson used letter drops, phone boxes and a tape recorder, along with stencils and alpha/numeric Dymo tape, to convey his demands. Sams used exactly the same tools and methods. Finally, there is this chilling statement that Neilson made to detectives after his arrest.

> *I discovered the drainage system in Bathpool Park while I was looking at the* railway line, *and planning that the money could be dropped from a* train. *[Author's emphasis]*

Of course, this was, more or less, the same plan that Sams had discussed with Carl Metcalf. Later in the same interview with police, Neilson had this to say:

> *My last act [with Lesley Whittle] would be to make sure she understood fully what was happening, and to make sure she was on my side. Throughout the entire plan, she was my ace. When released, she was the person who would have to give any information to the police.* She would tell them that I treated her well. *This would not have led them to pursue me with the same campaign of hatred that they did. [Author's emphasis]*

When we later examine Sams' treatment of Stephanie Slater, we will find him using identical tactics. If he treated the young estate agent well, he reasoned, she would tell that to the police, and he therefore hoped they wouldn't pursue him quite so vigorously. However, what Sams might consider 'good' treatment was experienced as something very different by his ultimate victim.

●

It is a matter of public record that, in November 1977, Michael Sams, Carl Metcalf, Roy Wood and Sidney Barnes were arrested and charged with criminal deception. This case involved the stealing of a young woman's motor car, altering its appearance and making a false insurance claim. Sams was the first to be interrogated – after he was spotted foolishly driving the stolen vehicle around Keighley. His first, somewhat selfish, reaction was to spill the beans and name his accomplices. Then he suddenly withdrew his admissions to the police. From then on, he was treated as a hostile witness, which did nothing to endear him to the judge at his forthcoming trial.

On 24 April 1978, he appeared for sentencing with his cronies. Sams received six months' imprisonment for taking a car without consent, three months (to run consecutively) for attempted deception, topped up with one month (to run concurrently) for fraudulent use of an excise licence. He also acquired a Criminal Record number: CRO 41894/78v.

Sams thought he'd been given a raw deal, for his co-defendants had all received lighter sentences. Not only that, but while he was awaiting trial, Oakfield had suffered serious fire damage. Although the police and fire brigade treated the incident as arson, no one was ever apprehended or charged. The fire was to have even wider-reaching consequences. The event proved to be the pivotal turning point in Sams' life, after which he slid quickly down the slippery slope into homicidal violence.

Several days after the fire and two months before his trial, Sams was trying to repair a window on the first-floor landing. His right knee – the cause of so much pain despite the minor operation in 1976 – simply gave way, and Sams plummeted to the ground, landing on a pile of debris.

Sams' medical records show that he was in agony after this fall, and he was prescribed large weekly doses of painkillers – Distalgesic and Fortagesic – which relieved much of his suffering. To help him sleep, he was given Mogadon, a relatively powerful sleeping pill.

Within days of being incarcerated in Armley Prison (where he was to catch sight of Donald Neilson), Sams started complaining of agonising pains in his right leg. The weekly supply of painkillers and sleeping pills had been withdrawn the moment he had walked through the prison gates.

The jail's surgeon, Dr Choudhury, prescribed mild painkillers, and when Sams' knee started to swell up like a balloon, the doctor referred him back to Mr Norton, the surgeon who had operated on his knee. The latter simply recommended 'activities'.

Unfortunately for Sams, neither the pain nor the swelling went away, and he was left to suffer excruciating pain 24 hours a day. It felt as if a drill was being inserted into his leg and was tearing every nerve, muscle and sinew to shreds. His mental torment was further increased when he learned that his brother John had been killed following a motorcycle accident while home on leave from the Royal Marines.

As the months dragged on, Dr Choudhury referred Sams to another specialist, who asked Mr Norton to forward the medical notes made when Sams had been operated on in 1976. Norton replied that they had been misplaced; however, he would look for them. It appears that Dr Choudhury was anxious to help inmate Sams, but the prison doctor was hamstrung. Despite his good intentions, he was only a medical piggy-in-the-middle, able only to pass the buck and prescribed aspirin or paracetamol.

Was Sams malingering? No. A visual examination of Sams' leg would have shown clearly that something was seriously wrong. Sams' medical notes – to which I have had access – confirm that he was prescribed large quantities of pain-relieving drugs and sleeping tablets right up to the week of his incarceration.

Here we should ask ourselves: why should these medical problems be of interest when studying the mind of Michael Sams? How does a swollen knee and unrelenting pain assist us in attempting to unravel the thought patterns of a killer?

Part of the answer lies with the fact that Michael Sams had cancer and it was spreading fast. If his sentence had been a few months longer, he might have died in the prison hospital. Deep down, Sams felt that he was going to die, and ultimately, the delay in treatment cost him dearly. The running fanatic would soon lose his leg.

This man had entered prison a small-time crook, perhaps a robber and, without doubt, a person who, at the very least, planned kidnapping and extortion. But in the eyes of the law, Sams had not committed a criminal offence – had received not so much as a parking ticket – until he became involved in the theft of that one car.

While in jail, with time on his hands, he reflected back over the years. He reasoned that he was an intelligent man, and God only knew how hard he'd worked to make good. His marriage had been on the rocks for years, and he had effectively lost his two sons and now his only brother. Perhaps he found it rather convenient, even comforting, to lay his problems at the feet of others, especially Susan.

Every brick of the prison reeked of the sweet stench of disinfectant, urine and stale sweat. There was never a moment's peace, day or night, with cons screaming at each other across landings and wings. To Sams, this was a human dustbin – a stinking warehouse storing only low life. Reality stared him in the face: he was one of them.

Sams' mind began to transform him into someone bitter and twisted. One evening, while racked with pain, he sat down to itemise his personal profit-and-loss account. Studying it allows us a rare glimpse into the mind of an emerging killer.

I have lost the following:
(1) Freedom for six months (with parole).
(2) A wife, 2 children and our £20,000 home. £7,600 was her share of the house.
(3) £500 I paid for the first car.
(4) £100 I paid for the second car (both cars were recovered by the police).
(5) £600 I have lost through having to sell my present car while in detention.
A total loss of £8,000.

But now consider the loss to others ... Over the next five years we have:
(1) Loss to over 1000 customers £300,000 (an average of £300 for each customer whose central heating would break down when I am unavailable to service it).
(2) Loss of money owing by me to my suppliers, whom I will not be able to pay when my firm collapses £4,500.
(3) Loss of my tax to the Inland Revenue, plus loss of VAT to Customs & Excise over the next five years £10,000.
(4) Cost to Government for my imprisonment for 6 months, £35 pw I am told = £875.

(5) Supplementary Benefit I will have to be paid when I am released as I do not forsee [sic] employment in the next 5 years £7,250.

A total loss to the Government and others of over £322,625.
(Government departments will directly lose or have to pay out £22,625.)
Add to this the loss to myself and you have a staggering loss of over £300,000. All for the loss of one motor vehicle to a young lady for 5–6 weeks.

By the time my release comes in October, I should be a very bitter person ... SOCIETY OWES ME AND I WILL BE REPAID.

Quite what punishment Sams would have recommended for himself is unclear. But one thing is sure: a few months later, the bitterness would grow to become an all-consuming hatred, when his right leg was amputated above the knee. What price would he place on that?

TWO

Jane Marks and Teena Aston

When Michael Sams was released from prison, he was referred back to Mr Norton. On 10 November 1978, the surgeon picked up his surgical saw and severed half of Sams' right leg. Although this operation undoubtedly saved the man's life, it did little to improve his state of mind, for he believed that, had the leg been treated much earlier, it might have been saved.

Just before Christmas, he was again seen by Mr Norton, who wrote in his notes that his patient was 'making excellent progress', adding, 'He has a sound stump.' Sams was not exactly buoyed up by these comments, for he was having to come to terms with a lifelong handicap. A few months later, when Sams remarried, his wedding photographs portrayed a gaunt, frail, grey-faced ghost – putting on a brave show for the guests.

While in prison, Sams had spent much time studying history and writing letters to a woman he'd met while awaiting sentence. Despite grieving the loss of Susan to Alfonso Grillo, he was always scouring 'lonely hearts' columns for prospective lovers. He met Jane Marks (*née* Hammond) after replying to her advertisement in the *Yorkshire Post*. She was younger than Sams, had been married twice before, and came from the seaside town of Cleethorpes on South Humberside.

Susan – now Mrs Grillo – had won the legal dispute for overdue maintenance payments owed by her former husband, and Oakfield had been taken by the bailiffs. With no roof over his head, Sams moved in with Jane at her house in Norman Row, Leeds. He was unemployed for the first time in his life, and still hobbling around on wooden crutches waiting for an artificial limb to be fitted. This, however, did not prevent him from driving a car. Sams was often to brag about how he'd fooled the law by illegally using a crutch to work the accelerator and brake pedals.

The couple had only been married a very short time when Jane realised that she'd married the wrong man yet again. Sams had become a listless, argumentative millstone around her neck. They started to row, and she went completely off sex.

Sams later agreed that he did change for the worse, but as usual, he has a convenient explanation, laying the blame for his behaviour at the feet of others. In a letter to me, he wrote:

> *Jane saw this change and told me. But I didn't believe her, or didn't want to believe her. To my mind I loved all women and wouldn't harm any woman. I certainly never did anything violent towards Jane. It was the reverse.*

Sams went on to allege:

> *She often pushed me over and had a go at me. But even though Jane kept telling me I had changed, I didn't believe her. The crash came when we were turned down for adopting due to the fact I had only recently been released from prison.*

In reality, Sams knew that his second marriage was going the same way as his first but a damn sight faster. He resorted to threats and intimidation to prevent Jane from leaving him, going as far as saying that he would get a pistol and shoot her dead.

Whether Sams had access to firearms at the time is unknown. Nevertheless, the threat so terrified Jane that she forced him out on to the street and slammed and locked the front door. She had been reduced to a quivering wreck. There had been something evil in her husband's eyes, and his quiet, soft voice had carried sinister undertones. She asked herself, 'What if he does come back to shoot me?'

In a state now bordering on hysteria, she fled that same evening to stay with a friend. The following morning she returned with a hired van and hired help, and removed as many of her possessions as the truck could carry. Michael Sams has neither seen nor heard from Jane since; they were later divorced.

The degree of loss that he claims he suffered at losing wife No. 2 can be gauged by a statement he made to me in 1992: 'Once more I surrounded myself with beautiful girls.' These 'beautiful girls' were prostitutes whom he met in a public house in Bradford. He was using the red-light districts of the north to trawl for nightly sex.

On 20 November 1979, Michael Sams answered an advertisement that he'd seen in the *Yorkshire Evening Post*, placed there by the tool-making firm Black & Decker, based in Leeds. A search by me through its personnel records revealed that Sams commenced work with the company on 2 January 1980 in the position of 'workshop repairman'.

During the next two years, he lived first at 1 Neville Mount, then at 16 Woodview Mount – both in Leeds. Just before Christmas 1981, he was asked if he would move to the company's workshop in Birmingham. Sams took up the position with the proviso that Black & Decker contributed towards his relocation costs.

He moved on 4 January 1982, taking up residence in a modest new property at 139 South Road. Then, in a burst of property speculation worthy of any serious Monopoly player, he sold that house to purchase 57 Short Heath Road, within a stone's throw of Witton Lakes and the Leak Hill Recreation Ground in Short Heath. It was while living here that he met the woman who was fated to become wife No. 3.

Teena Sheila Aston was born 31 May 1949. Her father, Robert Christopher Aston, had been a well-decorated soldier, having served with valour in the Rifle Brigade throughout World War II. Teena's mother, Elsie, had worked at a children's home before taking up long-term employment with Elbies, a handbag manufacturer.

Like Jane, Teena had already been married twice when she fell in with Michael Sams. Again, like Jane, each of her attempts at marital bliss had ended in dismal failure.

On 5 November 1968, the 19-year-old Teena gave birth to a

son, Paul. She was then living with her parents in Yardley Wood Road, Birmingham. Six months later, she married her child's father, William James Hegarty. The marriage lasted a mere 15 months.

For a few years, Teena brought up Paul alone in a flat in Sisefield Road. Then she met her second husband, Graham Cooper. By all accounts, he was a reasonable man who worked as a painter and decorator for the local council. This marriage might have lasted but for Graham's interest in Teena's very pretty niece, Denise. While Teena readily admits that she is a little 'dim' at times, perhaps it is more correct to say that she was naïve. Her marriage of two years came to an end when she discovered that her husband was enjoying a full-blooded affair with Denise, who had just left school. (They later married.)

If both of her marriages had given Teena sadness, there was the consolation that Graham had at least left her with some security in the form of bricks and mortar: 818 Yardley Wood Road, just down the road from her parents' house, belonged to her.

Sometime in early 1982, Teena placed an advertisement in the 'lonely hearts' column of the *Birmingham Evening Mail*. She received 20 replies, one of which was from Michael Sams. He sent her a photograph, she rang him – she liked his soft, quiet voice – and they agreed to meet. Teena later told me her first impression of Sams: 'He was very kind and considerate. We went out nearly every night. I would either visit him at Short Heath Road or he would come to my house.'

They frequented the Billesley Hotel, which, in those days, had a singles' club. The courting couple didn't smoke or drink to excess, and a few friends reckoned that they were marriage material. Therefore, it came as no surprise when they became engaged 18 months after first meeting. They would marry in November 1988, after living together for about six years.

It wasn't long before the rot set in. Teena and Sams started to argue about the most trivial of issues. However, the spark that ignited most of the blazing rows was unwittingly caused by Black & Decker, who had asked Sams to move once again, this time to their Coventry workshop. Teena put her foot down, refusing to let him go. Surprisingly, he acceded to her demands and accepted voluntary redundancy, with a pay-off of £3590.60, which he banked on 27 September 1985.

With over three grand in his pocket, Sams started up on his

own again. Black & Decker had taught him how to service power tools, so he looked around for suitable premises comprising a shop and workplace. The ideal choice proved to be 42 Oundle Road in Peterborough, for it included a small flat above a shop. Sams leased the building, which he transformed into Peterborough Power Tools Ltd. He opened a trading account with Black & Decker, and within weeks, he was repairing all manner of electrical equipment – not only that made by his former employer, but also Bosch and Skil products. Just as before, Sams did most of the work, in between travelling to and from London where he frequented trade exhibitions. The paper-work? Well, he listed his accounts in a scruffy, oil-stained notebook, which Teena would later transcribe into something more legible.

Sams quickly purchased another property, 10 Orchard Street, which he refurbished and rented out. Then came 22 Jubilee Street and 29 New Road. It seemed as if he were buying up half of Peterborough.

Teena was also in the property market, albeit not on the scale of her fiancé. She tried to sell 818 Yardley Wood Road in Birmingham, while taking out a mortgage on 215 Oundle Road. She and Sams never moved in, and eventually, at some serious financial loss to herself, Teena disposed of both houses before moving into the flat above Peterborough Power Tools.

Quite how many properties the Samses owned or rented between them remains a mystery. On the surface, it appeared that Sams had settled down, having learned something from his previous mistakes. However, a study of his Inland Revenue records paints another picture. When investigators finally tracked him down years later, they discovered that his personal finances had been in dire straits, and Peterborough Power Tools had fared no better. Given access to an Inland Revenue document, I noted this comment:

From records we can say that Peterborough Power Tools Ltd, throughout the period of trading, made negligible profits, indeed, in some years had substantial losses. We can also say that the remuneration drawn by both directors – Mr and Mrs Sams – was consistently low, supporting the belief that the company was not a very profitable concern.

Given that assessment and the fact that the Samses owned and leased many properties from which they drew rent, it is obvious that Michael Sams had been fiddling his taxes. In my exclusive interview with him at Full Sutton prison, I touched upon this subject. He said that, having been ripped off by the system far too often, he had enjoyed doing the same to the tax man.

Having yet again taken the self-destructive plunge into financial ruin, Sams was becoming violent and abusive towards Teena. Like the proverbial lemming, he was teetering on the edge of the abyss.

And there was something else worrying Teena during those fretful months. The causes for concern were her husband's frequent trips to London and his secretive digging in the garden of 29 New Road, Peterborough. Sams had always welcomed Teena to see any renovation work he carried out, but, she told me, he almost forcibly kept her away from this address. Her recollection – seemingly untainted by the passage of time – is that Sams excavated a large hole in the garden which he then proceeded to in-fill with rubble. This was no mean feat for someone with his disability – the effort required must have been enormous – and with just a third of the work done, he contracted some labourers to finish the job with hard core and top soil several metres deep.

Nine years later, the police half-heartedly excavated a well in the garden of 29 New Road in their search for the body of a missing woman, whom they thought could have been Suzy Lamplugh.

THREE

Suzy Lamplugh

At around 12.40 pm on Monday, 28 July 1986, 25-year-old estate agent Suzy Lamplugh left Sturgis Estate Agents in the Fulham Road, West London, to meet a prospective client. Her desk diary recorded the bare details. She was to meet a 'Mr Kipper' outside 37 Shorrolds Road, a property with vacant possession and an asking price of £128,000.

Driving her white Ford Fiesta, index number B396 GAN, the journey from her office to Shorrolds Road should have taken about eight minutes at most. There is every indication that she planned to return to her desk after the appointment, for she had left her handbag there.

A resident of 35 Shorrolds Road, 58-year-old unemployed bachelor Harry Riglin, spotted a young couple looking appraisingly at No. 37 next door. Riglin seems to have been quite taken with the man, whom he later described as 'handsome, 25 to 30 years, 5 feet 8 inches tall, medium build, clean shaven with thick, combed-back hair, looking prosperous in smart dark suit'. On the face of it, Riglin's description hardly seems to fit that of the 45-year-old, one-legged Michael Sams. Riglin took little notice of the young woman.

The next possible sighting of Suzy Lamplugh was made by Barbara Whitfield, a partner in a flat-finding company. Having met five months earlier, the two women had frequently gone to look at flats together. Barbara was sure that she saw Suzy driving her white Fiesta along Fulham Palace Road towards Putney and the River Thames at around 2.45 pm; a man was sitting next to her. 'I was absolutely certain it was her,' Barbara later told the police. She was unable to give a decent description of Suzy's passenger.

The estate agent failed to return to her office, and at 5 pm, the manager telephoned Suzy's mother to enquire about her whereabouts. Diana Lamplugh contacted the police, who started a massive hunt for the vivacious young woman who was described as 5 feet 6 inches tall, medium build, with blonde-streaked hair, wearing a peach blouse, black jacket and grey skirt, two rings and stilettos. But Suzy seemed to have simply vanished.

Details of her car were logged into the police computerised dispatch system and flashed to all mobile patrols and beat offi-cers in the area. Shortly before 10 pm that night, PC Chris Dollery reported from his vehicle that he had discovered the missing car, facing north, on the eastern side of Stevenage Road. This cut-through to the busy Fulham Palace Road ran parallel to the Thames. Nearby was Craven Cottage, the Fulham Football Club stadium, and between Stevenage Road and the river were various wharfs, warehouses and shady business premises.

A cursory examination of the car provided evidence that it had been abandoned in some haste. Not only was it badly parked, but the handbrake was off and the driver's door was unlocked. Suzy's straw hat was on the rear parcel shelf, and her purse was stuffed into the driver's door pocket.

As the search for Suzy gained momentum, Harry Riglin ela-borated on his story by telling a police officer that he now thought that the young couple had been arguing outside 37 Shorrolds Road, and that the woman had been bundled into a car. Although this later proved to be something of an exaggera-tion, the police were now very worried indeed.

According to a stream of other witnesses who now came forward, a young woman answering Suzy's description had been spotted all over south London. Then Riglin remembered that the good-looking man had been carrying what appeared to be a bottle of champagne. Another description of the man was given by unemployed jeweller Nicolas Doyle. He claimed that the man standing outside 37 Shorrolds Road was between 25 and 30, with dark swept-back hair and wearing an 'immaculate and expensive' charcoal grey suit. His nose looked as though it might have been broken at some time. Doyle had got the impression that he was an ex-serviceman or a former public schoolboy who had been injured playing rugby. Alternatively, he could have been a very well-dressed East End criminal.

In all serious criminal cases, a successful conclusion relies a great deal on the descriptions and timings given by witnesses. In this case of apparent kidnapping, problems over timings occurred from the outset.

A woman telephoned the police, saying that she lived in a house in Stevenage Road, almost opposite the spot where Suzy's Fiesta had been found. Mrs Wendy Jones recalled that she'd first seen the white car on Monday at about 12.45 pm. It had still been in the same place a couple of hours later, and when she had returned from the cinema at about 10.30 pm, the vehicle had been surrounded by police officers. If Mrs Jones's evidence was correct, Suzy must have driven straight from her office to Stevenage Road. There was support for Mrs Jones's first sighting of the Fiesta at about 12.45 pm: Mrs Mahon, a near neighbour, had also noticed the car parked there at the same time. The police quickly established that both women were reliable and level-headed witnesses, able to give accurate timings for their movements.

This new evidence cast doubt on whether Suzy had been Shorrolds Road at all that day. If she had left her office at about 12.40, she could not possibly have had time to drive there, meet 'Mr Kipper', show him around the property and get to Stevenage Road a mile away, all within five minutes. The alleged sightings and timings of Harry Riglin, Nicolas Doyle and Barbara Whitfield also now appeared distinctly shaky.

Over the years, the Suzy Lamplugh case would prove to be totally frustrating from an investigator's viewpoint. The facts – if one could call them that – merely tell us that Suzy left her office at about 12.40 pm on Monday, 28 July 1986, to meet a 'Mr Kipper' outside a house with vacant possession. She may have been seen viewing the property with a well-dressed man who may have carried what might have been a bottle of champagne. There may have been a struggle on the pavement, and Suzy might have been forced into her car against her will. Barbara Whitfield may have spotted her friend in the Fiesta with a man at around 2.45 pm, but then, Mrs Jones and Mrs Mahon might well have been right when they said that they saw the car parked in Stevenage Road well before that time, at 12.45. However, most police officers say that only two real clues exist: the time Suzy left her office and the time her car was found. What happened in between and after remains a mystery.

During the search for Suzy, many suspects were interviewed to no avail. There was nothing in her personal life that might have led her to run away – she was a very happy young woman. However, there were a few other things worth examining.

The first of these was the driver's seat in Suzy's car. It had been pushed back from its usual position, the notch used by any woman of Suzy's height. It could be that someone taller than the usual driver had driven the car that fateful day. We also know that the car had been parked badly askew in Stevenage Road, with Suzy's purse and a few other personal effects left inside the unlocked vehicle. Therefore one might conclude that Suzy had been hurriedly and forcibly taken from the car, moved into another form of transport and spirited away. Kidnapped.

'Mr Kipper' was obviously an alias; the police could trace no one of that name. People started calling them, suggesting that the first two and the last four letters in 'kidnapper' spelt 'Kipper'.

The Metropolitan Police later concluded that Michael Sams could not have been responsible for Suzy's kidnapping. One officer claimed that it was 'impossible' for Sams to have been in London on Monday, 28 July 1986, but he would not say why.

As later events would prove, Sams certainly thought of young female estate agents as victims. He was perfectly able – despite his artificial leg – to lure a victim into his own car, tie her up and move her long distances. We now know that he was quite capable of murder and the disposal of a body. Therefore, when we draw the strings of Sams' criminal history together towards the end of this book, we will find that it is quite conceivable that Michael Sams *was* Mr Kipper.

However, for the moment, we must return to his life with Teena in Peterborough.

Teena made every effort to support and please Michael throughout 1986, and the pattern lasted into the following year as she scraped together enough cash to buy a house for her son Paul.

During these turbulent times, Sams notched up GCEs in history, English language and geography at a local college. Nevertheless, none of these academic achievements appears to have assisted him in the management of his business and property affairs. He was constantly staring bankruptcy in the face, and needed money desperately.

In February 1988, Sams approached Joseph Jennings of DJD Financial Services Ltd at his office in Cross Street, Peterborough. This was very much a last-ditch effort to raise cash to pay off mortgage arrears and a string of Peterborough Power Tools' angry suppliers. Sams needed to explore the potential of raising capital on 10 Orchard Street, the mortgage of which was also in arrears.

Sams' application for a loan was successful, but the £30,000 he received didn't quite resolve his immediate problems. After repaying the arrears of another mortgage, he was left with the princely sum of £3000, which soon disappeared after he paid a few outstanding bills. Broke once more, he again turned his thoughts to kidnapping a woman and demanding a substantial sum for her release.

The first problem Sams had to overcome was finding a reason to leave Peterborough and Teena. However, accomplishing this was easy because he had a ready-made excuse. He would say that he was going off on one of his train-spotting adventures; there was nothing unusual about this to arouse Teena's suspicions.

His next task was to locate an estate agents' office in a town with quick access to the motorway network – for once he had the woman in his car, he had to be able to transport her as quickly as possible some distance to a hiding place. Sams decided to drive south-west towards Bristol via Birmingham.

He had to cover all eventualities. For one thing, it was obvious that he would have to return home to Teena with a clutch of photographs to substantiate this train-spotting trip, so he decided to drive and stop off at all the major towns and cities between Peterborough and Bristol, taking pictures while searching for a likely target. Photographs that I unearthed show that Sams did just that. One of the towns was, significantly, Worcester.

After arriving there, he wandered into Foregate Street. Nearby was a large post office which suited his plans exactly, and further down was the Star Hotel, which at the time was undergoing extensive renovation. With his Praktica MTL5 camera, fitted with a Miranda 28mm 1:2.8 lens, he snapped a picture of the estate agents Andrew Grants at 59/60 Foregate Street – one of seven branches of a chain.

Although Michael Sams admitted to me that he had looked

for an estate agent to kidnap during 1988, he would not give the precise dates of his reconnaissance. However, an examination of the photographs that he took during this trip point to July. The one of the Andrew Grants office shows not only the estate agents, which is clearly the focal point of the picture, but also the Star Hotel and a Citibus. The shadows show a time around noon, and the Citibus provides clues which further narrow the time frame. After I contacted the owners of this bus, Midland Red West, area manager Colin Aldridge sent the following report based on the photograph taken by Sams:

1. *The Wyvern sticker on the offside window of the bus was fitted from February 1987. The photograph could not, therefore, have been taken before this date.*
2. *The vents on the front of this vehicle were modified from January 1989, which means the photograph was taken before this date.*
3. *The blinds on the bus appear to have numerals on the left-hand side. This type of blind was fitted in October 1987. This means that the photograph was taken between October 1987 and January 1989.*
4. *I telephoned the Star Hotel – which, in the background of the photograph, had scaffolding erected around it – and spoke to David Galvin, operations manager. He advised me that, while the hotel was being refurbished in 1988, the scaffolding had been erected for only a month or so – after June 1988 and before end of August. It would appear, therefore, that the photograph was probably taken in July 1988.*

Fortunately, for whatever reason, Sams did not kidnap an estate agent in 1988.

In September, two months after Sams returned from his 'recce', Teena's son Paul, who had been training for a career as a male nurse, died from a viral infection that had affected his brain. Devastated, Teena appeared to lose all interest in life and in the business for which Sams had worked so hard. She begged him to agree to move away from Peterborough, and when he refused, she withdrew into a world of her own, which included rejecting all physical and sexual approaches from her husband. This led to many bitter arguments, and to nights when Teena slept in the spare bedroom.

Sams realised that he was in a no-win situation, so he decided to consider carefully Teena's demands to leave Peterborough, the town that now held so many sad memories. For a start, he wasn't getting any sex, and this was driving him wild. Added to that, he no longer had Teena's cooperation in Peterborough Power Tools, and his accounts and general paperwork were in a terrible state. Then there was the growing list of irate creditors – if he were to survive in business, he would have to pay these suppliers off quickly.

In the end, Sams decided to move his home and business out of the area. If nothing else, that would resolve some of his domestic problems. In addition, at the age of 47 he finally married 41-year-old Teena at the town's register office in November 1988. He promised that they would go house-hunting.

The idea of a move also appealed to his devious business mind: he could virtually dump Peterborough Power Tools. First, though, he would have to find other business premises close to his new home. The couple settled on the quiet Nottinghamshire village of Sutton-on-Trent for a house and the market town of Newark-on-Trent for a workshop. In a rare romantic mood, he decided to call the new firm T & M Tools – Teena & Michael's Tools.

FOUR

Plans for Kidnapping and Murder

With a move in mind, in June 1989 Sams was back in Joseph Jennings' office asking for further financing. This was timely as the arrears on another of Sams' properties were piling up, and indeed, 29 New Road, where he and Teena were living, was also under the threat of repossession.

Sams soon sweet-talked his financial adviser into looking for a mortgage for him, pulling out of his pocket estate agency details for Eaves Cottage, Barrel Hill Road, Sutton-on-Trent. The yarn he spun was simple: Teena owned 29 New Road, the house was now up for sale, and he anticipated a quick disposal. Of course, there was no mention of repossession. Eaves Cottage was selling for £88,000, and Sams needed at least £73,000 from a building society. He told Jennings, with hand on heart, that as soon as 29 New Road had been sold, the borrowing would be reduced by at least £23,000, leaving a mere £50,000 mortgage, which was well within his means.

Looking back over that period, Teena told me that she knew nothing of her former husband's application for a loan from Mr Jennings, and that the stories that had secured it were so much pie in the sky. Peterborough Power Tools had been losing money hand over fist, a fact that is substantiated by the Inland Revenue, which would report that Sams' business in Peterborough had been a financial disaster.

Nevertheless, the Halifax Building Society accepted without question Sams' application made through DJD Financial Services. Sams also took out a bridging loan for an unlimited duration, a loan that, even in his wildest dreams, he would never be able to repay legally. When he moved into Eaves Cottage, he rented out rooms at 29 New Road, but pocketed the cash payments rather than paying them to the Halifax.

As soon as contracts were exchanged, the couple drove up to their new home every weekend to decorate, ferrying paint and building materials back and forth in Sams' clapped-out gold Rover SDI. For a short while, Teena was in her element, and was thrilled to move into her 'dream cottage' with her Yorkshire terrier Mimi and two German shepherds, Tara and Bonnie.

The Samses soon realised that they could no longer run the failing Peterborough Power Tools from such a distance, so Michael Sams started to look for business premises. He found the ideal workshop advertised in the window of Richard Watkinson & Partners of 17 North Gate, Newark.

Part of this company's responsibilities was to manage premises in the nearby Swan and Salmon Yard off Castle Gate, on behalf of the owner, William Saunders. In early 1990, the latter decided to rent out Unit 32C, once a coaching inn but more recently a rundown sail loft and filthy warehouse. Sams wandered into the estate agent's office with an offer of £1950 a year. He went on to demand a rent-free period of three months, during which time of non-trading, he would, at his own expense, renovate the unit for his purposes.

References were required, but Sams had no problem providing them. Letters from Barclays Bank and his solicitors, Search & Company, were accompanied by a trade reference from Tec Power Tools – the only one of Sams' suppliers to whom he did not owe money. A lease for Unit 32C was soon drawn up, signed, and Sams moved in.

At first, Teena managed T & M Tools, where she spent much time painting the walls and generally tidying up the place. Sams would commute daily to Peterborough using his British Rail disabled-person pass. It seemed that hardly a day went by without a county court judgment dropping through the letterbox of the almost-defunct business. His Peterborough properties were being repossessed, he was £16,000 in debt (not counting the mortgage and bridging loan for Eaves Cottage), unpaid suppliers were freezing his accounts, and two credit card companies were chasing him for money. Peterborough Power Tools finally folded in March 1990, and Sams sold on the premises' lease to a former customer, Roger Tuttlebee. He moved his stock up to Newark, leaving a string of creditors in his wake and the taxman at his heels.

Finally in residence at Swan and Salmon Yard, Sams built a counter and put up shelves that doubled as a partition to separate the sales area from the workshop at the rear of the building. However, high on his list of priorities was an alteration to the wiring, for he intended to get his electricity supply free, and to do that, he would have to bypass the meter.

After cutting through the high-tensile wire to gain access to the terminals, he added an extra circuit breaker which was, in turn, connected to the live incoming cable set in the outside wall. He plugged the hole with an oily rag. All he had needed to make the connection was a cable clamp and piercing screw. Limping around in rubber boots, he added a junction box to his illegal system, into which he could plug all manner of appliances. The extra circuit breaker was insurance, just in case he overloaded his *gratis* supply and brought East Midlands Electricity engineers running from all directions.

In 1992, one of these engineers examined Sams' handiwork at the request of the police (who probably thought that, if Sams got away with murder, they could at least nick him for stealing electricity). Stewart Hall calculated that, over two years, Sams had extracted an average of 5.8 units of electricity a day – a miraculously low amount considering that this was an electrical tool repair shop.

During the early months of 1991, husband and wife argued frequently. Teena claimed that Sams spent far too much time at work, leaving little time for her – which was all very reminiscent of his behaviour towards his first wife Susan. Teena now says that Sams, when he *was* at home, would often provoke an argument just to give himself an excuse to leave the cottage. He would storm out, often not returning for hours or even days. A friend recalled Sams saying that, if Teena didn't buck up, he'd drive to Leeds or Bradford to find a prostitute. He certainly knew where to look.

Teena was a sad figure at this time. Plagued by memories of

Paul, she pulled out of the business. Sex with her husband was almost non-existent and she began to think of leaving him, but she changed her mind when Sams agreed to their adoption of a child. Because Sams had had a vasectomy, the question of adoption had cropped up frequently – Teena longed for another child, and this route was the only possible solution. Unfortunately, shortly after applying to the social services in Newark to adopt, Teena was forced to rescind the application, with the very real excuse of not being able to afford a child at this time. They would reapply when things improved. Sams must have secretly rubbed his hands with glee.

With Teena so depressed, Sams decided to cheer himself up. He decided to scrap his Rover and buy another car. He'd seen an orange Austin Metro on the forecourt of John Emmingham's garage in Skellingthorpe. Despite having had a string of owners (all of whom had lavished tender loving care on it), the car had only a genuine 40,000 miles on the clock. Sams paid for it with £1800 in hard cash.

His only other means of transport at this time was a plum-coloured Suzuki 'Love' moped, a gift from Teena. This, in partnership with the car, would be used to great effect when he came to kidnap Stephanie Slater.

With Teena no longer working at T & M Tools, the business's paperwork went undone, and inevitably, everything started to spiral out of control again. On the surface, Sams seemed calm and relaxed, a mask that provided a quite effective smokescreen for his ever-increasing despair and frustration. He was running up large accounts with suppliers, which he could never hope to settle; his cash flow had dried up; and a steady supply of customers had failed to materialise.

Added to this was the substantial sum he owed his mother. Iris Sams had loaned her son £1000 to help him set up Peterborough Power Tools, and in 1988, she had cashed a bond for £8000 to assist him in buying a property. Sams had only ever been able to repay the interest on these loans, which amounted to £100 a month. However, he continued to meet that obligation until the week of his arrest on charges of kidnapping and murder.

Mortgage repayments, rent for the workshop, purchases of stock, general living expenses – not to mention his twin obsessions, model railways and train-spotting, on which he spent hundreds of pounds – all these were weighty millstones around

Sams' neck. He took over the household budget, allowing Teena only £40 a week to pay all food and domestic bills, and he monitored her every purchase like a hawk.

Teena had become a prisoner in her dream cottage. Day after day, Sams would 'nit pick', constantly leaving sarcastic notes such as 'Fill up the kettle' and 'Don't move the cups.' He would force her to sleep in the spare bedroom – often leaving notes saying: 'Spare bedroom tonight.' He even berated her in front of an elderly neighbour for not having his dinner on the table, although she hadn't had a clue when he'd arrive home from wherever he had been.

Teena was now on the verge of a mental breakdown, and no longer knew the difference between right and wrong. Try as she might, there was no pleasing this Dr Jekyll and Mr Hyde character. Keeping the cottage spotless became her reason for living. But even as she tidied up and dusted, Sams claimed that it was done badly, and complained that his personal things were never put back in their right place.

In an effort to resolve her troubles with her husband, and realising now that T & M Tools was in financial straits, Teena drew out what little money she had in her building society account and gave it to Sams. But he snapped at her for keeping the savings a secret, and accused her of deceiving him. Teena's diaries during this period (to which she allowed me access) make depressing reading.

To ameliorate some of the financial problems that beset him, Sams signed on as unemployed – unfit for work due to his disability – at Newark's Job Centre in Lombard Street. The manager, Pamela Little, helped him complete form UB461. Sams, ever devious, made a false declaration, saying that he had merely been the service manager of Peterborough Power Tools when, in fact, he had been the proprietor and major shareholder. He made no reference to T & M Tools.

Sams collected his first 'Giro' cheque for £115.61, on 30 April 1991. An examination of his file shows that, from that date until his father's funeral on 17 February 1992, he illegally continued to draw state benefit totalling £5086.84.

Sams also found Income Support a soft touch. While unlawfully saying he was unemployed, he convinced the Department of Social Security to pay the mortgage on Eaves Cottage, as well as the bridging loan he'd accumulated on the still unsold property

at 29 New Road, Peterborough. Why was Sams so keen to keep
that property when all else had had to go?

The DSS obviously did not do their homework, for a stroll
into Swan and Salmon Yard would have revealed Mr Sams –
unemployed due to disability – beavering away over a backlog of
repairs, sending out statements of account to customers, including the local council, and filling in banking credit slips.

While Sams was quick to grab as much money as he could –
legally or otherwise – he was uncommonly slow when it came to
paying it out. He would employ all manner of subterfuges to
avoid meeting even the smallest debt. Many of the tactics he later
used against the country's most experienced police officers, he
employed on the Inland Revenue and every other creditor.

Beale Tools of Craywood had been one of Sams' suppliers
since 1990, and he still owed the firm several thousand pounds.
They had no intention of letting Peterborough Power Tools get
away with the debt, so they continually pressed for payment.
With court action being threatened, and knowing that his former
supplier could force him into bankruptcy, Sams sent them a
small cheque in an effort to buy time. With it, he enclosed a letter
that ended cheekily: 'We thank you for you [sic] support, and you
may rest assured you will continue to receive our custom.'

Sams was the last customer Beale Tools needed, and the small
reduction in his account failed to placate the company's solicitor.
On 11 April 1991, the month Sams signed on as unemployed,
the company issued county court proceedings against Sams' new
firm T & M Tools (to which they had traced him), in what was to
be a futile effort to recover the remaining debt. This sparked
Sams into trying one last time to prevent Beale Tools ruining
him. He typed another letter that was to become the prototype
for all his future correspondence to creditors.

> It may be the case you have other communication with other
> suppliers who used Peterborough Power Tools Ltd, and they have
> told you that I, out of my own pocket, paid their outstanding
> invoices. This was true. But this was done because they offered
> myself credit facilities on the understanding I did my best to
> secure monies for their outstanding invoices, it was therefore a
> goodwill gesture that I paid them out of my own funds, but I
> have no obligation to underwrite all outstanding invoices.

While this letter, full of false magnanimous gestures, might have
fooled some, it didn't impress Beale's. But although they pursued
their action vigorously, they received not a penny more for their
labours.

That April, Sams was also trying to get the Inland Revenue
off his back. His first task was to distance himself totally from
any involvement in 22 Jubilee Street and 29 New Road,
Peterborough. He wrote a letter to the Inland Revenue, saying:
'Mrs Teena Sams has now handed the property back to the building society. She will be living at Eaves Cottage until she finds a
suitable property to rent.' This was an attempt to suggest that
Teena owned all the houses in Peterborough, not him. Teena
herself knew nothing of any repossessions until 1994, when I
showed her Sams' letter to the tax man. She had been under the
impression that her husband had sold the houses and made a
profit. This letter gave her another jolt. She was the co-owner of
Eaves Cottage and had never intended to rent anything.

In June 1991, Sams sat down to think about his money problems.
Trying again to kidnap a female estate agent seemed, to him, the
only option. That summer at Crewe, he made a determined
attempt to kidnap two women who, for legal reasons, cannot be
named.

Using the same meticulous techniques as he had in Worcester
(and possibly in London), he drove to Crewe and spent most of
a day searching for estate agents and houses with vacant possession, eventually settling on 71 Westminster Street, which had rear
access through an alleyway.

His next stop was Derby where he posted two letters in
unsealed white W. H. Smith window envelopes, addressed to
himself in Newark. He needed a good impression of a Derby
postmark.

A week later, on a Wednesday, he drove to Crewe, and just
after the staff had left the office for the day, he pushed one of the
envelopes through the letterbox of Swetenhams estate agency.
The letter inside asked for a viewing of the Westminster Street
address that very day, and gave instructions to phone him at a
number in Ashbourne, Derbyshire, any day between 9.00 and
9.30 am to confirm the details. Sams hoped that, the following
day, the estate agents would think that the letter had been delayed
in the mail and would ring the number immediately. He would be

waiting for the call in a phonebox in Ashbourne, and would arrange the viewing for later that day, when he would kidnap the estate agent. Hopefully, a female.

However, after Sams had posted the letter through the door, a policeman drove up and asked if he was all right. Sams, lacking a disguise, worried about the risk of going ahead with his plan in case the officer remembered him and his car. Nevertheless, the following morning he drove to Ashbourne. When the phone failed to ring, he called Swetenhams himself and was told that they had only just received his letter. An appointment was made for a fortnight's time.

Back in his workshop, Sams reviewed his kidnap plans. He had constructed a chipboard box to contain his victim, and laid out a length of chain. In a corner of the room, hidden from view under a grubby sheet, was a set of false car number plates, as well as two signs that he would attach to the rear side windows of his car: 'BLOCKED AND BROKEN DRAINS'. These would cover the windows entirely, giving the vehicle the appearance of a small plumber's van.

His kidnapping kit consisted of two knives, rope and a gag, while he would disguise himself by wearing a pair of Michael Caine-like heavy-rimmed glasses, dyeing his hair darker and attaching a few plastic warts to his face. He then sat down to go over his route for the kidnap proper.

As we shall see later, Sams preferred to kidnap his victims from locations approximately 70 miles from his base in Newark. Crewe would be no exception. After he secured the estate agent in his car, he planned to drive north-east along the A534 and A54, crossing the Peak District he knew so well from his running days. From Buxton, he would take the A6 and A619 to the bypass at Chesterfield, where he would join the A617 to travel down to Mansfield and then on to Newark. But first he had to catch his prey.

Two weeks later – on 3 July 1991, and again on a Wednesday (his day off work) – Sams drove to Crewe for his 2 pm appointment at 71 Westminster Street. Disguised, he waited nervously outside the property. Then a man working on a nearby house walked up to him, offering his expertise should he decide to buy the property. This unwarranted interference may have saved the 41-year-old estate agent's life, for Sams was scared off by the persistent builder. When the woman arrived, accompanied by a schoolgirl on work experience, she was told that her potential client had gone.

Using the alias 'Lettin' – obviously a play on words, perhaps as 'Kipper' had been – Sams made another attempt at the same address. This time, a female colleague of the first estate agent booked the viewing. She later told the police about the builder who had annoyed all of her clients. She also remembered a scruffy man wearing Michael Caine glasses walking towards her with a peculiar gait. Then he had suddenly changed direction and disappeared.

With two more abysmal failures under his belt, Sams decided to pick an easier target: a prostitute. After all, he knew as much about them as he did about estate agents, with whom he had come into contact through his property speculation exercises.

Sams drove to Leeds' red-light district and spotted a prostitute plying her trade. His plan was to kidnap her and drive back to Newark; then after collecting £145,000 in ransom – which he believed the police would pay – he'd kill her and dump the body.

After striking a deal, the hooker climbed into the orange Metro. Sams drove to a nearby carpark, where she started to undress, but within seconds, he whipped out a knife and pushed it to her throat. With grim determination, she fought him off and, pushing him to one side, leapt from the car, grabbing what clothes she could. Sams was half in, half out of the door when a lump of house brick slammed into his windscreen. The woman stumbled off into the night.

She had a miraculous escape, as this letter from Sams to me suggests:

> *Had either of these too [sic] had gone ahead then the captive would not have been allowed to go home. When the 3 July 1991 at Crewe failed, I have no explanation as to why I thought the police would pay a ransom for an unknown, everyday person [the prostitute]. But I knew in my mind they would.*

A short time after this abortive kidnap attempt, he was back in Leeds once more. This visit would bring him into fatal contact with Julie Anne Dart.

FIVE

Julie Anne Dart

On 1 March 1973, a baby girl was born to Lynn Margaret Hill, *née* Atkin, and was registered as Julie Anne Hill. Three years later, the little girl's father, lorry driver Alec Hill, left Lynn with Julie and a two-year-old son, Paul. The family was living with Lynn's grandmother, Elsie, in a semi-detached house in the seaside town of Bridlington, when the divorce came through in 1977.

Lynn met her second husband, electrician Ian Michael Dart, that same year. They moved to Lynn's native Leeds, where they settled in council accommodation at 7 Buller Crescent. After a short wait on the council's housing exchange list, they were allocated a larger place at 36 Hollin Park Crescent. Lynn married Ian on 4 March 1987, and she changed her children's surnames from 'Hill' to 'Dart' by deed poll. Thereafter, they called Ian 'Dad'.

Little is known of Julie's early education; her last school was Foxwood High School. Nevertheless, she comes down to us as intelligent and a hard worker: to top up her weekly allowance from Lynn, she took a part-time job on weekends at the Grill and Griddle café on Harehills Road. She stayed there until she left school in 1990 with aspirations to be a driver with the Women's Royal Army Corps (WRAC). While working at the café, she met two people who were to play important roles in her life: Dominic Murray and Michael Walter.

Julie and Dominic, also an employee at the Grill and Griddle, became engaged and moved in together. Lynn disapproved of the relationship, which became the cause of many heated arguments between mother and daughter. This doomed the engagement from the outset, and just before Christmas, Julie moved back to her mother's home.

That December she got a temporary job with retailers Argos, and called into the Army Recruiting Office in Wellington Street, Leeds, to enquire about joining up as a driver in the WRAC. The job at Argos lasted only until the January 1991 sales. Then Julie went to work at the Oakwood Beefeater restaurant.

On 8 January, she was examined by John Kemp Scott, a consultant in chest diseases who, although semi-retired, was retained by the Army to check on potential recruits. As a result of this examination, Julie was referred to another specialist concerning her asthma. She told neither doctor that she was severely claustrophobic.

She was seen at the Duchess of Kent Military Hospital at Catterick Garrison by consultant physician Colonel Barry Hennigan, and on 18 March, she was passed as fit for service. Her final selection examination was to take place at the WRAC centre in Guildford, Surrey on 13 and 14 June, and a briefing about this was set for 10 June 1991 at the Leeds recruiting office. But there was a problem.

When she was 15, Julie had got a part-time job cleaning at the plush Weetwood Grove Mansion in Leeds, owned by 41-year-old Michael Walter, whom she had met at the Grill and Griddle. While doing this work, Julie had access to all of Walter's personal effects. When his Bank of Scotland Visa card went missing and £560 was stolen from this account – along with £100 from his NatWest account by similar means – Walter suspected Julie. He later alleged that, not only had she been the only person in his home during the period when the cards were taken and used, she had also known his PIN numbers.

When he confronted Julie, she agreed that she was responsible, and to stop him reporting the crime to the police, she promised to repay the money and signed a document to that effect. However, Walter also knew of Julie's plans to join the Army, and was concerned that, after she joined up, she would renege on the repayments.

On Friday, 7 June, Recruiting Sergeant Lesley Holt had a phone call from Michael Walter, who explained his concerns. Sergeant Holt decided to raise the matter with Julie at the 10 June briefing. Being free of financial liabilities was a condition of recruitment, and Julie had so far mentioned nothing of this matter.

When Sergeant Holt asked the girl about the money owed to Walter, Julie told her that not a penny was owed. The recruitment officer relayed this apparent contradiction back to Michael Walter, who was now sure that Julie would never pay back his money. The sergeant arranged yet another meeting with Julie, who would then have the opportunity to confront Michael Walter and sort the matter out. And there was something else – a slight query about the GCSE results that Julie had said she had achieved. These later proved to be false.

At the second meeting at the recruiting office, on 18 June, Julie promised Walter that she would pay back the money in full. It was made clear to her that, if she failed to do so, she would be turned down by the Army and Michael Walter would report her to the police. It may be that she felt that the only way to earn such a large sum was via prostitution. (However, there were some alleged sightings of her working on the street as early as January 1991.)

Julie had told her mother Lynn that she had taken work at a research centre near the Leeds General Infirmary, working between 4 and 9 pm. She also told her that, when she was staying out till all hours, she was with a girlfriend; in fact, she was using the friend as a cover for meetings with Dominic Murray. Julie had always taken pride in keeping herself smart and well-groomed, but now her mother noticed that her daughter, constantly short of money, had 'let herself go' and was always dressed in skimpy multi-coloured tops, a black mini-skirt and high-heeled shoes. Unknown to Lynn Dart, Julie was now 'on the game' and had started to pay off her debt to Michael Walter.

On 4 July 1991, Lynn bumped into Julie walking through the city centre just before lunch, so they went shopping. Later that afternoon, they caught a bus to the Travellers' Rest at Crossgates, and by 7 pm Julie was drunk. After another heated row, Lynn ordered her out of the pub, and the younger woman left and caught a taxi. Two days later, on Saturday, 6 July, Julie returned home for a change of clothes and asked to borrow £10 to get into town, promising to return with any change. Lynn Dart never saw her daughter again.

Julie was drunk again at about 1.30 am on Sunday, 7 July, in Rocky's nightclub, this time with Dominic. He had had too much to drink, and Julie could hardly stand up. As they staggered home, Dominic supported his girlfriend and slapped her face in an effort to sober her up. When off-duty Special Constable Paul Battye saw that Julie's face was swollen, she had a split lip and her clothing was in disarray, he tried to break up the couple, but as he did, Dominic fell over, breaking his left ankle.

It has been reported that Dominic and Julie were both admitted overnight to St James's Hospital, where Dominic had his ankle put in plaster. The following morning, it is alleged, he went to collect Julie from another ward, but she had apparently told staff that she was meeting him at the hospital exit. Another account has it that, after Julie had discharged herself, she met up with Dominic and they kept on walking, never to return.

However, new evidence has revealed that Julie Dart was admitted to the Leeds City Council's Emergency Unit Direct Access Hostel for single women. She had been referred by the emergency duty team, having suffered a split lip. (How she met up with the emergency team is unknown.) The hostel's night log shows that, during initial counselling, Julie claimed that she was 'fleeing violence'. The young prostitute stayed at the hostel that night, not at St James's Hospital, but she did meet Dominic the following morning, as previously claimed.

In addition, while there is no doubt that Julie was not working for any research centre, further new evidence shows that she had applied for a post with Catering by County through the Job Centre in Leeds. This firm was subcontracted to both the Leeds GHBA/Hazleton Clinic and a research centre, so there may have been room for misinterpretation here. Robert Smith, a manager at Catering by County, confirms that Julie had successfully passed the job interview. He'd taken a liking to her as she had enjoyed the same interests: sport, swimming and aerobics. He was disappointed when she didn't turn up for what should have been her first day at work.

During the police investigation that followed, a number of witnesses were interviewed by detectives keen to establish Julie's precise movements on the evening of Tuesday, 9 July 1991.

Two men said that they had seen her in Chapeltown between 8 and 9.30 pm. This caused a problem, for at that time, Julie was reported to have been in the company of two other prostitutes in the White Swan – locally known as the Mucky Duck – a pub several miles away in Call Lane.

Lorraine Kelly, a self-employed hot dog vendor with a fixed

pitch at the Corn Exchange behind the pub, remembered Julie as a 'very pretty young woman who spoke frequently with other prostitutes'. The last time she saw Julie was at about 9.30 pm that night, wearing a 'dark V-neck shirt and black skirt'. Because this description of Julie's clothing contradicted the many claims that she had been wearing jeans, it is now believed that Lorraine Kelly was mistaken.

Whatever the case, by 10 pm the three women were back in Spencer Place, where they all picked up punters. Afterwards, having earned some cash, they walked to a tandoori restaurant for a take-away kebab. When they arrived at the Health Centre, a profitable soliciting spot, the two other girls went home.

The last confirmed sighting of Julie Dart was made by an occasional prostitute, Evelyn Rowe, who first spotted her alone at the junction of Leopold Street and Spencer Place at around 11.15 pm. Julie was wearing blue jeans, she said, and carrying a black bag. At 11.30, with Julie still waiting alone for a punter, Evelyn went home to her husband and three children.

During the police enquiry, it was felt crucial to locate all the garments worn by Julie Dart that evening. Trace evidence such as cloth fibres and body fluids might be found on such items, which could eliminate a suspect or link him directly to her murder. Unfortunately, none of Julie's clothing was ever found.

No prostitute is safe on the streets at any time of the day – and least of all when in the company of an unknown man late at night. Most of them stop selling sex after 11 pm, when trade dies down. The streetwise majority know that lone, inexperienced girls, desperate for money, are extremely vulnerable to attack. But from either naïvety or stupidity, Julie was still offering her body just before midnight. The streets were almost deserted, and there wasn't another hooker in the area.

Sitting in the shadows was a human predator, one that may have passed as insignificant in his orange Metro car, or even more so if he had limped down the street. He was watching the girl as she stood, isolated, outside 69 Spencer Place. To Michael Sams, she looked provocative under the yellow street lamp. Like a moth and all other nightlife, she may have been attracted to the false security that beckoned from the light. Or Julie Dart may have been intent on highlighting her assets.

Sams wiped his stubby fingers across his lips. Deep within

his mind, the emotions that had begun to boil at the sight of this lone young woman became increasingly irresistible. He had entered what forensic psychologists call the 'wooing phase', for he had fantasised for weeks about kidnapping a hooker and demanding a hefty ransom for her release. But there would be no safe return – he'd kill her even if he did get the money.

Sams rubbed what remained of his right leg, trying to ease the nagging pain that troubled him day and night. Society had let him down, had crapped all over him. Now, right now, was the time to get even. As he had written in his own profit-and-loss account in prison: '*Society owes me and I will be repaid.*'

The man with hooded dark eyes betrayed no outward sign of emotion as he stared into the rear-view mirror, the car radio tuned to his favourite Radio 2. At that moment, he knew that this lonely woman was marked down to him and destruction. All it required was the usual chit-chat; he'd done that time and again in the past when talking to prostitutes. A well-timed blow, perhaps a terrifying threat; then the car door would be slammed shut, and she would be at his mercy.

The long search for a victim had only served to heighten his expectations, and the previous abortive attempts had simply added to his frustration and bitterness. This time there could be no room for error. Once the woman had been tied up, he would take all the time he needed to prepare her for the subsequent ritual – after, of course, first completing the ransom arrangements. It was a scenario in which he would be the star. It had been planned for years, planned with military precision. With cold-blooded anticipation, he mentally rehearsed how he would batter this woman to death, a ball-pein hammer gripped tightly in his hand. Michael Benniman Sams knew all these things as he patiently watched Julie Dart from the shadows.

Julie Dart is, of course, now dead, having been murdered by Michael Sams, and so is unable to tell us about her kidnap. Any description of that event has to come from the lips of Michael Sams, and over time, he has provided two versions. The first is now common knowledge for those who have studied the case, but it differs considerably from a lesser-known second account.

The accepted summary was discovered by murder squad detectives searching Sams' somewhat erratic business records on his computer – for he had also planned and edited his campaign of terror using the same software. The killer's intention had been to print out a letter he had written on his computer and post it to the police, to send the investigators on a wild goose chase in their search for Julie, and thereby remove suspicion from Sams if he became a suspect.

After printing out what he had written, Sams erased the relevant file – at least that was what he thought he had done. With his limited knowledge of electronic technology, he had been under the misguided impression that, once a file was erased, it couldn't be retrieved. Police computer experts were able to prove otherwise, recovering material from the part of the computer's memory called 'limbo'. In this way, they found 99.9 per cent of a document that referred to Sams' kidnapping of Julie Dart. The following is a transcript of what was in that computer file. The few gaps are due to technical difficulties encountered during the retrieval of the information:

> *... car and lowered the window. The young girl then called out, 'do you want business?', to which I replied, 'Yes'. She then ran across to the passenger side and opened it. A conversation went something like this.*
>
> *Me. 'Where?'*
> *Girl. 'Over there behind the wall [probably meaning the Health Centre].'*
> *Me. 'That's no good. Not outside. In the car.'*
> *Girl. 'In the car will be extra.'*
> *Me. 'How much now?'*
> *Girl. '£20.'*
> *Me. 'Okay. Is it a safe place?'*
> *Girl. 'It's money up front. Please.'*
> *I then held out two £10 notes which she took; it was only then that she got into the car. She immediately told me her name was Julie, and directed me down the road. On the way we had a little conversation in which she told me she was 24-years-old and lived in the Leeds area. I did notice she was tall, very good looking girl, and I asked Julie her height. She replied, '5ft 9½ inches.'*
> *Julie directed me to what I think was the Thomas Danby car park. I was a little apprehensive but she assured me that no other girls would bring anyone up there whilst a car was up there. I got*

out of the car to fold the rear seats up and placed a blanket on the floor, then got inside myself through the rear doors. Julie got between the front seats, she removed her shoes and before she would remove anything else I asked her if I could remove her clothes. She agreed for a further £5, which I did [gap] the buttons on her blouse and removed that. For the record Julie had on white lace briefs with a black lace bra. After a little while I had penetrative sex with a condom provided by Julie. After sex I as [gap] sex, I asked her to lay there a while and talk and that I would give her extra.

It was at this time that I noticed she had a couple of bruises on her body and numerous on her legs. I challenged her about these to which she explained that she had been beaten up previously and had then borrowed money from a friend to get away to recover, that was why she needed the extra money to the wages she got from work. She elaborated her statement by adding that she had just got out of the bath and that they were therefore looking worse. Also that she worked at the LGI [Leeds General Infirmary], and had got something from the Sister to put on them at nights. It was then that the lights went out in the car park. We both got dressed and returned to the corner of Leopold Street and Spencer Place.

I asked her if she had a boyfriend and if so what did he think of her doing this. She replied; 'He does not know anything about it.' She was going to give me his name but stopped the second letter sounding like the 'O' in 'Not'. Slightly before the car stopped she asked me about the extra I had promised her. Apologising I gave her a £20 pound note, saying that she had provided the best sex I had ever had and would be back. She did not place the note in her shoulder bag as she had before, but removed her shoe and placed it in. She then opened her bag, removed her various items, large earrings, perfumes, beer glass, plus a few pieces of paper. She was looking for a Biro. There was no skirt in the bag or any other clothing. Having found the Biro she placed the items in the bag and then wrote her name in inverted commas. It reads, 'Julie D', on one of my business cards that were about. She said, 'that's me. I will be around here some evenings. I get dropped off about 10.45 and collected around 11.30'.

It was then that another car drew up behind. Julie opened the door and looked behind and then said, 'Thanks, you're a great guy but I've got to go now'. She shut the door and seemed to run towards the car at the rear. I turned up Leopold Street and went a little way up to turn around. Upon returning Julie and the car had gone.

On the way home, I threw the business card and used condom out of the window around the Scamadam [Scammonden] Dam area. I did return a couple of days later to see her again, but I have not seen her.

The above is a full description as I believe you want in a statement. Only intimate details have been left out as irrelevant. I cannot give my name or any further details, due to the fact I am married.

I also once heard one of your Chief Constables saying that Police Officers thought of me who used prostitute [sic]. I'm sorry that should read – your Chief Constable saying what Police Officers thought of men who used prostitutes.

This rambling, somewhat incoherent letter, which was never posted, contains a matrix of fabrication and truth. For example, the reference to Scammonden Dam was a calculated attempt to lead the police away from the south-easterly direction where Sams lived in Sutton-on-Trent, to the south-west, between Leeds and Rochdale.

In an effort to ascertain the veracity of this first letter, I checked it against a statement written by Sams while in prison after his trial:

I set off from our house at about 7 p.m., 9 July. Teena thought I was going to decorate her house [29 New Road, Peterborough]. I called at an off-licence for a tin of lager to relax me. I stopped en-route to put false number plates on and went to the 'Mucky Duck' down the Calls in Leeds. There seemed no way there I would be able to pick a girl up without being seen. I had known that Chapeltown was the red-light area so I went to have a look.

After a bit of searching I found the corner where the Health Centre was about 11.15 p.m. There were three girls on the corner, so I parked a little way up the road. Two were coloured girls and one a tall white girl. Shortly after I parked where I could see the three girls, a white, largish car stopped across the road from the girls. The tall white girl ran across the road to the driver's side, spoke to the driver and then gave him something from her back jeans pocket.

At about 11.30 p.m., the coloured girls left. So I then went

*and parked opposite her. She called out, 'Do you want business?',
and I answered 'Yes'.*

*She then ran across the road passing in front of my car and
came to the passenger door and opened it. She told me it was £15
behind the Health Centre, which I declined, or, £20 in the car. I
paid her £20 and she got in and directed me to the Thomas
Danby car park. She told me her name was June and she was 24.*

*When we got to the car park she bent down to take her shoes
off. I leant over and grabbed her neck and pressed down. In this
doubled up position she couldn't scream. I told her I would let
her up if she didn't scream and she kept her eyes closed. I wanted
to talk to her.*

*She agreed, and so I let her sit back. I then slipped a rope I
had ready, over her head and secured it around her stomach.
Similar to a seat belt, but she couldn't undo [sic]. When I had
done that I said she could open her eyes, which she did, and saw
that she was tied and I had a knife. Her hands were tied by her
side with the rope. So I asked her to pull them out and I tied
them together in front of her.*

*I said, 'Right, we are going on a journey', to which she
replied, 'Do you want photoes [sic] or a video?' I thought this
was a good idea so I said, 'Yes'. She saw I had a knife across my
legs and so presumed I would use it if she screamed or anything.
She was not frightened one little bit.*

*We went down through the centre of Leeds past the station
and on to the M1. At no time when stopping at traffic lights etc,
did she try to attract the attention of any motorist. She just kept
talking to me.*

*It was about 2 a.m. when we reached Newark. On the M1, I
had put a jumper over her face. I said I didn't want her to see
which town she was in. She never objected to the jumper over her
head, and we both kept talking. I took her into the workshop [T
& M Tools] with it still over her head and guiding her. Then I
tied her to the chair whilst I put away the car.*

Even a cursory examination of the two accounts reveal a whole
series of contradictions. However, several points make for interesting comparison. Both 'statements' suggest that Sams had
picked up Julie outside the Health Clinic, and that she was
wearing jeans at the time. The amount he allegedly paid Julie was
also the same – £20. Sams was correct when he says he saw

bruising on Julie's body, so at some time, he must have seen her partially clothed. (This may have been when, as Sams alleges, he had sex with her; however, he later stripped her at the Newark workshop.) And there is every possibility that she gave him her name which was penned on to one of his business cards.

Of significance is the large white car. In the first letter found on his computer, Sams says that, when he dropped Julie off, she got into this car and drove away. The second document reverses the scenario: she spoke to the driver of such a vehicle prior to the abduction.

The Thomas Danby carpark also features in both narratives. Julie must have taken Sams to that carpark, which is situated half a mile away behind the two-storey educational block of Thomas Danby College in Roundhay Road. In fact, one can place murderer and victim in that carpark at a precise time. The place was, and is, a regular haunt for prostitutes and their clientele. Unlocked 24 hours a day, it is illuminated during the hours of darkness by three 400-watt sodium floodlights mounted on a ten-metre mast set into the middle of the carpark. At the time of the Julie Dart homicide, Robert Williamson was the building services manager with Leeds City Council's Education Department. His responsibilities included the care and upkeep of these lights. Williamson had set the 'Sangamo Solar Dial' time-switch so that the electricity to these floodlamps would be cut off at 11.30 pm British Standard Time, but 12.30 am in the summer. The time-switch was later checked by the police and found to be accurate to the minute. This information corroborates Sams' computer letter when he says that the lights went out while he and Julie were in the carpark.

Sams' second statement contains a previously unknown fact concerning that evening. He was also in the White Swan ('Mucky Duck') public house, and at the same time as Julie. That night she was accompanied by two other prostitutes, one of whom was the same woman whom Sams had attacked only weeks earlier. It was fortunate for him – and disastrous for Julie – that this woman didn't see her assailant in the bar. The suggestion is that it was there that Sams spotted Julie Dart and followed her back to the corner of Spencer Place and Leopold Street. Then, as soon as her two colleagues left for home, he made his fateful move.

SIX

Murder Most Foul

That night, Sams drove Julie about 70 miles from Leeds to Newark. At a steady 50 mph, that would have placed kidnapper and victim in Swan and Salmon Yard about 1.45 am. Sams would also have us believe that Julie entered his workshop as meek as a lamb, but there is some evidence to suggest that she did not go willingly into that dark and cold place – that she, in fact, put up quite a fierce struggle.

David and Diana Maund's motor barge was berthed at Cuckstool Wharf, a mere 75 yards from the workshop, on the opposite bank of the slow-moving River Trent. They were both sitting in the barge's lounge when they heard screaming, which David later described as 'hysterical'. He clearly heard the words, 'Leave me alone! Leave me alone!' Diana was to state that she had heard a man's voice say on a couple of occasions, 'You'll be all right now.' She also recalled hearing car doors slamming. The noise lasted for about four minutes, but the Maunds did not investigate its source.

When questioned by police after Sams' arrest, David was not sure of the exact time this event took place, but he estimated it to have been around 11.45 pm, no later. Diana, however, was a little more specific and claimed it was 11.30 pm. Although the Maunds' timing of this racket was much too early – Sams would still have been in Leeds – it should be remembered that Newark is a peaceful little town, and commotion such as this would have been quite noticeable.

A statement by another couple might shed more light on whether Julie put up a desperate fight for freedom. Shane Bush and Jane Clarke lived in a first-floor flat overlooking Mill Gate, with the River Trent at the rear of their building. One warm and sticky night, sometime between 1.15 and 1.45 am, they were roused from their sleep by screams coming from the direction of Swan and Salmon Yard, just 100 yards away. Although initially concerned about the noise, they mutually decided that it was a domestic dispute and went back to sleep. Unfortunately, they could not be specific about the date on which this unusual event took place – indeed, the police doubted the reliability of the evidence of all four witnesses. But it may be that, taken together, these four accounts reveal that Julie might have put up a struggle as she was taken into T & M Tools.

Having tied Julie firmly to a chair in the back of the rundown building, Sams left to park his Metro round the back, then returned to his victim. We have only his version of what took place next:

> When I came back I untied her from the chair and told her to sit on the mattress. She still had her hands tied, and her leg was also tied by a rope to a bracket over her jeans. When she saw where she was, she said she was not happy about removing her clothes in that cold building.
>
> I then told her that she hadn't been kidnapped for photoes [sic], but held until the police paid a ransom for her release. She actually laughed at this idea. She didn't think they would pay, and that I had kidnapped the wrong person as her mother had no money. I tried to tell her that I knew the police would pay. She then said she wanted some sleep and so she did. She had seen the P.I.R. [passive infra-red] light so I told her it lit up when she moved and would activate the alarm. I had disconected [sic] the audible alarm & phone. And she heard it work. That was to make sure she didn't move whilst I also slept.

If Sams had anything to contribute to society, it was his ability to adapt everyday items into something practical and cheap to operate. This inherent talent had surfaced months earlier when he had constructed a burglar alarm for his workshop. To under-stand the clever workings of Sams' mind, it would be worth pausing for a moment to examine the construction of this alarm system that, like his *gratis* electricity supply, was quite special.

Anthony Hawley, senior technical officer for the Nottinghamshire Constabulary, would later describe it as a 'somewhat primitive alarm system which was nevertheless effective'. It was powered by a car battery connected to a mains charger. This meant that, even if the electricity from the illegal supply was cut off, the alarm would still continue to operate. Sams never left anything to chance.

He had also fitted two passive infra-red (PIR) detectors. The one on the wall above and to the right of the sliding door would detect anyone entering the workshop or moving about in the shop area. The other, secured to a wooden ceiling beam further back in the workshop, would locate anyone who'd managed to climb through the rear window which Sams now kept shuttered.

The two PIRs were connected to a red alarm box, which contained a panel fitted with a rotary timer – a crude home-made device that was, in turn, linked to a cheap push-button telephone. The system was so wired that, if any of the detectors picked up movement, the timer would activate two micro-switches within the telephone.

Most modern telephones have a 'last number re-dial' facility, and this is where Sams' innovatory skill came into its own. The first micro-switch lifted the receiver half an inch from its cradle; the second switch brought into use the 'last number re-dial' facility. To set the alarm, all Sams had to do was call his home number, then replace the handset. If someone moved around in his workshop after hours, the alarm would automatically ring his telephone at Eaves Cottage, and this would tell him that he was being robbed. To deactivate the system, he would have to drive to the Newark workshop, switch off the system, then replace the receiver. It was as simple as that.

To complete the system, Sams had wired the whole lot to a bell. However, now that Julie Dart was his prisoner, he had disconnected this, so that, if she triggered it off, the bell wouldn't ring and attract the unwarranted attention of the constabulary.

Having pointed out to her the significance of the red flashing lights, Sams crammed Julie into the large box that he had constructed out of chipboard. He had bored holes through the top so she could breathe. What he didn't know was that Julie suffered from claustrophobia, so his claims that she slept soundly all night must be untrue.

Neither did Michael sleep that night at T & M Tools, as he has also claimed. He went home and climbed into bed during the early hours. There was little risk of waking Teena, who was, as usual, in the spare bedroom on his written instructions. He fell into a fitful sleep, knowing that Julie could not escape from the box; even if she did, the padlocked door would stop her leaving the workshop. Thirty minutes later, the phone beside his bed rang.

Breathless, he arrived back at T & M Tools to find the box smashed to pieces and Julie hysterical with fear. He gagged her and then secured her to a length of chain that was bolted to a ceiling beam.

He hadn't the time nor the inclination to rebuild the box, nor to spend the next night freezing while he babysat his hostage. Sams decided instead to kill her later in the day. Julie's death warrant had been signed.

Her first and only day in captivity was Wednesday, 10 July, the day T & M Tools was always closed for business. There would be few visitors to the yard, although Jane, who ran a small business directly above the workshop, would be open. However, at 10 am, Sams heard unwelcome voices calling his name from the front counter. If fate had dealt Julie a fairer hand, she might still be alive today.

Elizabeth and Eric Theaker were working in their antique shop at 36 Castle Gate, at the very entrance to Swan and Salmon Yard. While his wife dusted the stock, Eric repainted the exterior in Old English white, using brown paint to finish off the woodwork and cornerstones. He was so delighted with his handiwork that he extended the colour scheme on to the archway and entrance to the yard.

While standing back to admire his labours, Eric was tapped on the shoulder by a customer keen to find Michael Sams. The man had already visited T & M Tools, and he was concerned. The padlock on the front door was open, hanging by the clasp, but the interior was in darkness, and to heighten the man's sense of unease, he had heard someone, or something, shuffling around inside. This seemed a little sinister so he summoned the assistance of Eric Theaker.

When they arrived at Sams' premises, they discovered that, indeed, the padlock was open and the sliding door was ajar. Easing it open, they walked into the shop area, calling Sams' name several times. In a statement later given to the police, Theaker said:

> *Suddenly, Michael appeared from behind the counter area. He was holding his head by placing his hand on his forehead and appeared to stagger towards us. His face appeared as if he had just got out of bed and he looked unkempt. He said, 'I've got a migraine.' He said it in a fashion that he didn't want us in the shop, and he didn't want any business. Both of us left the premises and didn't return.*

Julie Dart probably heard every word. But, as the door slid shut behind Sams' unwelcome visitors, any chance of her staying alive walked out of the workshop with them.

Little is known of what happened in the cold and damp workshop during the rest of that day. The only account is from the pen of Michael Sams, and again, his recollections are published here for the first time.

> *I woke her in the morning and asked her to be quiet all day. If she wouldn't promise I would gag her. She promised. She had to be quiet as Jane was open on Wednesday about [sic] me. Jane always had her tape/radio on loud so this would drowned [sic] any noise we made talking.*
>
> *All day Julie never stopped talking about her plans for the future, her boyfriend's behaviour towards her, and the scraps she had with her mother. She also said it was the first time she had been on the streets. I said, 'Come off it. I don't believe that.' She said it was true, and that she had borrowed some money off a bloke to go on holiday to recouperate [sic] after [allegedly] being beat up.*
>
> *She pulled up her blouse to show me the bruises. She also said she worked at the LGI and had been given something by the Sister to make them go. But they looked worse because she had just got out of the bath. [Since Sams didn't allow Julie to have a bath, this sentence is a bit of a puzzle.] She did tell me her name was Julie, not June, but maintained her age was 24 and she was going into the Army because she wanted to get out of Leeds as everyone was violent towards her. She never once offered me sex, nor did I ask for it.*
>
> *She was given tea to drink and a few biscuits I had. She*

didn't want any [more] food. We chatted all day as a normal couple do. The fact that I knew I was going to kill her in a few hours in no way showed through to her.

I learned all about her life and running, and even told her I had run for the Bingley Harriers. At 5.30 when Jane, above, had gone home, I asked her to write a letter which I dictated. She initially wrote one to her mother. Then after a few minutes doodling, she said, 'Don't send that, I'll write to Dominic instead. He can tell my mother.'

So with shaking hands, Julie started to write:

Hallo Dominic,

Help me please, I've been kidnapped and I am being held as a personal security until next Monday night. Please go and tell my Mum straight away.

Love you so much Dominic ...

Mum, phone the police straight away and help me. Have not eaten anything but I have been offered food. Feeling a bit sick but I'm drinking two cups of tea per day.

Mum – Dominic HELP ME.

Dominic my Mum will be in at 5.00 everynight [sic] or phone, yes phone her ... If not there leave a message. If not working go to her house.

> *Love you all,*
> *Julie.*

Apart from the obvious falsehood that Sams woke Julie in the morning (it is hardly likely that she was in the mood for sleep after smashing the box to pieces) and omitting the fact that she was most certainly gagged when Eric Theaker called at T & M Tools, much of Sams' story seems to bear some resemblance to the truth. Later, when we examine the kidnapping and imprisonment of Stephanie Slater, we will see that Sams enjoyed talking with his captives. In addition, other sources have verified the fact that much of the information given in his account could only have come from Julie Dart.

There is no doubt that Sams dictated Julie's letter to Dominic and her mother. In it are echoes of Donald Neilson's thoughts on the welfare of his captive Leslie Whittle: look after the girl and the police might pursue their enquiries with a little less tenacity ...

Before and throughout his trial, Michael Benniman Sams categorically denied the kidnap and murder of Julie Dart, but finally, on 12 July 1993, the convicted man confessed to senior detectives at HM Full Sutton prison. Out of Sams' disclosure was born the 'official version' of Julie's terrible murder. According to this, Julie was exhausted after writing to Dominic, and fell asleep in a chair. Sams crept up behind the girl and hit her, twice, on the back of the head with a ball-pein hammer – the favourite instrument of death of serial murderer Peter Sutcliffe, who had savagely attacked seven women and brutally murdered 13 more between 1975 and 1980. However, those heavy blows delivered in quick succession were insufficient to cause the pitiful woman's immediate death, so he throttled her with a ligature. Julie succumbed shortly afterwards without regaining consciousness.

Unfortunately, the truth may be somewhat different. Again, I can reveal here, for the first time, another letter released to me by Sams, which, he says, is the complete truth:

> *After writing the letter she asked to be allowed to wash. I untied her hands but not her leg. When she finished I said I was tying her hands behind her back, so she lay on her tummy and I put her hands behind her back.*
>
> *She never had them tied because I hit her with the hammer I had with me, behind the head to render her unconscious. Believe it or not I didn't want her to feel pain, and then I put a cord round her neck and tightened it. I was fully convinced in my mind that she had not felt a thing.*

So, far from sleeping peacefully in a chair when Sams fell upon her, trusting Julie Dart was talking to her captor seconds before he rained blows down on to her pretty head.

That evening, an exhausted Michael Sams went home. Teena noticed nothing except that he appeared more distant than usual.

The next day, he went to the workshop at the usual time, taking a bowl of porridge to heat up in the microwave oven there. After finishing his breakfast, he started to tidy up the previous evening's mess. He wrapped the body in material, then pushed the gruesome bundle into a green wheely bin in a corner and covered it with rubbish. Sometime in the afternoon, he drove 50 miles south to Huntingdon where he posted two letters; one had been written by Julie and the other was a ransom demand for her safekeeping and life, addressed to the Leeds City Police.

Early on Friday morning, 12 July, Rose Neil, Dominic Murray's sister, climbed out of bed to take her twins to the nursery. Fifteen minutes later, a letter was posted through her letterbox; it was addressed to Dominic in what she recognised as Julie's handwriting. Rose left the letter on the kitchen table for a while, until eventually she opened it.

At first, she thought the ransom note was a joke; then the reference to the police and Lynn Dart's telephone number made her think otherwise. Within minutes she was on the phone to Dominic.

As chance would have it, Dominic had stayed with another sister, Mary, the previous night. Rose took Julie's letter to him at 9.35 am. A family conference followed, to decide what to do next.

The elder members of the family, with the exception of Rose, took the letter with a pinch of salt, while young Gemma burst out laughing. However, Rose and Dominic thought that it was serious, so Dominic called Lynn Dart at work. During the conversation, he began to cry, prompting Lynn to break down, too. But within the hour, suitably composed, Lynn was standing at the front desk of Gipton Police Station, reporting her daughter as missing and demanding to speak with a senior officer.

With thousands of similar reports being made each year, one might forgive the duty constable for not treating Lynn's problem with the immediacy it deserved. Nevertheless, the Darts are not people to be fobbed off, and if Mrs Dart wanted to see a senior officer, she would do just that.

Detective Chief Inspector John O'Sullivan pondered over the ransom note, weighing up the odds of it being a foolish prank (he'd seen a few in his time), an elaborate hoax (he'd seen some of those, too) or a genuine case of kidnapping. Something from all those years of experience in dealing with crime seemed to suggest that he should make further enquiries.

A two-minute interview with Dominic soon eliminated him from those enquiries. The letter had been posted in Huntingdon, Cambridgeshire, at 7 pm the previous evening, but Dominic had a solid alibi placing him firmly in the centre of Leeds at that time. In police parlance, the lad was out of the frame.

A few discreet telephone calls revealed the fact that – contrary to what Julie had told Lynn Dart, who in turn had told the police – Julie didn't work at any laboratory. Enquiries made of Chapeltown Police Station confirmed that she had no 'form'. There was no record of her name on the Criminal Record Index or collator's register (a police register of local criminals). She had 'no known criminal associates' either.

A constable then completed a Missing Person's Report (MISPER), and after consulting the force's standing orders, he decided that Julie was to be classified as 'Missing. Non-Vulnerable'. By now, O'Sullivan himself was receiving calls. It was becoming clear that Julie Dart had been on the fringes of prostitution. Working more by instinct – call it a gut feeling – the police officers now believed that Julie might well be in danger of losing her life. Recalling Peter Sutcliffe's reign of terror, they became more concerned as each hour passed.

The second letter posted by Sams in Huntingdon also arrived at its destination on 12 July. Initially, the contents were read by Special Branch, which has responsibility for dealing with threats of a subversive nature. They sent it by internal mail to the Divisional CID at Chapeltown, where it was sealed as a possible exhibit, to preserve fingerprints and saliva, and given to DCI O'Sullivan, who placed it side by side with Julie's letter. The investigator felt sick. Any doubts as to the veracity of the kidnapper's letter evaporated. Sams had written:

All misspellings and grammatical errors are Sams'.

[First page]

A young prostitute has been kidnapped from the Chapltown area last night and will only be released unharmed if the conditions below are met, if they are not met then the hostage will never be seen again also a major city centre store (not necessary in Leeds) will have a fire bomb explode at 5am 17 July.

1) A payment of £140,000 is paid in cash (one hundred & fourty thousand)

2) £5,000 is put in two bank accounts, 2 cash cards and P.I.N. issued, these two bank accounts to allow at least £200 per day withdrawal.

Next Tuesday 16 July a WPC will drive to Birmingham New Street station with the money, and await a phone call at the Mercury phone terminal in the waiting room on platform 9, she must wear a lightish Blue skirt with the money in a sholder bag. She must be there by 6pm and await the call at 7pm, she will then be given the location of the next phone call, (after receiving the call she must drive North out of the city on the A38M Aston Expressway to join the southbound M6, this information is given to avoid her getting lost in the city.) She must have enough petrol for at least 200 miles driving, and a pen and pad may also be carried, but no radio or transmittor,

All phone calls will be prerecorded and no communication will be possible or answered. No negotiations will be entred Into. Any publicity or apparent police action will result in no further communication.

The monies to be in equal quantities of £50/20/10 used notes and the cash cards to have their P.I.N. marked on them in marker pen. The money to wrapped in polythene of at least 120 microns then taped with parcel tape the bank cards to then be taped to the polythene then the package to be wrapped in brown paper and tied by a nylon cord with a loop handle. The whole package to be no more the 350mm X 350mm X 90mm.

Once the money has been received Leeds will receive a phone call at around midnight of the name and address of the store with the fire bomb in five hours should be ample time to gain entry to the store. The hostage will only be released when all monies have been withdrawn from the accounts.

The hostage will be well fed and well looked after in a home rented for the purpose, she will be guarded 24hrs a day by P.I.R. detectors connected directly to the mains. Once the monies have been withdrawn you will receive the address of the hostage, BEFORE ENTERING HOUSE THE ELECTRICITY MUST BE SWITCHED OF FROM OUTSIDE before opening the door or any movement will activate the detectors.

No attempt must be made to follow the WPC and as she will be followed over very quite roads which can easy be checked, aircraft can be heard.

LEEDS CITY POLICE
HEADQUATERS
LEEDS.

[Second page]
Tuesday the WPC will at all times carry the only packages with her. She will bring it to various phone boxes for phone messages. At one box a small plastic box with a small green L.E.D. illuminated will be inside the box, this must be picked up and placed ontop of the instrument panel of the car dashboard and must be visible through the front windscreen, this box will also have a large red L.E.D. (Antitamper) and a large amber L.E.D. (Transmitter detector) if either of these two illuminate then no further messages will be received. The money package as I said must be carried at all times and at one destination it must be clipped to a dog type clip that will be hanging from a tree, no downward pull must be made on the rope. The WPC must then return to the car which will be some 300 metres from this point within 60 secs and drive a further 800 metres before removing the plastic box with the L.E.D.s.

The money will be picked up by some-one unconnected with the writer but will be the only person who parks down this 'lovers lane' each Tuesday for a few hours, his female companion will be also held hostage until the money is picked up from him, he will have a short range two way radio which I can direct him. Should anything go wrong these two hostages will not be harmed.

This action has been planned for some time, but obtsining a small hand gun plus ammunition took longer than antisipated. If anything goes wrong or the ploice are not able to meet the demands then the hostage will never be seen again, plus the store will be fire bombed, the action will then begin again next time an employee of say the Electric/Gas/Water companies will be used, to kidnap them in course of there work will make the company pay the ransom.

No publicity must be given until the money has been received then a press statement may be released but must mention that no monies were handed over.

The extra £5,000 must not be added in cash with the main money, as the main package will be buried for a long while so that serial number will not be traced, serial number in cash dispencers cannot be traced.

The ransom letter was deadly serious, and the police had little time to react before the Tuesday deadline just four days away. However, an analysis of the demand provided a few clues that might be of value in any attempt to free Julie Dart and make an early arrest. It is immediately apparent that the writer was not good (or was pretending not to be good) with the English language or a typewriter. There were over 20 spelling mistakes and numerous grammatical errors. The typewriter was old and in bad repair, so it could be safely assumed that the kidnapper didn't use one to earn a living.

The drawing was a dead giveaway, for it showed that the individual had a knowledge of perspective, perhaps through making engineering drawings and plans. The fact that he used a ruler confidently indicated that this tool was part of his stock in trade. The references to 'PIR', 'LED' and 'polythene at 120 microns', along with other measurements in metres and millimetres, and the mention of two-way radio – all this showed an understanding of electrical gadgetry, either from employment or because the kidnapper had a related hobby.

Another clue was the instruction about the dog clip and length of rope to which the ransom money had to be attached. The writer specifically used the term 'dog type clip'. Why not just 'clip'? Could it be that the kidnapper was a dog owner? The Samses had three ...

Then there were the known and as yet unknown locations alluded to in the letter, which would later prove vital in catching this devious man. He obviously knew Leeds and Chapeltown – the red-light district – and, of course, Julie had been kidnapped from Leeds where she lived. The two letters had been posted in Huntingdon, Cambridgeshire, 115 miles south-east of Leeds. Both places were linked by the A1 motorway and the East Coast Railway. Then there was the fact that the courier had to be at Birmingham New Street Station to receive the kidnapper's first phone call – yet another link with the railways. Michael Sams was already mapping out his territory for the police.

Did the ransom demand give any clue to the kidnapper's age?

Sams had made an error in addressing his letter to the 'Leeds City Police', a title that had been defunct for 17 years, ever since the force had amalgamated with others to become the West Yorkshire Police. This mistake hinted that the man was not familiar with the present police set-up. Perhaps he was a past offender? A forensic psychiatrist later suggested that, by adding this clue to others, it was possible that the kidnapper was a man aged around 50.

To sum up, the following are the pointers and clues that the police may have garnered from this first of many letters from Michael Sams:

• The offender was a man aged 45–50 years, who had had an average education.
• He was perhaps a dog owner.
• He had no immediate criminal history.
• He had access to a motor vehicle.
• He might work as a tradesman dealing with electrical equipment.
• He was used to working with engineering drawings or plans, and was quite able to draw confidently and express himself freely in precise measurements.
• He knew Leeds and its red-light district Chapeltown.
• He had visited Huntingdon.
• He was familiar with Birmingham New Street Station.

Investigators could, or should, have made a careful note of three locations – Leeds, Huntingdon and Birmingham. If the enquiry developed, these places would become indicators of what forensic psychologists call 'spatial mapping', and they could link this with 'patterns of criminal behaviour', or *modus operandi*.

According to the theory of spatial mapping, we form mental maps of the terrain in which we exist, strongly related to our daily work and where we live. Try as hard as we can, we cannot remove these patterns from our minds, and they form a blueprint that affects our behaviour and our means of living. During the months ahead, the police would make correlations between a matrix of physical events and mapped locations, which would pinpoint the criminal's 'centre of gravity' and give them the general location in which Sams lived or worked.

●

The task of coordinating the operation to rescue Julie Dart and to arrest the kidnapper (and, into the bargain, save £140,000) fell to No. 3 Regional Crime Squad based in Wakefield. The officer in charge was Detective Chief Superintendent Norman Mould, an extremely efficient investigator. He had spent his career locking criminals away, and he was sure that Julie's kidnapper would be the next on his list.

The success of such an operation rests largely on excellent communications between crime squad officers responsible for the case and those from other forces. RCS detectives are able to move freely anywhere in the United Kingdom on these 'jobs', with the proviso that they inform a 'host' police force that they are working on their patch. They also, of course, work under direction of the senior investigating officer (SIO) on the case.

The operation to secure the release of Julie Dart was code-named 'CASTLE', and entailed the use of a trained female courier who would deliver the ransom money to an as yet unknown drop-off point. That location could be anywhere within the 88,619 square miles of Great Britain.

The selection of the woman police officer would prove a rigorous task. One name cropped up several times: Detective Constable Annette Zekneys. Known to her colleagues as 'Netty', the policewoman had been with No. 3 RCS for two years, and although only in her late 20s, she had proved herself time and again. In the end, DC Zekneys wasn't ordered to act as ransom courier; she volunteered. She knew that she was placing herself in the firing line. She was also aware that, if she failed in her duty, another woman might be murdered, and a department store could be set ablaze, possibly resulting in the loss of more life. This was a heavy weight to be carried on such young shoulders, but she was sure that her fellow officers would not let her down.

The 'wheely' rubbish bin that already held Julie's remains was one of eight that had been stolen by persons unknown in Newark that month. It contained Julie's naked corpse still wrapped in the material that Sams had given her to keep warm while she was alive. The lid had been sealed with tape, for the sweet stench of decomposition was awful.

In a letter to me, the cold-blooded killer had this to say:

After first wrapping the body up in a green curtain and putting the body in a wheely bin, there it stayed until Saturday afternoon when I thought there was a smell coming from it. I then laid the body out on a carpet still clothed. I was worried about fibres from her clothes being in the car so I removed them. As I was doing this her hair came away from her head. This was a shock as I couldn't understand it. The blanket that Julie's body had been wrapped up in was put on another sheet as it was smelling, probably from the body fluids.

It must have been this sheet, contacting the sheet hanging up, which resulted in the hanging sheet getting a 16" x 16" blood stain. Julie's body was then wrapped in another sheet so that people or a person would not be able to look at her naked body. Another sentiment I cannot explain.

Annette Zekneys knew none of this when she and her colleagues set out to comply with the kidnapper's demands at 3.30 pm, Tuesday, 16 July. The officer would, in fact, be striving to save a life already lost.

At 5.50 pm, Detective Constable Zekneys purchased a platform ticket at Birmingham New Street Station, and walked to the Mercury phone booth in the snack bar on Platform 9. At 7.06, the phone rang, and she took it off the hook and answered, 'Hello.' There was no reply and then the line went dead. After waiting a further 19 minutes, the operation was called off for the day. Dispirited, Annette Zekneys returned to her car.

Three days later, the body of Julie Anne Dart was discovered in a remote Lincolnshire field. Michael Sams later wrote an account while in prison, explaining what had happened and how he had disposed of the body:

On the Tuesday 16th July, I had arranged to contact the Police at Birmingham New Street at 7 p.m. At 7 p.m. I rang and after hearing someone answer it, I played a recording of my instructions. they were clear, but what I hadn't bargained for was the phone suddenly going dead.

I then went back to the workshop and put Julie's body, still in the wheely bin, into the car, and took her south on the A1. Just south of Grantham I turned left. Then came to a T Junction, turned right. A little way along the road I spied a lonely turning on my left. There were no cars up the lane so I turned up.

Removed the wheely bin and then placed the body underneath a tree and within sight of the road & lane. I did not know where I was in relation to Stoke Summit [a favourite haunt of train-spotting enthusiasts]. Nor did I know that I had placed Julie's body within 50 yards of a disused railway line. It was now about 11.30 p.m. on the Tuesday.

I then retraced my route back to the A1 and then went back to the workshop. I spent the next hour or two cutting up the wheely bin and putting all Julie's clothes, and the hair that had come away, in sealed boxes. The next day, Wednesday 17th July, I took all the boxes to the Peterborough waste disposal site.

SEVEN

The Talkative Corpse

Fifty-year-old Robert Derek Skelton farms 579 acres of pasture with his two sons, Christopher and Andrew. His land stretches from the busy A1 trunk road across the B6403 and a railway embankment near the quiet Lincolnshire village of Easton, five miles due south of the market town of Grantham.

During the weekend of 6/7 July 1991, he had been cutting and conditioning a crop of grass in Broadwalk Field, leaving it in neat rows to dry for 24 hours. It was to form part of his cattle feed for the next winter. At 7.30 am, Monday, 8 July, he returned to his field, collected the grass and left, after securing the five-bar gate behind him.

Nothing could have prepared Skelton for the grim discovery he made the next time he entered Broadwalk Field, on Friday, 19 July, to secure fences. On this occasion, he was accompanied by his son Andrew and a Youth Training Scheme farmhand, Grant Sutcliffe. In a statement to the police, Skelton described what happened:

> *I pulled into the entrance of the field which is adjacent to the railway line. I immediately saw on my right a bundle under a tree. It was clearly visible, and there had been no attempt to hide*

it. At that time I presumed it was litter left by people using the lane.

The farmer explained that, over the years, the lane had been used by courting couples, people stopping for picnics and to relieve themselves, and all manner of others. He'd got so used to this that passing traffic didn't worry him any more.

Returning to the 'bundle under the tree', Skelton said:

I went over to it and saw it was a white sheet with a pink candy stripe. The bundle was tied up very well with a bluish coloured rope. There appeared to be three wrappings around the bundle and one lengthways. It was very secure.

When the three men got closer, they could see that it wasn't rubbish, so Andrew made a small cut in the sheet with his penknife. Peering into the bundle, they could see the shape of a human arm. Leaving Andrew and Grant to guard the body, Skelton jumped into his Land Rover and sped off to phone the police. After a brave attempt to stay with the bundle, the two lads moved over to a nearby hedge, away from the sickening smell emanating from the bundle.

The police had completely sealed off the area from public scrutiny when Home Office pathologist Professor John Stephen Jones arrived, pulling off the B6043 exactly four hours after the body had been discovered. The welcoming committee included Detective Chief Superintendent Cowman and Detective Chief Inspector Gordon Readman, who had intended to spend that evening mowing his front garden. Detective Inspector Newmarch and other officers from the Lincolnshire Police, including members of its Scenes of Crime Department, made up the group.

The body could not have been in better hands, for Professor Jones was a Fellow of the Royal College of Pathologists, and had a diploma in medical jurisprudence among other qualifications. He began taking notes, recording his first impressions.

The body appeared to have been wrapped in the sheet in such a way that the top and bottom ends of the sheet were situated at the head end, while the centre of the sheet covered the undersurface of the body, the buttocks and the back.

At the head end, the sheet was heavily soiled with blood and fluid from the putrefying body, [and the head] – which was flexed and tucked into the right shoulder region – was badly decomposed.

Numerous flies, occasional beetles and earwigs were present in the vicinity of the head end of the body. Numerous small larvae were present on the outside and inside of the opened sheet in the vicinity of the head.

After making sketches on his pad, Professor Jones completed his initial examination. He left the scene at 12.24 pm, ordering the body to be placed in a body sheet and securely wrapped for transport to the mortuary.

Forensic pathologists only deal with the dead and silent. Corpses cannot tell them why they died so pathologists must find the causes in other ways. They are the detectives of death – not life. They visit the body where it has been found, then examine the remains under controlled and sterile conditions during a post-mortem examination. Finally, they study the once-living person's medical history, if one is available. It is through this autopsy process that the body can speak after death. The celebrated American forensic pathologist, Michael Baden MD, has said: 'Deciphering the message is an art as well as a science.'

At the request of Mr T. J. Peart, Her Majesty's Coroner for Grantham, Professor Jones was asked to carry out such an examination on the corpse discovered in Broadwalk Field. He started at 1.15 pm, within the chilly confines of Grantham & Kesteven Hospital, and the post-mortem examination lasted several hours.

It was clear to Professor Jones that this young woman, looking so vulnerable on the table before him, had been in the prime of her life when she had been battered and strangled to death. The body showed no evidence of forcible rape or buggery. If there had been sexual intercourse prior to death, the woman had acceded to it through coercion or threat, rather than penetration being forced upon her while she struggled.

There were ligature marks on the lower surface of the middle third of the left forearm. A similar mark was present on the back of the left lower forearm immediately above the wrist, and two marks forming a 'V' were present on the flexor surface of the right wrist. Further examination revealed no evidence of bruising or other injuries to the hands and fingers. Her coral-coloured nail varnish was immaculate.

Turning his attention to the lower limbs, the pathologist noted a ligature mark 8 cm long by 0.8 cm wide on the left leg. Although this resembled the upper limb marks, it did not appear to have extended all the way around the leg. There was an almost identical mark on the lower right leg, and immediately above the right ankle, a series of intermittent red marks could be seen around the limb. The woman was saying that she had been chained.

Professor Jones took 39 items from the body for further, more comprehensive investigation. However, he had already found that his subject had suffered severe head injuries. A later examination would result in the discovery that Julie had also been strangled.

Although the post-mortem proper had been concluded, the body still continued to speak to the pathologist as he wrote up his report several hours later. However, the professor was faced with a puzzle. The decomposition changes implied that the murder victim had been kept in a sealed space for a prolonged period after death. In addition, the absence of undigested food in the stomach further suggested that death had occurred at least eight hours after her last known meal.

After more checks by the Lincolnshire Police, the identity of the talkative corpse from Broadwalk Field was revealed as Julie Anne Dart of 36 Hollin Park Crescent, Leeds.

The following Monday, with a full murder investigation now under way, another typed letter arrived. Addressed incorrectly, as before, to the 'Leeds City Police Headquaters Leeds – re: Julie Dart', it was sent directly to Millgarth Police Station, which now housed the Julie Dart incident room.

Checking with the Post Office, detectives learned that it had been posted in the 'Leeds MLO' (Mechanised Letter Office) area – which covers all of Leeds and even parts of Harrogate – on the day before, Sunday, 21 July. Like the Huntingdon-postmarked letter, it contained many spelling and grammatical errors:

> Words will never be able to express my regret that Julie had to be killed, but I did warn what would happen if anything went wrong, at the time of this letter there has been no publicity, if you do not find the body within a few days I will contact you as to the location, it will have to be moved today as it appears to be decomposing.

She was not raped or sexually abused or harmed in any way until she met her end, she was tied up and hit a few blows to the back of the head to render her unconcious and then strangled, she never saw what was to happen, never felt no pain or know anything about it.

The fire bomb was not left as promised as the selant around the combustables must have got knocked in transit and smelled badly, so it was never placed. Owens furniture store in Coventry was to be the target.

The mistake I appear to have made is that I did not know the voice at the end of the phone. I still intend to carry out this campain until I receive the monies however many people suffer. In two weeks or so I shall demonstrate my fire bomb.

I still require the same monies as before under the same conditions if you want to avoid serious fire damage and any further prostitutes life, to contact me place an ad in the Saturdays 'SUN' newspaper personal column and a phone call will be made to the box at Leicester Forest East northbound services, the box nearest the R.A.C. box. On the following Tuesday at 8.30 p.m. The courier to be the same W.P.C. as used last time (I presume it was her of course at Birmingh New Street) and when answering the phone must say, 'Julie speaking' she will once again be given instructions, a little clearer next time, if she misses the instructions a reaet phone call will be made straight away, she must pick it up a second time if she has got it the first time as only one repeat call will be allowed. If any phone box is occupied then a call will be made as soon as available. The calls as before will be recorded, this time by a hostage picked up on the Monday evening in other cities red light district.

The ad in the Sun to read 'Lets try again for Julies sake'. If no message is seen in Sat 27th or Sat 3 August then the fire bomb will definately be placed on Tuesday 6 August. No prostitutes will be held until the message is received or until the fire bomb fails to bring any responce.

This totally contradictory letter and the discovery of Julie's body provided yet another set of clues that could have eventually led the police to Julie's killer.

Julie's body had been found at a location almost midway along a straight line between Leeds and Huntingdon, and these two places are linked by the A1 and the East Coast Railway. The letter added further geographical reference points for the police: Coventry and Leicester. And this time, the letter had been posted in Leeds where the case had started. This suggested that, from Leeds in the north, the murderer's territory extended south-east through Grantham to Huntingdon, then due west to Coventry and Birmingham. Each of these cities and towns were served by the national rail network and, between three of the locations, the East Coast Railway and a busy trunk road, the A1. The police must have realised that, somewhere within the base and right-hand side of this triangle, the murderer continued to plot his crimes.

It was obvious to the investigators that the letter writer and the killer were the same individual. He had described how Julie had met her death, and the post-mortem examination had verified the details. Both of the typed letters sent to the police had been produced on the same old Olivetti machine, which had a distinctive fault in the letter 'f'. The envelopes of the three letters sent by the killer all differed: the Leeds-postmarked letter was contained in a brown banker-type envelope, and the first two, sent from Huntingdon, had been in white wallet-type envelopes, one of which came from W. H. Smith and was made from recycled paper. However, the paper used for all three letters was identical – sheets of lined A4 with two punched holes in the left-hand margin.

Later, Paul Rimmer, a forensic scientist based at the Home Office Forensic Laboratory, Birmingham, would examine the letter apparently written by Julie Dart. After comparing the writing in this with correspondence taken from Julie's bedroom, he would state categorically that the handwriting matched in every respect.

However, the mammoth task now facing investigators was to find the typewriter with the faulty 'f' from among the hundreds of thousands in existence. Then they had to discover a person who not only had access to this typewriter but also had the same paper and three different types of envelopes in his possession. They started by trying to trace the route of the Leeds-postmarked letter.

The envelope may have been handled by a dozen people, so it was necessary to interview everyone who might have touched it, in order to isolate the murderer's fingerprints. And, of course, the killer might have been wearing gloves ...

The irksome task fell to Detective Sergeant Shilleto. He began by visiting the chief inspector of Leeds Mechanised Sorting Office, Norman Bonarius. The detective watched as Bonarius closely examined the envelope while expounding on the mechanics of postal delivery. Shilleto learned that the letter had been posted 'after the Saturday collection and prior to the Monday morning collection – viz., between 1.30 pm, 20 July, and 8.30 am, 22 July 1991'.

The first-class postage stamp yielded an even more interesting clue. It depicted the head of a teddy bear, and Carol Daykin, assistant manager of Post Office Counters Ltd, confirmed that this particular stamp was sold only in presentation packs, each containing 10 different stamps and 12 gummed labels.

In an effort to leave no stone unturned in this homicide investigation, Detective Constable Harland later made enquiries at the British Philatelic Bureau in Edinburgh. Terry McMahon, the operations manager there, told him that Michael Sams had been one of their customers and regularly received details of all new stamp issues. Moreover, after looking through the computer sales ledger, McMahon confirmed that, on 26 March 1991, Sams had purchased a set of first-day covers including the teddy bear stamp. At the time of the Julie Dart enquiry, Valerie Tomlinson, a chartered biologist and member of the Institute of Biology, was a senior scientific officer based at the Home Office Forensic Science Laboratory at Wetherby, West Yorkshire. In this case, her job was to examine the items released to the police by Professor Jones. Just as Julie's body had communicated with the forensic pathologist, the material and rope used to parcel up her corpse would now talk to Valerie Tomlinson.

She first examined a number of intimate body samples for the presence of semen. She found none, but this did not rule out sexual intercourse: the killer could have worn a condom. She then turned her attention to the rope that had tied up the gruesome bundle. Constructed of green polypropylene, each of its constituent strands comprised nine twisted threads, each of which in turn were made up of a helical arrangement of 30 fibres. Armed with this information, detectives soon determined that this rope had been manufactured in Portugal by Cerfil (Compania Industrial de Cordas Artificiais), the British importer was Oakhurst Quality Products Ltd of Edenbridge, Kent, and they supplied the green monofilament polypropylene rope to, among other retailers, Parkers of Peterborough.

Of more significance was the finding of two tufts of carpet fibre entangled in the rope strands. The fibre was made up of 50 per cent yellow wool and 50 per cent brown nylon. If some of this rope could be discovered at the same place as this carpet, or even just fibres from each, this could help bring a killer to justice.

But perhaps the most important finding resulted from Valerie Tomlinson's examination of the sheet. This was flannelette with a pink-and-white candy-stripe pattern. Attached by metal staples to the underside, close to the bottom edge, was a laundry mark bearing the inscription: 'MA143'. In Tomlinson's experienced hands, the sheet revealed even more potential evidence. She applied several strips of clear one-sided sticky tape to the striped material and pressed down firmly. Then she pulled away the tape – with, sticking to it, any fibres or debris that may have been on the sheet – and sent this for further analysis at the Birmingham Science Laboratory. There, the tape revealed carpet fibres identical to those that had been found entwined in the rope. Pieces of that rope, along with the very same carpet fibres, were later found in Michael Sams' workshop.

On Thursday, 25 July, Sams worked at his workshop as usual. He'd spent the previous day alone and closed for business, checking his carefully laid ransom plans that, for the moment, had gone awry. It occurred to him that, as it was now getting darker earlier, he had to make sure that it would be easy for the police to find and follow his ransom directions, pointing the way to the next stop-off point.

Looking around, he hit on the idea of painting three heavy bricks with white emulsion paint – he would attach the instructions to these. The bricks would act as excellent markers, and there was no possibility of them being blown away if it became windy. Sams selected the bricks from a stack right outside T & M Tools.

As requested by Julie's killer, the police placed the item in the *Sun*'s personal column for Saturday, 27 July. Detective Constable Annette Zekneys was to be the courier again, if for no other reason than the killer might recognise her voice. Then, on Tuesday, 30 July, a third letter arrived at the incident room in Millgarth Police Station.

Postman Peter Bywater was aware that the police were interested in correspondence directed to 'Leeds City Police Head-quarters' – there was a notice pinned to the sorting office wall saying just that. As he was sorting through a pile of letters, he noticed an envelope bearing all the characteristics of this wanted mail.

It bore a York MLO postmark dated 10.15 am the previous day. Bywater rushed the letter to his supervisor, who hotfooted it over to postal executive Duncan Edwards. He had the sense to place it in a plastic bag to avoid further fingerprint contamination.

When the police opened the letter, they saw that both envelope and letter had been written by hand, almost if the person who had penned them had done so on a fast-moving train. As expected, the correspondence was littered with the usual mistakes:

> *Re Julie Dart.*
> *Seen message will phone 8.30 Tue 30 July. WPC will answer Julie & give make & colour + Reg number she will be given name & place from where hostage (prostitute) has been picked up Sun/Mon – Lets hope she has been reported missing by then – WPC will be given location of next call – operation may be called off if young lovers car is not in lane – if 'go' then location of detector will be given – the young lovers will not be harmed provided there is no-one else at the pick-up and the detector has not detected anything – the money will be picked up by the male in the lovers car whilst the female is held hostage – so marksmen shooting him would cause embarasing headlines for the police.*
>
> *After 2hrs pondering & writing this on the train (To post W Leeds) I am still at a loss to understand why the police are going ahead – will fall back on the Japanese production principles and can only come with the following.*

What followed was quite bizarre, for the killer seemed to have turned into a bookmaker, giving himself excellent odds against being arrested.

> 1) *I am sucessful (Good Chance)*
> 2) *Could be seen withdrawing. (Very long odds)*
> 3) *Could be seen profiting. (Very long odds)*
> 4) *Police try to follow WPC – Have second person in car – bug car – pick-up designed to block nearside doors – others observed – bug detector will detect transmitter. (Long odds)*

5) *Police to use aircraft/sattelite observation to follow – some device not known to me – good possibility – but escape route designed to overcome this + young female & prostitute will be in car police won't gamble with 2 lives – Therefore (Long odds)*

6) *Police set up road blocks over wide area possible as not one police car was observed on M1 on 10 July – My advantage – only I know pick-up area – escape route designed to overcome this.*

7 *Money will be marked. (Odds nil)*

8) *Serial numbers recorded – definate – money can be spent but not deposited in banks B/S for months.*

9) *Explosive device or marker dye in package of money – package to be opened by one of hostages – no risk.*

10) *Could be traced later – possible – think harder Sun/Mon/Tue.*

11) *Could be caught committing further offence – 1st & last crime.*

12) *Could be identified by lovers – No risk covered face.*

13) *Could be identified by prositute – little risk – darkness + bribe possible.*

14) *Must be more – keep calm – think and plan hard.*

GAME ODDS

Police <u>win.</u> Win money back – loose receive writers

female lovers
Prostitutes bodies.

<u>loose</u> Win no-one hurt – loose £145,000
Bluff   Win loose no money
loose receive
1.2.or 3 bodies.
Me Win
£145,000 Loose death of Julie
once same was finished will feel grief – contemplate death suicide in RTA.

<u>Loose</u> Death.
<u>Bluff</u> win? Loose?

I am tempted to ask why the bit of onfor relesed to press has been wrong – also why no T.V. coverage when found?

Julie was not blugeoned to death (Jim Oldfield – D Mirror) She was rendered unconscious by 3–4 blows to the back of the head & then strangled.

She never felt a thing. She wrote the letter herself Wed 11 pm, 10 July. Full typed details will be available next week whatever the outcome – also how Julie's body decomposed so quickly.

Just like the previous letters, this one contained more clues. It had been posted in York, which extended the murderer's range northeast of Leeds. York was also another major station on the East Coast Railway. The Post Office confirmed that the letter had been posted on Monday, 29 July, at the Leeman Road letterbox directly outside the York District Sorting Office, which is just 100 metres from the railway station.

Of course, the murderer's reference in the letter to spending two hours on a train might well have provided a vital clue to the killer's base. There now existed a direct rail and road link between Huntingdon, Leeds and York. Letters had been posted in all three locations, and indeed, Julie's body had been found not far from that very same East Coast Railway track. Sams worked in Newark where there is a mainline station, and he lived at Sutton-on-Trent where the same rail link cut across the bottom of the garden at Eaves Cottage. On Sundays, the journey time by rail from Newark to York – changing at Leeds – is just two hours.

On about 29 July, the senior investigating officer, Bob Taylor, rang Professor Paul Britton at Arnold Lodge, a high-security hospital for the criminally insane. A forensic clinical psychiatrist, Professor Britton is one of Britain's foremost crime and offender profilers, and works closely with colleagues at the FBI Academy in Quantico, Virginia.

Having been briefed about the kidnapping of Julie Dart, and having read the letters sent by the kidnapper, Professor Britton formed an initial opinion as to the type of person who had abducted Julie. He decided that he was a 'games player' – a criminal who thought he could outwit the public and the nation's police. He would be set in his ways – after all, he had written that he had planned the kidnapping and the ransom demand months beforehand. Britton also concluded that the man might be a psychopath – one of the most dangerous of our human species – who would kill without feelings of remorse or guilt, and who would stop at nothing until his dysfunctional requirements were satisfied.

At 8.17 pm, Tuesday, 30 July, Detective Constable Zekneys stepped into the telephone booth at the northbound Leicester Forest East motorway services between junctions 21 and 22 of the M1.

At 8.31, the phone rang. The officer answered as instructed: 'Hello, Julie speaking.' A male voice was heard amid music in the background, but the message from Sams was incoherent. Zekneys said: 'If you are listening, I cannot understand what is being said. Do you want details of my car?' All the detective heard was 'services', then the line went dead and the phone didn't ring again.

Two days later, on 1 August, a fourth letter, this time post-marked Coventry, arrived at Millgarth Police Station. It had passed through the Coventry main sorting office in Bishop Street at 7.30 p.m, on 31 July. Handwritten, it contained the usual mistakes, was written on the same lined paper as some of its predecessors, and was sealed inside a brown banker's envelope identical to those previously posted in Leeds and York:

No go last night was not free Monday afternoon for make-up to get hostage Monday evening – make up takes hours. Your WPC should have been able to hear I have tried it on an extension. Will post this Coventry next one Bristol/Manchester may as well cover all parts of country. Next week I will definately be free all Monday & Tuesday so will have no problem with hostage or insendary – you will like incendary similar to one shown on TV the other night – seems to be the same timing system but nicads (Nickel Cadmium Batteries) for ignition system.

 Still have not worked out who police would gamble with 3 lives – cannot see you providing £145,000 for nothing without proof of further action by me.

 Nor can I see you providing an empty package which will result in 2 further deaths (both females – the male only used for collecting from pick-up.

 Still all my affairs in order. All life insurance paid up – so I'll gamble. I did say last time to WPC to answer Julie speaking & then give the car make and reg number. I need to see her pass me at one point before returing to drop package.

Bye ring Tuesday.

P.S Paper – WHS recycled envelope.

In an effort to narrow down where the letter had been posted, Post Office shift manager Stephen Hughes could only tell DS Shilleto that the relevant letterbox could have been any one of the several thousand within the Coventry CV1 to CV35 postcode areas.

The fact that the blackmailer had previously mentioned fire-bombing a store in Coventry and then went on to post a letter in the same city gave added weight to a developing theory that a line running from Birmingham through Coventry to Huntingdon in the east was the southern border of the offender's territory. With York and Leeds to the north, the shape of a possible triangle was beginning to form.

Linguistic experts were called in to examine the correspondence for signs of a phonetic rendering peculiar to certain dialects. Two villages in South Yorkshire, Grimethorpe and Worsborough, were selected as likely candidates because the misspelled 'Headquaters' could be pronounced 'Headkwatters', which was the way this word was rendered there. The two mining communities were just 40 miles from Newark and from Sams' cottage.

Grimethorpe is situated on a direct line between Leeds and Huntingdon. It was also between the M1 and A1 motorways and just four miles from the East Coast Railway. At a later date, Worsborough would become of major significance. Situated just eight miles south-east of Grimethorpe, it is three miles away from the tiny hamlet of Dodworth and junction 37 of the M1 motorway.

As Sams had so cockily pointed out to the police in the postscript to his latest letter, he had used W. H. Smith recycled stationery. In an effort to find out where this particular envelope had been sold, officers turned to the large retail chain of stationers for assistance, but it was like looking for a needle in a haystack. One of the Huntingdon envelopes had particularly excited police attention. Detectives met Norman Featherstone, controller of W. H. Smith's Dunstable warehouse, who was able to confirm, through his extensive knowledge of stock control, that this particular envelope had come from a batch of 140,000 delivered to his branches in June 1991. Police forensic experts later found that the Huntingdon envelope had a flaw in it, and Featherstone was then able to confirm that it ran through every envelope in that particular batch. He also said that, among other W.H. Smith branches, the one in Newark had received a supply of the very same.

The laundry tag – bearing the legend 'MA143' – which had been stapled to the sheet used to wrap Julie's corpse, became the source of another line of enquiry. It was established that the tag had been manufactured by Isaac Braithwaites & Sons of Kendal, Cumbria, and that they had supplied millions of these items throughout the country since 1940. Detective Sergeant Field was given the thankless task of tracking down the last person to possess the tag and the sheet. He eventually arrived at the Laundrama in Kenilworth in Warwickshire, where he spoke to a 72-year-old man called Roy. He recalled a laundry agency that had doubled as a corner shop in Moseley Avenue. The initials 'MA' could signify 'Moseley Avenue'. The search was hotting up.

Tracing Eld's Newsagents at 92 Moseley Avenue took DS Field no time at all. The proprietor, John Eld, confirmed that he had issued laundry tag number 143, and promptly handed over his ledger. Unfortunately, there was no record of the customer's name or address. Interviewing the entire population of Kenilworth, and nearby Coventry, asking if they remembered the tag, was clearly impossible. However, the police did compare the electoral roll of 1940 with the one for 1991, and interviewed all those who appeared on both. But no one remembered the laundry tag.

Michael Sams had been furious when he had failed to make contact with the police at Birmingham New Street station. In a letter to his solicitor, he tells of his actions as he tried to arrange collection of the ransom money:

> I still thought the Police would cooperate so on the Thursday (18 July) I typed another letter to the Leeds Police. Which I posted in the Leeds Railway Station letter box on Sunday 21 July. The letter was between two other letters which I was also posting. For some reason or other I thought I no longer needed the typewriter to write anymore letters so I threw it away.
>
> I saw the Police message in the Sun on Saturday 27 July,

and I then realised I needed a typewriter, so I decided to write it by hand.

Teena & I were expecting visitors on Sunday 28 July. So she told me I could stay later at the shop or station so it would give her time to prepare. I travelled to York on the train & posted the York letter on the station. The P.O. were wrong when they sat it was posted at Leeman Road P.O. 3.30 am – 10.15 am on the 29/7/91.

I had then intended to try again on 30/7/91 but I had a problem with the moped. I [sic] would not run or tick over. So I went to the phone box just south of Sheffield and phoned the courier at Leicester. I then had to write another urgent letter to arrange another run on 7 August.

I then hit a bigger problem on 6 August, MON[*]. Teena wanted to go to Peterborough with me to see her friends at 31 New Rd. I had arranged to pick the rent up 6 Aug (MON). So I could be free all Tue evening – when Teena went to Peterborough with me she saw that I had finished the decorating. This ended my reason for being out Tuesday evenings. Further runs would have to be Wed.

On 7 August, Detective Constable Zekneys returned, as instructed by Julie's killer, to the telephone kiosk at Leicester Forest East motorway services. She was accompanied by an élite team of the Regional Crime Squad. Arriving at 8.16 pm, she found herself among a group of 'squaddies' rushing to use the same phone. Luckily she was first in the door, and refusing to vacate her position despite the young men's protests, she stayed there until the operation was called off at 9.15. Teena hadn't allowed her husband out to play.

The following morning found the Samses at a local auction: Michael Sams needed another typewriter. In due course, Lot No. 89 – a machine once owned by the late Esther Webster who had passed away in July 1991 – was knocked down to Sams, who paid £10.06. That afternoon, Michael returned to his workshop and altered the typeface with a mini-drill and grindstone. He then typed another letter (again full of mistakes) and drove to Nottingham where he posted it.

---

*The 6th of August was actually a Tuesday, so Sams must have meant the 5th.

Re Julie,

Could not make it Tuesday evening due to the fact that there was no suitable hostage in the Huddersfield red light area on Monday evening, also our young lovers are not down the lane on Monday evenings, the latter more important than the prostitute, as a prostitute can be eliminated any time should the police no co-operate. But another suitable couple have been located but the day will have to be changed to Wednesday. This being the case a phone call will be made to the usual box on Wednesday 14 August at 8.15 pm (not 8.30 pm). The extra 15 min being needed due to location change.

Also this time your W.P.C. will need a Stanley type knife, with a sharpe blade, she will be traveling to the box where there is one located. this will be the last time you will receive a call at the usual location, should anything go wrong, then you will be given the location of the incendary device or the location of the prostitutes body, mind you, you found Julies within 24 hours. I did think of hiding her body till it was all over but felt sorry for her, she was only killed because she saw where I was, but this time the second prostitute will only be needed to be kept for 24 hrs also so there should not problem if nothing goes wrong.

I will also need to know the phone number of where you want to be told the location of the incendary, this phone number must be given at the second box not the first box at Leicester.

This letter arrived at Millgarth Police Station the following day, 8 August. The police were quick to notice that the typeface differed from that of the previous letters, but the usual errors showed that it had been written by the killer of Julie Dart. The paper was also the same, but it had been sent in a white Croxley Script envelope.

Nottingham added another location to the growing list of places visited by the murderer. After drawing a few straight lines on a map, it appeared that Nottingham was – at least for the time being – the central point of the offender's territory.

EIGHT

A Bomb, Bricks and a Claypit

he pressure on Michael Sams was now building up. His previous attempts to get his financial affairs in order had failed. Now, all he had to show for his efforts was a brutal murder and several botched ransom demands. His life was falling apart.

Sensing all was not well, Teena took her husband out for dinner on his birthday on Sunday, 11 August. He moaned throughout the meal. Later, Teena noted in her diary: 'We argued all the time. He did not appreciate what I had done. I have had just a belly full. Never been so fed up in my life.'

The day when Sams would try to collect the ransom for the fourth time was a Wednesday, his day off. On Tuesday night he stayed at the workshop and repaired his moped before placing it into the back of his Metro. Then, at the crack of dawn, he drove off to Toton Railway Depot on the outskirts of Nottingham, where he planned to do some train-spotting – take a few photographs and list train numbers. However, when he arrived he realised that he'd forgotten to bring his Praktika camera, so, to pass the time, he sat on a railway embankment deep in thought. Then, as the time approached to phone the police, the one-legged man climbed into his car and drove north towards Wakefield.

At 8.16 pm, Sams stepped into a telephone kiosk somewhere along his route and, in a fake Pakistani accent, spoke to Detective

Constable Zekneys. Then he drove south along the M1 until he reached Barnsley, where in a callbox he taped a message underneath the directory shelf.

As requested, Annette Zekneys answered the telephone at Leicester Forest East with the words: 'Hello, Julie speaking.'

The voice on the line said: 'I am going to tell you where to go because my tape recorder's broken.'

For a few seconds, the speaker's words were garbled and the police officer thought that she'd lost the caller once again.

Then the man's voice said: 'Walkman Gardens. I abducted her last night. I want you to take the M1 northbound to junction 40, not junction 39. Then take the A638 to Wakefield. Go an eighth of a mile, and on your right-hand side, there's a telephone box by a bus stop ...'

Annette Zekneys interrupted the caller, asking if he wanted the details of her car. Sams said he did, so the police officer gave them to him. Then she enquired about the name of the girl he'd just kidnapped.

The man replied: 'Sarah Davis. She lives at Walkman Gardens, or something like that. I'm not quite sure. In Ipswich.'

When he rang off, Detective Constable Zekneys knew the route she had to take to the telephone box near Wakefield, and that she had to be there within 90 minutes – by 9.45 pm. She sped along the motorway with the better part of 100 miles to cover – at times, her speed exceeded 100 mph – with her police colleagues in unmarked cars leap-frogging her every mile or so.

This time Michael Sams was turning up the pressure on the police by introducing the name and address of a fictitious woman whom he had supposedly abducted in Ipswich. He knew that they wouldn't be able to check out his story before he collected the money. Although they quickly discovered that 'Walkman Gardens' didn't exist, a phonetically similar place did, which was a prostitutes' haunt in Ipswich.

On her arrival at the A638, DC Zekneys found that there was no callbox an eighth of a mile down the road. Conferring with her superiors by radio, it was agreed that she would go to a telephone kiosk at the junction with the Broadway, and another detective constable, Yvonne Archer, would cover the one opposite the junction with Eden Avenue.

At 10.35, the phone in DC Zekneys' callbox rang. She picked

up the receiver, then the line went dead.

At that moment, she noticed the figure of a man standing outside in the darkness, watching her. This sudden presence sent icy shivers down her spine. She knew it couldn't be a police officer, for her colleagues in the operational command vehicle were parked at a discreet distance.

The stranger seemed impatient, so she opened the kiosk door. The man asked, 'Have you broken down, love?'

Looking across at her parked car, DC Zekneys swallowed nervously. 'No,' she replied.

The man persisted. 'Are you waiting for the AA? It's just that I drove past earlier and you were here then. Could I use the phone, please?'

The police officer said that he couldn't because she was waiting for a call to sort something out, and with that, she closed the door and turned her back on him. Over her shoulder, she watched as he walked towards a row of houses and disappeared. At 10.55 the phone rang again. It was the enquiring stranger.

'Hello, love,' he said. 'It's the lad again that was outside the phone box. Are you sure you're all right? It's just that it seemed you were a bit panicky and I didn't want to leave you on your own.'

When she assured him that everything was all right, the line went dead. Five minutes later, the evening's operation to catch Julie's killer was terminated.

Sams never said a word to Annette Zekneys while she waited in that telephone box. It was Yvonne Archer who took his call. She had arrived there dead on 9.45 pm, and 11 minutes later, the phone rang. When she picked it up, she found that the telephone cradle had jammed down, but she was able to release it by striking it with her fist.

'Who's that?' she asked.

The killer replied: 'Is that Julie?'

'Yes, this is Julie speaking,' said the detective.

'Hello. It's me again. Problems. I'll have to ring you back in half an hour.' But Michael Sams didn't phone back.

He had been watching the traffic speeding along the M1 from a footbridge that spanned the motorway, then left to make his call to the telephone box where DC Zekneys should have been to receive his instructions. On hearing a strange voice – that of DC Archer – he became suspicious. He couldn't figure what the police were playing at, or what they would do next. It crossed his mind that they might be about to tap him on the shoulder and arrest him. Then, when he spotted a vehicle near to the drop site (which could have been one of theirs), he took fright and left.

For the previous four months, 26-year-old David Herring had been employed to clear up rubbish thrown out of car windows along the M1 motorway – what he described as 'litter picking', even though the job came with the somewhat grand title of 'motorway maintenance worker'. At 10.50 am on the morning of Thursday, 15 August, he was wandering along the southbound carriageway of the motorway, due south of junction 37 – the Dodworth/Barnsley turn-off. As he approached a disused railway bridge, he spotted what he called an 'article' at the side of the ARMCO crash barrier that protected the bridge supports. The 'article' turned out to be a brick that had been painted white, and taped to it was a brown envelope with the number '(3)' written in the top left-hand corner.

Herring stopped and peered closer. Then he saw a cylinder-shaped silver tin. The top was sealed, and Herring formed the opinion that it couldn't be opened easily. Not that he wanted to, of course, for on the lid there were two red lights and one was illuminated.

Taking a well-advised step backwards, Herring started to consider what might happen to him if he picked up this thing. A small piece of coiled wire on the lid seemed to enter the container. Curiosity getting the better of him, he picked up the device, and then the penny dropped: it might be a bomb. Gently he put the device down again, took three steps backwards, then hightailed it down the hard shoulder to his workmates.

They were equally puzzled, and in a moment of decision, they flagged down a passing police traffic vehicle. A radio call was made to Superintendent Melvin Miles who was in charge of traffic support for the South Yorkshire Police. He put in a call to the Bomb Squad, requesting them to attend. Then he jumped into the fastest car at his disposal and tore up the motorway with blue beacons flashing.

What Herring had picked up was now being treated as an explosive device. For two hours, the police sealed off that section of the M1, despite the ensuing traffic chaos.

Staff Sergeant Ian Akeroyd had been looking forward to

lunch at the Royal Army Ordnance Corps' Beeston Barracks when the call came through 'scrambling' him to the incident. On his arrival, he studied the object through binoculars at the sensible distance of 130 metres. A remote-controlled vehicle was moved into a position where Sergeant Akeroyd could examine the device in more detail. The vehicle's television monitor showed him exactly what Herring had seen from close up.

Using the expertise in bomb disposal that he had gained over the previous 14 months, Akeroyd recommended blowing up the device in a controlled explosion, and South Yorkshire Police agreed. After police officers had removed themselves to a safe distance, a loud bang was heard and the device disintegrated in a cloud of smoke and debris.

The suspect bomb was now in a thousand pieces. However, the brick and the envelope remained undamaged. Inside the envelope was a stencilled message.

Moving at high speed, the police travelled a short distance to the next bridge, where they found David Herring staring vacantly at a second white-painted brick.

Some might say that the South Yorkshire Police acted somewhat hastily in ordering the almost complete destruction of what might have turned out to be vital evidence. However, at the time they believed Sergeant Akeroyd's assessment that it was a bomb of some sort. Then again, they were not aware of the possible importance of the tin in the investigation of Julie Dart's murder.

Unfortunately, neither No. 3 Regional Crime Squad nor the West Yorkshire Police had informed their South Yorkshire Police colleagues of the operation to catch Julie's kidnapper and killer. However, it must be emphasised that many police operations require secrecy, even within the service, with everyone concerned operating on a 'need to know' basis.

Sams' sixth letter arrived at Millgarth Police Station, having been posted in Grantham, Lincolnshire on 19 August. In it, the killer explained his actions in mocking and almost incomprehensible terms:

> *Re Julie,*
> *Thank you for your message that the South Yorkshire Police had closed the motorway between J36–J37, for bridge structure*

checks, I know & you know the real reason was that you were looking for message 4. That was the problem mentioned to your W.P.C. I drooped the brick out of the passenger door by accident and the envelope fell from my grasp and blew away, message 5 was not placed, I did not think that you would think that the trail was to have stopped at the bridge, but somehow you guessed there was a message missing or it seem blowing about the motorway, when I heard your message I was on my way back to try to retreive message 3, had you kept obsevation rather than broadcast the message, then yourstruly would have been seen that evening trying to recover it.

Game is now ababdoned, Crimewatch U.K. will tell me most of what I wanted to know, but what I was realy looking for was the package, I never envisaged any money in the package, but had made arrangements for the bug/transmitter would have been in, to be made inoperative, I wanted a sample of the type police would use. I did not need the car number from your W.P.C. as I saw here at Leicester Forrest East on 6 August, hence the reason for no calls that week, she will never know just how near she came to the writer, my 'proper' detector did not pick anything up in Leicester, that was the reason for message 4, I needed your W.P.C. to be directly underneath so that the detector would see if there was any bug/transmittor in the package, so I still do not know the frequency used.

You will have to file your papers until I try again, which is what this was all about, as you know I never picked anyone up in Ipswitch or planted and devise, I didn't need to following Julies unfortunate death, you would co-operate in anthink I said.

For your records Julie was picked up on Tuesday 9 July 11.30 pm just off Roundhey Road and was wearing jeans not a skirt, I believe I mentioned last time the date and reason she died. The body detiated so quick, was that it was kept in a wheely bin in a greenhouse for two very hot days, I thought this was the best way to keep, the body, her head was wrapped in a towel, but when this was removed to clean her up before dropping her, her hair came away, stuck to the blood on the towel. The wheely bin was used to transport the body to where you found her, although you will know that by the tracks.

This letter tells us more about Sams' state of mind than the previous correspondence he'd sent to the police. It contains far more grammatical errors and misspellings – surprising for a man with an 'O' level in English language. To my mind, there are two possible explanations why Sams should write such an illiterate letter: that he was mentally falling apart or that he was very drunk (and Sams never drank to excess). The police have a third explanation – that Sams was being exceptionally cunning, having carefully thought out the letter with the object of dispersing disinformation in part to disguise where the drop point for the courier was to have been.

An even closer study of the letter shows Sams' true hand, for it reveals that much of what he threatened was so much 'huff and puff'. No prostitute had been abducted in Ipswich, and the 'detector' with its red lights was nothing more than an elaborate hoax. However, knowing that the police couldn't take any chances, he still had the upper hand, and he was quick to remind his pursuers just what a cold-blooded bastard he could be.

The final pieces of the ransom failure puzzle fell into place at 8.30 pm on Saturday, 24 August 1991. Twenty-two-year-old Alan Moore regularly made telephone calls from a kiosk outside a small restaurant called La Bohème in Dodworth Road, Barnsley, which leads from the town centre towards the M1. On that day, Alan rang his friend Paul Turnball, and as he was waiting for the call to be answered, he began tapping his fingers under the directory tray. He touched something and, to his amazement, pulled out an envelope that had been stuck to the underside of the shelf. In a statement he later made to the police, he said:

> Out of curiosity I pulled the envelope off which tore the paper. I looked inside the envelope and saw a white note inside. I read the note and it said something about a device with a flashing box having been planted on the motorway. There was also a razor blade contained in the envelope. I remembered that there had been some recent incidents on the motorway involving some kind of devices, and although I thought I had found some type of practical joke, I attended Barnsley Police Station later that night and handed it to the officer on the front desk.

It was now a simple matter of detective work to figure out the blackmailer's intentions on the night Annette Zekneys received her phone call from Michael Sams at Leicester Forest East. Leaving the motorway service area, she drove north and should have arrived at the phone box on the A638 at the junction of Eden Avenue by 9.45 pm. Sams would have then directed her to the kiosk outside the La Bohème in Dodworth Road. There, the note later found by Alan Moore would have sent her to the M1 and the white-painted brick and a second note that read:

MESSAGE NEXT BRIDGE 400 METRES 2 MIN ALLOWED
DETECTOR ON PANEL
CARRY MONEY

The blackmailer had explained in his letter that another note of instructions had blown away, and that was why there were no details attached to the second brick found by David Herring. However, the police now believe that there never was any note at the second white brick – it was simply a marker.

But from here on, the plan was obvious. Sams would have stood on the next bridge, south of the structure carrying the Dove Valley Trail across the M1. He would have dropped a length of rope over the top, attached to which was a dog clip. After the police officer attached the package to this, Sams would have hauled it up and made good his escape.

What was left of the tin was forensically reconstructed, and it turned out to have been an 'Aquarium' brand fishfood container. Perhaps, as had been suggested by the dog clip, this indicated that the criminal had a pet or two – a dog *and* fish? Sams owned both.

The enormous task of tracing the white-painted bricks fell to Detective Sergeant Tim Grogan and his partner Detective Constable Hadley. They were aware that Julie's killer could have picked up the two bricks anywhere, and that the chances of the offender being a 'brickie' were very remote.

Their enquiries took them from a forensic laboratory to the Steetley Brick Company at Chesterton, Newcastle-under-Lyme in Staffordshire, where Grogan spoke with Andrew Biggs, the firm's senior technologist. After a short examination, during which one of the bricks – which were actually called, in the jargon of the brick industry, 'channel blocks' – was sliced in two and examined under a microscope, it was deduced that, unlike modern bricks, this had been pressed rather than extruded into shape.

The next day, several fragments were analysed by Professor Ansell Durham at Leicester University. X-rays proved that the 'blocks' were made of a clay known as 'Lime Rich Upper Etruria Marl', and the professor was able to pinpoint the claypit at Bradwell, just up the road from the Steetley Brick Company. The investigators set about tracing the customers of the Bradwell clay works, not an easy task since the firm had gone out of business in the late 1970s. After many hours of fruitless chasing of company records and clients, Grogan and Hadley had to admit defeat.

After Sams' arrest, a pile of old Imperial Staffordshire Blue bricks with shallow frogs and three fluted channels – Class 'A' engineering bricks made from the same clay as the 'channel blocks' – were found in a rear garden that adjoined Swan and Salmon Yard. Sams had 'liberated' a few and taken some to the former premises of Peterborough Power Tools, and two half-bricks were found propping up shelves at T & M Tools.

NINE

Millmeece

On 15 October 1991, 35-year-old Oonagh Clarke sat down at her desk to start work. She was employed by British Rail as personal secretary to the Chief Executive (Railways), John Welsby, and worked in an office at Euston House, Eversholt Street, London. Among her responsibilities was opening the mail. That morning, one letter aroused her interest more than the five others in her tray. It was marked:

FOR THE ATTENTION OF A SENIOR EXECUTIVE ONLY

Oonagh would later tell detectives that this type of instruction on letters sent to British Rail was not unusual, and was normally associated with passengers with something to complain about. However, on opening the envelope she was surprised to find another sealed envelope tucked inside, which contained a two-page letter with a technical diagram on the first page. Scanning the letter, she realised it was a threat to British Rail and required immediate attention. She took it and the envelopes to Pat Murphy, secretary to another executive, and asked that the items be dealt with urgently.

Pat placed the letter and envelopes on a window shelf, saying, 'We get some nutters.' Between sips of coffee, she called the British Transport Police, who have jurisdiction over British Rail property and crime. Within the hour, Detective Chief Inspector Pacey arrived to study the letter.

Unless we receive a cash payment OF £200,000 we shall cause the derailment of an express train, either the D.T.V. of an East coast 225 or the D.T.V. of a West coast push-pull. A high speed section has been selected and some materials already concealed nearby, below is a drawing of how we intend.

We are extreemly serious about the course of action should you ignore this letter or no money is forthcoming. We expect you shall call the police, but any publicity or visible police action will result in us not communicating again. Should you ignore this letter then you will be able to see how serious we were.

Should you also pretend to go along with our demands but do not deliver any money then this will make us even madder than ignoring the letter.

The £200 thousand to be made up as follows, exactly.
£50,000 new £50 notes packed in 4 bundles. Not consecutive numbers.
£50,000 used £50 notes packed in 4 bundles.
£40,000 used £20 notes packed in 8 bundles.
£40,000 new, new type £20 notes packed in 8 bundles. Not consecutive numbers.
£20,000 used £10 notes.

The money to be transported in an unlocked case, as the money will be transfered to our case along the route. The money will of course be scanned for any transmitting device, and a metal detector to check for any metal object or reflector etc, police communications will also be monitored with two frequency scanners, one for land, one for aircraft etc.

We would also mention at this point that no-one in our families knows anything about this action, and the person making the phone calls knows not what action we are taking. He is only being paid to make a few phone calls.

Next Monday 21 OCT you will insert the following advert in the 'Evening Standard' personal column, 'The train is ready to depart', we will then know that all is ready, on the following WED 23rd two female employee's of B.R. (Preferably two members of the transport police), must be at Crewe station at 3pm and park in the 'Police vehicles only' space for 30 mins, they must be in the car they will be using to deliver the money, the car must be a small Metro or Nova type due to the width restriction later in the journey, it must be a three door and have no ariels or phone etc, the rear seats must be folded up completely, after 30 mins they can leave. They must return at 6.30pm and park in the same spot, the only item in the rear must be a case containing the money, one woman must stay in the car, the other to go to the phones on platform three and await a phone call at around 7pm, she must wait until the call is received, this call will only givea name of a B.R. station and a time, they must travel to this town and await a phone call at the time given. The phone box is located 50 yards the other side of the cross roads which are just down the road from the station given, the phone box in the station cannot be used, for certain reasons. The phone box (two of them) are located outside the Post Office, When she answers she must say 'This is Amanda speaking' so that we know we have the right person, she must then just listern, it must always be the passenger who takes phone calls, the driver to remain in the car at all times. The person receiving the calls must wear a skirt and shoes with heels, we want no Olympic sprinter in trainers, the two woman must have a good road atlas and have good road direction sense.

If at any time both of the phone boxes are occupied, wait, but after receiving each call she must then open the boot door for 30secs, at some stage this will be checked to make sure no-one has been picked up.

Note. As security against a police ambush we have an ace card to be played at the time the money is picked up, this you will learn of later. But your females will not be harmed in any way if they attempt no heroics, there will be a firearm trained on the driver at the time of the pick up, but she will not see anyone.

WILL NEED TORCH

WARNING YOUR FEMALES WILL BE IN
DANGER IF MONEY NOT REAL

As DCI Pacey considered how to deal with the blackmailer's demands, Sams was having problems of his own. His stepfather had had a stroke and was now lying in Airdale Hospital. Sams had to visit him with Iris, and then discuss the money his mother had loaned him. After a few hours at Sidney Walker's bedside, Iris and Sams drove to her house at Silsden, north-west of Bradford, where Iris cooked an evening meal before he left for Sutton-on-Trent at 7 pm.

It was a stormy night, with gale-force winds battering the area. Nevertheless, reluctant to drive straight back to Teena and her whining, he made his way through Bradford to the M606 and M62, heading for the turning for Huddersfield. By now he was extremely upset. The sight of Sidney dying before his eyes and the tears rolling down his mother's cheeks were almost too much to bear, especially on top of his own domestic problems. For a brief second, he almost lost control of his car, swerving to miss a lorry. He pulled himself together and parked in a layby. After all, he was an 'advanced motorist' with a certificate to prove it. He didn't want a smash-up and lose his other leg.

The rising gale rocked his little Metro; driving rain lashed down and the windows quickly misted up. He'd had enough. He was sick and tired of life. Cock-up after cock-up. Job after job. Marriage after marriage. So many homes and the women. Then his sadness turned to anger. Julie Dart and the police. The bastards had hacked his leg off. He despised Teena, her weakness and demands. Then there was the spectre of the tax man, the court judgments. Peterborough Power Tools was now only a painful memory, but oh, how hard he'd worked to succeed. Now his mother wanted her money back; he was in the shit with T & M Tools, in serious debt. He owed money all over the shop and was living off the state. Michael Sams was one angry mother of a killer in that layby.

'I was mad,' he told me. 'I had no option but to teach the bastards a lesson.' And it was then, in the little orange Metro, that he hatched another plot to keep the 'Old Bill' busy. Pulling on a pair of heavy industrial gloves to avoid leaving fingerprints, he grabbed pen and paper to write the following letter:

Re Julie (with no hair)

As you are no where near on my tail the time has come to collect my £140000 from you. I do not get any bigger sentence for 2 murders and prostitutes are easy to pick up but as this time you know I mean business I dont need to pick one up until Monday & I have purfected the pick up. The money to be the same as before

On Wed 21 Oct the same WPC will be at the phone box on Platform 3 of Carlisle Station (bottom of ramp) at 8pm for message (recorded) at 9.15pm approx.

I believe you will deliver the money as you will not risk life of WPC or prostitute

Hard luck I have nothing to do with Bradford or Sheffield prostitutes battering I will kill for money not sex anyway I wouldnt have sex with a prostitute

Letters are stamped and dropped on train havnt you ever wondered why that are stamped

Hope you can read writing hard writing in large gloves

He addressed the envelope to 'West Yorkshire Police, Millgate, Leeds'. In his anger, he might have made a slip by referring to 'Millgate' when it should have been 'Millgarth'. Then again, was he playing a cat-and-mouse game with the police? His workshop was just 50 metres away from Mill Gate in Newark-on-Trent.

Sams now appeared to be running two separate plans to extort money. The British Rail scheme would commence on Wednesday, 23 October 1991, when two female officers from the British Transport Police would be at Crewe railway station waiting for a telephone call from Sams at 3 pm. This was to be a re-run of his previous attempt to extort a large sum of money, but this time, he'd upped the ante to £200,000.

The second plan was for the usual £140,000 plus cash cards. However, the scheme was flawed for, in his letter to West Yorkshire Police, he had specified Wednesday, 21 October when it should have been Wednesday, the 23rd. Had he intended the

Carlisle plan to take place on the Monday, the 21st? Surely he couldn't carry out two collections simultaneously? Or was he using one plan as a smokescreen for the other? Which was the true plan and which was the false?

DCI Pacey of the British Transport Police had handed the British Rail letter to the Cheshire Police (who cover Crewe), who in turn passed it on to Detective Chief Superintendent Pat Fleming, coordinator for No. 9 (Metropolitan) Regional Crime Squad in London. Fleming decided that it was likely that the writer would carry out his threat to derail an express train, which, if the police didn't act swiftly, could entail the loss of many lives. The two officers set up an operation codenamed 'ORIENT', possibly with the Orient Express railway in mind. As the detectives called their colleagues together, they had no idea of the links between their crisis and the Julie Dart murder enquiry several hundred miles to the north.

DCS Fleming circulated every other police force in Britain with details of the blackmailer's letter. On Saturday, 19 October, a copy fell on to the desk of DCI Eddie Hemsley, manager of the Dart enquiry office at Leeds' Chapeltown. He immediately noticed the significance of the 'demand with menaces' and tele-phoned Fleming at New Scotland Yard.

Over the telephone, the two investigators discussed the simi-larities between the letter now in the possession of the Yard and the ones in Yorkshire. The sums of money demanded differed, but there had been almost identical instructions to provide the cash in bundles of £50, £20 and £10 notes. The BR letter had been sent in an envelope identical to the one used for the third in the Julie Dart series (W. H. Smith/white/window). In both cases, the female police couriers would attend telephone boxes where they would receive their first set of route instructions. The day chosen for both transfers of money was a Wednesday, which indi-cated that this was a day off from work for the blackmailer. All the letters were badly spelt and contained almost identical gram-matical errors. Finally, and particularly significantly, railways featured prominently in each scheme – not only the use of tele-phone kiosks at railway stations, but also the detailed knowledge of the railway displayed in the BR letter.

Hemsley briefed Fleming, including the forensic psychia-trist's opinion that their man was a 'games player' who enjoyed outwitting the police. This came as no surprise. This cunning criminal seemed to be attempting to smokescreen a genuine operation with a decoy. But which was which?

George Clayton enjoyed the same interest in railways and rolling stock as Michael Benniman Sams. However, whereas Sams' enthusiasm was limited to model railways and train-spotting, the 55-year-old Clayton had a whole railway system to play with. As head of British Rail's department at the Railway Technical Centre in Derby, there was nothing this expert didn't know about trains.

When British Rail received Sams' extortion letter, they called upon Clayton for professional advice. He responded with a ten-page report that spelled out the real threats to life and property if the blackmailer did as he said he intended and derailed a train. Although many of Sams' technical terms and abbreviations were slightly askew, George Clayton reckoned that British Rail had a serious if not lethal maniac on their hands.

After studying Sams' sketch and considering all the factors, he concluded that such a device could indeed derail a fast-moving train. In his mathematical calculations, he had taken into consideration the speed and weight of a train travelling at either 225 kph or 170 kph, along with the angle and stiffness of the two RSJs (rolled steel joists), and how securely they had been set into the track bed. He concluded with what seems an understatement of the awful scenario resulting from a fast-moving train being lifted and shifted just a few centimetres by what Clayton described as a 'formidable obstacle'. A £2 million train travelling at least 170 kph would be hurled from the rails. The front bogies and axles would be ripped away, and several carriages would probably cartwheel into the embankment or, worse still, a bridge, killing dozens of passengers and injuring and maiming a hundred or more. The offender would become Britain's most notorious mass-killer overnight.

On Monday, 21 October, senior detectives from both Regional Crime Squads met the Julie Dart enquiry team in an effort to avoid the confusion that would be inevitable if both courier runs were made at the same time. Running two complex surveillance operations side by side had inherent command-and-control problems. There might be hundreds of policemen from different agencies and jurisdictions chasing a dangerous man over the same ground. Coppers might end up tripping over each other in their determined efforts to catch Julie Dart's killer. If communications broke down, this could result in officers arresting their own colleagues. The whole operation could end up a farce straight out of the Keystone Cops.

Crewe station had been checked out. The 'Police vehicles only' parking bay would be in clear view of the offender should he be watching from a nearby car, so the police would have to be both close by and very much undercover. Buses and coaches frequently stopped outside the covered entrance to the station foyer; there was a taxi stand to the west, and double yellow lines to the east. The officers realised that there was no good cover to allow anyone to watch the phone kiosks undetected, police and offender alike.

The telephone kiosks at Crewe were side by side, between platforms 1 and 3 – the one with telephone number (0270) 255370 was for phone cards only, and number (0270) 255254 was coin-operated. Both were in clear view of passing travellers.

The layout of Carlisle station was quite different. This old building with its Gothic architecture could only be entered by driving through gates into a 10 mph speed restriction zone. An antiquated phone box stood on platform 3 at the bottom of the ramp that led to platforms 4 to 8.

Despite the fact that the killer's BR letter was purposely written to convey the impression of a gang, the West Yorkshire Police reckoned he worked alone. Therefore, he could hardly be at two locations at once.

Just as Sams had reflected on his past botched attempts to collect a sizeable ransom, the police at the joint-authority meeting were ruing their failed attempts at catching their man. Then someone had the idea of stalling the blackmailer, keeping him off balance, playing him at his own game. If they could take the initiative, keep *him* guessing for a change, this might leave him exposed. In any event, No. 9 RCS of the Met had already independently decided not to run a full operation (which, in the opinion of at least one senior police officer, could have had dire consequences if Sams had eventually killed Stephanie Slater as he no doubt started out intending to do).

DCS Fleming took responsibility for the decision to play for more time. It could be a dangerous move, and he conceded as much. However, the benefits might prove invaluable for, at the very least, it would give the police more time to coordinate a comprehensive operation.

That evening, No. 9 Regional Crime Squad placed a message in the personal column of the London *Evening Standard*:

> *Amanda*
> *Could not make it on the 23rd. Could not get on the train due to your mother's illness. Please ring me on 071 922 6925.*
> *Michael*

The police could not have known that this message just might give heart failure to the man they were hunting. Not only had they signed off with Sams' Christian name, but at the time, his mother was not at all well.

On Monday, 21 October, Sams went out to buy a copy of the *Evening Standard*. However, since it was a London paper, this purchase involved more than popping into a local newsagent's. As Sams later explained in a letter to his solicitor:

> *So I therefore travelled to Peterborough by train. This was because I wanted to catch the 1800 hrs from Peterborough to Cleethorpes. The train where I used to catch it regularly nearly emptied at Peterborough, and there were always copies of the paper [the* Evening Standard*] left on it. On this night I could not find one. I joined the train at the rear, 1st Class, and walked the whole length. But could not find one. I could there-fore not tell if the B.T.P. [British Transport Police] had inserted the message.*
>
> *I decided then and therefore made arrangements to go ahead Wed 23rd.*

At precisely 7.08 pm, on Wednesday, 23 October, WPC Susan Wooley, attached to No. 1 Regional Crime Squad, was in position inside the phonecard kiosk on platform 3 at Crewe station when the phone rang. She allowed it to ring five times before picking up the receiver. Her instructions were *not* to answer 'Amanda speaking', but merely see if a call came through. The caller – Michael Sams – asked 'Hello?' several times, to which Susan answered 'Hello' in return. The caller asked, 'Who's that? Who are you?' Then the line went dead.

WPC Wooley left the kiosk, but waited nearby. Eight long

minutes passed before the phone rang again. The voice seemed to have a northern accent and to be 'slightly well pronounced'. Wooley thought the man sounded more nervous than angry. No instructions were passed to the detective and the phone was put down.

While Susan Wooley took Sams' calls, 12 other RCS officers were discreetly keeping track of everyone moving around the station and its approaches. Every visitor to the station and all people boarding and alighting from the trains were monitored and the details of their appearance and movements were logged. Operation Orient continued until 9.46 pm, when all surveillance officers were sent back to their vehicles. They stood down four minutes later.

An almost identical operation had been carried out by No. 3 Regional Crime Squad at Carlisle station, which also failed to entice the killer from his lair. Fifteen detectives watched every inch of the station but to no avail. The 9.15 pm deadline came and went without incident, and the operation commander stood down his team at 10.30 pm.

With hindsight, the police now believe that Sams never intended to run two extortion plans. The Carlisle operation was a hoax, simply intended to direct the resources of West Yorkshire and No. 3 RCS away from Crewe, which was the one plot Sams did plan on running.

Having taken part of the game away from the murderer, the police had effectively bought extra time to plan the man's capture more carefully. At another conference, they decided to throw the ball back into his court. On Monday, 28 October, the personal column in the first edition of the *Evening Standard* carried a second message for 'Amanda':

Amanda
We need to talk. we would like to help. Please call Michael.

The problem was that Sams, since he hadn't seen the first police message, didn't know the number to call. But if the police were concerned that he might not surface again, they were wrong to be. He had already written.

On 29 October 1991, David Cox, a 50-year-old clerical worker, was busily sorting through the mail at British Rail Headquarters in Euston House, London. With him was Pat

Murphy, who had handled Sams' previous letter. She immediately recognised another with the same particular style of envelope and distinctive typewritten address: 'Senior Executive, British Rail, Euston House, Euston, LONDON.' Inside the envelope, which was postmarked Nottingham and dated 28 October, was yet another envelope on which was written: 'To be opened by the same senior Executive who opened the last demand'.

Congratulations you have now qualified for retribution, but on this occasion I would like to think that there were mitigating circumstances so avoiding the full penalty, for it could have been that my fine college [colleague] indicated the wrong time for my phone call, or infact something could have gone wrong at your end. He missed the copy of Monday's 'Standard' so could not be certain as to whether the message was in that night, but I myself saw a car parked in the designated spot in the afternoon. However, this time I will lay out the agenda and keep a copy so that there can be no dispute as to the content.

Within a week or so a small penalty will be imposed in the form of the removal of an electric locos pantagraph, and with a little luck the downing of a section of line, a suitable place has not yet been located, but studies are under way. This is the small demonstration I wished to perform initially to prove our determination.

Following this, we shall await a message in Monday's or Friday's 'Daily Mail' personal column, within two weeks, that, 'The train is now ready to depart'. Failing this, then our initial threat will be carried out to the letter.

The day of the message in the 'Daily Mail' your female employee will be at the two phone boxes between platforms 1 and 3 on Crewe station at 3pm for a message, everything must be ready at that time, I shall then indicate the day and time she is to return, when we are once again ready to collect your offering.

No further communication will be sent, should you fail to respond to this letter, then our satisfaction will have to be the considerable cost we will have incured [sic] upon yourselves, I shall be hoping this will be well over £2m by the time we call it a day.

It was claimed that Sams had typed this letter (using an italic typeface) on his computer because, as he had done with the first typewriter, he had got rid of the second one, too. 'I didn't think I would need it again,' he would later tell me. How wrong he proved to be. But something more sinister must also be considered: the possibility that this letter was written by someone else. It has hardly any spelling mistakes and is altogether more coherent than Sams' other letters. Perhaps he had an accomplice.

The device Sams finally decided to use in an attack on a train late on Sunday, 3 November, no longer resembled the lump of wood and two RSJs he had shown in the diagram sent to British Rail on 15 October. He had now chosen something more portable and very easy to put into place.

While pottering in his workshop, he had gathered together a length of steel wire, a sash cord, a sizeable lump of sandstone and a large concrete block, which to an outsider might seem to have no intrinsic value. However, Sams' scheming mind had worked out that the items might just wreck a train and cost BR hundreds of thousands of pounds. He didn't even consider the cost in human life.

With his Black & Decker hammer drill, he bored a hole through the centre of the sandstone. He fed the wire through this and joined the two ends of the wire together, to create a loop. He cut off four metres of sash cord and tied one end to the wire loop. Then he tied the concrete block to the other end of the cord. With his handiwork completed, he wrote a message on the sandstone, placed his derailment kit in the back of his Metro and drove west.

The place he had chosen for his intended crime was at Millmeece, a tiny Staffordshire hamlet lying about eight miles south-west of Stoke-on-Trent and three miles from the M6 motorway. It sits astride the A519, and is near Bridge 30, under which pass express trains whistling north and south along the West Coast InterCity line. This particular spot had always been a favourite with railway enthusiasts.

It was as much as Sams could manage to lift his device on to the bridge's brickwork parapet. As well as guiding the sandstone block into the path of any oncoming express, Sams also had to contend with the weight of the concrete block that would act as a counterbalance.

For a man with one leg, the task was very difficult and also extremely dangerous, for just a few feet below the bridge ran cables carrying 25,000 volts of electricity. One false move, a sudden gust of wind, and Sams would have resembled a charred artefact left over from Guy Fawkes night.

When he had finished setting up the device, he stood back for a moment to admire the view stretching away to the south. White-painted steel gantries crossed the tracks for as far as the eye could see and on to distant Birmingham. To Sams, this was a magnificent sight; to the locals, a blot on an otherwise unblemished landscape.

Then Sams heard the familiar humming of wires and rails as a train approached, moving at almost 170 kph. Now was the time for him to leave.

The following morning, track chargeman Dennis Parton was inspecting eight miles of track between Whitmore and Norton Bridge on the Staffordshire stretch of line. At 9.30 am, as he walked under Bridge 30 at Millmeece, he saw – in the 'Up Fast Lane', directly under the south side of the bridge – a broken concrete block with a rope tied around it, along with several chunks of sandstone. A message had been written on the sandstone: 'CHIEF EXECUTIVE, LONDON'.

Using the trackside telephone, Parton called the British Transport Police who, in turn, contacted Robert Winfield, technical manager of electrification who was responsible for all the power supplied to the InterCity West Coast route from Euston to Gretna Green and on through the Scottish Borders to Glasgow.

After examining the obstacles that had been placed at Bridge 30, Winfield reported to the police. He first explained that the trains collect their power through an extendable roof-mounted frame known as a pantograph, which is raised by spring pressure to the overhead power line. He then pointed out that, apart from the obvious danger of electrocution to the culprit responsible, the least danger to a train and its passengers would have been an unscheduled stop several hundred metres along the line if the rock and pantograph had collided – what, in locomotive engineering terms, is called a 'traction failure'.

Winfield couldn't think of a way in which this device could have completely wrecked a train, but there had been a strong possibility that the damaged pantograph could have trailed into the power lines, tearing down live cables carrying 25,000 volts of single-phase alternating current. He described this as a 'potentially fatal hazard', but providing no one had left the carriages or touched the cables, they would have been safe since the current would have earthed itself through the wheels.

So with the potential of a disastrous loss of human life removed from the equation, the engineer turned his attention to the financial loss had the object performed as intended. The complete line, north and south, would have been blocked for 24 hours while all traffic on the permanent way was brought to a standstill. The cost in labour and materials for repairs would have amounted to more than £18,000. The financial impact on InterCity services on a typical day would have been £35,000, based on 500 minutes of delay to 'class one services' at £70 per minute. The total would have been in excess of £53,000, making Sams' lump of rock a pretty expensive item.

On Sunday, 3 November, an inspection had been carried out on all trains using the West Coast route and no damage had been found. Therefore, it was assumed that the draught preceding a train had blown the pendulum-suspended block to one side before it could strike the pantograph, before it then fell from the bridge parapet and broke up on impact with the track below. In a later effort to mitigate this offence, Sams wrote to me, saying: 'Just in case I wanted to use the B.R. extortion I threw the brick & block off the bridge at Millmeece to make it look as though it had been attempt [*sic*].'

Julie Anne Dart was finally laid to rest on Thursday, 7 November, at St Wilfred's Church, Leeds. The inquest into her death had been delayed for months in the hope that the police would arrest her murderer. Eventually the coroner recorded a verdict of 'unlawful killing by a person or persons unknown'.

The Reverend David Booth told the congregation: 'We are here today because we believe that evil, human evil, whether it was done by one man in Leeds, or Lincolnshire, or wherever, cannot triumph.'

Julie's nearest and dearest spent a few hours with her for the last time. The media and police kept a discreet distance throughout a service that had brought many tears, although six police investigators had been asked to and were present at the funeral, including Detective Superintendent Bob Taylor, the senior investigating officer on the case. Julie's brothers left final gifts. Paul tightly held a framed photograph of his sister, while boyfriend Dominic Murray nervously fiddled with his rosary beads. When they left her in that cold place, a simple wooden cross bore grim testimony to a lovely young woman who had fallen foul of an evil monster:

JULIE ANNE DART. DIED JULY 1991. RIP

DS Bob Taylor had reason to feel frustrated. The money spent on police time in the hunt for Julie's murderer was already running at £500,000, and the police were no nearer to catching him. The BBC series *Crimewatch UK* had screened a chillingly accurate reconstruction of Julie's abduction, but with disappointing results. The search for laundry mark MA143 had stopped dead in the water, and investigations into the two white-painted bricks had fared no better. Police officers all over the country had been working flat out, with little to show for it.

Sooner or later, Sams thought, he'd collect the better part of £200,000. However, for the time being, he would have to be patient. He would sit down, take stock, rethink the whole scheme through. He had time on his side; the police didn't. He now knew just how the law might react to his telephone calls, letters and threats. True, British Rail had been slow off the mark in responding to his first letter – later, in a moment of sick humour, he would say to me, 'They never did run on time anyhow.'

But not everything was going Sams' way. By now, the police knew something about their target. Professor Paul Britton, who had conducted the initial profile on the killer, was constantly updated as the enquiry progressed. Again he was asked to form an opinion on what the offender might do next, and, more specifically, he was asked to suggest ways for the detectives to continue playing the deadly game.

The police had a number of options. They could shut down the investigation as far as releasing information to the media was concerned – lay a blanket of absolute secrecy over the case, allowing it to take a very low profile. This could help because Julie's killer might have become so disturbed over the actual mechanics of homicide that there was little or no chance he would kill again. There was some support for this theory: the offender had threatened to destroy a train using one of two methods, and he'd opted for the one that would have been most unlikely to destroy human life, while the alternative almost guaranteed it. There had been the threats to abduct and murder other prostitutes, but these were regarded as mere posturing. If the killer were as cold-blooded as he claimed to be, surely he would have already killed again? But he hadn't. In addition, the killer's 'bug detector' found on the motorway had been found to be a hoax, and he hadn't fire-bombed a department store, although he'd threatened to more than once.

Perhaps it would be fair to say that Sams had already proved his point. He could easily take human life, and in doing so, he had set out the parameters of his *modus operandi*. It might be necessary to repeat the inhuman performance – he knew that. The police? Well, they couldn't be so sure. The man was unpredictable, therefore he might kill again. That being so, when he surfaced, the police had better be ready for any eventuality.

A second option was for the police to collate every scrap of information and go over it all again, for somewhere in the reports were clues they might have missed. The more the man communicated with them and the more they learned about him, his *modus operandi* and his way of thinking, the sooner he – like most attention-seeking criminals – would become ensnared in a trap of his own making.

The police's ace was the killer's reaction when they had delayed the operation, causing him to backtrack, thus taking the initiative away from him. The last two courier runs, set up independently of each other for Wednesday, 23 October, had been dismal failures for the killer, and this had allowed the police to control the game to a degree. It was also obvious – or should have been – that Sams had bitten off more than he could chew. In later correspondence, he made it clear that he had become worried and confused at that crucial time. Those emotions had then turned into rage, and when that had subsided, he had acted like a spoilt brat, dangling a rock in front of a passing train.

It was agreed that the police would adopt the second option, with the proviso that they would move swiftly when he resurfaced. The only way they could contact him was through a newspaper, but would he read the message? On Monday, 11 November 1991, the following message appeared in the personal column of the *Daily Mail*:

To all members of travelwise
We can confirm that your train is now ready to depart. Your
bridge messages received.
Representatives can be contacted on the numbers supplied.
Michael

Had Sams travelled on the train to Peterborough that Monday and found a copy of the *Daily Mail*, he might have read the message and known that the 'representatives' – the police – would now be waiting for him to ring them at Crewe station. However, Sams did ring the station, on the off chance, and when the receiver was lifted, he spoke briefly to someone before slamming the phone down.

As 1991 drew to a wintry close, Michael Sams began to make full use of his Amstrad computer. He had never quite mastered the intricacies of the 'Locoscript' word-processing program, but his stock and accounting programs were to pay dividends. Night after night he would sit in the spacious front room of Eaves Cottage, spilling reams of paper from the printer. T & M Tools was owed in excess of £2000, and he rightly believed that, having done excellent work for these customers, the overdue money was better off in his pocket than in theirs. After sorting out his accounts, Sams wrote a letter to each customer requesting settlement within 30 days. These letters often contained misspelt words such as 'accont' (account) and 'settlment' (settlement). Nevertheless he was accurate to the penny when it came to calculating the total bill, along with any interest charge levied for slow payment.

However, he didn't pay his own bills when they fell due for payment – in fact, he wouldn't pay them at all if he could get away with it. Here he was, signing on the dole, drawing a disability benefit and having his mortgage repayments and arrears paid by the DSS, while at the same time fiddling his electricity. Any cheques he received from customers who did pay up were banked at Barclays in Newark. His banking statements show that the account hovered between red and black with remarkable consistency. He would request the bank to clear any sizeable cheque he received within three days; then he would draw out the cash and rush to Teena's building society, where he would deposit the money in her Halifax 'Maxim' account. This he called 'laundering'. However, by far the most attractive alternative was simply to stuff the notes into his back pocket.

Financial documents shows that, after the Christmas holiday 1991, he was performing four and five of these financial juggling acts a week. On one particular afternoon, he deposited £240 at the Halifax; less than an hour later, Teena strolled through the door to bank a further £650 in cash. This surprised the female cashier enough to mention it, months later, in a statement given to the police.

January 1992 found Michael Sams seemingly awash with cash. He cheered up quite noticeably, even having a change of heart about adopting a child. Buoyed up with the anticipation of having a youngster to care for, Teena wrote again to the Social Services asking for her and Sams to be reconsidered for adoption now that their finances had improved. She might have been forgiven for thinking that all her Christmases had arrived at once.

However, the New Year wasn't a fortnight old before Sams started to write more bitchy notes for Teena's benefit: 'Too lazy to move back' (referring to a sugar basin she had moved and not put back in the identical spot on a kitchen shelf), 'Haven't touched these' and 'The kettle needs filling'. It had started again. The monster inside was resurfacing.

For the police, it was a time of mixed emotions. Christmas, New Year and the January sales meant little to dozens of officers who had previously vowed never to take their work home. Dectective Constable Helen Dover, who had been one of those closest to the Dart family throughout their ordeal, had felt their grief acutely. At 10 am on New Year's Day, she phoned Lynn Dart, wishing her all the best for 1992. And such was the dedication of that fine detective Bob Taylor that, on Thursday, 2 January, he was back at his cluttered desk with a slight hangover, poring once again over all of the evidence. It was a waiting game: he knew that the killer would resurface.

TEN

Stephanie Slater

Twenty-two-year-old Stephanie Slater was single and lived with her adoptive parents, Warren and Betty, in Newton Gardens, Great Barr, a suburb to the west of Birmingham. 'Steph' had been born at Dudley Road Hospital, Winson Green, to Audrey Margaret Green and Roger Frederick Powell. She had spent the first six weeks of her life with Audrey before being placed in a children's home in Harbourne, from where the Slaters had adopted her.

From the age of five, Stephanie had attended Hamstead Infants and Junior School. Then, aged 11, she had gone to Churchfield High School, West Bromwich, leaving at 16 with a number of qualifications. She had started working life as a trainee hairdresser at a salon called Edgar's where she remained for only a month. In September 1984, she was placed on a Youth Training Scheme at Toby Sounds, working as a clerk. A year later, she moved to Hayes Spires, an estate agent in West Bromwich. Then, in August 1988, the firm was taken over by Prudential Property Services, and her new employers promoted the dark-haired young woman to negotiator.

In March 1991, the Prudential agency was sold to Connell Estate Agents. Stephanie resigned, considering herself underpaid compared with her colleagues working for rival companies. On 16 December 1991, she started working for Shipways Estate Agents at 905 Walsall Road, Great Barr, a wholly owned subsidiary of the Royal Life Estate Group of Companies. Shortly after joining the agency, Stephanie was given a company car, a royal blue Ford Escort that she nicknamed 'Gizmo' after the creature that had 'starred' in the 1984 film *Gremlins*. It soon became her pride and joy.

The manager of the small office was 34-year-old Kevin Watts, who had been in that position since 1983. The rest of Stephanie's co-workers were: David Thompson, the 33-year-old financial adviser; Jane Cashman, a 20-year-old junior, who had been recruited only seven months earlier; and the eldest member of the team, 54-year-old Sylvia Baker, the office secretary.

Around 4.30 pm, Tuesday, 14 January 1992, Sylvia took a phone call, one of the dozens of enquiries about property the office received every week. She later recalled that the man had given his name as 'Mr R. Southwall', and that he had said he was from Wakefield. He was looking for a property in the £60,000 bracket. It had to be a two- or three-bedroom semi-detached house, and he specified gas connection as well as a garage. As Sylvia jotted down these details on her pad, Southwall went on to say that he intended to renovate the property quickly and then move on quickly – he was obviously a small-time speculator. Finally, he insisted that the house be in the Calshot Road area of Great Barr.

The company's usual policy was for their staff to complete a 'Customer Requirement Form' (CRF), but when Sylvia asked 'Mr Southwall' if he wanted to be added to the firm's mailing list, he replied, 'No.' The potential client had already asked for Sylvia's name, which she freely gave. Now he asked her to sort out a few details for the following morning when he would call at the office at 9 am. Just as the telephone conversation was ending, he said: 'Sylvia, you won't let me down, will you?'

After searching through his files, Kevin Watts selected about 20 suitable properties for the mystery client. He placed the details into a brown envelope which he marked 'Mr Southwall', ready for the next day.

Michael Sams, alias Southwall, left Newark at 7.30 am, Wednesday morning, for the long drive to Great Barr. He arrived as the clock struck nine, having stopped along the way to alter his appearance by dyeing his hair black and adding a few stick-on warts to his face. He again wore the thick-rimmed Michael Caine-style spectacles and deliberately made himself look in need of a good brush and wash.

Jane Cashman later remembered Mr Southwall as scruffy,

solidly built, with piercing eyes set under heavy eyebrows. He'd asked for Sylvia by name, mentioning that he was Bob Southwall. Sams wanted everyone in the office to note his appearance – it would, he reckoned, throw the police off his scent later. But Sylvia had little time to take much notice of her client that morning. 'All the details are here,' she said, passing Sams the sealed brown envelope. 'There are too many to go through each one. If you select the ones you want, I'll go through them with you. If you'd like to view any of the properties, please phone the office, and we'll arrange it for you.'

Minutes later, Sams was sitting in his car flipping through the contents of the envelope, looking for a particular address that he knew would be suitable to his quite specific purpose. But when he did not find the sheet pertaining to that house, he wasn't bothered. He didn't need to read about the place – he'd already been there.

In November 1991, Sams was still smarting from his failure to collect the £145,000 from the Julie Dart ransom bid. On Tuesday, the 5th – Teena's late son's birthday – he drove his wife to her mother's home in Yardley Wood Road, Birmingham, so that she could place flowers on Paul's grave. Sams had little interest in sharing the day with her. Instead, he went off in search of estate agents, with a well-planned criminal purpose in mind. He selected the Shipways branch in the Birmingham suburb of Erdington. Here the staff gave him a free company magazine called *Home Hunter*, which contained, among other properties for sale, a vacant house at 153 Turnberry Road, Great Barr.

He found the address using the Birmingham *A to Z* street map. He drove past the house twice before parking and ambling round to the back garden, peering in through the grimy windows. He particularly noted the property's rear access to a muddy track – ideal for his plans, which certainly did not include buying the rundown property, much less renovating it.

When I interviewed him, Sams claimed that he could have gone ahead with the estate agent kidnapping before that Christmas. But why hadn't he? The answer came in a letter written by Sams in prison: 'I didn't really want the person that was kidnapped to have a rotten Christmas, believe it or not.'

Sams next left Newark more than two months later, on the afternoon of Tuesday, 14 January. Darren Waterhouse, an 18-

year-old sales assistant, was working at the Barnsley Outdoor
Centre in Peel Parade, Barnsley, South Yorkshire, when Michael
walked in wearing a sky-blue bomber jacket and jeans. Darren
and his colleague, Cathy Shaw, were later to remember this
customer, who was wearing heavy-rimmed glasses with what
appeared to be tinted lenses.

Sams asked where the maps were kept. He then specified in a
quiet voice that he was only interested in one that detailed the
Barnsley/Penistone area. Darren selected Pathfinder No. 715, an
Ordnance Survey map that covered the district on a scale of
$2\frac{1}{2}$ inches to the mile.

Three days later, Kevin Watts, on arriving at work, opened his
mail. One particular letter caught his attention and he smiled.
This enquiry could develop into a deal that would help raise the
office success rate.

143 Wakefield Road;　　　　　　*Shipways.*
Durkar;　　　　　　　　　　　　*905 Walsall Road;*
Wakefield.　　　　　　　　　　　*Birmingham.*
West Yorkshire.　　　　　　　　 *B42 1TN.*
WF12 6RR.

f.a.o. Mr Kevin Watts.

15 January 1992.

Dear Sirs;

*I called into your offices last Wednesday, 8 January, and Sylvia
gave me some leaflets on properties, although she was unable to
tell me anything about the properties. I did manage to view a few
later that afternoon and have a couple in mind. I have returned
to ones that I do not require.*

*However there was a property at 153 Turnberry Road, for
which you did not include a leaflet, this could be very suitable to
myself as I am able to undertake most property repairs, this will
then give a potential for a good profit when I next have to move
again in a few years.*

I do require that gas is installed and at the time was unable to see if there was any supply to the property, I do not require any telephone, as when I am on duty I am supplied with a mobil phone. Could you please enquire from the vendors as to whether there is any gas into the house.

If this is the case could you also enquire of them if they are prepared to accept £47,000 for a quick sale, and by quick sale I mean around 14 days, I require no mortgage.

If the vendors will accept my offer could I please make arrangements for yourselve to show me the inside of the property on Wednesday 22 January, at about 10.30am, if this is unsuitable then about 3pm would be O.K. At that time if you would bring the vendors details then I could get the ball rolling immediately.

As I am not on the phone at the above I shall contact you around 9.30am on Monday 20 January.

Yours faithfully

The letter was signed 'Bob Southwall' – and, like the name, the address was fictitious. The written offer remained on Kevin's desk until mid-morning when it was passed to the sales negotiator Stephanie Slater.

Although the offer was for something less than the asking price of £49,950, Stephanie thought the cash transaction might appeal to the vendor, Mr Nazim. She penned 'Mr Southwall's' details into her desk diary, and made a provisional appointment with the client for 10.30 am, Wednesday, 22 January.

Promptly at 9.30 am, Monday, 20 January, Mr Southwall phoned Kevin Watts to see if his offer had arrived. The manager tried to put him through to Stephanie, but she was engaged with another call, so Kevin gave the caller further details, and suggested that he call back. Southwall instead gave a number where he could be reached, but when no call came through, and he lost his patience, he rang Shipways at 9.55 am. Taking the call, Kevin apologised and confirmed that, although his firm had not been able to contact Mr Nazim, an appointment had been booked for Southwall to view the house. The prospective client asked if it would be Kevin showing him around. Watts replied: 'No, not me. I have two other appointments. It will probably be Stephanie Slater.'

Stephanie left her office at 10.30 am, ensuring that she would be at least ten minutes late for her appointment with Bob Southwall. He was already waiting outside the front door of 153 Turnberry Road when she arrived.

Violet Darling was a neighbour to the former occupants, and on this particular Wednesday morning, she'd decided to clean her bedrooms. She started her chores around 9.15 am. While Violet was beavering away, another neighbour, Diane Medford, was leaving to do her shopping. As it later transpired, both women were able to give the police excellent descriptions of the man who kidnapped Stephanie Slater.

As Diane drew close by No. 153, she saw a man standing outside the front door with what looked like a clipboard in one hand. Sams was annoyed at being kept waiting. The longer he stood hanging around, he thought, the more chance there was of some nosy person taking careful stock of him. He was right to be concerned. Diane, although trying to mind her own business, was observant enough to describe him later as being between 40 and 50 years of age, medium build and around 5 feet 8 inches tall. He had straight, collar-length, dark hair brushed back from his face; it was not gelled or greased back. The man had a broad chin with a five-o'clock shadow, was wearing thick, black-rimmed, Michael Caine-style glasses, and appeared scruffy and unkempt. On her return from the shops, about 30 minutes later, she noticed a young woman enter the house with the same man, who closed the door behind them. Stephanie Slater was now in Sams' carefully laid trap.

Stephanie, mindful that she had kept her client waiting in the cold, struggled for a moment to open the red front door, which was swollen with damp and required a good push before it finally gave way. She walked inside, placing the keys on a meter cupboard in the hallway.

Having been empty for a considerable period, and without heating and ventilation, the house was damp and musty – a sad welcome even for the most optimistic first-time buyer. The hallway's only redeeming virtue was the lavishly varnished interior surface of the front door. On the floor were several free newspapers, a Labour Party circular and a water rates bill, along with a card from B&W Radio Cabs, setting out their reduced rates and wishing everyone a 'Merrier Christmas'.

Stephanie felt that she was on to a losing streak from the moment she and 'Mr Southwall' entered the house. Nevertheless, as she walked through into the kitchen, she tried to be as cheerful and enthusiastic as possible under the circumstances.

Mr Southwall, obviously unimpressed, stamped his feet on the floor, asking: 'Are they wooden?' Stephanie replied that they were indeed wooden floorboards. But like the rest of the property, the kitchen had nothing to recommend it. The linoleum was ripped, old newspapers had been stuffed under a black plastic-covered stool, and a pair of rusty gardening shears were lying on the floor.

Stephanie got the distinct impression that her client was avoiding looking her straight in the eye. He was shifty, and there was something else that made her feel uneasy: he wouldn't touch anything – he went out of his way not to. Stephanie was becoming a little worried.

Climbing the stairs, covered by a red-and-beige diamond-pattern carpet, she found herself alone in one of the bedrooms. She looked vacantly out of a window, totally oblivious to the fact that she was tracing lines with a fingertip in the frost that virtually covered the glass.

Suddenly, Mr Southwall, who was in the bathroom, asked: 'What's that up there?' He was pointing towards the right-hand wall, above the bath. Stephanie peered around the doorway at what seemed to be the flannel holder, a cheap plastic bathroom accessory.

Then, in a much harsher voice, the man said, 'All right.' Spinning around, Stephanie saw that he had both hands raised and extended in front of him in a threatening manner, and in his right hand, he held what appeared to be a knife or chisel. For the first time, she noticed that he was wearing dirty grey gardening gloves.

Stephanie's first reaction was to scream. Then, grabbing at his hands, she cut herself on the blade of whatever he was holding, before being forced backwards into the orange-coloured bath, dislodging the accessory panel as she slipped down. Still struggling, she tried to lift herself up. 'Shut up, be quiet!' he shouted. 'Put your legs into the bath.' With what she now saw was a knife at her throat, she begged, 'Don't kill me. Please don't kill me. Please remember I'm human.'

'No one's going to kill you,' he said. 'You're not going to be harmed. Where are your car keys?' She thought for a few panicky seconds before telling him that they were downstairs on the meter cupboard, along with the house keys. Stephanie later told the police that this had been a ruse to get him out of the room so that she might attempt an escape. But the ploy didn't work. Instead, Sams tied her wrists together with a length of translucent washing line. Stephanie then decided to be honest with her assailant, and told him that the car keys were, in fact, in her coat pocket.

Sams placed a pair of dark glasses over Stephanie's eyes and ordered her out of the bath. She accomplished this with much slipping and sliding, and at one point, she caught a glimpse of his face. 'Don't look at me!' he shouted.

Stephanie later told police what followed:

> He was standing behind me and to my right, adjacent to the doorway, when he put his left hand on my left shoulder, and his right hand on my right shoulder. I was not aware of any weapons in his hands at this stage, and I have no idea what happened to them.
>
> He took hold of me firmly and pulled me back to the doorway. Whilst pulling me backward he asked how my brooch holding my scarf in place fastened, and whether it was a 'pinned brooch'. I explained that it was not a pinned brooch. He then pulled the scarf from around my shoulders whilst behind. I did not know at this time where my brooch had gone. He turned me round to face him and wrapped my scarf around my bound wrists, securing it tight. I do not know how he secured it as I was unable to see through the glasses.

Stephanie went on to tell how 'Mr Southwall' tied another length of washing line around her neck and held on to the other end like a dog lead. 'I was not tied tightly around my neck,' she recalled, 'but I could feel it being tugged.' She thought that he might be going to hang her, and it came as a relief when he told her that they were going down the stairs, and she'd be 'OK'.

Slowly they made their way down to the hallway, with Sams guiding her over every step until they reached the bottom, where he sat her down. The glasses hadn't been such a good idea, for they constantly fell off, so he untied the scarf, ripped it in two, and used one piece to blindfold her. As he did this, he apologised for ruining the scarf. It had been a Christmas gift.

Stephanie could now see nothing. Then he stuffed what she took to be 'industrial material' into her mouth. 'It had a bitty texture,' she later told the police. 'Fragments came off in my mouth.' This gag was secured with another strip from the scarf secured over her head and under her chin. 'It was tight but not uncomfortable,' she said in her statement. Finally, with another length of washing line tied loosely around her legs, he guided her to the french windows and out into the back garden. Stephanie later remembered what took place after leaving the house:

> *I stepped up on to a hard surface which I think was a garage floor. Although I did not touch anything, I felt the man move forward as if to open or pull something aside. I felt as though there was a wall to my left. I could also smell damp wood. He said: 'There's a car there. Get in.' I sat down bottom first into what I believed to be the front passenger seat. He said: 'Swing your legs in.' I then realised that the seat was approximately [at a] 175% angle and laid back. I heard the passenger door shut and he got into the driver's seat, shutting the door behind him.*

Michael Sams passed another length of washing line under her chin, which pinned her firmly into the seat. By now she was simply frozen with fear. 'I thought he was going to rape and kill me,' she said later.

Sams threw a blanket over her head, but it was so full of holes that she could breathe easily. On top of this, he laid a lightweight jacket. Finally the kidnapper placed a heavy toolbox on her lap, saying: 'This won't be there very long. It's just to keep you down.' After securing her seat belt – the only legal form of restraint he employed – Stephanie felt the point of a knife touch her stomach. 'Right', said Sams. 'Don't make any moves or I'll use this.' Then he started the car, ready to drive off.

At this point in her abduction – which was a carbon copy of the technique he'd used when stealing Julie Dart from the streets of Chapeltown – Stephanie was very unsure as to what was going to happen to her. She had imagined that rape or death could come at any moment – but it hadn't. He had not viciously assaulted her either. There was the very real threat of stabbing and strangulation, but again, none of this had taken place. Neither had he pushed her roughly down the stairs; he had gently but firmly guided her down to the garage and into his car. Perhaps, the cool-headed young estate agent reasoned, if she played ball with 'Mr Southwall', she might survive. And, if that happened, the only chance of the police catching the man might rest solely on what she could remember.

The only witness to these events was Violet Darling. From one of her bedrooms, she saw a 'bright red van' – as she described Sams' orange Austin Metro – being driven backwards and forwards several times as it was manoeuvred on to the track at the rear of her home. She even watched it as the car disappeared in the direction of Turnberry Road. The 'van' had, Violet said, writing along the side: 'BLOCKED AND BROKEN DRAINS.' She estimated the time as 11 am.

ELEVEN

Ride into Captivity

Stephanie Slater was a level-headed young woman who was good at communicating with people – a distinct asset for a sales negotiator. She would now have to use this ability to great effect if she were to save her own life. She would, in effect, have to negotiate her freedom. Yet, perhaps because of something in her captor's quiet, well-spoken voice and in the occasional offers of reassurance, she believed that, if she kept her head, she just might survive to tell the tale. What followed was an extraordinary example of pluck, common sense and courage.

From the moment she got into the car, she made a conscious effort to remember as much as possible. Concentrating on these details accomplished two things: she might later help the police catch her kidnapper, and she could push far more frightening thoughts to the back of her mind. Even though blindfolded, she would later be able to describe Sams' car in great detail and to give a broad outline of her journey.

After she and Sams had driven for about 40 minutes, he stopped the car behind what she thought might be a parade of shops:

> Once stationary, the man turned the engine off and he said, 'You probably know you have been kidnapped,' and I thought, 'Oh, my God.' He then said, 'Everything will be all right if you don't cause any trouble. You'll not die if you don't cause any trouble. Do you understand?' I said, 'Yes.'
>
> He said, 'Fine. We're going to make a tape for your boss. What's your name?' I said, 'OK. My name is Stephanie Slater.'

Sams removed the jacket and blanket from Stephanie's face and then removed the gag. He brought out a tape recorder, and into the microphone, she repeated a message that he had dictated to her. It took her three attempts to get it right.

She didn't know what the man did with the tape, but he did write on something before asking her to lick an envelope flap, which he then sealed. He obviously knew that DNA could be extracted from saliva.

At that point, he replaced the blindfold and gag, securing it in the same manner as before. Then as he prepared to get out of the car – presumably to post the packet – he mentioned something about a man being outside the vehicle. He said something like: 'Aye up, there's a man. Keep still. Keep quiet.' Then, after a minute or so, Sams left the car.

At around noon, Sylvia Baker received a telephone call at Shipways.

> SYLVIA. *Good morning, Shipways Estate Agents. Can I help you?*
> CALLER. *Can I speak to Mr Watts?*
> SYLVIA. *I'm sorry. He's not in the office at the moment.*
> CALLER. *Who's in charge?*
> SYLVIA. *I'm here. Can I help you?*
> CALLER. *Listen, Sylvia. Stephanie Slater – she's been kidnapped. There will be a ransom letter in the post tomorrow. All right? Phone the police and she'll die.*

The man had sounded agitated, if not nervous, and he had known Sylvia from her voice and he obviously knew Stephanie Slater. Despite being greatly shocked, Sylvia Baker made a note of the conversation on her desk jotter pad.

Kevin Watts' second appointment that morning was at a house at 27 Dunedin Road, Great Barr, and to give her experience, he had taken along young Jane Cashman. They arrived at the property at 10.55 am, and left for the next appointment around 30 minutes later. As chance would have it, the journey to that one took them along Turnberry Road, and at about 11.30 (give or take a few minutes), Kevin spotted Stephanie's car parked outside No. 153. He remarked to Jane that Stephanie must be running late. There was nothing at the Turnberry house to suggest that anything sinister had occurred, so, blissfully unaware that their colleague was now in the clutches of a killer, Kevin and Jane proceeded to 49 Calshot Road, arriving at 12.15 pm. Kevin Watts would later tell the West Midlands Police:

Whilst at 49 Calshot Road at around 12.15 pm, I received a telephone call on the owner's phone. It was Sylvia in the office, and she said a man had telephoned the office and told her that Stephanie had been kidnapped, and that he would kill her if we told the police. She asked me what to do. I told her I would return to the office immediately. I told Jane what had happened, and returned to the office.

Still sceptical, Kevin asked Sylvia to ring directory enquiries and ask for the telephone number for R. Southwall at 143 Wakefield Road, Durkar, Wakefield. This drew a blank. Then he rang the number given by Mr Southwall. It rang and rang before a man answered. But it turned out that he had simply been walking past a telephone booth at a service station on the A1 at Blyth, Nottinghamshire, when the phone rang. Blyth was just 15 miles from Sams' cottage at Sutton-on-Trent.

Meanwhile, Sylvia had reached the estate agency's regional manager, to whom she passed on the details. Further telephone enquiries confirmed that, although there was a person named R. Southwall living in the Leeds area, there was no one of that name at 143 Wakefield Road. Kevin realised that his mysterious client must have been using the Blyth service station phonebox to make and take his calls.

Within minutes, Kevin climbed into his grey Rover 216 GSi and, with David Thompson for support, drove at speed to 153 Turnberry Road. There they found Stephanie's car 'Gizmo' still sitting by the roadside. The men then made a quick but thorough search of the house – they found the house and car keys on the meter cupboard – and looked into the garden. Taking both cars back to Shipways, Kevin phoned his regional director, Kendal Head. Then he called the police.

Until recently, the exact details of Sams' route from Birmingham to Newark remained a mystery to the general public, but he gave me this information.

On leaving Great Barr, he drove out towards Walsall – stopping near the RAC Headquarters, where he had Stephanie make the tape recording and posted the letter. From there he drove north up the M6 motorway as far as junction 14, turning west on to the A5013 towards Eccleshall, the eastern edge of which he skirted by driving along the A519. Four miles north was Millmeece, where he had dangled the rock in front of a northbound express. It was here he stopped, ate his sandwiches (Stephanie, a vegetarian, refused to share them), removed the sign from his car and his own disguise, and helped Stephanie to go to the toilet.

At first, she had politely refused. He mentioned the long drive in front of them, and said, 'I'll help you. If you have any modesty now, you won't have by the time you leave me, 'cause I'll be the one taking care of you. So forget your modesty. I've got to babysit you for the next eight days.'

He drove north once again, joining the M6 near Newcastle-under-Lyme, before taking the A53 across part of the Peak District National Park. This bleak expanse of moorland was familiar to him – years before, he had three times completed the Three Peaks race in the area. When they stopped here to fill up the petrol tank from a can he had in the boot, Sams said, 'I bet you don't get hills like this in Birmingham.'

From Buxton, he drove north to Glossop, then turned east towards Silkstone and the Dove Valley Trail – the disused railway line that had already featured in Sams' earlier attempt at a ransom collection, and would feature in his crimes again. Here he parked up close to the Rob Royd pithead until it grew dark, at about four o'clock. Sams, previously chatty, had now become quiet, and as they drove on, Stephanie, having by now lost any sense of direction, started to feel car sick. Sams drove across the M1 at junction 37 towards Barnsley and the A1(M), before heading south towards Newark.

The car finally slowed and almost stopped. Sams turned the wheel to descend down a rough unmade track. He ordered his captive not to scream, adding: 'Not that anybody's gonna hear you out here.' Stephanie lay still, not daring even to breathe. She was about to be locked behind the closed doors of T & M Tools, to spend days in the damp, cold building where Julie Dart had met her dreadful death.

Police Constable Richard Board was on duty at Walsall Road Police Station when the call came from Kevin Watts, reporting

Stephanie missing. 'Excuse me,' asked the constable, 'but are you suggesting that we would possibly have a kidnapping here?' Kevin's answer prompted PC Board to contact Sergeant John Rowley of C1 Sub-Divisional Control at Thornhill Police Station. He immediately created a 'command and control' computer log – serial number 893 – into which all actions pertaining to the incident would be filed.

Four uniformed officers converged on 153 Turnberry Road, and carefully picked their way through the premises, noting what they thought was a spot of blood on the wall at the top of the stairs. Hastily they retreated into the garden via the french window and 'preserved the scene'.

A neighbour who had been peering at the activity through her net curtains could contain herself no longer. Slipping on her coat, she wandered across to explain that she had seen a man talking to a young woman before they'd entered the house earlier. Her description was well worth taking down.

Colin Tansley, a senior officer, arrived and instructed some of the other officers present to begin house-to-house enquiries. Then he told the Scenes-of-Crime Department, the Operational Support Unit and the Air Operations Unit to begin their work.

With so many of his officers involved in the one incident, it was only a matter of time before Chief Superintendent Tom Farr, head of West Midlands CID, contacted Assistant Chief Constable (Crime) Phil Thomas. With the Chief Constable away on holiday, the latter's recently promoted deputy, Richard Adams, assumed overall charge and rapidly convened a conference. Deciding that this was no hoax, Adams and his men had to assume that it was a genuine attempt to extort money from Shipways and its parent, the Royal Life Estate Group of Companies.

A tape-recording device was ordered to be installed at Shipways. DC John Domachi collected the equipment from the Technical Support Unit and quickly set it up in the office. Now they had to sit and wait for Stephanie's kidnapper to make contact by phone. If he did, the police would trace the call – probably.

It had crossed the officers' minds that this abduction bore all the hallmarks of the Suzy Lamplugh case, way back in July 1986. Suzy, also an estate agency negotiator, had had an appointment to show a 'Mr Kipper' around 37 Shorrolds Road. Like Stephanie's 'Gizmo', her car had been later found abandoned, only in that case it had been a few miles away. Like Mr Kipper's, Bob Southwall's name was obviously phoney, and like 37 Shorrolds Road, 153 Turnberry Road was 'with vacant possession'. And both Stephanie and Suzy had vanished into thin air. A study of police documents show that, even this early into the kidnapping of Stephanie Slater, Suzy Lamplugh's name had cropped up.

With all the police activity at Turnberry Road and at Shipways, it was only a matter of time before the press got wind of the kidnapping. Any press coverage could jeopardise the enquiry, so a fax was sent to every news agency in the country invoking a blackout. No reporter was to go near Shipways or Turnberry Road; in return, the police promised a controlled press conference for that evening. It was decided that, since 'Mr Southwall' had given a Wakefield address, Assistant Chief Constable (Crime) Phil Thomas would liaise with his West Yorkshire counterpart, ACC Tom Cook, while Thomas and the Acting Chief Constable, Richard Adams, would both field any questions fired by the journalists.

Links had already been formed between the West Midlands and West Yorkshire police forces concerning the abduction and murder of Julie Dart. The investigation into the attempted extortion from British Rail had been widened to take in the serious prospect of the same criminal attempting to derail a train. Now there was the kidnapping of Stephanie Slater, which was beginning to have terrible echoes of the most famous case for decades – the mystery surrounding Suzy Lamplugh. If the press were not controlled, there might soon be headlines claiming that a homicidal maniac was at large.

At around 6 pm, Stephanie entered T & M Tools – she later recalled being guided through an open doorway into what she described as a 'large building' – and was then forced into a hard wooden chair, the same one Julie Dart had sat in six months earlier.

Sams tied up Stephanie with more washing line before sitting down on the floor himself. To him, the bound woman represented £175,000 in hard cash, more than enough to get him out of his present financial difficulties. But Stephanie was no hooker. She was also quite attractive – although Sams found her a 'little large' for his taste – and well-spoken, nicely dressed and very vulnerable. This appealed to Sams, and he started to feel some pity towards the terrified estate agent now sitting, blindfolded, at his mercy.

In a letter released to me by Teena Sams, Sams said:

> *The reason I showed emotion when talking about my treatment of Stephanie was simply because she was the first person that had ever been frightened of me. The question the police & press always ask is, 'Why Julie had to die, but Stephanie lived?' The plain truth is that I kidnapped Julie with the intention that I was going to kill her. Whereas with Stephanie, my intention was, that whatever went wrong Stephanie would go home. Nothing could have saved Julie & nothing Stephanie did would have got her killed.*

As we shall see, this was as so much hogwash.

Stephanie would later give two accounts of what happened in the Newark workshop. In the first, she said that she had been in the workshop for about ten minutes when Sams said he would tidy her hair. He cut through the elasticated band at the back of her head, then tied the hair in a ponytail with part of her scarf. He removed the washing line from her waist and had her stand up. 'We're gonna have to change your clothes,' he told her. 'I've got some others here for you to wear.' She kept on her T-shirt, briefs and boots, but everything else was provided by Sams. First came a woollen round-necked sleeveless jumper, and then a thinner cotton cardigan, which he buttoned down the front. Stephanie was also given a pair of denim jeans and a pair of heavy woollen socks. Then, with metal cuffs around her wrists and ankles, she was linked to a chain that, in turn, was bolted to a strong point in the wall. Finally she was retied and made to sit down in the wooden chair.

Years later, Stephanie made a startling confession in her book, *Beyond Fear*. In this second account, she wrote that, having been undressed by Sams, he began touching her. 'Open your legs,' he ordered. 'Open your legs properly.' She felt he was scrutinising her body, and he asked if she was a virgin, which she wasn't. Then he entered her. Stephanie wrote: 'I just cut out as he humped and grunted his way through this obscene travesty.' Then he washed and towelled her dry before dressing her in the other clothes. Upon her safe release, Stephanie mentioned nothing of this rape to the police or to her parents because she had felt totally humiliated by the experience.

Although I learned of Sams having sex with Stephanie from the murderer/rapist's own lips during our interview in Full Sutton prison, the incident was not included in this book until it was made public by Stephanie herself.

After redressing and securing his captive, Sams ambled up to the Jubilee fish-and-chip shop in Castle Gate, returning ten minutes later with a bag of chips. Then, after her spartan meal, he helped her to a wide-rimmed bucket full of disinfectant which was to be her toilet for the remainder of her captivity. That first night she slept inside a wooden box and wheely bin that she would later call a 'coffin'. Sams drew a sketch of the container for me, titling it 'Stephanie's Box'. The box was a chipboard construction, similar in shape to a coffin, that was placed inside a large green wheely bin. Sams had cut off the bottom of the bin with an angle grinder and the foot of the box/coffin poked out of the end, which was rammed against the workshop wall.

Stephanie later told the police how she entered and left her 'coffin':

> I did not have to negotiate any ridges or dips before entering this coffin. My hips got stuck, and I said, 'I can't get down anymore.' He replied, 'You should be able to get down. I can get down it.' I shuffled further at an angle, so my hips could fit. I lay on one hip, with the other pointing up and my knees were slightly bent. Although my hips were twisted, my shoulders were flat against the base of the coffin. Whilst entering the coffin the man was kneeling behind me. When my body was inside, he took hold of my wrists by the handcuff chain and tied it above my head to what I believe was a metal bar. My elbows were now extended outside the coffin and my hands crossed directly in front of my face.
>
> The man said, 'Don't pull down on the bar because there are boulders above you. If you pull on the bar, you'll pull them down and crush yourself. No shouting, no screaming. I don't want to hear any noise from you. When I open this door in the morning, I want to see the gag is still on you and blindfold still on.' I just said, 'OK.' He also told me there was a wire in the box with electrodes on it, and if I moved during the night, I would get an electric shock.

While locking Stephanie into her box, Sams said, 'I can't understand why you're so calm. Why are you so calm?' She explained that, far from feeling relaxed, she was terrified to death. Stephanie Slater obviously had the temperament to handle such a difficult, even bizarre situation, and this may well have saved her life, despite what Michael Sams has since written and told me.

That first night in captivity was the worst experience of Stephanie's life. At any moment, her captor could have returned to rape her again and perhaps kill her. It was bitterly cold, for a biting wind swept along the River Trent and up into Swan and Salmon Yard. Sams' workshop had no heating at night, and the old building was full of holes that let in the freezing air. Stephanie thought she might die from hypothermia. At times, she hallucinated, seeing angels and the face of Christ. Then her mind started to blank out into a sort of void, in which she was slipping towards the doorway of death. Her arms and legs ached with the damp cold that pervaded the coffin. Waves of terror and shock, interspersed by brief periods of half-sleep, brought her back to reality and a living nightmare.

Michael Sams spent that night tucked up in a warm bed at Eaves Cottage, with Teena, as usual, in the spare room. Sams knew that, if Stephanie broke out of the box, she would set off the infra-red passive detectors linked to his bedside telephone. And if she struggled free, she would be impaled on nails set into wooden boards that were arranged around the workshop, which would cripple her until he returned to kill once again. But Stephanie didn't break free from her coffin, and the telephone didn't ring.

Detective Constable Bullas and DC Domachi had gone to the Royal Mail sorting office at Great Barr with the intention of intercepting, before night-shift workers touched it, any mail from the kidnapper sent to Shipways. The officers sat drinking tea from 4.55 to 6.20 am, when a sorting officer found something addressed to Shipways Estate Agents. DC Domachi took possession of the brown envelope with the address written with Letraset letters. Opening it with a knife, he found an unsigned letter and another brown envelope. Inside that was a BASF LH E190 audio cassette. He immediately sped off to Nechells Green Police Station, Birmingham, where all the items were handed over to the exhibits officer, DC Hart; the integrity of this evidence had to be assured at all costs. But the typewritten letter did nothing to relieve the tension building up in the officers involved in what was now officially designated 'Operation Kaftan'.

Your employee has been kidnapped and will be released for a ransome of £175,000. With a little luck he should be O.K. and unharmed, to prove this fact you will in the next day or so receive a recorded message from him. He will be released on Friday 31 January 1992 provided:

1) On Wednesday 29 January a ransome of £175,000 is paid, and no extension to this date will be granted.

2) The police are not informed in any way until he has been released.

On Wednesday 29th at 4 pm (on line 021 353 2281) you will receive a short recorded message from the hostage. To prove he is still alive and O.K. he will repeat the first news item that was on the 10 am Radio 2 news. He will then give further instructions. A second and more detailed message will be given at 5.05 pm the same day. Your watch must be synchronized with 5 pm pips on Radio 2. The location of the second call will be given at 4 pm, so transport with a radio must be available.

The money must be carried in a holdall and made up as follows precisely: £75,000 in used £50. £75,000 in used £20. £25,000 in used £10 packed in 31 bundles. 250 notes in each.

Kevin Watts (if not the hostage) must be the person to receive all messages and carry the money to the appointed place. However, please note that all messages will be pre-recorded, and no communication or negotiations can be made.

YOU HAVE BEEN WARNED. HIS LIFE IS IN YOUR HANDS.

This letter posed more problems than it answered. First, it implied that a male employee of Shipways was the intended hostage, and referred to Kevin Watts by name. Since Sams' imprisonment, he has maintained that he had hoped for a male hostage the second time around because he had thought that a man would be easier to control. Some police officers believe just the opposite: they reckon that the implication that the victim would be male was intended by Sams to avoid any connections with the Dart enquiry. According to them, he always sought female victims, believing that they would be easier to manage in a rough and tumble.

The second point raised by this letter was that Sams had apparently intended to leave the ransom letter at 153 Turnberry Road, for it says that the audio cassette would arrive a few days later. Sams says that, in his confusion, once he had realised that he had to take a female hostage instead of a male, he had forgotten to leave the letter. This has a ring of truth.

But what the letter did tell the police was: the sender listened to Radio 2; he wanted the money to be parcelled into bundles, not unlike the demand in the Julie Dart case; he would communicate by telephone; and he made spelling mistakes, fewer but again similar to those in the Dart case.

The cassette only served to confirm the obvious. It was definitely Stephanie Slater talking into the microphone, and she was very frightened:

> *This is Stephanie Slater. The time is now 11.45. I can assure you I'm O.K. and unharmed. Providing these instructions are carried out, I will be released on Friday, 31st January. By Wednesday, you will need an Ordnance Survey map between Blackburn and Burnley. Kevin Watts must be the person that acts as courier and use his car. Sylvia or Jane may be passengers to act as guides, but only these two people must be in the car. The passengers must never leave the car. Next Wednesday at every point, clear instructions will be given. The boot of the car must be open for 30 seconds. Money must not be marked in any way whatsoever, or contain any device whatsoever.*

The West Yorkshire police were now firmly convinced that the killer of Julie Dart and the British Rail extortionist was putting words into the young estate agent's mouth. (However, right up to Sams' trial for Julie's murder, some West Midlands officers had doubts that Sams was responsible for anything but Stephanie Slater's kidnap.) Supplying the £175,000 was no problem; Royal Life Estates agreed without reservation to put up the money. It was up to first-class police work and a top-notch surveillance team to make sure that Stephanie was returned safe and well.

Counting their blessings, the police were at least happy that the kidnapper had written a letter and allowed them to hear Stephanie's voice, but they were all too aware that, if they messed things up, they'd have another body on their hands.

There was one final clue. 'Mr Southwall' had told them to get a map of an area including Blackburn and Burnley. This was Ordnance Survey map 103, but the seemingly helpful advice was yet another smokescreen, as the map doesn't cover the South Yorkshire area, in which Sams was about to be operating.

For his part, Michael Sams had learned a great deal from his past dealings with the police, and he reckoned that they might just have learned something about him. He understood the law of diminishing returns: the longer he took to bring a ransom bid to a successful conclusion, the more he risked getting arrested.

TWELVE

Operation Kaftan

Just before 8 am, 23 January, Stephanie woke from her first night in captivity to the sounds of music from a radio that had switched itself on automatically. She could just see a pinprick of light through her blindfold. Then she heard the door behind her head open, and standing above her was Michael Sams.

'What's the matter?' he asked. Stephanie got the impression he was surprised at the terrible state she was in. He unfastened the chain, pulled her out of the box on to a mattress and removed the gag. Her arms had locked solid during the freezing cold night, so he massaged her elbows in an effort to increase the circulation in them. 'Is that better? Is it getting better?' 'Yes,' she replied weakly.

Sams switched on a small electric fire and offered her a bowl of hot porridge heated in the microwave oven. Hungry, Stephanie willingly accepted the food, and slowly, her body warmed up. She also sipped hot, sweet tea from a mug that Sams held to her lips.

Stephanie's welfare started to worry him. He was beginning to care for her, and he would later claim that he'd never felt this way about a woman before. He would also say that, from that moment on, he knew that he could never hurt her – not unless she caused him serious problems. Then he would be in a fix.

He removed the cuffs from her ankles, attaching instead a chain placed around her lower right leg, which gave her a little freedom of movement. (Julie Dart had been restrained in an identical manner before she died.) Stephanie could now hobble to the chair, mattress, toilet and 'coffin' without her shackles hurting her too much. Sams then replaced the gag, telling her to be quiet. She lay down on the mattress and he covered her with a blanket. Tears rolled down her cheeks.

For several hours, she listened to the music, voices, a large door opening and closing – Sams was still open for business. A dog whimpered and barked from time to time. Sams told her it was a disobedient six-month-old Alsatian bitch. Then he started using an electric saw, which upset the animal even more. Shouting, he ordered it to shut up.

After lunch, Stephanie needed to use the toilet. Getting to it was no problem; undressing was something else. She coughed to attract Sams' attention, and called out 'Bob' through a gap in her gag. He replied, 'I'm not having this every day,' and told her that she could only use the toilet twice a day. When she had finished, he guided her back to the mattress. Of some comfort to Sams was the fact that Stephanie had summoned him discreetly, so he decided to remove her gag completely, instructing her to stay very quiet.

Later that day Sams cut the coffin into two, leaving just the bottom half. Twice he offered her chocolate. Then, at teatime, she ate another bag of chips. The local chippy was doing good trade with Mr Sams.

In a later police interview, Sams made a comment that he was to substantiate for me. It had been his intention to make Stephanie frightened of him. 'It was that day only,' he said. Sams did not anticipate any further problems after that first day in the workshop:

> I went out of her sight on many occasions. I knew, when I went back, that she wouldn't have taken the blindfold off. I was confident. In quieter times, I went out and left her. I even went out of the building when she was sat on the chair, without tying her down or anything. All she had on was the blindfold.

Yet, Michael Sams was nobody's fool, as a later remark illustrates: 'At times, I gave her the impression that I was going out of the building, and I actually sat and watched her, and she never moved.'

Stephanie's second night in her 'coffin' was a little more comfortable, for only her feet, calves and knees were enclosed; at the bottom was a rag-filled plastic bag, and underneath her was a blanket. Once she was inside, Sams handed her an 'air blanket' which was similar to the one that he'd used to cover her in the Metro. He wrapped her in a continental quilt without a cover. Finally, he gave her a foam-filled pillow, and a couple of Kit Kat chocolate bars. Her toilet, should she need it in the night, she described as a 'seed tray without holes in the base'. She never used it. The last thing Sams said before he left her was, 'I'll be back in the morning.' For ten minutes, he busied himself tidying up, laying the boards spiked through with long nails, and setting his alarm system, before closing and locking the sliding door at 10 pm.

It was to be yet another tearful night for Warren and Betty Slater, Stephanie's parents. They had heard their daughter's voice on the tape, and confirmed that it was her speaking. Both husband and wife had been quizzed by detectives about the possibility of a domestic dispute, or Stephanie being in league with her kidnapper. They also asked whether she held a grudge of some kind against her employers. Did she have a secret lover? Was she in debt?

Warren and Betty said Stephanie was a quiet young woman who had few boyfriends. She was decent, liked ice skating and did the usual things a woman of her age would do. Above all, the distraught couple thought Stephanie would be able to cope with her terrible predicament – and they prayed to God she would.

On Friday, 24 January, Stephanie was allowed to wash for the first time. She could remove her blindfold with the proviso that she kept her eyes closed. On this and every other occasion when she washed, she was aware of the man sitting in front of her.

Sams placed a square plastic bowl on her lap, which was filled with hot water and a bar of soap. He asked if she needed a flannel. She said a towel would do. When she cleaned her teeth using the corner of the T-shirt she was wearing, he asked if she would like a toothbrush.

Following another short period in her box, she was taken out for a meal of vegetable soup and dry bread. Supper would always be the same: Heinz soup. She remembered it because she enjoyed the brand.

That day he brought her a pair of his Y-front underpants to

wear. A new blindfold was provided. On a more chilling note, he told her that in the building was a large wheely bin – which he had originally planned to use to remove her body had he murdered her. He actually told her: 'I was going to wheel you out in it, but you're too big. I'll have to get rid of it now.' This slip of the tongue was the first indication that Sams had planned to kill this kidnap victim.

Instead, he now found himself becoming increasingly concerned about her health. He'd noticed that the cut on her hand still hadn't healed, so he told her that he would bring in a tube of Germolene the next morning to treat the wound. He would also give her a pair of 'moon boots' to keep her feet warm.

For her part, Stephanie was trying to remember as much as possible about 'Mr Southwall', whom she called 'Bob'. He had stubbly, workmanlike fingers with hairs on the back of his hands. His voice was always quiet, calm yet firm. He never used foul language and did not smoke, and she never smelled alcohol on his breath. His accent was northern, maybe Yorkshire, with a soft, slow tone. He pronounced strongly the Ks and Ts at the end of words. He seemed middle-aged.

Every night, Stephanie tried to figure out what sort of building it was in which she was being held captive. She formed the impression that it was 'just like an old warehouse or workshop'. She could hear occasional traffic, perhaps two or three times a day, but it varied; nothing went past after 4 pm. At night, a cold wind whistled around her prison – it was a godforsaken place.

Stephanie and Sams were talking more frequently to each other now. In fact, he would ramble on and on for ages at a time. He asked her personal questions: her address, former occupations, salary, details of her car, her hobbies. Answering truthfully, Stephanie was unconsciously allowing her kidnapper to identify with her as a human being. She was no longer just a commodity to him. However, she was still a means to an end for Michael Sams, and he knew that, if all his carefully laid plans failed, he could never let her go free despite what he had said to her and would later tell the police.

They talked about food, and he complained that she was not eating enough. Sams mentioned getting a big bowl or pot of soup and putting garlic in it. She loved garlic – he hated it. Sams asked if she'd heard about Marks & Spencer having to withdraw all their garlic dips because someone had put glass into them. He claimed that he preferred a more professional approach to extortion and, seemingly oblivious of his double standards, censured the Marks & Spencer blackmailer for risking innocent women and children.

Stephanie heard how Sams liked *Coronation Street* and knew all the cast by name; although he watched *EastEnders*, he couldn't recall the actors. They spoke about astronomy, one of Stephanie's interests: *The Sky at Night*, Patrick Moore, black holes, constellations such as Cassiopeia, Great Bear, Little Bear and Orion. Sams knew about the weather, the fact that the sand in the rain came from the Sahara Desert. Weather cycles and how they can be used to predict the weather was another topic he enjoyed.

Stephanie responded. She told Sams that it would take a person, travelling at 100 mph in a sports car towards Saturn, 950 years to reach the giant planet. Sams found this amusing, and made a little joke about the size of the petrol tank needed for such a long trip.

Sams told Stephanie that he had liked school, that he had been athletic and had once participated in hockey. He didn't like cricket. They chatted about marriage, and Sams was quick to say that people married too young. He didn't agree with divorce, and wanted children. Stephanie sensed that this was a sore point.

Sams mentioned his computer and the work he was putting on disk. He said he had to leave it switched on all night because he hadn't figured out how to save his files. He would not drink in pubs or brag about his criminal intentions and exploits, he told her: 'That's how people get caught.'

Stephanie was interested in the doomed liner, *Titanic*, but when Sams expressed a distaste for the subject, she changed tack, bringing the conversation on to travel. Sams talked about his visit to Egypt as a merchant seaman. Trains were the best way to travel long distances, he advised her. She had been to Spain but had not liked the heat, while he enjoyed relaxing on the beach while on holiday, soaking up the sun.

Sams later reckoned that, under more pleasant circumstances, he and Stephanie would have made an ideal couple. (Stephanie thought otherwise.) In fact, he was falling for her, even though he knew that this was bloody stupid and told himself as much in his quieter moments. But this helpless young woman was so refreshing, such a change from the everyday drab existence of his marriage with Teena, who couldn't even fill up the kettle or have his dinner ready on time.

He once mentioned that the disappearance of a missing woman had nothing to do with him. He was referring to Julie Dart, but Stephanie thought he meant Suzy Lamplugh. Then, in a moment of compassion towards Stephanie, he said that he hoped this horrible experience wouldn't ruin her life. 'You're just a victim. You've done nothing wrong, and you're gonna go home. You could make a lot of money out of this and become a celebrity.' Stephanie, starting to believe that he was telling the truth, instinctively reached out and hugged him tightly.

For Stephanie, Sunday, 26 January, brought the usual routine. Out of the box, toilet, wash, breakfast. Sams cleaned and dressed her cut hand and sores with Germolene. Then he sprang a surprise. She could talk to her parents on tape. He asked her to listen to the ten o'clock news on Radio 2, and remember the first three news stories. The lead item was something about Parliament, then there was a report about Imelda Marcos being released on bail, and finally there was news of the reopening of an enquiry into the Zeebrugge ferry disaster. At one o'clock, after lunch, he gave her a message to read into the microphone. The day before, he'd asked her what her father's favourite foot-ball team was. 'Albion,' she had answered, 'West Bromwich Albion.' Sams gave her the microphone to read out the following message to Warren and Betty Slater:

> *Hello. It's Stephanie here. They've allowed me to make a message to you, just to let you know that I'm all right. I'm unharmed. I honestly think West Bromwich Albion lost yesterday to Swansea, 3–2. I want you to know I love you. I'm not to say too much, and, whatever the outcome, I'll always love you. Look after the cats for me.*

Once the tape had been completed, Sams explained that he would have to put her back into the box for a short while; he had to go out. After locking up T & M Tools, he drove along the northbound carriageway of the A1, passing through the tiny villages of Carlton-on-Trent, Tuxford and Ranby, towards Doncaster where he arrived at two o'clock. He found a telephone box and rang a Birmingham number. At 2.11 p.m, Warren Slater picked up the receiver, simultaneously pressing the 'record' button on a police tape recorder. He asked, 'Who's speaking please?' The caller spoke firmly. 'Is that Mr Slater?' Warren Slater confirmed he was. 'Just listen' came the order. Then Sams pressed the play button on his machine, and for the second time since Stephanie's abduction, Warren Slater heard the wonderful sound of his daughter's voice.

When she realised what had happened, Betty Slater collapsed. Detective Constable Donna Cooper threw her arms around the distraught lady, who cried and cried. After making a pot of tea, the police officer played the tape again to confirm that it was indeed Stephanie speaking. The couple hung on every word, then signed a statement verifying that the voice was their daughter's.

On his arrival back at the workshop, Sams told Stephanie that he'd disguised his voice while talking to her father. Unknown to her, he had also modified his plans about where he would release her. Strangely, he was worried that she might be assaulted if she were dropped off at a remote spot, so he'd decided on a place within 100 yards of Uttoxeter Police Station. He gave her several cans of Suncharm lemonade, then threaded a wire attached to a switch through the bottom air hole in her 'coffin', saying it worked a light. If she wanted anything, she merely had to operate the switch. She was to use it twice.

Monday came and went. As on every morning of her captivity, Stephanie would exercise with Sams standing by her, watching every move. During breakfast, he passed her another pair of clean Y-fronts and a pair of well-worn corduroy trousers that fastened on the right side with a button and zip. Stephanie even noticed (and told the police) that there was glue or something similar above the right knee, which she picked at from time to time. Sams told her that, as she wasn't going to be killed, he had to cut up the wheely bin. Later in the morning, he plugged in another electric fan heater. It would help to keep her warm.

After a particularly cold night, Stephanie was released from the box on Tuesday morning as usual. She did a little running on the spot to improve her circulation, ate the porridge and was quickly returned to the box. There she stayed until around 1 pm, when she was allowed to use the toilet and given refreshment. Her captor had to go out that afternoon, so she was returned once again to the box and stayed locked away until 4.40 pm, when Sams came back, shutting the heavy door behind him.

That afternoon, Darren Waterhouse had recognised the

customer the minute he had walked through the door of the Barnsley Outdoor Centre. Sams needed another map of the Penistone area for he'd mislaid the one he had purchased earlier. This time the store was out of stock. Darren did, however, sell the man a pair of gaiters, a pair of thermal gloves and a battery of the type that cavers use in their helmets. Sams paid in cash and left.

Just before five o'clock, Kevin Watts received a telephone call at Shipways. It was Stephanie Slater's kidnapper.

Jane had answered the telephone. 'I want to speak to Kevin Watts, quickly,' said a man's voice. Jane put the caller through to Kevin, who punched the 'record' button on the police taping device.

'Kevin Watts?' Sams asked abruptly.

'Speaking.'

'Have you got the money?'

Watts wanted to speak to the kidnapper on his own without distraction. He asked David Thompson, who was standing next to him, to leave the room.

'Have you got the money?' the man asked again.

By now the police were trying desperately to trace the call, and Watts needed to give them as much time as possible. He knew exactly to whom he was speaking, but was intent on stalling. 'Who's this, please?' he asked.

'Never mind. Have you got the money ready for tomorrow?'

'For tomorrow?' asked Kevin, who was becoming more confident by the moment.

'Yes. Have you got it?'

'I'm getting it. Yes.'

'Three o'clock. You'll get a message at three o'clock,' said Sams.

'A message at three o'clock,' repeated the manager.

'Yes, and do you want a password? If you give me a word, I'll get her to repeat it to say she's all right.'

'Yes,' answered Kevin. 'Could I have her mother and father's Christian names, please?'

Sams now realised that he'd been on the phone for too long and that the police might be tracing the call. 'Mother and father's Christian names. OK. Three o'clock tomorrow.' Then he slammed down the receiver.

Although the call had lasted only a minute, British Telecom

engineers had been able to trace it to a phone box on the A52 dual carriageway at Gamston, a small village between Nottingham and Radcliffe-on-Trent. A radio message was flashed to the Nottinghamshire Constabulary, which dispatched several fast police cars to the location. They arrived within minutes, and Sams grinned as he saw their blue beacons tearing past him as he drove home. Within less than an hour, he would be safely back in Swan and Salmon Yard.

'I've just spoken to Kevin Watts,' Sams told Stephanie. She breathed a sigh of relief. 'Who is David?' he asked her. Stephanie told him that David was the financial adviser at Shipways. 'Well, I heard Kevin tell Dave to "get out".'

Sams had rightly suspected that the police had been called in by Shipways – the police cars racing towards Gamston were too much of a coincidence. The one thing he couldn't afford right now was complacency, for he was only a day away from success.

But he had already sealed his fate. It had been his habit to disguise his voice when talking over the phone by clipping a clothes peg over his nose. However, when he'd spoken to Kevin Watts, he had forgotten this important precaution. It was an error that would later lead to his arrest.

As soon as he had learned of the ransom demand, Eric Willetts, personnel director of Royal Life Estates, had spoken to the firm's 'crisis management team' coordinator about the feasibility of raising the £175,000 demanded for Stephanie's safe release. Now the details of the operation were firming up, and the actual mechanics of drawing the cash had commenced. The company's treasury department had liaised with the West Midlands Police and transferred the required sum to them. At midday, Friday, 24 January, Detective Inspector Gwyn Wright – seconded to No. 4 Regional Crime Squad from the Warwickshire Constabulary – arrived at the financial department at Lloyd House, the West Midlands Police headquarters, where he received (against signature) a cheque for £175,000. Wright was then conveyed in a marked police car to the Tamworth Bullion Centre where he exchanged the cheque for cash. He then speedily returned to Lloyd House where the money was placed in a safe. During Saturday and Sunday, each note was diligently recorded on video at the Regional Technical Support Unit. (Unfortunately, it transpired that, for some of the time, the camera was out of focus, and a great many of the serial numbers were blurred and later proved unreadable.)

It was getting close to the time when Kevin Watts, acting as courier, would play his part in Operation Kaftan. He had been briefed by police officers and had spent time with Professor Paul Britton. The exact nature of those discussions remains a secret, but it would be fair to say that Kevin was left feeling confident and prepared for anything untoward that might happen.

That Tuesday night, Stephanie was placed in her 'coffin' around 9 pm. Telling her that he was expecting a telephone call from his mate about the ransom, Sams drove home to collect everything he needed for the next day. He told Teena he was off to a model railway exhibition with a pal, and her diary shows that he left the cottage that evening at 10 pm.

Back at the workshop, Sams jammed his moped into the rear of the Austin Metro, then loaded the car with a crash helmet, a drawer from an old-fashioned wooden sideboard, a washing line, two orange-and-white traffic cones, a bag of builders' sand, an Osram light-bulb box with a silver-painted cigar tube attached, and various messages and signs, including four indicator markers on which had been stencilled 'SHIPWAYS'. His ransom collection kit was completed by a roll of two-sided adhesive tape.

Sams had washed and ironed all of Stephanie's clothing, and now placed them in a small suitcase. It was pitch black in the building so, before he left, he removed her blindfold. She saw, above her head, a red light blinking on and off. Although Sams had actually disconnected the alarm, she believed that the light was 'watching' her and would continue to monitor her movements as she slept.

The following morning, she went through the familiar routine. When she refused the porridge, Sams ate the lot. 'I'm going to be busy today,' he told her, 'so don't worry. You'll be OK. Before I go, I want to take a photograph of you as a keepsake, but keep your eyes closed.' While she posed in that grim building, Sams focused his battered Praktica MTL 5. There was a flash and the snap was taken.

Stephanie complained that her feet were sore, so he gently bathed them. He took her damp socks and dried them by the heater. At 9.15 am, she was returned to the box, and Sams gave her several Kit Kat chocolate bars along with a can of cold drink.

Having done all he could to make Stephanie comfortable, he left the workshop to make his final preparations for the day. He was almost home and dry; if all went according to plan, he would be £175,000 better off that night. There was no way he'd turn back now. If he failed, Stephanie would have to be killed, despite what he had told her.

In Great Barr, Kevin Watts was steeling himself for the worst day of his life. He had been up since early morning. His two older daughters, Natalie and Sarah, were still in bed when he left home. His wife Julie, holding ten-week-old Sophie in her arms, kissed him goodbye on the doorstep. She pressed a St Christopher good luck token into his hand. The patron saint of travel seemed quite appropriate under the circumstances.

Kevin Watts had signed a disclaimer, saying that he had volunteered himself for the job of ransom courier. With this document in their pocket, the police went over with him their respective parts in the operation again and again. He was told to carry a pen and paper with him; a torch was to be provided. Apparently he was to be backed up by undercover detectives using sophisticated surveillance and tracking equipment, and his car had been fitted with a two-way radio. A transmitter had been sewn into the lining of the holdall which would contain the money, which he had to keep with him at all times.

Kevin had to obey the kidnapper's instructions to the letter. Messages and telephone calls would be used to direct him to the cash drop-off point. Finally, he was asked to relay all of the criminal's instructions over his radio, repeating them twice in a loud voice so that his controller back at the operation's headquarters in Birmingham could hear them and organise the covering vehicles and manpower that would hopefully give him total protection. Then he was given a bullet-proof vest to put on.

Sams' first problem of the day was a slow puncture. There was no point in trying to outwit the police running on a flat tyre, so he changed the wheel and had the tyre repaired at a local garage in Newark. Then he called Teena, telling her that he was in London having a drink with his friend.

He returned to Stephanie and got her out from the 'coffin'. He gave the hungry woman a slice of dry bread, a can of drink and more bars of Kit Kat, before returning her to the box. He promised that he would be back to free her by 9 pm. By then, if all went well, he would have his money and she could go home.

Detectives from No. 4 Regional Crime Squad had tested the tracking device fitted to Kevin's Rover car, and a police helicopter would watch over him from the air. Every vehicle involved in the operation would receive its instructions from a mobile command post that, in turn, was in direct communication with the West Midland Police HQ. Over 100 officers from around the country were gathering for this operation, and others had been put on standby in case they were needed. Everything was being slotted into place like a giant jigsaw puzzle.

Senior officers met the directors of Royal Life Estates and Shipways, who had a vested interest in both the money and Miss Slater. Of course, Stephanie's welfare was the priority; she had to be rescued whatever happened, even if it meant losing the money. Catching the kidnapper and killer of Julie Dart followed a close second. If he pulled out a firearm, the police would shoot to kill, and the money would be recovered in due course.

In anticipation of success, a press conference had been booked for that night or, at the latest, the following morning. A team of female officers led by Detective Inspector Elaine Baker had been placed on standby. Their task was to debrief Stephanie after her release. Ellie Baker had been responsible for searching Stephanie's bedroom, and had collected numerous samples and personal items for possible forensic comparison, depending on how things progressed. To assist her, she had chosen her colleague and close friend DC Donna Cooper and another detective, DC Denise Wright from Rose Road Police Station at Harbourne. They had worked together as a team before, and were expert at handling traumatised rape victims.

At 12.50 pm, Gwyn Wright took from his safe the £175,000 and sorted out the money into 31 bundles – each containing 250 bank notes, a total of 7750 notes. These he packed – amid jokes about him leaving the country on unlimited leave of absence – into a sports holdall.

Just after 2.20 pm, Wright handed the bag to Kevin Watts who was patiently waiting for the kidnapper to phone him with the first set of instructions. These were tense moments at Shipways.

A number of police vehicles were parked outside the estate

agency. A grey Peugeot saloon seemed innocuous enough, but it contained two highly trained Regional Crime Squad detectives, both armed. DS Martin Keys was the driver and his partner was DC John Rawlings, and the car fairly bristled with electronic gadgetry. Across the street, another unmarked police car waited by the kerb. 'Bravo 9' contained four detectives wearing casual clothes. Detective Constables Pete Roberts and Paul Fowler of the West Mercia Constabulary sat with Simon Hurst from the Leicester Constabulary, and next to him in the back seat was DC Jose DeFreitas, seconded from the Metropolitan Police. In over a dozen cars, the cream of British police were checking and rechecking their radios and tracking equipment. They all worked perfectly, at least in Birmingham.

Meanwhile, Michael Sams was driving north-west towards Glossop. The two-hour drive took him along the A1, then the A57 through Worksop. Crossing the M1 motorway at junction 31, he travelled west, through Sheffield and on towards the Peak District. After 90 minutes, the car crossed the Ladybower Reservoir, arriving in Glossop just as the clock struck 3 pm.

Parking just down the hill from the railway station, he checked the phone in the station foyer to see if it was working properly. Then he limped a few hundred yards down the street to a pair of telephone kiosks outside the Norfolk Arms public house. In the first of these, he taped a brown envelope under the directory shelf, before phoning Shipways to talk to Kevin Watts.

The police had been getting concerned. Had it all been a hoax? they had asked themselves. Was Stephanie already dead? Was her kidnapper one jump ahead of them again?

Watts received the call at exactly 3.25 pm. When the phone rang, the police moved quietly around the CeeMarc recorder and listened intently. They recognised the voice immediately, and British Telecom engineers started tracing the call.

'Hello,' said Watts.

'Hello. Kevin Watts?'

'Yes. Speaking.'

'Have you got it?' asked the kidnapper.

'Yes, I have.'

Sams then told Kevin the names of Stephanie's parents as the password. Twelve seconds had passed and BT were working flat out on the trace.

Sams then ordered Kevin to drive to Glossop railway station.

He was to go to the telephone kiosk inside the entrance hall where he would receive a message at 7 pm. He assured Watts that Stephanie was OK, and if all went well, she would be released just after midnight. Then there was a click and the police heard the young estate agent's voice: 'It's one o'clock, Wednesday afternoon. My parents are Betty and Warren Slater. I'm frightened but unharmed.'

Sams asked Kevin if he'd received the message. Stalling for time, Watts replied it was OK but not very clear. Then the line went dead. The call had lasted just over a minute, ample time to trace the call box had it been on the latest digital exchange system. But it wasn't. Sams had done his homework thoroughly.

Outside in the street, several police cars moved off. It was getting misty and they didn't want the operation hindered by fog, if for no other reason than that the helicopter would be grounded because of poor visibility.

In his office, Kevin shook hands with the police officers, and they wished him luck and reminded him to keep calm. They told him that their colleagues would never be very far away from him at any time.

Shortly after 4 pm, Kevin took the holdall, got into his car and drove to junction 7 of the M6 and drove north on the motorway, leaving it at junction 20. Then he skirted south of Manchester via the M56, M63 and M66 and took the A57 to Glossop.

THIRTEEN

The Pick-up

On his arrival at Glossop, Kevin Watts drove to the town centre where he asked for directions to the railway station. After a few minutes' drive, he pulled into the carpark to the left of the station foyer, got out of the car and located the phone booth. A few minutes after 7 pm, the telephone rang, and Watts was given specific route instructions by Michael Sams.

As soon as Watts replaced the receiver, he left the station. Turning right at the entrance, he walked down the hill past his car to the telephone kiosks outside the Norfolk Arms, entering the first as instructed. Taped under the shelf, he found an unsealed envelope. Inside was a typed message on a sheet of white paper that looked as if it had been cut down. There was also a punched hole in the top left corner.

The message was much the same as the instructions given to Watts over the phone in Glossop station:

> Take B6105, (which is the road outside station) uphill and continue until joining A628.

> Right on A628 to Barnsley.

> At junction of A628 & A629 turn right at roundabout. to Sheffield.

> Phone box 1.6mls from roundabout on left hand side. just past cross roads.

Stay in car and enter box at exactly 7.40pm, if phone is not ringing there is a message taped under the small black shelf. Open boot before going in box and leave open until returning.

Warning. Enter boxes only at times given. At sometime you will be observed.

After reading the message, Kevin walked back to his car. He had been instructed to relay any instructions to the police over his two-way radio, and now he did just that. The next stop-off point – another phone box – was only about five miles from where Sams had left the two bricks on the M1 motorway and was close to the Dove Valley Trail.

Kevin drove out of Glossop and on to the B6105, going north. 'I was driving very slowly,' he said later in his police deposition. 'All of a sudden, as I reached open country, I was in thick fog.' After obtaining directions from a group of joggers, he found the A628.

By now, the fog was as thick as pea soup in places, and he was reduced to driving along the unfamiliar roads at a snail's pace until he reached a mini-roundabout. He took the third exit on to the Huddersfield-to-Rotherham A629 where he zeroed the tripometer so he would know exactly how much further he had left to travel.

Ten minutes later, he found a new-style BT kiosk on the left-hand side of the road, in the tiny hamlet of Four Lane End. He parked and, carrying the holdall, opened the boot as instructed. He knew that he was running late, so without waiting for any telephone call, he took the kidnapper's message from under the shelf as before. He then returned to his Rover, slammed the boot shut, threw the holdall on to the back seat, and sat in the car, reading the instructions with the aid of a torch.

THIS ROUTE WILL SHOW IF YOU ARE BEING FOLLOWED.

BACK TO CROSS ROADS. (50yds).

RIGHT UP HILL (B6449 TO DODWORTH).
LEFT 100 yds (signposted Public Bridleway) This is a small lane on LHS before main B6449 bears right.

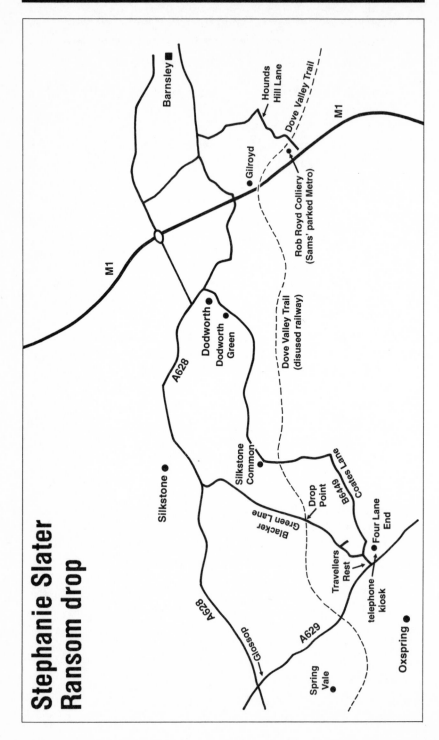

Stephanie Slater
Ransom drop

(Left) Michael Benniman Sams aged about three, with his mother, Iris.

(Above) Michael with his father, Ernest Sams.

(Right) A smiling Michael Sams receives a cup after winning a race with the Bingley Harriers – the same running club Julie Dart later belonged to.

Music and running: the two leisure pursuits in which the young Michael Sams excelled.

(Left) Eleven-year-old Sams' student certificate (junior division) from the Trinity College of Music, for his proficiency on the piano.

(Below) Sams (centre) at one of the racing meetings he participated in his youth.

(Right) The certificate Sams was awarded for the last Three Peaks race he entered, in 1972 when he was 30.

(Above) Sams, aged 19 in 1960, after joining the Merchant Navy, dressed in his Clan Line dress uniform.

(Left) A grey-faced Sams with new wife Jane Marks, in 1979 - a few months after his right leg was amputated.

(Left) Eaves Cottage, the home of Michael and Teena Sams in Sutton-on-Trent.

(Left) Jane and Michael Sams, with Sams' mother, Iris, and her second husband, Sidney Walker.

(Main picture left) Sams' squalid workshop in Swan and Salmon Yard, Newark-on-Trent, Notts, where he held his victims Julie Dart (above left) and Stephanie Slater (left). It is also possible that Suzy Lamplugh (above) may have met her fate here.

(Photos: Workshop © West Midlands Police Photographic Department;
Dart © Syndication International;
Slater © *The Sun*, Rex Features;
Lamplugh © Rex Features)

(Right) Bridge 30 at Millmeece, Staffs, on the West Coast InterCity line, where Sams rigged his device to damage or derail a train during his British Rail extortion bid.

(© British Transport Police)

(Above) Dove Valley trail, where it crosses the M1, along which Sams rode his moped during the Stephanie Slater ransom collection.

(© South Yorkshire Police Photographic Department)

(Left) The bridge over the disused railway line, where the Slater ransom money reached Sams.

(© South Yorkshire Police Photographic Department)

(Above) The utility room at Eaves Cottage, with Sams' Suzuki 'Love' moped and railway memorabilia, including the Paddington station sign which had special significance for Sams, perhaps in connection with the abduction of Suzy Lamplugh.

(© West Midlands Police Photographic Department)

(Above) Police photograph showing how the moped would fit into Sams' car.

© West Midlands Police Photographic Department)

(Right) Artist's impression of Sams (wearing Michael Caine-like glasses as a disguise), drawn from a description given by Stephanie Slater.

(© West Midlands Police Photographic Department)

(Above) Andrew Grant's Worcester estate agency, where Sams admits searching for an estate agent to kidnap circa June 1988.

(Left) Sams' third wife, Teena, in happier days.

(Above) Sams at Swindon railway station, just one of the hundreds of photographs that record his train-spotting activities.

Take care to turn right 100yds down lane.

LEFT FORK BY FARM HOUSE. (Down the hill).

150yds DOWN LANE IS A SMALL BUILDING ON LHS.

PICK UP BLACK BAG BY RED/WHITE CONE.

TRANSFER ALL MONEY FROM YOUR HOLDALL TO INTO THIS BAG.

2 MINS ALLOWED FOR THIS.

DO NOT MOVE OFF UNTIL YOU HAVE DONE THIS.

MOVE OFF EXACTLY AT 7.47pm.

TAKE MONEY AND BAG WITH YOU.

FURTHER MESSAGE IN BAG.

Kevin turned his car around and turned right at the crossroads, on to the B6449 Dodworth Road. A large grey saloon slipped out of the pub carpark behind him as he disappeared over the brow of the hill and into the gloom. 'It was extremely foggy and visibility was down to five to ten yards,' Kevin said. 'I travelled along this road but missed the turning. I turned round and went back. I had only travelled a short distance at this time. I reached a road on my right marked "Public Bridleway", and I turned into it.' Kevin then missed another sign that read 'SHIPWAYS' and an arrow that pointed down the track, known locally as Blacker Green Lane.

The surveillance team were also experiencing problems in the fog. In addition, the helicopter that should have been nearby had been grounded because of the poor visibility, and for some reason, their electronic tracking device wasn't giving them proper directions. They might well have reflected on the famous FBI observation: 'The trouble with surveillance is you don't get to see anything.'

Shears, Dempsey and Thake in one of the undercover vehicles had been listening as Kevin relayed the criminal's directions over the two-way radio, and passed this information to their operational control back in Birmingham, where the route was being followed on a large map pinned on a wall. They followed Kevin Watts at a discreet distance along the Dodworth road, and they observed him as he stopped in the fog, turned round and drove back towards them. But by the time they had repeated the manoeuvre, they could only hazard a guess as to where Kevin had gone. Their guess was wrong. While Kevin turned right, down the lane, they drove straight back to the pub.

When the officers realised what had happened, their vehicle was driven back up the road and reversed 30 yards down the track. DC Dempsey then stopped the car, switching off its lights. This had the dual purpose of blocking the lane should the kidnapper attempt to make good his escape in their direction, and stopping anyone who lived along the track from getting in or out. But no one blocked off the north end of the lane.

Moments after Dempsey parked, just before eight o'clock, 'Charlie 1', a grey Peugeot containing DS Keys and DC Rawlings, was driven into Blacker Green Lane. However, when they saw their colleagues, who were doing their best to be inconspicuous, Martin Keys reversed the vehicle and shot back to the Travellers' Rest pub at the crossroads, where Rawlings hopped out to take up a 'covert position' in a damp field to watch the telephone kiosk. Then DC Shears finally saw, through the fog, a handmade sign at the bottom of a telegraph pole at the entrance to the track.

Disaster then struck. The radio link between police and courier started to break up because of the atrocious weather conditions, which played havoc with the frequencies. Now, Kevin Watts was effectively on his own. When news of the radio breakdown was passed back to Birmingham, pandemonium ensued.

Paul Burkinshaw, a 39-year-old accounts manager, was struggling through the fog on his way home from work in the Manchester area. He had stopped briefly in nearby Penistone, then travelled down the A628 Manchester-to-Barnsley road, and was now, at about 8.10 pm, entering the south end of Blacker Green Lane. He drove north when, suddenly, his headlamps picked out another vehicle inconveniently blocking access to his property.

Initially, sighting two people in the car with their heads down, he thought this might be a courting couple, a not uncommon sight in this neck of the woods. However, Burkinshaw's curiosity was aroused when he saw that the car's boot was open and someone was rummaging about inside. He reversed his white Peugeot 309, believing that the offending car would move. He waited, and he waited. When his patience finally evaporated, he tooted his horn and, for good measure, flashed his lights, but still the car didn't budge.

Burkinshaw then decided that caution was the better part of valour. Not wishing to become embroiled in a punch-up with three strangers in the middle of nowhere, he slowly eased his car past the other Peugeot, just clipping its wing mirror in the process. Somewhat peeved by the incident, he walked into his house to find his 16-year-old son playing upstairs on a computer, and a note from his wife telling him that she'd gone to the local pantomime at Penistone theatre and his dinner was in the oven.

Burkinshaw quickly washed and changed his clothes; then he heard the sound of a revving engine outside. Through a window, he peered through the swirling fog and saw red, then white lights turning on and off, as if the car that had blocked his way was trying to reverse. He was just about to investigate further when the vehicle shot forward, skidded to a stop, then sped off.

By now, the penny had well and truly dropped at both of the RCS operational headquarters. As the fog thickened and swirled, plucky Kevin Watts could be lying dead in an icy ditch and the money could have disappeared, along with the kidnapper of Stephanie Slater, who herself might then be murdered. Gone, too, was the British Rail extortionist and the killer of Julie Dart. To ameliorate the situation, a back-up vehicle was sent to the area, and 'Bravo 9' drove away from the lane to park within spitting distance of 'Charlie 1'.

But what of Kevin Watts? He had indeed turned into Blacker Green Lane and, after creeping down the track for some 100 yards, had seen the 'SHIPWAYS' sign with an arrow leading him to an even narrower bridleway. He didn't stop, but continued on for another 150 yards until he spotted a small building about the size of a shed on his left. In front of it was a red-and-white traffic cone with a dark-coloured bag next to it. He stopped the car and collected the bag, in which there was another message. Kevin transferred the £175,000 into the bag, then read the message, which had been written in blue felt-tip, using a stencil:

GO TO END OF LANE – TURN LEFT BACK TO ROUNDABOUT (A628/9)
TURN RIGHT – PHONE BOX 3.5mls LHS MESSAGE TAPED UNDER SHELF
15 mins ALLOWED

Watts continued to speak into the defunct microphone, relaying the kidnapper's instructions, just in case anyone could hear him. They couldn't. However, if the police had heard him, they would have moved to the wrong location, for this message was a ploy by the criminal to divert attention away from the actual ransom drop.

Kevin Watts continued driving down the track, which now led through a wood. In a break in the mist, he saw what he took to be a low brick wall and, right in front of his car, a second traffic cone. Pinned to it was a large white cardboard notice:

STOP

60 SECS ALLOWED

ON WALL BY 4 SIGN – WOOD TRAY – DO NOT MOVE TRAY SENSOR
INSIDE – PUT MONEY & BAG ON TRAY – IF BUZZER DOES NOT SOUND
LEAVE MONEY THERE – REMOVE CONE IN FRONT OF CAR AND GO –
MONEY WILL NOT BE COLLECTED UNTIL YOU HAVE LEFT

Removing the drawing pins from the cone, he returned to his car with the notice, placing it on the back seat. 'I picked up the bag,' he later explained,

> *and as instructed placed it very carefully on the tray which was on top of the wall. This tray was made of wood with about a 2-inch lip round the edge. It was about 2 feet by 1 foot, and in the top left-hand corner was a galvanised metal box about the size of a cigarette packet. I presumed this to be the sensor. The tray seemed to be purpose-built to take the bag without touching the sensor.*

Kevin got back into his Rover and locked the doors. Outside it was icy cold and foggy; the only sound was water dripping as ice thawed in the trees. He thought that he had stopped on a bridge over a river because of the blue metal railings that ran along some of the wall's length, but he had no inclination to find out more or stay longer than necessary. He drove off.

The police back-up vehicle containing detectives Roberts,

Fowler, Hurst and DeFreitas was now hurtling along the B6449. They had been positioned at junction 37 of the M1, where there was a road block in case the kidnapper was daft enough to join the motorway at that point. At 8.35 pm, they pulled into the carpark of the Travellers' Rest and, wearing balaclavas and dark combat suits, made their way across fields to the farm buildings in Blacker Green Lane. Now, without radio contact, they were left very much to their own initiative.

Pete Roberts took charge and extended the area under investigation. He directed Hurst and DeFreitas to search the lane, while he and Fowler walked off down the track. Although they were going in the right direction, nothing came of this, and as they returned to the farm buildings, a dog started to bark.

Paul Burkinshaw was taking the first bite of his dinner when the family pet started howling, so he got up and let it off its lead. 'I couldn't see anyone,' he said later, 'but they must have been very close. I heard a man's voice whisper: "I've just seen somebody." Someone else said: "Where is he?"'

When Burkinshaw challenged the strangers, one of them replied: 'We are on a map-reading exercise and following the path to the pub.'

The surveillance team finally found the 'SHIPWAYS' sign pointing down the bridleway, and although they had just walked up that track, the officers turned around to retrace their steps, which only served to infuriate Burkinshaw's dog even more. They then discovered the second sign and, shortly afterwards, the traffic cone halfway along the track. Three hundred yards further, they came across the second cone on the railway bridge. Pete Roberts managed to contact his fellow officers with a combination of muffled calls and whistles.

Among the first to arrive on the bridge was Simon Hurst, who had just regained radio contact with the operational commander on the ground. He was told to conduct a finger-tip search of the bridge. Initially, nothing was found because of the fog. Then, groping around, Hurst touched the traffic cone that Pete Roberts – unbeknown to him – had removed from the bridge parapet moments earlier. As the fog lifted a little, Hurst spotted the number '(4)', which had been spray-painted on the wall. Jose DeFreitas found traces of sand above the number, then peered over the side of the bridge into the gloom below. What, the police wondered, had happened to Kevin Watts?

After leaving the money, Watts had driven across the bridge, passed a few farm buildings and eventually reached a main road – the A628. Here, as instructed by the kidnapper's penultimate message, he had turned left, and then right into the A629 at a roundabout a couple of miles along the road.

But after driving three-and-a-half miles further on, there had been no telephone box to be seen. (If he had read the note Sams had left in the bottom of the tray in which he had deposited the money, he wouldn't have bothered to look: the note told him to disregard the previous instructions and return to Shipways.) At this point, he had been met by policemen who escorted him to a nearby factory site, where he handed over virtually everything left behind by the kidnapper, which he had been told by the police to collect – notes, envelopes, tape and drawing pins.

Unfortunately for the police, luck was not with them yet again. While trying to collect as much evidence as possible, Kevin had thrown into his car only one sign, but it was the vital one that pointed directly to the kidnapper's escape route along the disused railway line below the bridge.

So what exactly were Sams' movements that icy, foggy night? Until recently, the answer to this has been shrouded in an equal amount of fog. With Sams being an inveterate liar, sorting the wheat from the chaff has proved a difficult task. However, I have received valuable assistance from others, including a small group of people who live in the Dodworth and Oxspring area, and have been able to cull something resembling the truth from Sams himself. The result is new evidence that sheds a completely different light on the events that occurred the night of the ransom drop.

Evidence from Kevin Watts and the police show that, on 29 January, Sams telephoned the branch manager of the estate agency at Glossop railway station around 7.10 pm. However, there is another person who could possibly confirm this timing: 55-year-old Frank Hudson.

Frank was in the habit of walking his dog most evenings between 6 and 8 pm. That Wednesday, he allowed the animal to wander almost at will at the end of a 15-foot extending and retractable lead. As the dog eagerly sniffed its way towards an old-style telephone box at the junction of Manor Park and the A628, a few minutes' walk from the northern entrance to Blacker Green Lane, Frank noticed a small hatchback car, either orange or grey. He wasn't sure of the make or model – in fact, he probably could not have recognised it again – but he did comment later to the police that it was dirty, as though it had done a lot of mileage. The street lamps near the kiosk would have altered the true colour of the Metro, the fog not helping either. And Sams rarely washed his car – it was always dirty.

This evening, Frank's over-excited dog managed to get its lead wrapped round the kiosk, and in his efforts to untangle the dog, Frank couldn't help noticing a man using the phone. He couldn't make out what he was saying, but the person appeared to be doing all the talking. 'It appeared to be a one-sided conversation,' Frank told the police. 'I have no idea what he said, and I could not say what accent he was speaking in. It was a slow tone.

'The man kept moving around,' Frank continued.

It appeared as if he was trying to keep his back to me. I didn't get a good view of him, but I would describe him as follows: white male, approximately five foot seven inches tall, short dark-coloured hair combed back, and he gave the impression of being aged between 40 and 50 years. I didn't take particular notice of him as I thought he might think I was being nosey going right up to the phone, and that's why I thought he turned his back towards me, for privacy. I then walked home.

This description bears a likeness to Michael Sams, and the description of the car resembles the Metro. The timing is important as Sams has since confirmed that he used this telephone box to speak to Watts at Glossop station, and that he did this just after 7 pm, which fits in neatly with Frank Hudson's statement. But perhaps the most important fact is that Sams agrees that he parked his car nearby at seven o'clock.

However, he was in this locality much earlier that evening. Brian Rushforth is a self-employed butcher whose shop adjoins his home at 1 Station Road, Dodworth. At 5.30 on Wednesday, 29 January, he was working alone in his premises when a man walked in, asking for directions to the nearest fish and chip shop. Brian began to give directions when the man cut him short, saying: 'Have you got any pies?' Rushforth sold him two standard-size pork pies, priced 45 pence each, which he placed into a white plastic bag. The customer left the shop and walked off down the B6449 in the direction of the northern end of Blacker Green Lane.

Brian later described his customer as '45–50 years, short at perhaps five foot seven inches, medium build, wearing glasses, clean shaven. He was wearing a cap with the peak pulled down over his eyes. He also wore a three-quarter-length coat or overalls. The trousers were the same colour as the coat, either dark blue or green.' He also recalled that the man wore either Wellington boots or substantial climbing boots.

According to Rushforth, the man had a Yorkshire accent, although he didn't think it was a local one. He seemed furtive and on edge. His manner was abrupt, and he seemed in something of a hurry. Rushforth's overall impression was that the customer was scruffy, untidy and needed a good wash. The entire description fits Michael Sams that evening.

So Sams was in Dodworth at 5.30 pm, and was spotted at about 7 pm by Frank Hudson at Manor Park, within a short walking distance – a few minutes – of the northern end of Blacker Green Lane. So what were Sams' movements during the 90 minutes between the two sightings?

Sams has told both the police and me that, after he'd left instructions under the telephone shelf in Glossop, he drove cross country, checking the mileage and driving time from Glossop to Four Lane End. However, because he was able to leave a message at the Four Lane End kiosk giving an approximate arrival time of 7.40 pm, and repeated this time to Watts over the phone, Sams must have checked the route and driving time on an earlier occasion – in fact, the police found all the information on his computer, as he had intended to use the same run for the British Rail extortion.

Sams has said that, after taping the second set of instructions to the telephone box at Four Lane End, he drove along the B6449 through Dodworth and checked out the place where he would later park his car – the pithead at the Rob Royd colliery at the end of Hound Hill Lane. Having done that, he stopped at Dodworth where he bought the two pork pies from Brian Rushforth. It was now 5.30 and he had to be in a phone box to call Kevin Watts at 7pm. Sams says that he spent 20 minutes eating the pies in a layby on the road between Dodworth and Manor Park. What he did between leaving the layby at around

5.50 pm and ringing Kevin Watts at 7 pm is only known to Michael Sams. However, I am now able to shed a startling new light on the evening in question, one that I believe shows that it was impossible for Sams, alone, to have carried out the ransom collection and driven back to Newark.

FOURTEEN

The Accomplice Scenario

After his arrest, while being interviewed by DC Kednay, DS Evans and DI Maxwell at Newark Police Station on 21 February, Sams was questioned about his movements directly after he'd called Kevin Watts from Glossop at 3.25 pm.

Sams told the investigators he left Glossop and drove straight to South Yorkshire where he parked his car and got the scooter out. This was not quite true, for we know he was still using the Metro between 5.30 and 7.02 pm, when he phoned Watts who had just arrived at Glossop from Birmingham. It is here that the plot thickens.

The telephone call to Watts confirmed that the £175,000 was ready. Sams now had the green light, and proceeded with his plan. According to him, he left the call box at Manor Park just after 7.10 pm. Entering from the northern end where it joins the A628 from Glossop, he drove the Metro to the other end of Blacker Green Lane – a bridleway that was all of 1½ miles long – in pea-soup-thick fog, turned the car around and began dropping off the cones and signs as he went. When he reached the railway bridge spanning the Dove Valley Trail (making his entire journey on Blacker Green Lane a total of about 2½ miles), he painted the number '(4)' on the wall with a can of spray paint, then tipped sand on to the edge of the parapet before placing the wooden drawer in position. (The sand was intended as a form of lubrication, to enable the drawer to slide easily down to the old track beneath.) Sams attached a length of washing line to the drawer, then threw the remainder over the side of the bridge. He would pull the rope to bring the drawer and money down to him. Sams told the detectives that he then removed the moped from his car and, with much difficulty, dragged it down the thickly wooded embankment to await the arrival of Kevin Watts on the bridge. As soon as he had the money, he would escape by riding his bike along the Dove Valley Trail to the Rob Royd pithead where his car was waiting.

But there is a fundamental flaw in all of this. Who drove Sams' car back to the pithead?

Sams' car (or one very similar) was seen by Frank Hudson at the telephone kiosk near the northern end of Blacker Green Lane at 7.02 pm. Sams confirms this: to set up the signs, cones, sand, wooden drawer and washing line along the bridleway, he used his car.

He left the first sign by the telegraph pole at the extreme southern end of the track. Unwilling to use his headlamps for fear of arousing suspicion, he drove back up the bridleway very slowly, and the whole exercise was made more difficult because he had to place each item in turn. He dropped the cones out of the window of the car, but when he set up the signs and drawer, he had to get out of the car. For an able-bodied person, this would have been easy; for Sams, it was not quite so. He had to unlock the knee joint of his artificial leg as he climbed out of the vehicle, lock it to walk, and reverse this procedure when he needed to drive off.

It is accepted by the police that Sams did all of this after he had phoned Watts at 7.02 pm. In perfect weather conditions, this drive up and half-way down the bridleway would have taken a total of ten minutes. However, Sams did it in foggy conditions without headlamps. Today, a number of experienced police officers say with hindsight that this trip in darkness and fog would have taken at least 30 minutes to complete.

That being the case, Sams could not have completed the task of dropping off all his paraphernalia until around 7.30 pm. This doesn't make sense of Sams' statement that he was back with his moped at the bridge just after 8 pm, while his car was parked in

Hound Hill Lane, at the Rob Royd pithead, six miles away. In fact, Sams' instructions to Watts, had been to move off to the drop-off point 'exactly at 7.47 pm' and it is inconceivable that Sams would not have been in position below the bridge close to that time.

If we examine Sams' statement that he dropped his bike off at the bridge after setting up his cones and signs, then drove the car to the Rob Royd pithead, we are left with the question of how he returned to the bridge.

Sams knew the courier would be at the ransom drop-off point before eight o'clock, and he had to be waiting on the track beneath to receive the money. He would need time to get the moped out of his car, walk it along the slippery railway embankment, drag it down a very steep wooded hill (a 18.25 m/60 ft almost sheer drop) in total darkness and in icy conditions to the railway bed below, then arrange the washing line so that he could pull down the cash when it arrived on the bridge above. But how did he get from the bridge to Hound Hill Lane and the Rob Royd colliery and back again – a round trip of 12 miles – and then get down the embankment, all within the space of some 20 minutes?

Sams might well have lied about his movements and timings that night. However, the evidence of two police officers may bring us closer to the truth.

After Sams was arrested, PC Richard Davidson of the West Midlands Police's Central Traffic Department initially had reservations about the ability of Sams' Suzuki moped – which weighed 52 kg (115 lb) – to fit into the boot of the tiny Metro, and he decided to put it to the test. With a little practice, the officer found that he could complete the task (albeit with some difficulty) in 12 seconds. Since PC Davidson is much younger and fitter than the disabled Sams, it would have taken the latter marginally longer to accomplish this.

Davidson, with 15 years' experience as a Grade 1 police motorcyclist under his helmet, carried out another test with the Suzuki, to evaluate its handling characteristics on the highway. He literally risked life and limb while riding the scooter on anything other than the quietest of roads, and at night, he could hardly see where he was going. The beam from the very dim headlamp was directed towards the middle of the road quite far in advance of the moped, instead of illuminating the surface relatively close up from the centre to the nearside of the road. Davidson could only make his way with the added light from a police van's headlamps following him closely. PC Davidson summarised his opinion in his report: 'As an experienced motor-cyclist, I would prefer to ride this type of machine as a fun/shopping bike, and in no way would I consider riding this machine on the roads out of choice.'

He added that the scooter was prone to buffeting from passing heavy goods vehicles, even though he had been some-what protected by his colleague driving a Ford Transit van. When lorries and coaches did pass him, the scooter became very unsta-ble, and he was sucked along in their slipstream. The upshot was that, because of poor illumination and passing traffic, anyone riding the scooter would inevitably reduce their speed in the interests of safety and self-preservation. Sams was not an experi-enced traffic cop, and did not have the same sense of balance. His chosen two-wheeled conveyance was slow and dangerous at the best of times.

PC Gerard Savage is a colleague of Davidson's at West Midlands Police's Central Traffic Department. He has been employed as a police traffic motorcyclist for 12 years, and also has a 'Grade 1' rating. At 4.57 pm, Wednesday, 11 March 1992, PC Savage rode Sams' moped from the level crossing at Hound Hill Lane to the bridge over the Dove Valley Trail – where Kevin Watts had placed the money. The officer measured the route at six miles, and the ride – which, incidently, he completed in broad daylight and perfect weather – took him 21 minutes.

In his comprehensive report, PC Savage said:

> *The Suzuki 'Love' scooter I was riding has a maximum speed of 30 mph on the flat. Over this journey the roads are mainly winding, undulating, country-type roads, and although I rode the machine as fast as I could, at one point on this route there is a long severe hill which caused the scooter to drop its speed to about 2 miles per hour on occasions.*

The traffic officer did go a little further: '... One might reason-ably add ten minutes to the timed police test of 21 minutes,' which would make the journey time more than half an hour. But this test bears no comparison to the reconstruction carried out by PC Davidson at night, when he could hardly see where he was going. And neither attempted duplications were executed in the fog that Sams would have had to contend with on that January night – if he had made the journey at all.

Then there is the supposed drive in the Metro from the bridge – where Sams alleges he first left his bike – to Hound Hill Lane. I have established that, under conditions similar to those experienced by Sams that night, this outward journey to Hound Hill Lane would have taken 15 minutes, not taking into account parking the Metro and removing the scooter from the boot before riding back to the bridge.

Taking the outward car journey of 15 minutes and the return ride on the bike of at least 30 minutes, this makes a total travelling time to and from the railway bridge of 45 minutes. If all this was accomplished from 7.30 pm, Sams could not have been back under the railway bridge before about 8.20 pm. However, Sams says that he was under the bridge waiting for Kevin Watts before 8 pm and almost certainly he would have been there by 7.47 pm, the time stipulated by Sams when Watts should 'move off' to the drop-off point. The police claim Watts did not finally leave the ransom money until 8.40 pm, but even if true, Sams could not have taken a chance on such a delay.

Sams' problems were compounded when he tried to descend to the abandoned railway line beneath the bridge. He had to get himself and the heavy scooter down on to the track 18.25 m (60 ft) below, and matters were made worse because he'd left his torch back at the workshop. He could hardly see more than a few feet in front of him. Sams later told detectives:

> I couldn't really get down in the place where I thought I could get down. I thought I could just take the bike down the side, but once I looked at it, I realised I couldn't get it down there, so I went about 100 yards further towards the Barnsley way, you might say, on the track. And then there was a track that led down to the old railway line. Took me bike down there, and when I got to the bottom, I realised it was icy.

In an effort to substantiate this part of Sams' ever-changing story – how he miraculously managed to drag his heavy scooter down the steep railway embankment with its two-in-one gradient, through the thick scrub and trees in icy cold, fog and pitch darkness without a torch – PC Savage attempted the same feat in broad daylight and in excellent weather, and came off much the worse for wear.

> *The embankment is too high and steep to have afforded me access with the scooter down to the track bed, so initially, I rode the scooter along a narrow path to the right of the bridge which runs above and alongside the track bed. After 150 yards [50 more than Sams had calculated] I was able to gain access to the track bed down a steep muddy slope. This was extremely difficult and the only way I could do it was to dismount and, standing alongside the machine applying both handlebar brakes, gingerly slide the scooter down the slope gaining the best possible footholds I could see; constantly, gently releasing, braking, releasing, braking, all the way down the slope. Even then it was a struggle to keep the machine upright and prevent it going down on its own and also myself from slipping and falling.*

PC Savage failed to give the time it took him to complete this almost lethal exercise, but whatever it was, it must have been appreciably faster than it would have taken one-legged Michael Sams in fog and darkness.

Everyone, including the police and myself, agrees with Sams' statement that, having picked up the ransom money after pulling it from the bridge, he rode his moped along the disused railway bed to the Metro parked six miles away. Again it fell to PC Savage to reconstruct this ride along the Dove Valley Trail.

Setting off in daylight, the officer enjoyed the experience. Puttering along through a few puddles and over the rough ground, he was in his element – until, that is, he arrived at a formidable obstacle about 150 metres from the Rob Royd pithead: a securely padlocked five-bar gate in an almost impenetrable, chest-high, wire-link fence. This was to cause the officer major problems, as his report relates:

> *I could see that the lower portion of the wire fence had been twisted and pulled up previously from the floor, but this was not high enough to get the scooter through. Even then I had to drop the scooter on to its side, push the front wheel and forks through the gap, then climb the fence, and from the other side physically pull the machine through the gap on its side, obviously with the engine off.*

If this fit policeman couldn't lift the scooter over the gate on his own, Michael Sams wouldn't have been able to do so either. Instead, PC Savage opted to pull it through the previously made gap, but he couldn't even do this until he had ripped out four steel staples holding the fence to a post, to lift the fence higher. He had to use all his strength to do this. According to Barnsley Borough Council records, no one had repaired the fence by replacing any pulled-out staples before PC Savage carried out his reconstruction – which leaves us with the only possible scenario: Sams *did* lift the scooter over the gate, but someone was there to help him. In fact, Sams has intermittently claimed both to the police and to me that an accomplice waiting in the car helped him lift the bike over the gate.

In a letter sent to me from HM Prison Wakefield on Monday, 24 January 1994, Sams wrote:

> *At our meeting at Full Sutton I disclosed one bit of information to yourself with advise [sic] on how to use it. You made a hash of that. I have now agreed with the person concerned not to reveal it, and the person concerned agrees to keep out of the public eye.*

This somewhat vague comment has a double edge. It is a veiled reference to Suzy Lamplugh, which we will look at later. But the final sentence suggests that there was an accomplice – 'the person concerned' – with him on the night of the ransom collection for Stephanie Slater. Later in the same letter, Sams says:

> *I would suggest you try for a March 94 release [of this book]. For I plan an April or May 94 release of my 'knowledge' as I term it through a National Newspaper. You will then appreciate just how inaccurate the Police's, Rod Chaytor's [crime reporter on the Daily Mirror] & your versions are.*
>
> *By the theories you put to me in your December 93 letter, I would suggest you haven't bothered reading much. The truth is in them [the case papers] ...*

After speaking to a number of officers who were involved in the Stephanie Slater investigation, I have learned that, within police circles, there are three schools of thought about Sams having had an accomplice. The majority pour cold water on the idea – and it is hardly surprising that they should. After all, they have their man and Stephanie is safe. However, a growing number of police officers are prepared at least to keep an open mind. Finally, a small minority firmly believe that Sams did have an accomplice.

When considering everything to do with this aspect of the Slater inquiry, one is left with a number of important, unanswered questions. Would it not have been impossible for Sams to have completed about an hour's work inside 20 minutes? How did he get the 52.5 kg scooter down the railway embankment *and* over the locked five-bar gate – alone? There is also the fact that approximately £8000 of the ransom money was never recovered. Did that money go into the pocket of an accomplice who played no small part in this cryptic crime?

FIFTEEN

Safe Return

Sams returned to Newark and Stephanie around 10.40 pm. She had expected him much earlier and she was starting to panic. 'I feared he had been arrested,' she was to tell the police. 'I had decided that if he hadn't returned by midnight, I was going to smother my face with a pillow in an attempt to commit suicide.'

On his arrival in the workshop, Stephanie blurted out, 'Did you get the money. Did everything go all right?' Sams answered, 'Yes.'

Stephanie was anxious to get out of the box, but he told her she'd have to wait a few minutes. Then she heard him moving about the building and shifting a few items. She also heard some loud banging (presumably Sams' taking the moped out of his car). Ten minutes later, she was released from her confines.

She asked him again, 'Did everything go all right?'

He replied, 'Yes. Apart from my mate falling off his motor-bike three times because of the weather conditions.' (Sams would later say that *he* fell from his scooter three times while negotiating the disused railway track.) Stephanie also recalls him saying that there had been a fence by the disused railway which had caused a problem and which had not been there when 'they' had planned the ransom pick-up. In addition, during this hurried exchange, Stephanie remembers Sams saying that his 'mate' had used a metal detector to check that the money hadn't been marked.

Stephanie then dressed in the clothes she had been wearing the day of her kidnapping, with the exception of her coat. Sams carried that to the car waiting outside. He was releasing her early, rather than waiting until Friday, 31 January, the date he had specified in his ransom demand to Shipways. Why he did this is not known. Perhaps he genuinely wanted to end her ordeal. Perhaps he thought that he would catch the police off guard. The truth probably lies in both these possibilities.

When Stephanie got into the car, her first impression was that the Metro seemed very cold – '... as if it hadn't been driven very far,' she recalled. Apparently the heater took a while to warm up. This is rather strange, for Sams had supposedly just driven 53 miles in the vehicle, and after 10–15 minutes, the engine and interior should still have been warm.

After leaving Swan and Salmon Yard, Sams headed for Birmingham. In his later interviews, he told DS Evans that he'd driven along the A46 to Bingham, where he turned right and carried on along the A52, past Radcliffe-on-Trent and Gamston. Although blindfolded and covered with a cardigan, Stephanie remembered him driving at speed over what she took to be country roads with slight curves. At one point, he remarked, 'You wouldn't believe how many police were around when I brought you here.' Shortly afterwards, he pulled into a layby on the dual-carriageway at Gamston, the small village three miles south-east of Nottingham where he had previously used the callbox. Now he told the blindfolded Stephanie that he would dial her parents' telephone number so that she could let them know that she was safe.

Sams had already told his captive that he would be dropping her off near the police station and hospital in Uttoxeter, and he obviously thought that she would tell her parents this. But it was patently a ruse to divert police attention away from Birmingham, since Sams' real intention was to leave Stephanie outside her own home. In any event, the pay phone was broken, so they drove off.

Ten miles on, travelling down the A453, they passed Ratcliffe-on-Soar, with its massive power station billowing clouds of superheated steam into the south Nottinghamshire sky. They passed under the M1 motorway at junction 24; then driving through Ashby de la Zouch, they hit the M42 with a clear run to the M6 and Birmingham.

Throughout the journey, Sams and Stephanie chatted as usual. He explained that he had had a contingency plan in case he had been caught picking up the money or if he had been injured or killed in a road accident: he had carried a note in his pocket, telling the police where she was being held prisoner. Then to reassure Stephanie, Sams started to count down the mileage, making reference to place names as they drove through. But it was only when they entered Spaghetti Junction that she realised that she was almost home.

At one point, he said, 'You have to thank the police helicopter for your safety. That's where I knew the money was, as Watts made a mistake.'

To check this out, I contacted the West Yorkshire Police Air Support Unit based at Carrgate, near Wakefield. The duty inspector checked through the technical log for that evening and confirmed that none of his aircraft had been flying, due to thick fog.

This return journey was a time of very mixed feelings for Stephanie Slater. While part of her was sure that she'd be safely home very soon, there was the ever-real possibility of her being murdered en route. This fear was fuelled by one incident: 20 minutes after leaving the callbox at Gamston, Sams stopped the car to clean his headlamps. She thought he was going to kill her then, but he got back in the car and they drove on.

As they approached the outskirts of Stephanie's home city, he said, 'Can't you smell Birmingham?' He mentioned the Bull Ring and a steel flyover that had been built by the army in the late 1960s. Stephanie was now picturing the route as if she had a street map in her head. When he mentioned traffic lights, she asked if there was a hotel nearby. There was. She thought they had come off the motorway at the top of Walsall Road, at the A34 Ray Hall interchange. In the direction they were travelling, towards the city proper, the Scott Arms public house was a local feature.

She now knew she was minutes away from freedom. Later, she told the police, 'When we approached the Scott Arms, and changed lanes left to right to turn right into Newton Road, he said, "I've got the Scott Arms in front and an electrical shop on the left. Am I going too fast?" I said, "No. Go on," and I knew that we were going down Newton Road towards my house.' Sams finally told her to remove her blindfold, 'But keep your eyes shut,' he asked her. She did.

The young woman's heart was pounding as she gave him directions for the last few hundred yards. 'When you get to the

"SLOW" sign in the road, turn left into Hamstead Road by the church. Turn right and right again. Right at the crossroads. On the left here, there's a house for sale with a Cornerstone "For Sale" board. Is it there?' She was nearly home.

All in all, Stephanie reckoned that they had been driving for just over 90 minutes. Before they stopped, Sams gave her some final instructions on how to leave the car – he had planned everything to the last detail. She was to hold her coat in her left hand, open the door with her right hand, and swing her legs out on to the pavement. Standing with her back to the car, she was to keep her eyes closed until he had driven away. She followed his orders to the letter. Sams' last words to Stephanie were: 'Now remember what I've told you. I'm sorry about all this. It's not your fault. Get back to your normal life as soon as possible. You may need counselling. I'm sorry it had to be you.'

So there it was. The killer, kidnapper and extortionist parted company with the young estate agent whose life could never be the same again. As Stephanie got out of the car, she squinted in the bright light from a street lamp – the first time she'd seen light for eight days. Then she stumbled. The car door wouldn't close properly. She heard it click shut behind her. Looking as if she was tipsy, Stephanie staggered along Stella Grove into Newton Gardens, where she hammered on her parents' front door. Finally she was home.

Michael Sams drove away along Howard Road with tears flooding down his face. He knew he'd miss her terribly, now it was all over. She had been the nicest girl he had ever met in all of his shabby life, or so he later claimed.

Not a single police officer was waiting outside in Newton Gardens for Stephanie's safe return. No one could have anticipated that the man who had battered and strangled a woman to death would dare to drive the missing estate agent, unharmed, to within 100 yards of her front door. However, Michael Sams and his little Metro were seen by one person, and that man was to become a vital witness in the hunt for a murderer.

Pervis Barnaby was a 32-year-old car sprayer, married with two children, who lived at 42 Bowstoke Road, Great Barr, on the corner of Bowstoke Road and Stella Grove. That night, his wife asleep beside him, he was watching the end of a film on television when he heard the sound of a car engine right outside his house:

'I got out of bed and went on to the landing. I saw lights from the car beaming through my glass front door. Somebody was on my drive.' Looking out of the front bedroom window, he saw what he called a 'Mini Metro', later describing it:

> *I know the colour is 'vermilion red', which in fact looks a horrible orange. I know that the car must be old because of that colour and the fact that it had small black plastic push-on caps on the wheels. The tyres were very muddy. The mud was dried on the sides of the tyres.*

Pervis thought that somebody was dropping someone off. 'They were talking,' he told the police next day. 'Then the passenger door fully opened and I saw a girl get out of the car. I thought she was drunk because she got out of the car unladylike. She wore a dark blue or black overcoat. She looked in a mess and scruffy. I remember her hair was a mess as well.' Pervis recalled that she seemed quite dazed, as if she didn't know where she was. 'She then ran off in a staggering run from the front of my house into and along Stella Grove,' he said. 'I remember she ran with her arms out as if to keep her balance. She looked upset.' He finally mentioned that the car looked as if the back windows were either blacked out or filled with 'stuff'.

Michael Sams returned to Newark by the same route, his feelings of sadness soon replaced with anxiety, the chances of being stopped ever present. Then he realised that he was almost out of petrol. He had just skirted Sutton Coldfield and was heading along the M42 when the gauge dropped into red. After a few miles, he spotted the welcoming lights of Granada Services at junction 10.

At 1.17 am on Thursday, 30 January, 21-year-old Craig Gardner was working the night shift at till no. 2 – the busiest of the three cash registers. Although he later couldn't describe this particular customer or his car, he did remember him. The driver had only had just under £4.00 in his pocket, and had asked if he could pay for the fuel using a company cheque. Craig had to refuse: Granada had a company policy that forbade its staff to accept such cheques when purchasing products. The driver had complained bitterly, even trying to seek pity by saying he had an artificial leg. Craig would have none of it.

Sams, with £175,000 stashed away, cursed his stupidity for

coming out with so little money. He was forced to put in his tank exactly £3.97 worth of petrol – 8.18 litres of four-star, just enough to allow him to creep carefully back home. He was given receipt no. 300192, which linked the sale to pump no. 7.

Just after midnight, Detective Inspector Adrian Bowers, the Slaters' family liaison officer, had chosen a rather inopportune moment to use the toilet. Hearing banging on the front door followed by the bell ringing, he hastily zipped his fly and shouted to Warren Slater: 'Leave it! Leave it! I'll get it!' The door was flung open to reveal Stephanie, panting and sucking in lungfuls of air.

The officer didn't realise who she was until Warren forced his way past and threw his arms around his daughter. Betty, who had been in her bedroom, rushed to Stephanie and hugged her. Both were tugged away by DI Bowers. 'Remember what I've told you,' he said. 'We need to recover her clothes for forensic examination'.

Dr Calderwood, the police surgeon, conducted a thorough examination. Stephanie complained of feeling rather disorientated and her eyes were sensitive to light, the result of having been blindfolded for such a long period. All the injuries that he recorded were minor and required no treatment – accidental bruises and scratches – apart from the cut hand. When asked by the doctor if there had been any physical or sexual assault, Stephanie categorically replied: 'No.'

Arrangements were then made for Stephanie to undergo full medical screening by a consultant physician, who would also arrange any future management. Dressed in fresh clothes, she was rushed to the exclusive private Priory Hospital, where she could sleep before her debriefing commenced.

West Yorkshire Chief Constable, Tom Cook, was given overall charge of both the Julie Dart and the Stephanie Slater investigations. It was decided that Detective Superintendent Bob Taylor would manage the Dart enquiry, while another West Yorkshire officer, Detective Superintendent Mick Williams, would run the Slater job.

The police officially lifted their communications embargo at 6 am on Thursday morning. West Midlands Chief Constable Ron Hadfield told a televised press conference that he was 99 per cent sure that Stephanie's kidnapper was also responsible for the

murder of Julie Dart. He revealed to journalists that the ransom
drop site had been a bridge, and that this was just a few miles
away from the motorway bridge where a device, similar to the
sensor used in the Slater kidnapping, had been discovered by
officers dealing with the Dart murder. Washing line had been
used in both cases. On the motorway bridge, the intention had
been to hoist the money up; in the Slater ransom drop, the cash
had been pulled down. But Hadfield held back one vital piece of
information. He told reporters nothing of the tape recordings
made when the kidnapper had phoned Shipways and Stephanie's
parents. Apparently the police had learned a few lessons since the
Peter Sutcliffe and Donald Neilson cases.

Armed with information that the drop-off site had involved a
disused railway line and a bridge, the press put two and two
together and rushed to their cars, cameras at the ready. But
someone else beat them to the Dove Valley Trail.

Andrew Shaw lived at Silkstone Common, and like Pervis
Barnaby, he worked with cars. Every morning, he would walk his
dogs – a boxer, a Welsh border-type mongrel and a small terrier –
along a set route that included the disused railway. At 7 am that
Thursday morning, he walked down on to the track bed. It was
still a little misty, and though cold, a gentle thaw had set in. Just
before reaching a row of cottages, he saw a polythene bag in the
middle of the track. He picked it up and, to his great surprise,
took out two bundles of notes sealed with a bank wrapper. There
was also some loose money in the bag. His first thought was that
this was drugs money and someone had dropped it. So – quite
naturally, some might say – he put the notes into his pockets and
hurried home to count the money – it totalled £2500. That very
day he paid part of this sudden windfall into his account at the
Midland Bank, Barnsley, keeping £137 for some trips he'd
arranged for when he went on holiday. He later deposited a
further £200 into his bank account and spent the balance.
Months later, Andrew Shaw was charged with and convicted of
the offence of 'stealing by finding'.

By late afternoon, scores of reporters and photographers had
descended on the trail. There they found an equal number of
detectives and scenes-of-crime officers scouring the trackside
and mounted police officers trotting along the old railway line.
On the railway bridge, Acting Detective Superintendent Allan

King of the South Yorkshire Police could barely conceal his embarrassment as microphones were pushed under his nose. What could he tell the media? Someone joked that it had been a 'king's ransom', but Mr King's only statement simply confirmed that the South Yorkshire Police were assisting two other police forces by searching the area, for his force knew nothing of the previous night's events.

The West Midlands force held the ace card with Stephanie Slater. Having got nowhere in their hunt for Julie Dart's killer, the murder squad in Leeds had to admit that their only chance of catching their man lay firmly within the grasp of three West Midlands Police detectives. These were the women who would debrief Stephanie, who was under 24-hour guard at the Priory Hospital.

After giving an 'Initial Debrief Note', Stephanie 'assisted' the police for a further 19 sessions, totalling 12 hours and 53 minutes, stretching over seven days. Several disturbing issues emerge from them.

The first and most important has to be the blanket denial of sexual assault that Stephanie made then, although she now claims that she was raped. The second matter is that Stephanie made no mention of Sams' artificial leg. This man walks with a very pronounced limp, and virtually all those who have met Sams have noted this and heard its distinctive click, too.

At 2 pm on Saturday, 1 February, Stephanie was introduced to freelance artist Julia Quenzlar, who had driven from her Sussex home to draw a likeness of Stephanie's kidnapper. As a starting point, she used a detailed description of the criminal, which Detective Inspector Elaine Baker had obtained from Stephanie after quizzing her for 48 minutes. Patiently, the detective had probed the woman's memory. She began by asking about the man's build and height; the colour, length and style of his hair; his ears and forehead (which Stephanie thought looked like Frankenstein's monster). Did he have sideboards, glasses, scars, freckles? What colour were his eyes? Did he have rosy cheeks? Were his nostrils flared? Did he have hairs up his nose? Did he grow stubble – a five o'clock shadow? What did he wear?

Julia Quenzlar, whose courtroom sketches often appear on television, has a remarkable ability to listen, observe and draw at the same time. It is as if she can visualise the picture inside someone's mind. She sat beside Stephanie, talking to gain her confidence as well as details of Sams, and as she did so, she created a portrait in pastel pencils. Stephanie commented that it was a very good likeness of her kidnapper, right down to the thick, Michael Caine-style spectacles he had worn.

After Julia left the hospital on that Sunday, she visited Lloyd House police headquarters, where she met Stephanie's work colleague, Jane Cashman. Jane looked at the portrait and said: 'The man I saw in Shipways' office I would say is identical to the man in the picture. I can recollect that the man's hair that I saw was longer than in the drawings, and when I saw it, it was more windswept. The man that I saw was not wearing spectacles.'

On Thursday, 6 February, Julia drew a sketch based on Jane's recollections – the two likenesses were almost identical. Now the police not only had a description of the offender's car, but two first-class portraits of the man who had probably killed Julie Dart. The West Midlands Police were naturally elated, having re-established themselves as the prime movers in a national hunt for an extremely dangerous kidnapper and murderer.

Julia Quenzlar's sketch was published nationally on 4 February. Here for all to see was the face of a killer in his 40s with straight, thick, dark hair brushed back. He had a broad face, a square, high forehead indicating intelligence, and a straight nose tipped up at the 'round bit' (as Stephanie described it). The drawing was to prove almost identical to later mug shots of Michael Sams, although the sketch flattered him by removing almost ten years from his actual age of 51.

Stephanie's description of his clothing suggested that he wore a duffel-type coat. On the breast pocket was a motif that resembled a blue train on its tracks. She had told Ellie Baker that the train looked like Thomas the Tank Engine with its round front. It was, in fact, a rail enthusiast's badge issued by a railway magazine in 1989, and depicted a Class 25 diesel in blue livery. The coat itself had been issued free to Sams by Tech Power Tools, along with an order for stock.

But like even the cleverest of criminals, Sams had made one mistake: he had allowed his true voice to be recorded by the police. This – along with the 537 pages of debriefing notes obtained from Stephanie, the two artist's impressions, the clothing, the railway badge and the description of his car – ultimately led to his downfall.

SIXTEEN

Game, Set and Match

It has been said by the police that Michael Sams buried the better part of the £175,000 ransom in a red metal toolbox in a field near his garden at Eaves Cottage. He was a patient man, content to spend the money gradually, paying off the odd overdue account and slowly improving his lifestyle. He knew that it would have been foolhardy to deposit it in his bank or Teena's building society, so the bulk of the cash had to stay hidden until things cooled down and the heat was off.

He did, however, use some of it immediately. He was able to exchange a few of the notes for railway tickets, and travelled by train to London with a camera slung round his neck, looking like any tourist. He told Teena he was off train-spotting.

Then on Wednesday, 5 February 1992, Teena made a significant entry in her diary. For the past few weeks, she had noticed that her husband seemed a lot happier. He claimed that business had picked up, and now he wanted to reconsider adopting a child. Thrilled, Teena made a note of it.

But when Sams read the daily newspapers later that Wednesday, his mood changed drastically. On the front page of the *Daily Mirror* was a picture of the man wanted by police for the kidnapping of Stephanie Slater (Julia Quenzlar's 'artist's impression' drawn during her session with Stephanie), and the accompanying news story linked him to the murder of Julie Dart. The same paper also showed a sketch of the railway badge worn by the kidnapper, which was at the very moment pinned on Sams' duffel jacket. He trembled with fear, which rapidly turned to rage. He was simultaneously terrified and livid.

Teena noticed this sudden change of mood. She saw her husband turn white, and was not surprised when he stormed out of the house. He did not return until 8.15 pm that evening. Twice during the day, she telephoned T & M Tools, but it was Sams' day off and she wasn't particularly upset when he didn't answer. But Sams *was* in the workshop, trying to clean it up.

There was now no doubt that the net was closing around him. Other papers carried the picture that closely resembled the person Sams saw in the mirror each day, and the *News of the World* had placed a £175,000 reward on his head. Oddly enough, although Teena read the same papers, she never linked these details with her husband.

Sams had to throw the police off his scent, so he sat down in his workshop and thought the problem through. So far, he had outwitted them at every turn, and he was sure he could do it again. It just needed a little planning, that was all. He switched on his word processor and began to type:

The Facts.

I, being the kidnapper of Stephanie Slater, am not the killer of Julie Dart. It is impossible that there can be any positive connection between the two cases.

I am also not the person who idiotically tried to blackmail B.R. The idear was a variation of an idear I had discussed with another, I now believe that he may have used my word processor to make his demands. The reason for the sudden cessation of communications between B.R. and the other, was my intervention when I learned with horror that he was to use my idears about picking up the ransome monies.

It could have been to my advantage to allow the police to continue to believe that the cases are all connected, but my concerns are for Stephanie and her parents, and how they must be now feeling after reading the reports. I promised and gave my word to Stephanie on a few things, and with only one exception I kept them. Some of the promises were; a) I had not killed before, b) Provided she did not remove her blindfold she would be relaesed and not be harmed in any way, both at that time or any time in the future. At that time it was not envisaged that anything could go wrong with the plan, all safeguards were in triplicate.

The only time I ever broke my promise to Stephanie was on the Wenesday she was released. In the morning I knew she was getting very nervous about me not returning, so I gave her my word that I would be back by 9.30pm at the latest and she would be home by midnight. But a slight delay, probably deliberately caused by the police, meant that Kevin Watts did not arrive at the spot until 8.30pm and not 7.49pm as planned, many times during this 40 min delay my thoughts were for Stephanie, but the presence of the police helicopter hovering overhead indicated that they were still going ahead with the drop. Incidentally this was not the first time I suspected the presence of police, for on the Tuesday at 5pm I unexpectedly phone Kevin Watts, he panicked for 4/5 secs and this confirmed what I expected, that the police had been called in immediately and that all calls would be taped.

After trying to dash back to the car over sheet ice, a stop at a petrol station to fill up both the tank and spare to allow a non stop trip to Birmingham and back, I arrived back to Stephanie's hide at 10.30pm. I informed her that everything was O.K. and she was now going home. It was the first time I had seen her cry, she virtually collapsed in my arms with relief. Fortunately she had her blindfold on and could not see my tears for her, stream-ing down my face.

Dropping Stephanie off near her home was not part of any game, it never entered my head that police surveillance would extend beyond the fence of her parents house. Initially it was discussed with Stephanie about dropping her off at Uttoxeter police station, but this was abandoned as I was worried that they would delay her return to her parents, the second option was Uttoxeter hospital, where I knew doctors would have kept her away from police for a while, but this again delayed her return to her parents, for during the long chats we had, her love off her patents was uppermost in her mind, it was this reason and only this reason that I decided to risk dropping her off a minute or so *from her house. It was not any bravado on my part I was terrified, not about the car being spotted, but I knew the police could win any ensuing chase.*

No blame can be attached to the West Midlands police for any of there actions, they did not know which direction they were heading, let alone into South Yorkshire Territory, they did not know or could not have known where the money was to have been dropped until at least 30 secs after it had been. They were not expecting her release until Friday.

There was no way they could have made any arrest that evening, unless, by accident, I had been stopped and searched for any traffic offence or accident, for in my car and pocket were letters informing the finder the whereabouts of Stephanie, I did not want Stephanie starving to death had anything happened to me, for her location could have remained a secret for weeks.

The fact that I knew, could, and did carry out the crime extreemly successfully is my only satisfaction, I am ashamed, upset and thoroughly disgusted at my treatment of Stephanie and the suffering I must have caused to her parents, Stephanie will most likely insist she was well looked after, but during the time we talked and I tried to make her laugh and smile, the sudden change of her smiling face to one taught and terrified was heartbreaking, and I knew I was doing that to her. Even now my eyes are filled with tears, I wake up during the night actually crying, with a little luck Stephanie will get over it shortly. Myself? I do not think I ever will.

Sorry Stephanie. Sorry Mr & Mrs Slater.

Before I destroy the last bit of forensic evidence, this W/P, I shall put onto paper a full and detailed account of everything from June 1991 to date, this will be given F.O.C. to any paper or periodical who thinks that Stephanie's exclusive story could be of use to them. this, in my own little way, seems to be the only way I can hope to offer any repayment for what I did to her. This case will never come to court as I have contingency plans should the police be two steps behind.

Mr Melvin Measure, solicitor, will be given these details, he will also have details of how to contact me.

c.c.
Melvin Measure.
Mrs Lynne [sic] Dart.
West Midlands Police.
West Yorkshire Police.
News of the World/Sun newspapers.
Yorkshire Television.
BBC Television.

Sams sat back to admire his handiwork. As usual, there were the spelling mistakes, but he couldn't know that these errors would be part of the evidence that would link him to murder, kidnapping and extortion. But most of all, this letter clearly illustrates the devious, cryptic mind of Michael Sams at work.

In the letter, he categorically denied being involved in the killing of Julie Dart. Then he hatched what he imagined was a brilliant idea to remove himself from culpability in the British Rail extortion. Yes, it was his idea, but someone else had modified it and carried it out, even going so far as to use his wordprocessor.

Moving on to his apparent concern for Stephanie and her parents' feelings, he states this ominous proviso: his captive would not be harmed in any way *as long as she didn't remove her blindfold.* One is left asking: what would have happened to her if she had removed it? Of course, Sams would have killed her as he done with Julie Dart.

He is incorrect when he says that Kevin Watts arrived at the bridge at 8.30 pm. Watts turned up and dropped the money at 8.05 pm. He is also wrong when he says that a helicopter was hovering above him – it had been grounded that night due to the fog.

And if Sams did stop for petrol on his way back to Newark to release Stephanie Slater (as the police also claim), why wasn't there enough petrol to allow a non-stop trip from the ransom drop to Newark, then to Birmingham, and back to Sutton-on-Trent and Eaves Cottage? Sams almost ran out of fuel shortly after releasing Stephanie.

After reading through the letter several times, he printed out a copy and then, making slight changes to each one, did this six more times. He neatly stacked all the letters on one side, being careful not to leave fingerprints on the paper. He then pressed 'DELETE FILE'. There, it was gone for good, or so he thought. However, Sams never did destroy his word processor (it is now in my possession), and police were able to retrieve much of this file later. After carefully addressing the envelopes – and sealing them using a small brush and tap water – he drove to Barnsley and posted them. This, he hoped, would give him breathing space.

Later that night, on returning home, he even apologised to Teena for being spiteful that morning. He ate his dinner and discussed finances with her. He had £542.00 in cash, plus a small cheque to pay into Teena's bank account at Barclays the following day, and there was another £240.00 to pay into her building society.

On 6 February, while Sams was counting his money ready for banking, a West Midlands detective chief inspector at Lloyd House was reading his latest letter. Immediately he contacted the incident room at Nechells Green Police Station. Detectives were split into groups and given the task of recovering all the copies sent to the other parties. The one received by the West Midlands Police (and its envelope) were sent off for forensic examination.

The first thing that struck the police as 'highly significant' was, in the address of the West Yorkshire Police, the misspelling of 'Millgate' instead of 'Millgarth'. The writer was denying all knowledge of Julie Dart's murder, yet here he was repeating the same error that had appeared on the Huddersfield note received by the police on 10 October the previous year. There were also similar grammatical errors. Unbeknown to Sams, he was telling the police that he had killed Julie Dart.

Professor Paul Britton read through the letter and instinctively felt that its author was feigning contrition. He was to advise ACC Tom Cook that the man they were hunting felt threatened, and this could be the beginning of his defence.

Releasing the first artist's impression and the details of the railway badge had done the trick. Wisely the police decided to keep up the pressure, and Friday brought little relief for Michael Benniman Sams, who was sweating it out at home. He contemplated flying to Saudi Arabia with his ill-gotten gains, but difficulties in getting the money out of the country and a fear of being picked up at the airport made him put that idea on the back burner.

His leg was playing up, and he wandered painfully to the newsagents. When he got there, he recoiled in horror. A new artist's impression, this time based on Jane Cashman's description of Sams, had been published. This picture portrayed a man without glasses, and the deep furrows on his forehead were almost a dead giveaway and he knew it. Sams almost staggered out of the shop, his cap pulled down for fear that someone would recognise him – someone with an eye on the £175,000 *News of the World* reward.

Teena read the newspaper that day but didn't put two and two together. However, to be fair to her, what wife would dream that her husband could commit such evil crimes? But someone could – Sams' first wife, now named Susan Oake. When she saw both police sketches, she knew: it was Michael all right. But then she asked herself: 'Why hasn't anyone mentioned his false leg?' It was that question that prevented her from immediately phoning the police.

That weekend, the media covered Stephanie's return home to Newton Gardens from the Priory Hospital. Welcoming her back was a uniformed constable holding a bunch of flowers. However, this gesture was somewhat spoiled by the police swarming around the house and immediate neighbourhood, some armed and others with dogs, as if they were protecting Stephanie from the possibility of assassination. The police had decided that it was better to be safe than sorry.

The *Sun* newspaper outbid its rivals, offering Stephanie an 'undisclosed amount' – thought to be £80,000 – for her exclusive story. They also nabbed Kevin Watts, then out came the cameras as the Slaters posed with Stephanie's two cats, Pipkin and Swiftnick.

And it was a 'swift nick' that the police wanted very badly. Back at the Nechells Green station, officers were, at that very moment, combing through each page of Stephanie's debriefing, with good information being found every minute. Two detectives had been assigned the job of tracking and timing Stephanie's description of her outward journey after she had been taken from 153 Turnberry Road to wherever, as well as the route by which she had been returned home. The kidnapper had driven north, for his first letter had been posted in Staffordshire. Staffordshire,

Millmeece, British Rail extortion bid, M6 motorway. Yes, he had been heading north. He always took the police north. The M6 was the western edge of Sams' territory.

They had driven up and down hills, and he had said to Stephanie that she didn't have hills like this in Birmingham. It had to be the Peak District. Yes, he had headed towards the east coast. The bastard had driven in the direction of, maybe, Nottingham, Grantham, possibly Barnsley, the M1, or Oxspring and the Dove Valley Trail. The detectives noticed that Crewe fitted the criminal's previous itinerary.

Tracing with their pencils across the map, while bearing in mind the timing of each leg of Stephanie's journey in the car, the officers pinpointed Leeds where the trouble had started. Now they knew that they were getting close.

Pausing for a coffee break, the detectives returned to the map. After switching into H.O.L.M.E.S., the national police computer into which every clue from Sams' crimes had been logged and cross-referenced, they called up every place name mentioned in the Dart and Slater enquiries. Then they drew a line from York to Leeds. Then one from Leeds to Huntingdon – which took in Sutton-on-Trent, Newark-on-Trent and Grantham. The base line was formed by Huntingdon, Coventry and Birmingham. The western perimeter – the M6 – had already been established before the refreshments. These officers had found Sams' working triangle. Somewhere within those 1000 square miles was the killer's lair.

Stephanie's return journey from her place of confinement was much easier for the detectives to figure out. In addition, as Stephanie hadn't been moved to different locations during her imprisonment, the police placed more importance on this home-ward-bound drive. Working on the premise that her kidnapper had wanted to spend as little time on the road as possible, and noting the duration of the drive and the time of day in which it was completed, the police were able to glean from Stephanie's debriefing notes detailed information that could narrow down the location of the kidnapper's base.

First, the homeward trip had taken much less time than the outward journey and it had been carried out when traffic was light, at night. As well as counting down the mileage for Stephanie, which Sams had done in an effort to put her mind at rest, he had told her when they'd passed a sign informing drivers that they were 47 miles from Birmingham. After making several phone calls, the detectives discovered that this sign was at Clifton on the A453, south of Nottingham. (Later they realised that just a few miles up the road was a phonebox that the kidnapper had used before.) The journey from Clifton to Birmingham, Stephanie reckoned, had taken an hour and 45 minutes.

She was also 100 per cent positive that, right after Sams had collected her from her prison on the night of her release, he had driven at speed down a long straight road for some time. Using a calculator and a ruler, as well as the brains of traffic officers from the Nottinghamshire Constabulary, the officers realised that the kidnapper must have used the arrow-straight A46 – an old Roman road known as the Fosse Way. This road links Lincoln in the north to Leicester in the south, and Newark-on-Trent is right on the route, halfway between the two larger conurbations.

Noting these details on an overlay over the map, the detectives felt able to tighten up the limits of the offender's territory to a triangle within the A46, the A606 and the A52. Smack in the middle was the small mining community of Cotgrave, Radcliffe-on-Trent was right on the A52 and Gamston was five miles to the west, while Tollerton and Plumtree nestled in the south. Nearby was RAF Newton, and it was there in a hut that the police set up a special operations room – a base for more localised enquiries. They called this area the 'Golden Triangle'.

Having completed this excellent detective work, the police didn't follow it through. They completely discounted Stephanie's recollection: 'We were driving for about ten minutes when I felt that we had got on to a motorway.' This is exactly the time it takes to drive from Swan and Salmon Yard, through Newark proper, to the roundabout that forms a link with the Fosse Way. She then remembered 20 minutes of fast driving in an almost straight line, and this again is exactly the run from the roundabout to the Granada service station and the A52. The motorway didn't exist, but how would Stephanie have known that, being blindfolded? With 35 minutes of the journey to Birmingham still unaccounted for, and centring on the 'Golden Triangle', it was vital to find that motorway that wasn't there. There is not 20 minutes of hard driving in a straight line within the 'Golden Triangle'. But there was along the Fosse Way.

There isn't a fish and chip shop within the 'Golden Triangle' either. During her first evening of captivity, Stephanie's kidnapper had bought a bag of chips – definitely 'chip shop chips', she said. Stephanie remembered that he was gone just ten or fifteen minutes, and she didn't hear him use the car, which was parked right outside. That being the case, the chip shop must have been only a few minutes' walk from where she was being held.

Newark is around 25 miles from Clifton, and Stephanie said they had only been driving for 35 minutes at about 70 mph before Sams had mentioned the sign 'BIRMINGHAM 47 MILES'. She wasn't far out: Sams had covered the distance in 35 minutes, averaging 71 mph – a rate that, at that time of night, he would have had no trouble achieving.

Unfortunately, this extra half-hour's driving at high speed along a straight road wasn't added to the equation. If it had been, Grantham and Newark, where there were chip shops and which were both on a major railway line, would have come into the picture.

Yet as the days passed, the investigation was getting no closer to Michael Sams, snug in Eaves Cottage.

As Tuesday, 18 February drew to a close, Michael Sams eased himself out of his armchair and told Teena that he was going out to collect soil for her seed trays. Instead, using a torch, he found the spot where he had buried the money.

Sams had no doubt that the police would get round to interviewing him sooner or later, so the money had to be moved. He had cleaned up his workshop in Newark, but finding somewhere to stash the money was another problem.

The red metal tool box and packets of notes came up easily and were quickly moved to the Newark workshop. There he counted out nearly £19,000 and placed this back in the box, which he had quickly rinsed off. (Traces of earth were later found on it when police found it tucked under a workbench alongside a broken blue and grey Black & Decker drill and a length of pink electrical cable.)

Teena's diary has no entry for Wednesday, 19 February, but Sams' movements can still be plotted with some degree of accuracy. It was a typical February day. There had been a little light rain and drizzle overnight, but this had dried up just after 8.30 am, although there were patches of morning mist. Alan Dorwood, principal meteorological officer at the Leeds Weather Centre, says that the minimum temperature was around 2 ˚C

(35.6 °F) with a touch of ground frost.

Tenant farmer John Berry works 600 acres around Westby in Lincolnshire, his land straddling the main East Coast Railway line. He crossed the tracks at a bridge about one mile from Stoke Summit. Mid-morning on that Wednesday, he was out in his green open-backed Land Rover with his golden labrador Freebie, intending to shoot the pigeons who were damaging his growing rape.

As the farmer pointed his gunsights at the sky, he encountered a stranger. 'You shouldn't be doing that,' said the man abruptly. 'I live in the country and pigeons shouldn't be shot.' John Berry explained that he was the farmer, and that was the end of the conversation. When questioned later by the police, Berry couldn't describe the man who had spoken to him, nor had he seen a car. But he did recall that the man had carried a walking stick.

Michael Sams knew that to bury the money and keep it hidden successfully, he had to dig a hole out of sight of inquisitive people. In addition, the site had to be both accessible to him and unlikely to be disturbed for months to come. Bridge No. 230 over the East Coast Railway near Stoke Summit seemed ideal. He stashed his loot in the two holes he had dug, several yards apart. This location is just seven miles south of Grantham (where he purchased his pet food) and 1.7 miles east of the spot where he had dumped Julie Dart's corpse.

On his way home, he stopped for a few minutes on the A1 near Great Gonerby, a small village two miles north of Grantham. From a callbox here, he telephoned Shipways once again. Jane Cashman took the call at about 3.15 pm. What follows is taken from a statement she gave to the police on 20 February 1992:

> *I said, 'Good afternoon, Shipways, Great Barr.'*
> *He replied, 'It's a friend of hers.'*
> *I recognised the voice as that of a man who I had spoken to on several occasions who I know as Bob Southwall.*
> *I asked, 'Who's calling?'*
> *He replied, 'It's a friend of hers.'*
> *I depressed the hold button on the telephone and said to Sylvia Baker, 'You'll never guess who this sounds like, it's him.*
> *I signalled for Sylvia to leave her desk and move to the financial adviser's desk where the telephone is fitted with a trace facility and a tape recorder.*

I then put the call through to Sylvia.

As Sylvia received the call from her colleague, she pressed the 'P' button on the telephone, which activated the search facility linking the digital exchange to Nechells Green police station. There, as Sylvia spoke to the kidnapper, information flickered on to a screen pinpointing a callbox near Great Gonerby. A 'flash call' was immediately made to the Lincolnshire and Nottingham police forces, and officers were scrambled to converge on the B1174 from every direction.

Sylvia knew the voice at once. Again what follows is taken from her deposition dated 19 February 1992:

> He said, 'I just want to talk to you for five minutes and then I won't speak to you again. I'm the person who kidnapped Stephanie. Stephanie and you are the only two persons that can identify me and Stephanie won't because she knows what will happen. Do you understand?'
> I replied, 'Yes.'
> This shook me up a lot and I was unable to concentrate on what he was saying as I was very distressed.
> He said something about if he was caught with the money, I can't remember his exact words.
> He said, 'If I'm not caught, I've got enough money to look after you.'
> The way he said this, I believed it to be a threat rather than the offer of a bribe.
> He then said something about Jane and Kevin, but I can't remember what. He made some more threats against me but I can't remember the exact words because I was finding it hard to think straight. He said something about, if he were caught, he would know where the information came from.
> He said, 'Do you understand?'
> I said, 'Yes.'
> He said, 'I won't speak to you again.'
> He then hung up.'

Following the phone call, Sylvia burst into tears. She later said that the man was sure Stephanie wouldn't identify him, and that he knew where Sylvia lived with her family.

The police had found the callbox within minutes, but once again the one-legged killer had vanished into thin air.

For some weeks, the police and the BBC had been putting together what Nick Ross, co-presenter of *Crimewatch UK*, called a 'considered package'. This included a profile of the offender, details of the car, the artist's impressions and a tape recording of the kidnapper's voice. The badge would also be shown. To keep the other media happy, the tape recording was to be made available to all interested parties at 9.30 pm on Thursday, 20 February – when *Crimewatch UK* was to be screened. *News at Ten* on ITV would run it as well. The police felt this was a last-ditch attempt to catch their man, but also their best chance yet. Millions of viewers would tune in, hoping to hear the voice of a person they knew so that they could claim the £175,000 reward for his capture.

On 20 February, rehearsals had gone well. Tom Cook, who was to appear on the programme, had briefed the producer methodically, saying: 'If someone knows the face, knows the voice, knows the car, knows the location and it's within an area that we are particularly interested in, then clearly that's going to score six out of six, and that will be a first-priority action. That's the way we are tackling it.'

Fifty telephone lines with an 0800 number would trip through to three specially adapted incident rooms in anticipation of a flood of calls. In front of each officer was a 'scoresheet'; as the information came through, the calls eliciting the highest number of 'ticks' would obviously be given top priority. British Telecom had worked overtime fitting tape facilities in case the killer decided to ring in, and each line was linked to the digital tracing network.

Sams' former wife Susan Oake was going out that evening, and she set her video to record the programme. Her and Sams' sons, Charles and Robert, would watch it live.

That evening, Sams arrived at Eaves Cottage with chocolates and crisps. He changed out of his overalls into a pair of tracksuit bottoms and a casual sweatshirt. He was about to see and hear himself on the television, and he intended to be comfortable while watching.

As the red battery-operated clock between the Georgian window and the bag of pegs showed 8.30 pm, Teena washed up in the neat little kitchen. She wiped the cream formica worktops with a cloth, quietly moved the chrome chairs back under the table and watered her plants, before joining Sams on the beige velvet sofa in the lounge. He was very quiet, just staring vacantly at the Royal Tank Corps engine name-plate hanging above the stone fireplace. The television's sound had been turned down for a moment and there was only the murmur of the fish tank next to it. This evening he had poured himself a glass of wine – he always kept a rack of 'plonk' in an alcove in the lounge in case visitors arrived.

Teena, distracted, intently gazed at the hundreds of brass ornaments and horse brasses that she had to keep clean. Had she missed any of them and would Sams notice a speck of dust?

As soon as *Crimewatch UK* came on, Sams turned up the volume and settled down next to his wife. For the first time in months, he held her hand. He needed her tonight. Then he heard his own voice, saw the artist's impressions, heard a description of his car and of the railway badge. It was him.

Fifteen million people watched that programme, and the switchboards simply couldn't cope. Charles and Robert Sams recognised their father immediately; both were stunned. But as Teena watched every minute of the programme and took in the description of the killer – who was sitting right next to her, holding her hand – it didn't cross her mind that Michael Sams was the man everyone was looking for.

When the programme finished, Sams got up to take Bonnie, the Alsatian, for a walk. As he closed the kitchen door behind him, he called out: 'Don't be surprised if the police don't come about the Metro. It could take six months.' However, they would certainly call about the Metro, but not in six months. They'd be at Eaves Cottage in the morning.

When Susan Oake returned home and switched on her television, and the video, she, too, heard her former husband's voice, and recognised it immediately. 'I was entirely convinced it was his voice,' she told detectives later. 'There was no doubt in my mind. Hearing it had such an effect on me that I became traumatised and suffered shock.' Then her two sons telephoned her, confirming what she already knew. In a state bordering on hysteria, she rang the police.

The Julie Dart incident room's number hadn't been displayed on the programme, and Susan Oake's call came as something of a shock to DC Wayne Greenwood who wasn't expecting any that evening.

'At 11.15 pm that evening I received a telephone call from a woman who sounded highly distressed and in a shocked condition,' the detective later said in evidence. The call lasted just a few moments and it is published here for the first time:

> SUSAN: *I've just heard a recording of his voice and I know who it is.*
> GREENWOOD: *Can you give me his name, please?*
> SUSAN: *His name is Michael Sams. I've been married to him. You don't have to look any further.*
> GREENWOOD: *Can you give me your name please?*
> SUSAN: *Susan Oake. I live at Riddlesden, near Keighley. You've got to believe me, I know it's him.*

DC Greenwood then asked her if she would like a police officer to visit her that evening and she said she would.

Detective Superintendent Bob Taylor instructed detective constables Dover and Newboult to call on Susan to obtain more information, and within 55 minutes, they were knocking on her front door.

Susan was clearly distraught. She explained that her former husband, whom she called Mike, had a power tool repair business in Newark, and that he was married to Teena, with whom he shared a cottage in Barrel Hill Road, Sutton-on-Trent. Bit by bit, she slowly went through the links that had convinced her and her two sons that Sams was their man. He liked trains, he drove an orange car, the artist's impressions were portraits of him, and the voice on the tape was definitely his.

'But he's got a limp,' she said. 'He had his right leg amputated years ago, he's got an artificial leg. Why hasn't someone mentioned the leg?' Months later, Susan would describe that interview as some of the most frustrating moments of her life. 'I felt awful,' she said. 'Like I was betraying my family, my sons. This was their father.' (However, that night Charles Grillo, Sams' son, rang the West Midlands incident room.)

The detectives stayed a while and noted down everything she had to say. As a parting gift, she handed them an envelope and three typed letters from Sams, which were destined to become exhibit 366 at his trial but were never required as evidence.

With some 600 calls being received that night from people who were sure they knew who the man was, it was not surprising to learn that Sams was low on the West Midlands' list (primarily because they were told by Charles that Sams had only one leg), although Leeds put him down as No. 1. During the following days, over 1000 possible suspects were named, but only Susan and her sons got it right.

Sams spent his last night of freedom in a restless sleep. His leg was playing him up, and his mind was playing tricks. He knew they could come at any moment, but he couldn't let Teena suspect anything, so although he needed her, she would have to sleep in the spare room once again. At dawn, he was already awake, and he made some tea and ate some porridge.

He shouted goodbye to Teena, and looked for the last time at his Suzuki moped standing next to her scooter in the utility room of Eaves Cottage. Even this area was covered in railway memorabilia and engine number and name plates: 'The White Rose', 'The Talisman' and 'Yorkshire Pullman'. Only one item looked out of place: a white plastic plant box filled with damp earth. Sams had brought the dirt back after his walk with the dog. It would fill Teena's seed trays.

Early that morning, Bob Taylor listened intently as DS Tim Grogan and detective constables Greenwood and Dover briefed him about the previous night's events (DC Newboult had the day off). Taylor made several short phone calls to other officers, then despatched DS Grogan, DC Paul Leach, DC Greenwood and DC Dover to Sutton-on-Trent, where they arrived at 10.40 am. They were allowed entry into the cottage by a nervous Teena.

The presence of railway memorabilia indicated a deep-seated interest in trains, but the Suzuki moped meant nothing at all at that moment. The officers asked where Michael Sams was, and Teena explained that he would be at his workshop, T & M Tools, in Newark. As they walked back to their car, Teena called out: 'He's probably expecting you. He said you might be wanting to talk to him about his Metro. He'll be home at five o'clock.'

The detectives drove slowly up Barrel Hill and turned right. From there, they drove like hell to Newark, where they arrived at 11.10. After a little searching, they found Swan and Salmon Yard, and as they swung under the archway, the first vehicle they spotted was an orange Austin Metro, index no. VWG 386Y. It matched precisely the description given by the eagle-eyed paint sprayer, Pervis Barnaby. And the downward slope of the yard fitted the details given by Stephanie Slater. Tim Grogan was moved to say, 'This is like driving down Wembley Way.'

At 11.20 am, the extremely excited detectives left their vehicles and entered the shop via the heavy wooden sliding door on its metal runners. Inside was another door, on which a sign indicated that the business was closed on Wednesdays. Tim Grogan called out, and Sams limped into the retail area from his rear workshop. 'What is it you want?' he asked abruptly. Grogan identified himself as a police officer, telling Sams that he was conducting enquiries into the murder of Julie Anne Dart. Walking past Sams, the policemen noticed a long wooden beam in the roof running the width of the premises. 'I've been expecting you,' said Sams. 'My wife has just phoned me.'

Tim Grogan noticed the hairs on the backs of Michael's hands – just as Stephanie had described. Leach saw the old-fashioned telephone, while DC Greenwood pointed to a number of stencils on a shelf. An old radio on one of the workshop's shelves was playing music, and DC Dover asked Sams: 'Can you tell me the station that your radio is tuned to?' He replied: 'Radio Two. I have it on all day.'

Grogan had seen more than enough. He led Sams to the shop counter. 'I am arresting you,' he said, and followed this with the customary caution. Sams said: 'You've got the wrong man. You're making a big mistake.' Sams was told to empty his pockets, and while DC Dover went to telephone Bob Taylor to tell him of the arrest, the shop doorbell rang, sounding like the old-fashioned cash register that Stephanie had heard. Michael Sams was taken into Newark Police Station at 11.40 am.

Meanwhile, Tim Grogan rang Bob Taylor to detail to him all the evidence at Sams' workshop that matched what they already had. When he hung up, the detective superintendent paused. He needed time to think before he broke the news to his colleagues in Birmingham. He had to be sure.

SEVENTEEN

The Cryptic Killer in Custody

At Newark Police Station, DS Tim Grogan identified himself to the custody officer and explained that Michael Benniman Sams had been arrested on suspicion of murder and kidnapping. Sams had nothing to say while his rights were read to him again, but gave his name, address and date of birth for the custody record and asked that his wife Teena be informed of his arrest. The duty solicitor was called, and a pair of spectacles and a pen were confiscated from Sams to prevent self-injury.

At 11.48 am, the prisoner, looking pale and shaken, was escorted to the custody suite. While there, he confessed to a rookie cop, PC Dale Barnett, who was supervising him. Barnett, then a 26-year-old graduate police entrant, asked Sams what he had been arrested for, and Sams answered, 'On suspicion of murder and abduction. Didn't you watch *Crimewatch* last night?' 'No', replied the constable. 'Is it about Stephanie Slater?' 'Yes,' said Sams. 'The evidence is in the workshop. I didn't do the murder. I don't know how they linked the two.' Barnett asked, 'Did you abduct Stephanie Slater then?', to which Sams replied, 'Yeah, but I didn't do the other one.'

Michael Sams supports Barnett's story in a letter to his close friends Kim and Amy Rusby:

Until my solicitor arrived, he [PC Barnett] was given the job of supervising me. Probably to make sure I didn't harm myself. Anyway when I was arrested I was releived in a way and I started talking to him and telling him I had done the kidnapping. When another PC came into the room I stopped talking and the young PC went out. He could hardly contain his excitement. The countries most wanted person was telling him he had done the kidnapping.

At 12.15 pm, the duty solicitor arrived and introduced himself to his new client as David Payne, of David Payne Solicitors, 48 Lombard Street, Newark. After Payne had 'taken instructions' from Sams, the prisoner was returned to PC Barnett. Inspector Baker received a telephone call that instructed him to have Sams watched very closely as he was considered a suicide risk. Since Sams could well be charged with other serious offences, he was categorised as an 'Exceptional Risk Prisoner'.

At 1.13 pm, Sams was told he would have to remove his artificial leg – someone had come up with the idea that the false limb might contain explosives. However, when the prosthesis was searched it proved to be empty. All of Sams' clothing was placed in polythene bags to be marked with exhibit labels. Sams was then redressed in a white anti-contamination suit.

The remainder of his time at Newark Police Station was uneventful. The killer had obviously taken a shine to PC Barnett, for he chatted to him about the kidnapping for quite a long time and the young officer was able to take down quite a detailed account of the abduction, the ransom pick-up and Stephanie's release. Sams made one startling unguarded admission: if Stephanie had taken the blindfold off, he might have had to kill her. (Unfortunately, since Sams had not been cautioned, all of the admissions that Barnett obtained were worthless as evidence.)

The task of officially interviewing Michael Sams about the kidnapping of Stephanie Slater fell to the West Midlands Police and two of their most experienced interrogators. DC Geoff Kedney and DS Ron Evans sat down to interview Sams, with DI Paul Maxwell from Leeds as an observer, at 2.56 pm. They would question him until 3.40 pm, when the first tape ran out. They would learn a lot about Michael Sams during this first interview.

He began by admitting to kidnapping Stephanie Slater. DS Evans said, 'You freely admit that you kidnapped Stephanie Slater ... Would you like to go to the beginning and tell us, slowly and clearly in your own words, exactly how you planned it. All the way through to its finalisation, please?'

Sams wasn't happy being asked to relive everything from day one, and protested: 'Well, that's gonna take too long.'

'No it isn't,' snapped Ron Evans.

'It is ...' argued Sams before being cut short.

'No, it won't. No, it won't take too long, seriously,' said Evans, in an attempt to regain control of the interview.

The prisoner was becoming more upset by the minute. Wiping his eyes, he started to relive the planning that had culminated in him being temporarily £175,000 better off, and then explained all about the abduction.

When giving details of the ransom collection, Sams said that he had chanced upon the Dove Valley Trail by accident the previous year, when he had been out walking his dog. He also stated that he hadn't been near the place since the ransom collection, but the police had evidence to suggest otherwise.

When asked where the rest of the money had gone, besides the £19,000 found in the workshop, Sams lied and said he'd buried it while taking Stephanie home. He also volunteered the fact that he'd only spent a few hundred pounds of it. Asked why he had chosen £175,000, Sams explained weakly that he had 'worked out a certain weight and a certain volume', going on to say that he'd planned the operation just to prove it could have been done. Then he said that he had intended setting up the job before Christmas, but had second thoughts: 'I didn't really want the person kidnapped to have a rotten Christmas, believe it or not.' The officers didn't believe a word of it.

DS Evans then turned to the question of an accomplice. Sams took a sip of tea and said, 'No, I had nobody helping me whatsoever. The only thing is ... somebody else knew what I was doing. Yeah. But he had no involvement with it whatsoever.'

The officers picked up on this ambiguity, and Sams sensed their unease. The cryptic killer decided to play on it and said that, in his diary, was a reference to a red Suzuki jeep. A vehicle of this description had been seen in the area on the night of the ransom drop. Despite a nationwide search by the police, neither the vehicle or its owner was ever found. 'I knew where that car was,' taunted Sams. 'It is something which I had discussed with another person. We joked about it.'

At 5 pm, he was asked and consented to supply non-intimate and intimate body samples, including hair, nail scrapings and saliva and blood samples. Then, after more interviews, he was finally locked up in a cell to await transport to Birmingham.

At the end of his first hours in custody, the police had a pretty good idea how Sams had planned and executed the kidnapping, and DI Paul Maxwell could return to Leeds with a pocketbook full of vital information. Now the Julie Dart murder squad could definitely place Sams near junction 37 on the M1 where the first ransom bid had been made – just a few hundred yards from the disused railway line and six miles from the bridge at Oxspring. The kidnapper of Stephanie Slater had used the same *modus operandi* as the killer of Julie Dart. 'Bob Southwall' had used the address '143 Durkar Road', and the laundry mark on the sheet used to wrap up Julie's body had borne the number 143. But Sams had now taken things a stage further. He had explained how he had used the post and telephone to convey his ransom demands to the police, and the links between towns and railways, used in both ransom bids, would become more apparent as the interviews progressed.

At 8.45 pm, the Nottinghamshire Constabulary signed Michael Benniman Sams over to the custody of the West Midlands Police. Within minutes – under heavy escort – he was speeding down the Fosse Way towards Birmingham and Belgrave Road Police Station, where he would spend the night. Tom Cook walked out on to the front steps of the police station in Newark and gave a statement to the horde of journalists who had gathered there. Cook would answer no questions, but it was obvious to everyone that he was delighted with what he had to say:

At 11.25 today, a 50-year-old man was arrested in Newark, Nottingham, and is being held in connection with the kidnapping of Stephanie Slater. He was arrested by detectives investigating information received in telephone calls to police following the Crimewatch *appeal. The man is presently being held at Newark Police Station and will later be transferred to the West Midlands Police area. He is expected to be charged in the near future.*

Eaves Cottage was stripped and picked clean by scenes-of-crime officers and forensic experts. Not a thing was left untouched, and everything was photographed and listed. Even the floorboards were lifted, the garden dug up. The once spotless cottage – Teena's pride and joy – was systematically wrecked.

T & M Tools fared no better. For a man who forced his wife to keep their home immaculate, Sams' workshop revealed quite a different facet of the man. Certainly the retail and display area was neat and well stocked, but behind the counter, the workshop was a veritable tip. The scientists and scenes-of-crime officers split into two teams, while a photographer focused his camera on every item, ranging from tools to specks of dust.

Among the first items photographed was a drawing pin tacking a sign to the counter front – identical to those used by Sams to secure a 'SHIPWAYS' marker to a traffic cone on the night of the ransom collection. Then there was the wooden chair that Stephanie and Julie had used, a radio tuned to Radio 2, money jammed into a red metal toolbox, an axe, a filthy cylindrical vacuum cleaner, striped curtains draped over a pile of junk, a microwave and model trains – literally dozens of them in various stages of disrepair. Nothing escaped the photographer's lens.

Systematically groping around on all fours, the forensic scientists hunted down the finest hair, the smallest fibre and stain. This painstaking work would pay dividends. Hairs found during the search matched Julie Dart's. Fibres were identical to the sheet used to wrap up her body. Blue strands of rope matched exactly those of the rope that had tied up the gruesome bundle. Green plastic shavings were from a wheely bin, and there was a brick. Not just any old brick, for this was a Wettern Channel Block – one of some 40,000 made for Croydon-based builders-merchants, Wettern Brothers, by Metallic Tileries of Chesterton – and, of course, this brick was identical to those left by Sams on the M1 at junction 37. Some of the evidence found at T & M Tools provided overwhelming proof that Stephanie Slater had been held in that building. Other evidence linked Julie Dart to the workshop and to her killer – Michael Sams.

Forensic biologist Valerie Tomlinson examined no fewer than 118 items. Her first significant link came with the rope used by Sams to tie up Julie's body. Trapped in the strands was a small tuft of yellow and brown carpet fibre. Tomlinson found this to be indistinguishable in colour and microscopic appearance from tufts of fibre found in the workshop.

Her second find was a blood group match. The green, brown and yellow curtain discovered at the workshop had a watery stain along the lower edge. This contained human blood of group PGM 2-1+. Michael Sams and Stephanie Slater both belonged to blood group PGM 1+1-, and Teena Sams was blood group PGM 1+. DNA tests later carried out at the Forensic Science Laboratory, Chepstow, showed that the blood on the curtain had come from Julie Dart.

In addition to this, hairs recovered from the sheet were similar to those taken from Sams' two Alsatians, Bonnie and Tara. The biologist concluded: 'I consider the most likely explanation is that the sheet, Item (SJ10), and the rope, Item (SJ6/SJ7), had been in the workshop at T & M Tools, or kept together with items from this workshop.' Effectively, this placed Julie Dart in direct contact with items belonging to Michael Sams.

It now fell to Paul Rimmer and his vast expertise in the field of document examination to seek other clues that could either link, or dissociate, Sams from the murder of Julie Dart. He examined 129 items in his laboratory, ranging from 'Item (PK1) – Handwritten letter and envelope' to 'Item (JL2) – Letter to Lynn Dart'. Referring to this letter, which had informed Mrs Dart of her daughter's kidnapping, Rimmer said:

> *While the questioned handwriting on Item (PK1) is not particularly fluent, it corresponds in detail and variation with specimens of Julie Dart's writing, and in my opinion she wrote this letter. The evidence is such that the possibility that another person was the writer can be discounted.*

Rimmer went on to associate with Michael Sams many of the handwritten letters and envelopes sent by Julie's killer, and did likewise with typed material and correspondence generated by Sams' Amstrad computer.

Michael Sams found himself in a trap of his own making, and his first interview at Belgrave Road Police Station buried him even deeper. First, he admitted to DS Evans that he had bought white envelopes – identical in every respect, down to the faulty watermark, to those used in the Slater, Dart and British Railway offences – at W. H. Smith's in Newark. But then, having made much progress, the detective asked a question that would cause his colleagues problems for weeks.

When Sams had returned to take Stephanie home, he told her that his 'mate' had fallen from a motorbike. DS Evans now raised this issue. 'Have you got a mate that uses a motorbike?' he asked, to which Sams replied, 'No, apart from my wife.' Pressing on, the detective asked, 'Did you ever suggest that a mate might have been riding a motorbike and fell off it to anybody?' Sams said that he might have mentioned this to Stephanie because she could have noticed that he had a limp. This sent DS Evans scurrying to scour through Stephanie's debriefing notes for a reference to a limp. There was nothing to be found.

By the time he returned to Sams, the prisoner had changed his story: 'I knew she hadn't seen my tin leg. I'd never come close enough to her. All the time we were talking, all the time she suddenly grabbed me and cuddled me, I made sure that me leg was on the opposite side.' If this weren't confusing enough, Sams made it worse when trying to extricate himself: 'She said she'd seen me limping in the house. I put it to her, "I'm glad you saw me limping because ... nobody [outside] had seen me limping," and I used the excuse to Stephanie that I'd fallen off me motorbike.' DS Evans was left with the dual possibilities that either Sams or a possible accomplice had fallen off a motorbike at some time.

At 11.27 am the following day, Sunday, 23 February 1992, Sams was taken to the interview room where DS Leach and DS Evans waited with his solicitor David Payne, who had driven down from Newark. After Sams was cautioned, Payne said that his client had something to say. The previous evening, he had written a statement, which Payne was about to read, but before doing so, Sams launched into a preliminary statement designed to impress everyone present.

A second man had been involved in the kidnapping of Stephanie Slater, he said, and he had been paid £20,000. Sams then explained that his Suzuki 'Love' moped wouldn't fit into the back of his Austin Metro. 'You'd have to cut it in half to do that,' he said. Then he told the officers, 'Also, not one person would be able to lift a Suzuki "Love" into any kind of car. It would need two to do it.' Another man – the accomplice – had picked up Sams in his car that day and together they put the scooter in the back. The accomplice drove Sams to Glossop, dropping everything off with the bike. The ransom collection went ahead as previously described, and Sams rode back along the disused railway track to meet his partner in crime. 'We both put the bike into the rear of his car, and with him driving, I still only counted 29 bundles. I agreed the missing would come from my share.' Then according to Sams, an argument developed over whether Stephanie should live or die.

At this point Sams broke down and started to cry. His solicitor read the remainder of the statement:

> *A few minutes later I said, 'Christ, I've forgotten to fill my car up, I won't make it to Birmingham and back.' My partner replied, 'What the fucking hell are you on about, we're going to kill her now and I'll dispose of the body,' I being the other man. 'P off,' I said, 'she's going home.' 'No, she isn't,' he said. 'She'll identify you, dead people don't identify.' A heated argument broke out in which I received a cut to my wrist from a knife he had. I was adamant and convinced Stephanie would not identify me, but this did not satisfy him. In the end I agreed to give him all the money except around £20,000, not to identify him, and not to tell the Police where the money was until I had been charged. I then insisted he returned the workshop key, with[out] that he couldn't get at Stephanie, and drop me and bike there, where we were, the junction of the M1 and A57 to Worksop. I got a few packets of money, put them in the tool box and returned to the shop on the bike, it was the reason I was late returning ...*

DS Evans then said, 'Name him.'

'Oh, I can't do that.'

'Why not?' demanded DS Leach.

Evans interrupted: 'It's the only way that we can verify this story, isn't it?'

Sams started to choke up, tears rolling down his cheeks. 'Because ... if I did that then there's no reason why he shouldn't take it out on somebody else, on, on Stephanie herself. He, he could take years, if I'm right he might wait years, but he assured me, he will bury the money and involve somebody else who will do it, and I, I wouldn't want the risk.' Sams was now sobbing his heart out so DS Evans adopted a softer attitude:

EVANS: Michael, that's not your decision.

SAMS: No. I won't take the risk.

EVANS: It's not your decision, Michael. There's another man involved in this offence according to you in this latest statement. We want to know who he is. You said yesterday the money was buried, is that incorrect?

SAMS: He said he would bury it ...

EVANS: You said it was buried.

SAMS: I don't know where, no, yes, I, I said I knew where it was buried, I decree as I said in that statement there, I decree I would not even mention this until I have been charged.

EVANS: Er, if I could step in. Do you know where the £150,000-odd is?

SAMS: No, no.

EVANS: Well, the only way we can verify this story, is we need desperately to know who the other man is.

SAMS: You don't to verify the ...

EVANS: We do need to know for Stephanie's, er, safety. For Stephanie's sake, we need that other man.

Having muddied the waters by saying there was an accomplice, Sams was now being forced into a corner by being asked to name him. Otherwise, the police would take it that Sams was lying. The detective, who was fast losing his temper, accused Sams of ducking the issue.

'I refuse to name him!' snapped the prisoner. 'Well, that doesn't do a lot for your credibility, Michael,' argued DS Leach. 'Well, I'm not worried about my credibility, am I?' retorted the kidnapper.

DS Leach tried something designed to trick Sams. 'So, really your meticulous planning has not been totally foolproof because you've not picked a really good partner. You've lost £150,000 of the deal. It's your plan, not his. He was your assistant and yet he turns turtle on you, and turns round and says he's gonna kill her because she can identify you, and not him.'

Sams still refused to name his so-called accomplice. Then DS Evans unwittingly dug a hole for himself: 'You could've taken the moped there earlier and then got a lift back, or what, left it secreted there. You could have used another vehicle. There's all sorts of things, Michael. So let's not play games about that. Let's just find out who this man is.'

The time ticked by, with Sams evading almost every question put to him. The detectives had laid out several scenarios by which Sams could have collected the ransom money and escaped, one of which included the possibility of using an accomplice. Michael Sams sat back in his chair and smiled.

DS Leach accused Sams of playing with them. 'Are you trying to taunt us ... trying to mess us about? ... Because you've done everything on your own, then all of a sudden this wonderful method of picking up the money in South Yorkshire on a disused railway line, all of a sudden you need somebody else's assistance, and I'm saying, "Why?" You've planned everything, the money's for you, it's not for anybody else, the least that anybody knows, the better. You've looked after her, you've left her there, she's not able to escape, you've not needed any guard, any assistance, any advice, nothing. All done on your own out of your mind. A well-, well-, well-planned exercise, and then all of a sudden, on the final day, you need some transport and you need somebody to drive you, and that – in all fairness, Michael – doesn't quite ring true with the sort of individual you are.'

Sams was adamant that the moped wouldn't go into his Metro, although we now know that it would just fit because the police tried it.

DS Leach concluded: 'I don't believe you. This has done nothing, it's not helped us at all.' Sams could only reply, 'Well, I was wrong then.'

The police officer was now at his wits' end. 'You're totally wrong. It's thrown us into total disarray, because now we don't know whether to believe you. We'll be looking for another man. We don't know whether to believe you or not. We don't know whether we're looking for an estate car at Newark that was involved in the kidnapping [an indication that Sams' disguising of his car with the signs on the rear side windows had been effective].'

Having won his little game, Sams now smugly told them that, since they had already solved the kidnapping case, he wouldn't name anyone else. For his part, DS Leach was concerned that Stephanie was still in danger if the accomplice existed. But this approach – appealing to Sams' better nature – got nowhere.

Sensing that they were barking up the wrong tree, DS Evans backtracked to the missing money, and pulled out a scrap of paper that had been found in one of the prisoner's pockets. The notations on it seemed to allude to a grid reference:

North				
LHS	*9T*	*15ft*	*90%*	*50*
MID	*5T*	*12ft*	*135%*	*20*
RHS	*3T*	*9ft*	*45%*	*10/20/5 0*

On the same paper were the numbers 35 and 63. DS Evans asked if they were important. Sams replied, 'Not important at all in this case. They were, but they're not, now.' Ten minutes were then used up with DC Kedney begging Sams to explain the numbers, ending up asking for 'just a clue'.

Sams admitted that he had six copies of this 'code', as the officers called it, and apparently they were all secreted away. DS Evans thought it pertinent to ask why he had six copies. Sams repeated that the numbers had nothing to do with the kidnapping, but DS Evans would have none of it. 'Do you actually want us to spend hours and hours and hours trying to break that code just ... for your pure entertainment?' Apparently the killer did.

Michael Sams was now enjoying himself. The following exchange took everyone into the realms of fantasy:

> *EVANS: It is relevant to this case because it's relevant to us eliminating those as being a possible place where that money is being put.*
> *SAMS: Well ... let's put it one way. If you went to one of those locations and dug up a big IRA arms cache at one of those locations, you'd say that were me because I knew about them. Now I do not know what is in those locations and so I am not gonna tell what that location is.*
> *KEDNEY: Yeah, but the odds on us finding an IRA cache in there is ...*
> *SAMS: Yes, I know it is.*
> *KEDNEY: Phenomenally ...*
> *SAMS: But I do not know what is in that location.*

The questioning ended with DS Evans saying that Sams was 'sticking up a shield ... trying to have a little bit of entertainment' at their expense.

On Monday, 24 February, Sams appeared at Birmingham magistrates' court for the second time. The magistrates acceded to a request from the West Yorkshire Police to remand Sams in custody at Millgarth Police Station so that they could interview him about the murder of Julie Dart. Believing that West Midlands had been pampering Sams, Bob Taylor felt that it would be a good psychological move to get the murderer on their own ground.

This was a move he had been dreading. The West Yorkshire Police would come down on him hard. This time it wouldn't be silly games over kidnapping – this was murder. The magistrates gave the murder squad detectives three days to wring a confession from the killer before he was to be produced before the court again.

Detective Sergeant Tim Grogan was already fully aware of Sams' evasiveness, having watched the West Midlands force's interviews with him relayed to a monitoring suite in Leeds. Deciding to treat the prisoner gently as they drove together to Leeds in a white van, the police officer remained silent while Sams chatted away about the Black Panther, Donald Neilson, whom he'd seen at Armley Prison in 1978. Sams admired the Black Panther's high security-risk status, saying to Grogan 'I suppose they'll say that about me now.'

DS Grogan timed this remark at 1.15 pm. Earlier in the journey, Sams had made two other significant statements. At 11.30 am, he said: 'I'll be OK at Millgate, won't I?' Referring, of course, to Millgarth Police Station, he had made the identical mistake he had committed while writing the Julie Dart letter the previous October. Then, at 12.55 pm, the van passed under the railway bridge that carried the Dove Valley Trail over the motorway. Sams cheekily piped up: 'This is very familiar,' and once again DS Grogan discreetly noted the comment in his pocketbook.

Although, while at Leeds, Sams did not confess to the Julie Dart murder, the police then and later, after Sams was charged, were able to amass an impressive array of evidence, forensic and otherwise. As well as the fibres, hairs, wooden coffin, wheely bin, bricks and ransom-demand envelopes, Tim Grogan could show that Michael and Teena Sams kept goldfish, and sitting on top of the tank in Eaves Cottage had been a fish food container identical to the one used for the 'device' found by the painted brick at junction 37 on the M1. In addition, Paul Rimmer was able to 'hack' into Sams' computer, where he discovered letters on file that matched material sent through the post in his ransom demands. Then there was the paint used to 'decorate' both the motorway device and the sensor that had been placed on the wooden drawer with the Slater ransom money – Sams had a tin of similar paint in his workshop, which he used on his model trains. Brian Soper, the managing director of Parkers of Peterborough, who sold the same kind of rope that had been used to tie up Julie's body, couldn't be sure if Sams had bought rope from them, but by sheer coincidence, the company rented 42 Oundle Road to the killer.

All Sams could say was that his 'friend' had used his computer to write the ransom letter and the confession, it had been his 'friend' who had planted trace evidence in an effort to fit him up, it had been his 'friend' who had taken Julie to a 'holiday house', and when she had tried to escape, it had been his 'friend' who had killed her.

To give himself an alibi for Wednesday, 10 July 1991 – the day of Julie's disappearance – Sams had invented a day-out to the Toton marshalling yards near Nottingham. That information he had craftily programmed into his computer, which was cross-indexed with his extensive photographic records: he must have been at Toton because he had snapped a few trains. The police developed hundreds of the murderer's pictures and soon found shots which appeared to be of Toton. However, a remarkable piece of detective work blew the alibi to pieces. DC Sadio called on John Woolley, the operating supervisor at the rail company, who had been working at Toton for two decades. Using Sams' photographs and studying records held at both Toton and Worksop, Woolley was able to say that it was impossible for the engines in the pictures to have been at Toton and Worksop on the dates Sams suggested. The net result of all this was that, having failed to establish an alibi for that fateful day in July 1991, Sams had implicated himself further by attempting to fabricate one.

On Tuesday, 17 March 1992, at the request of the West Midlands Police, a retired SAS colonel, Mark Winthrop, was called in to help pinpoint the missing cash. Winthrop is a world-acknowledged expert on search techniques, and on the resolution of kidnap and ransom demands on the Continent – especially in Italy, where such offences are relatively commonplace.

Colonel Winthrop's first port of call was Barrel Hill Road and

Eaves Cottage. In an incident report dated 19 March, DI Bache wrote:

> *I visited the area around 3 Barrel Hill Road with the Colonel. He examined several spots where his training led him to believe something might be hidden, unfortunately with negative result. After being shown the spot where Sams had originally buried the loot, the Colonel formed the opinion that 'external pressure must have forced Sams to have reinterred it'.*

Colonel Winthrop prioritised two railway lines – the Dove Valley Trail and the disused rail bed just a stone's throw from where Julie's body had been found. In an effort to tighten up the search areas, Winthrop suggested that the location would have vehicle access to the line and would not be overlooked by roads or houses. His 'Search Guidelines' listed five pointers to be followed by anyone looking for the money:

> *1. Newly disturbed earth.*
> *2. Natural hiding places.*
> *3. Disturbed brickwork.*
> *4. Markers relating to the figures 3–5 & 9 & letter 'T'.*
> *5. Areas not exposed to public view.*

A description of the stolen property was given as:

> *Approximately £155,000 in Bank of England notes of various denominations. At this stage it is not known whether the money is contained in one large recepticle [sic] or a number of small, possibly metal cantilever tool boxes. The size of the recepticle [sic] to hold all of the money would be something like a small holdall or the size of an office waste paper bin.*

The equipment required to locate this stash was outlined as:

> *Metal Detectors (Particularly for the area around Eaves Cottage).*
> *Pick Axes.*
> *Jemmy Levers.*
> *Dragon Lights.*

Aerial Photographs.
Ordenance [sic] *Survey and Fire Service Gazeteer* [sic] *Maps.*

Armed with this information, scores of policemen began looking, but despite all their efforts, there were nil results, and the West Midlands police gave up the hunt. Meanwhile, Sams was still claiming that his accomplice was out there spending the ransom money. The West Yorkshire force reckoned that, if they were to find the money, this would go some way towards destroying Sams' defence. So DS Tim Grogan began to apply a little old-fashioned detective work to the problem, which in the end was to pay real dividends.

Michael Sams was doing all he could to confuse the investigation. For instance, his notebook had revealed a weird clock and compass diagram. The police thought it had to be a formula by which Sams (and his accomplice, if he existed) could return to the hidden loot and recover it. However, this was another of Sams' foolish games. He had drawn it out of sheer bloody-mindedness in his cell at Winson Green prison, knowing that everything he said, did or wrote down would be passed on to the police.

And he had other cards up his sleeve that were guaranteed to exasperate the police. While he was in custody, Teena told detectives of a scrap of paper that she'd found in her husband's shoe, on which was written the numbers '373 282'. She was positive it was a girlfriend's phone number. The detectives thought otherwise – perhaps it was a map reference of sorts? Actually, it was the stock number for a Black & Decker hedge trimmer, a fact that was confirmed by the manufacturer. Sams had never ordered this item; he didn't even have one in stock. He'd merely written down the number and dropped the scrap of paper, and it had ended up in his shoe.

Finally, there was the fictitious name and address that Sams originally claimed belonged to a long-lost penfriend.

MAVIS BLAND	*143 RIDGE AVE*
(PENFRIEND)	*WEST FIELDS*

As soon as he realised that the police were taking a more than casual interest in this, he invented another yarn to keep them busy: he said it was a 'code' involving 'word association'.

'Mavis' and the number '143' rang alarm bells in the officers' minds, for hundreds of hours had been devoted to a Mavis and her partner Phil during the investigation into one of envelopes sent by Sams. Perhaps double that time had gone into examining the relevance of the number 143, which had first surfaced on the laundry tag attached to the sheet used to wrap round Julie's body and had reappeared as 143 Wakefield Road, Durkar – the phoney address of 'Bob Southwall'. Then the police realised that Sams had been arrested years beforehand at 143 Doncaster Road, Selby, on suspicion of car theft. 143 obviously meant something to Michael Sams, and he wanted them to think about it.

The killer was later to write (in a letter dated 18 May 1992): 'The figures were not any code etc – merely a poke at Police.' 'Mavis', he said, had come from his favourite programme, *Coronation Street*. In this letter – to his best friend Kim, who was dying of cancer – Sams denied killing Julie Dart and, on the subject of the missing money, offered up yet another tantalising cryptic clue: 'I don't know where it is. My mate dos'nt [*sic*] know where it is. But together we do. But how do I persuade them to give me bail to recover it?' The police read this letter before it left the prison. It was to give them even more problems to solve because it indicated that the accomplice did exist.

While all this was going on, DS Grogan and his small team had been patiently sifting through the transcript of Sams' interviews, looking for a clue that might lead to the missing money. Grogan started with the premise that Sams had buried the cash after Stephanie had been released, and the time frame he needed to examine was between 30 January and 21 February. The officers would look closely at Sams' movements for that period. In his deposition dated 5 February 1993, Grogan said:

> *On 16th July 1992, Michael Benniman Sams was interviewed at Birmingham in respect of new information concerning the murder of Julie Dart. The full details of that interview are recorded in a separate statement.*
>
> *Prior to this date the closest Sams could be associated with Easton and the area at which Julie Anne Dart's body was found, was at Grantham where he admitted buying dog food.*
>
> *During the interview Sams admitted knowledge of Stoke*

Summit which he used for his train-spotting activities.

Enquiries revealed Stoke Summit to be an area south of Grantham, 1.7 miles from the location where Julie Anne Dart's body was found. It is a high point on the East Coast Railway famed as the region at which the 'Mallard' steam train broke the British speed record in 1937.

In effect, Stoke Summit is a viaduct carrying a farm track over the railway line from Westby Lane, Westby, to agricultural fields where it peters out. There is a flat-topped embankment on either side of the viaduct. Each embankment consists of open grassland and thickly scrubbed vegetation.

On 12th September 1992, Michael Sams was interviewed at Leeds regarding further developments concerning the murder of Julie Anne Dart. Details of that interview are recorded in a separate statement.

During that interview, Sams was questioned more closely relative to his knowledge of Stoke Summit, which revealed the following information:

1. He knew that a signal box existed in the vicinity 10 to 15 years previously.

2. He had known it for 'Donkey's Years', which he later clarified to mean 3 years.

3. He describes seeing a farmer in the area many times, detailing the farmer's vehicle and dog. In addition, he recalled his last visit to the viaduct was on a misty/drizzly Wednesday in February after he had collected the ransom money and released Stephanie Slater.

In view of Stoke Summit's sudden emergence in the enquiry, efforts to recover the outstanding ransom payment were focused on the ground area adjacent to the viaduct. In addition, Sams' version of how the money was disposed of after he had collected it on 29th January 1992 was re-examined. In effect these were as follows:

1. Sams hid the money personally in 3 places, 100 miles a part.

2. Sams buried all but £19,000 of the money en-route to Birmingham with Slater on 29th January 1992.

3. Sams had intended burying the money in a field at the side of his house, but the plan changed when the alleged accomplice took all but £20,000 on 29th January 1992. Alleged accomplice then buried the money in an area not known to Sams.

4.   Sams hid the money personally in one place now known by the alleged accomplice.

5.   Sams alleged on the night of the ransom drop that £15,000 in two bundles was dropped at the scene therefore indicating that only £140,000 was outstanding after including the money found in his possession at the time of his arrest.

As a consequence of this information, factors identifying Stoke Summit as a likely area to bury the money, and theories to support Sams having buried the money at this location were considered. These included:

1.   Sams having an excellent knowledge of Stoke Summit.

2.   Sams admitted visiting Westby Viaduct on a Wednesday morning between the time he released Stephanie Slater and the time he was arrested. He maintained he spent 3–4 hours at this location. At that time the weather was cold and drizzly. He stated he went specifically to train-spot and described a conversation he had with a farmer on that day.

3.   The farmer, John Berry, was traced and confirmed this meeting.

4.   This occasion could only be one of the following dates: 5.2.92, 12.2.92, 19.2.92.

5.   Alan Dorwood, a meteorologist, confirmed that the weather conditions on Wednesday 19th February 1992 were misty with light rain in the Grantham/Westby area. Weather conditions in the same area on both 5th and 12th February 1992 were fine and dry with good visibility.

6.   Sams would have no need to train-spot at Stoke Summit as his home is on the same railway line and details of all trains passing his house are recorded on his computer, quoting exact times.

7.   Similarly, Sams recorded all details of his train-spotting activities on his computer. There are no records whatsoever of him ever visiting Stoke Summit, nor are there any photographs of this location.

DS Grogan's theory was based on the premise that Michael Sams had acted alone throughout. This was in keeping with Professor Paul Britton's advice, as it was apparent to him that the criminal would need to control the money in order to control the game. And it seemed that Stoke Summit was an area that fulfilled all the prerequisites relative to specialised search techniques.

By now Grogan and his team were warming to their task. There had been no reason for Sams to have dug up the money from land adjoining his cottage unless he had feared that it would be discovered. The detectives began to try to identify any event that might have forced him into transferring the money elsewhere.

On 19 January, the media had announced that the police were searching for a railway enthusiast. The photo-fit had been released on 7 February, followed by details of the Metro on 19 February. On the 19th there had also been massive publicity about the intention to transmit a recording of the voice of Stephanie Slater's kidnapper.

DS Grogan has said:

> *This could, we believe, have accounted for him being at Stoke Summit for 3–4 hours on a Wednesday in February. If this was indeed Wednesday, 19 February 1992, as the evidence available appeared to indicate, it might well have fitted in with him being at Great Gonerby at 3.15 pm that day when, in a moment of panic, he made a threatening phone call to Sylvia Baker at Shipways. This concerned her preparation of a photo-fit. Great Gonerby is 4 miles from Stoke Summit, yet 18 miles from Sutton-on-Trent.*

As a consequence of this information, the area was visited and a cursory examination carried out. Then on 10 November, Stoke Summit was examined by Professor Hunter, a forensic archaeologist, but he found nothing.

The flat-topped embankment had seemed the best bet as the criminal would be effectively hidden behind thick bushes and out of sight of any farmer who might drive along the track. There was also, for this particular killer, the *frisson* of knowing that passengers on passing trains would unknowingly be riding past the better part of £150,000 every 20 minutes.

On 17 November 1992, as a result of information from the West Yorkshire Police Technical Support Unit and Oxford University, the merits of ground-probing radar were discussed. The Atomic Energy Authority at Harwell was consulted, but the task was allotted to Oceanfix International of Aberdeen.

Oceanfix International employ SIR – sub-surface interface radar – which is highly portable and self-contained and can give a real-time display of sub-surface information. It may be used on land and ice and in fresh water. The system works by firing a pulse through the material at a speed proportional to the electrical characteristics of the material. If the material changes, the pulse speed will change and some of its energy will be reflected back to the SIR system receiving antenna. The results are fed to a graphic display unit.

At 8 am, Tuesday, 1 December 1992, Peter Simkins, Oceanfix's survey manager, and Ian Angus, an assistant radar field operator, turned up at Stoke Summit with a crowd of policemen armed with pickaxes, shovels and forks. The two surveyors began a sweep of the field boundary on the west side of the railway line. By 4 pm, they had discovered a number of 'targets', which included four large stones and pieces of metal. Each item was dug up by the police, whose day-glo jackets and wellington boots brought wolf-whistles from passing trains. As dusk settled, they packed up for the day.

The following morning, they were at it again, searching farmland on the west side of the line, closing in to survey the embankment on both sides. At 1.30 pm, they started on top of the west embankment, in a grassed area with small saplings and hawthorn bushes. Ten minutes later, Simkins shouted: 'Target.' A few moments later, the police dug up a package with howls of delight. They had literally struck pay-dirt.

The money had been buried 20 cm (8 in) beneath the surface. The packaging it was wrapped in comprised a black plastic seed tray containing the bank notes, which was covered with newspaper and then sealed in polythene.

Michael Sams heard about the find on the television news that evening. He was furious, and spent the rest of the night listening to the radio and limping up and down in his cell on 'D' Wing at Winson Green Prison. The following morning, he asked Prison Officer Bill Standford if he could make a telephone call to the police. He told Standford that, according to what he'd heard on the radio reports, the police had not found all the money: 'I can describe the boxes I put it in.' The officer told him that he would contact prison security, and as he walked away, Sams shouted after him: 'I don't want the police to leave the scene because everyone is going to start digging for it then.'

Many have argued that this effectively blew Sams' accomplice scenario out of the window, as it proved that not only did he know where the money was buried, but how it was packaged and divided up. However, if you consider Sams' remarks more carefully, that is not the case. He merely said he knew how the money was wrapped up, and since the whole ransom amount had not been found, it was obvious that there was more nearby.

Following a quick police conference, it was decided to speak with Sams in the presence of his solicitor. At 4.05 pm, on 3 December, DC Kedney from the West Midlands Police and DS Tim Grogan and DS Paul Leach from West Yorkshire trooped into the prison governor's office, where Sams was holding court.

He had concocted yet another pack of lies. He began by reminding the officers that he hadn't actually invited them along – he had merely wanted to pass on a message. He then said, 'Although I don't know where the boxes are, I know that there are two boxes, and once the scene had been published on TV, I'm worried that the other box will disappear if you leave that site. The other box is an ice-cream box, either a 2-litre or a 5-litre ice-cream box, and the one you've found sounds to be the big black plastic box.'

Cockily he went on to explain that he had packed the money into two almost identical amounts of around £60,000 each. He said that the money had been buried on Wednesday, 5 February and not, as originally thought, the 19th. He had visited Stoke Summit again on the 12th just to see if he could locate the money. On 19 February, he said, he had simply phoned Shipways from Great Gonerby and returned home.

There were definitely two packages, according to Sams. With his accomplice, he had driven to Stoke Summit in his car, right up to the bridge itself. He had dropped off the other man and had then gone back to the gate, about 700 metres (2300 ft) away. Then he had waited in the Metro with the lights switched off until his accomplice signalled with a torch that he'd buried the money. Sams refused to tell the detectives how long this took, only saying that he would tell all in court.

Sams told the bemused officers that he had always wanted them to get the money back. 'It's in my best interest,' he said. He confessed that he was 'mindful of the people who were trying to find the money. Mindful for quite a long time.' 'I've been trying to get the money back,' he said. 'I have been discussing this with my solicitor for a long, long time now.'

When asked why he wanted to give the money back, Sams

answered, 'Because it makes a difference to my sentence. I didn't want it missing.' The problem for Sams was that it was the police who had found most of it without his assistance. If there had been any chance of a small deal being cut – which there wasn't – it had gone after the first package had been found. But Sams couldn't see it that way. He argued that he had 'indirectly' told the police he had been at Stoke Summit, to which DC Kedney responded: 'I think you told us you went to a lot of places as well, didn't you? You went to London and all over the place, didn't you? You didn't tell us you went to Stoke Summit to bury the money, did you?' Sams could only answer meekly, 'No.'

He then claimed that, after taking the spade, his accomplice had been gone for almost an hour before he flashed his torch. This was intended to send the police all over Stoke Summit and through the nearby fields, looking for something that they had almost trodden on earlier.

When asked by Kedney why the other man hadn't returned to dig up the cash before now, Sams said, 'He doesn't know where he was.' The detective asked if the accomplice was a railway enthusiast as well, to which Sams replied, 'You believe so. I won't answer that question.' Grogan put it to the killer that, if this so-called partner-in-crime was a railway buff, he might have looked at the bridge number marked on the parapet and been able to trace the bridge that way. But Sams simply burbled on about nothing.

DS Leach tried another tack by appealing to Sams' self-esteem: 'You're an intelligent man, Michael. It makes sense to tell the truth, doesn't it?' Sams agreed: 'You've got a point there, yes. But I'm not prepared to go into it at the moment.'

When asked if the second package was close to the one already found, he replied, 'I've no idea. You're asking me for something which I cannot tell you. If I could say, "Yeah, I saw him dig a hole there," and I didn't see that. That's all I'm saying. It must be four, five hundred yards away.'

When Sams was told he was frustrating everyone in their attempts to find the last package of money, he responded, 'Well, that's total rubbish.'

The next day, Friday, 4 December, the police visited Stoke Summit for the third time. Within two hours, PC Calter had dug up the second cache of money. It was sealed within a white Black

& Decker carrier bag emblazoned with the eerily appropriate logo: 'WE KNOW HOW, DO YOU KNOW WHERE?'. Inside was a Tesco ice-cream container, and the money consisted of 24 bundles of £50 notes.

However, even with this prize firmly in their grasp, there still remained one small outstanding matter: to find out on which day Sams had buried it. The possibility of him slipping through the net by firming up the 'second man' scenario still existed if he could prove that he was elsewhere on the day the money was hidden. He had told the detectives at Winson Green prison that he'd stashed the loot with his accomplice on Wednesday, 5 February; enquiries pointed towards the 19th. How could they disprove Sams' claim?

In the first cache discovered, the money had been wrapped in a copy of a local free newspaper, *The Newark Trader*, dated 5 February. DC Shilleto contacted the paper's distribution manager and then its Newark agent. Ian Jones confirmed that 378 copies of the paper were delivered to his home very early each Thursday morning and that Sams' house was on his delivery route. Thus Sams would not have received the paper until the 6th, the day after he had claimed he had buried the money. DS Grogan had been right all along.

EIGHTEEN

Life in Prison and the Life of Riley

On Wednesday, 9 June 1992, the trial of Michael Benniman Sams was about to begin. As he arrived at Nottingham's Crown Court, cameramen rushed to snap that ever-elusive photograph but the vehicle's windows had been blacked out. Sams was wearing a smart, well-pressed blue suit for the occasion, and to give himself a studious appearance, he wore gold-rimmed spectacles.

After Mr Justice Igor Judge had settled on his bench, the clerk rose to her feet to read the indictment:

> *Members of the jury: Michael Benniman Sams is charged on Count One of this indictment with murder, in that on a day between the 8th and 20th days of July 1991, he did murder Julie Anne Dart. On Count Two of this indictment, he is charged with kidnap, in that on a day between the 8th and 11th days of July 1991, he did unlawfully, and by force or fraud, take or carry away Julie Anne Dart against her will. On Count Three of*

this indictment, he is charged with blackmail in that on the 12th day of July 1991, with a view to gain for himself, in a letter postmarked Huntingdon, the 11th of July 1991, and addressed to the Leeds City Police, he made an unwarranted demand of £140,000 from the police with menaces.

The other charges were slowly read out, with Count Four being the second blackmail attempt against the police contained in the Leeds letter of 22 July 1991, and Count Five being the attempted blackmail of British Rail. Sams pleaded 'Not guilty' to all counts.

In view of Sams' disability, the judge offered him the option of sitting, but Sams refused. He wanted to show the court and the world that he was still a proud man. Sams had pleaded guilty to charges of kidnapping Stephanie Slater and of blackmailing her employers before he went to trial. He had admitted kidnapping Stephanie Slater to save her the pain and anguish of giving evidence (although, in fact, Stephanie did give evidence about her abduction and imprisonment). This was to be his only concession. Now, like a cornered rat, he would fight to the end.

Sams' defence was managed by David Payne, and pursued with vigour in court by John Milmo QC, but for them, it was an uphill struggle from day one. The prosecution, led by Richard Wakerley QC, adopted a firm line of attack that, at times, left Sams snivelling and sobbing. Nevertheless, he still refused to name his accomplice and lied at every twist and turn.

Wakerley listed 21 solid links between the kidnapper of Stephanie Slater and the killer of Julie Dart. Yet when he put it to Sams: 'The game is up, Mr Sams. Come on, you killed Julie Dart, didn't you?' the defendant, wiping tears from his eyes, replied: 'No, I didn't – absolutely and definitely not.'

He sobbed again when he explained that Stephanie had grown to trust him. 'I would never be able to hurt a woman,' he muttered quietly, drying his eyes with a soaking-wet handkerchief. 'Never be able to hurt a woman?' snapped Wakerley as he produced a board spiked with nails which Sams had put down in case his barefooted victim attempted to escape. The jury were left under no illusion that, had Stephanie made a run for it, her feet would have been impaled and Sams would have killed her.

In a final effort to dig himself out of trouble, Sams argued that his friend had killed Julie Dart, that he'd assumed her death was accidental.

'An "accident"?' echoed Mr Wakerley incredulously. 'An "accident" ... This girl was beaten over the head and then strangled. How can that be called an "accident"?'

'Well, that was my interpretation,' said Sams.

When pressed on why he hadn't told the police where the money was hidden, he changed his earlier yarn: 'Because I was in danger in Winson Green prison. Violent prisoners were demanding to know where I had buried the money, wanting treasure maps ...'

Wakerley said: 'You failed with British Rail and then couldn't bring yourself to admit you killed Julie Dart. And so, like a little child, you invented this friend ... To think there is another man involved is an affront to common sense.'

In his summing up, Sams' barrister drew attention to the fact that no one had seen Michael Sams in the Chapeltown area of Leeds on the night in question. Milmo went even further by saying that three law-abiding people had apparently seen Julie alive and well the day after it was claimed that she disappeared. He argued forcibly that there was no forensic evidence linking Julie Dart with Sams' orange Metro. He conceded that there was trace evidence that indicated that she'd been in the workshop, but none directly connecting Sams with Julie Dart.

Milmo pointed out that the murder of Julie Dart and the kidnapping of Stephanie Slater were as different as chalk and cheese. 'Why kidnap a prostitute?' he asked. 'Who will produce a ransom – the object of this exercise?' Then he literally begged the jury to accept the possibility of the existence of an accomplice who could have been responsible for both the murder and the attempt to extort money from British Rail.

The judge spent all of Wednesday, 7 July, summing up the evidence. He told the jury that Sams was not to be convicted of one crime simply because he had admitted his guilt in another. Urging the jury to use their common sense, he said:

> The defendant's case is that another man was the criminal. He does not have to prove it ... You are entitled to say that this account of an unidentified friend is untruthful fiction, designed to deceive you, to enable the defendant to avoid responsibility for the crimes. But on the other hand, if you believe his account, then you must acquit him ...

The following morning, the judge spent 90 minutes finishing his summing up. He brilliantly encapsulated the entire case with the words: 'The question may be: is he hiding someone else, or is he hiding himself?'

At 11.42 am, the jury retired to consider their verdict. Three-and-a-half hours later, they walked back into court and returned guilty verdicts on all counts of murder, kidnap and blackmail.

As Sams stood in the dock, not a flicker of emotion crossed his face.

'You are an extremely dangerous and evil man,' the judge told him.

> *The jury has convicted you of murder, a murder in cold blood. You deliberately strangled her to death when your kidnapping went wrong because she saw more than she should. You tried to turn her death to your advantage. You were heartless at the grief you had caused. It was misplaced pride and callous arrogance.*

The judge who had remained dispassionate throughout the entire trial was now allowed to show his contempt towards the criminal in the dock: 'The letters that you wrote make chilling reading – no qualms, no remorse, heartless at the grief you had caused.'

Turning to Stephanie Slater, the judge remarked:

> *I have not the slightest doubt that she was in desperate and mortal danger for the first two or three days of her captivity. If it seemed necessary to you, she, like Julie Dart, would have been murdered in cold blood. Her survival was entirely due to her remarkable moral courage and the unostentatious display of qualities of character. The ordeal which you inflicted on her is something the rest of us can only imagine. The reality must have been far worse. You are, for an indefinite future, a menace to the community. There is an urgent necessity to protect the public from harm by you.*

Mr Justice Igor Judge then imposed four life sentences – one for each kidnapping, one for Julie's murder and one for Stephanie's unlawful imprisonment. Michael Sams was also sentenced to ten years for each charge of demanding money with menaces. All these sentences were to run concurrently, which means that, one day, Michael Benniman Sams might limp painfully back to freedom.

He was led down to the cells by five prison officers, and within the hour, he had been whisked away under heavy escort to Winson Green prison in Birmingham, to start what most people would assume to be a miserable existence behind bars. However, a few days later, he was comfortably ensconced at Full Sutton, the most luxurious establishment within the British penal system. Sams was about to start living the life of Riley.

On Monday, 12 July 1993, Inmate No. HP2510 Michael Benniman Sams held court for two senior police officers – Detective Inspector Paul Maxwell and Detective Superintendent Bob Taylor. He wanted to confess.

During an interview that lasted an hour, he told the officers what they had already figured out for themselves: he, and he alone, had killed Julie Dart. Then he gave his reason for finally confessing. It was because he had seen a press picture of Lynn Dart at Julie's grave. The inscription on the headstone was incomplete for it couldn't record the actual date on which she had died. It simply read: 'DIED JULY 1991.' He wanted to set the record straight. He explained that, while Julie was asleep during the late afternoon of Wednesday, 10 July, he had crept up behind her and struck several blows to the back of her head using a ball-pein hammer; then he had strangled her to death. Yet even now, Sams was being untruthful. As we now know, Julie had been very much awake when he had murdered her.

Since his arrest, Michael Sams has spent time in three of Her Majesty's prisons. While on remand, he enjoyed the confines of Winson Green, Birmingham. He spent the long hours writing to his wife, decorating each letter (all 50 or so which I later obtained) with quite competent drawings of roses coloured in with crayon. He was locked away in protective custody because it was thought that the other inmates would treat him like scum or worse. Nevertheless, he wrote to Teena that he was constantly being offered £5 for his signature and that the other prisoners treated him like a lord.

His earlier letters indicated a desire to help his wife with the obvious financial problems she was encountering during her husband's incarceration. He advised her to change her name and open up a different bank account. Then he asked her to make sure that he received the *Star* and the *People*, along with the monthly *Railway Magazine*, which, in happier days, had been his favourite reading. This she was to pay for, at £6.50 a month. Time and again, he would demonstrate his love of figures and calculations, at one point going to perhaps extreme lengths to work out his prison sentence in terms of years and months, with time off for good behaviour.

What with the excellent food (which Sams claimed he ate too much of), the sweets, listening to football matches on the radio and the long hours of 'peace and quiet' in a place he called 'home', Sams had little else to complain of except how he 'suffers the most by the time delays in getting to trial'.

For page after page, his letters contain little more than sentimental drivel about his undying love for Teena. This was somewhat balanced by descriptions of his busy prison life – the hours of sleep and rest, excellent medical treatment, hot food three times a day. Then there were all his new friends, how they wanted his autograph and how his fellow cons cheered him every time he walked out to meet them.

For a time, he immersed himself in writing poetry. One particular piece of literary work began:

> *At the end of the day, I just sit and pray.*
> *I say thank you Teena for being my love today.*

Even when eating his breakfast porridge, Sams was capable of bursting into rhyme:

> *Did you remember what I did say.*
> *That you eat your porridge every day.*
> *For just each day to gain that extra pound or two,*
> *More if you want but a pound will do.*

As his trial approached, Sams' feelings towards Teena underwent a sea change. Another woman had been writing to him, and her name was Victoria Vinchelli.

The *Star* would later describe 41-year-old Vicky as 'Sams' Bit on the Side' and his 'Lonely Divorcée Pen Pal'. Sams would spitefully tell Teena that 'V' – as he called Vicky – was the best-looking woman he'd ever seen.

As the relationship deepened, Vicky would visit Sams at Winson Green. Once, as Teena arrived at the prison gates, she recognised 'V' because of her 'full figure', low-cut blouse and mini-skirt. Sams refused to see Teena, preferring instead his busty admirer.

In letters to Vicky, Sams would lust over her figure, brag how other inmates treated him like a prison overlord and gloated about the 'happiest days of his life', when he'd held Stephanie Slater captive. He also freely confessed to cruelly beating two of his three wives.

In her defence, Vicky later told reporters that she had felt sorry for Michael Sams, whom she had originally thought was innocent. She was lonely, and he seemed as if he needed someone to love him. However, when my assistant and I met Vicky in her council flat, which was adorned with French underwear hanging from every hook and nail, out came the photograph albums showing her posing in a French maid's outfit, extremely tight swimming costumes and low-cut dresses. Twice, as she tried to sell us Sams' letters to her, she received 'dirty phone calls'.

Perhaps Vicky did feel sorry for Sams; perhaps she felt lonely and sorry for herself. And, to be fair to this sad soul, she later claimed that she was horrified by his chilling crimes and she regretted the relationship. But this didn't prevent her from selling her story to the press, or flaunting her body, half naked, across the front pages. However, she now has a complaint: she has been forced out of her council flat for fear of reprisals. She now lives in London at a secret address.

The relationship between Sams and Teena rapidly disintegrated. Although she continued to profess her love for him, Sams' correspondence to her became increasingly vindictive.

He wrote that he'd previously bedded a former Miss Venezuela while she was staying in England. (The lady in question has categorically denied such a relationship.) He also claims that he was fortunate to escape the bathing beauty's clutches: 'Luckily, I went to Thailand the next day on business,' he said. (His employers at that time – Black & Decker – say that he was never sent abroad on business for them; he did, however, go to Bangkok on holiday in December 1981.) And in all these letters, he continued to swear undying love for Teena.

After his trial, Sams was moved to the prison hospital at Winson Green. It is standard Home Office procedure to place all newly convicted 'lifers' under close observation immediately after a verdict, in case they attempt suicide. After a short time, he was packed off to the relative luxury of Full Sutton prison in York.

The killer was allocated a room on 'A' Wing, with carpet and curtains to make his life comfortable. He was soon writing to poor Teena demanding jeans, trainers, a Walkman with earphones, train books, his Seiko watch, a calculator, coloured pencils, a dictionary and a paper punch. 'The food,' he said, 'is very good here. There are thousands out there who would love three hot meals a day like we get in here.' He told her that his favourite television programmes were *Last of the Summer Wine*, *EastEnders, Coronation Street* and *Every Second Counts*, 'plus a lot of snooker at Dinner & Tea times'.

Michael Sams was indeed living the life of Riley. In another letter, he wrote:

> *I saw the Education Officer on Tuesday afternoon. He told me this morning that I can now do the gardens & lawns in the mornings and do education in the afternoons. I do Sociology Mon. English Language on Wednesday afternoons. History & Business Studies from Aug/September. As I am doing part time gardening (Cleaner's job) and part time education, they don't have a wage rate for that so I should get about £5.50 per week.*

Letter after letter alleges that Sams was revelling in his new environment. He had the run of Full Sutton, informing his wife not to phone him as 'although the staff don't mind taking calls, they have trouble finding me. I could be in any one of a hundred rooms.' Besides, Michael Sams had plenty of phonecards, so many in fact that he loaned them out to other inmates for a fee.

He could wear civilian clothes. His favourite outfit in quite an extensive wardrobe was a jogging suit. He asked for some wire so he could extend his radio aerial, and net to make up better curtains. However, he told Teena not to send him so many odds and ends because each inmate was issued an *Argos* catalogue; he could choose more or less what he wanted from that.

One might be forgiven for thinking that Sams was not being punished for his heinous crimes, for the gardening suited him as well as the accommodation and food: 'I am left to roam around and get on with the digging and planting. When my back aches from one job, I then potter off elsewhere and do a different job.'

Teena would always reply to this drivel by return of post. However, the cumulative effect of her husband's evil crimes, which haunted her dreams, and the constant hounding by reporters eager to snatch up any tasty morsel that could be dished up for greedy readers only added to her emotional insecurity. She also received a letter from East Midlands Electricity, threatening court action to recover an outstanding bill. And all during this period, she was deluged with letters from Sams, professing his love on one page and showing contempt for her on the next.

Teena's problems were further exacerbated when the police returned the Metro and moped to her at her mother's Birmingham home. People would stop and stare at the grisly exhibits parked in the front garden. Then a car dealer offered Teena cash to tow the car away, but on closer inspection, he decided against the purchase. The interior had been trashed by the forensic experts: the seat belts cut away; swatches of seat cloth removed; and areas contaminated with the purple dye used to reveal trace evidence.

In a letter to me, dated Tuesday, 28 September 1993, Sams said that he didn't know whom he could trust. 'My problem is I don't know who I can confide in. I will have to trust you and take your word that what I will tell you will remain a confidence unless you feel you are able to publish it.'

Quite what Sams was alluding to was a mystery, for I had merely asked him to tell the truth if a book were to be considered. I had also requested that he talk about any other offences he might have committed – including any against Suzy Lamplugh.

In the next letter from Sams, dated 20 October 1993, he wrote:

> *I was only going to ring you when you had been approved to arrange when you wanted to visit. There are things I wish to discuss with you. The first one being what the book means to me or will do for me. There are things I wish to talk about that I could not put in this letter in case it is read. I also don't want my solicitor to post one to you in case he reads it. Also I couldn't trust any inmate to get one out for me, as I'm quite sure it would be opened first. I am quite sure we can come to an agreement, and when you hear what I have to say, I'm quite sure the National Press will rush to your door for Exclusive Rights.*

Looking back through Sams' letters, I was left with the distinct impression that he had something interesting to say, even though he was extremely secretive. But what was so important that reporters would rush to my door asking for 'Exclusive Rights'? It could not have involved Stephanie Slater or Julie Dart – virtually everything about their cases was known. What was it?

Home Office regulations regarding visits to 'Category A' prisoners are strict. The inmate may ask anyone to visit him, and providing the visitor is a member of the immediate family or a close relative, the application is usually accepted after a careful and very thorough vetting procedure. However, without exception, authors and journalists are *persona non grata*.

Unfortunately for the Home Office, Sams was about to outwit the authorities again. He arranged for another inmate, whose category was something less than 'A', to send me a 'VO' (visiting order).

A few weeks later, in the company of Sams' mother, I strolled through the security of Full Sutton prison to spend two hours with the killer and kidnapper. This would be the first and last time any journalist would interview Sams, and I was determined to ask him about any unsolved crimes he might have committed.

He set the stage by denying that he had tried to kidnap the first Leeds prostitute, despite her excellent description of her assailant and his little orange car. She had told the police that she had thrown half a brick at the windscreen when escaping, and the Metro's windscreen still bore damage that supported this allegation. She also mentioned the artificial leg. And, of course, we know that Sams later committed kidnap and murder using almost identical methods.

He admitted killing Julie Dart and, with an almost expressionless face, went into some detail about the dreadful mechanics of this crime. (Sams' mother Iris sat with us during these revelations, apparently oblivious to what was being said.)

On the matter of Stephanie Slater's kidnapping and subsequent imprisonment, Sams discussed details that, at that time, could not be corroborated. These formed the basis of three separate stories he wanted to sell for £50,000 apiece. It was his contention that he'd had sex with Stephanie Slater, that they'd formed a relationship, and that she knew of his false leg. If she did form some bond with him, then it would be because (say the experts) she developed what is now often called the 'Stockholm syndrome' (after an earlier case in that Scandinavian capital), in which a kidnap victim identifies with her captor(s) as the only means of staying alive. However, any way you look at it, she was subjected to rape.

With regard to Suzy Lamplugh, Sams said that this was why he wanted to meet me face to face. For £50,000, he would reveal the whereabouts of her body, and tell me the name of an accomplice, one who enjoyed the same train-spotting and railway interests as Sams. He also made specific reference to Paddington station. Get my photographs, he said. 'It's in them.'

Looking back at that interview, and in the light of Stephanie Slater's claim that she was, in fact, raped by Sams, there is a ring of truth in what Sams had to say. Despite denying that he had attacked the Leeds prostitute, he told the complete truth about how he killed Julie Dart, and his assertion that he had had sex with Stephanie Slater is indeed now corroborated by the victim herself. So why should the police be so quick to discount the idea that he murdered Suzy Lamplugh?

As the interview drew to a close, he outlined another plot to raise a further £50,000 from a newspaper. A camera had been smuggled into the prison and he was to be filmed in his cell and the garden. The money, he claimed, was to be used for a specific purpose.

Within days of my visit to Full Sutton, it was clear that three rolls of film had already been smuggled out of the prison. Warders were later to locate one roll of undeveloped film and the camera. On Friday, 16 December 1994, the *Daily Star* published three of the pictures under a headline written by John McJannet: 'EASY LIFE, EVIL KILLER KEPT IN LAP OF LUXURY.' In an article, McJannet reports: 'Now he has less time for the game [snooker] because he is busy writing his crime memoirs, teasingly called "Mr Kipper". The title is a bizarre and cruel reference to the unsolved 1986 kidnapping of London estate agent Suzy Lamplugh whose body has never been found.'

The picture in the *Daily Star* is proof that Sams is quite capable of smuggling photographs out of jail. What of the sealed envelope that Sams had passed to his mother during our interview? Within a few days, the letter arrived on my desk. The contents revealed just why Sams didn't want it to be vetted by the prison's censors.

Undated, it was headed: 'ALSO PUT MY DRIVING LICENCE IN.'

Dear Teena,

This hasn't my number on the top as I shall pass it to my mother Thursday to post.

My mother & Christopher Berry-Dee are coming Thursday. Berry-Dee wasn't passed to visit me as Cat 'A', so all we do is send a VO to my mother from me & a VO to him from a mate who doesn't get many visits. I'll give him an ½ oz of tobacco this week and he will be as happy as a lark.

There is one thing I want you to do. This may sound a strange request. I want you to put my passport and birth certifi-cate in one of the boxes of books. DO NOT HIDE THEM. I want them to be found by security when they check the boxes. Next time you write, put the expirey [sic] on my passport at the top of the first page, e.g, 1992, just the date. I'll know what it means. As I said it sounds a strange request, but there is a reason for it.

At this point in the secret letter, Sams mentions that a national newspaper – I withhold the name for legal reasons – was inter-ested in the photographs. He then wrote:

A camera was smuggled in but the lad was caught bringing an extra film in. The first film had been used on his mates. So another lad had to bring in another film next visit.

Sams goes on to allege:

The Governor couldn't find the camera, so he had to strike a bargain with the lad. Hand the camera in and there will be no disiplinery [sic] proceedings. So we took the shots Sunday and handed the camera to the Governor Monday. I now have the film hidden. The Governor not knowing that another film had been brought in.

The remainder of the letter (which Teena later admitted had been posted to her) is devoted to his bad teeth and the fact that he had turned the West Midlands Police away when they had called to interview him about two other serious offences. 'I told them to write for an appointment,' he said.

Quite how the film was smuggled out poses questions, for

every visitor passing through the normal security barriers is subjected to X-ray, and the roll of film would have shown up.

I persuaded Teena to give me Sams' passport, birth certificate and driving licence. Sams' request for these documents was immediately passed on to the Humberside Police, and after a late-night telephone conversation with me, the prison governor moved Sams to a security cell. The next morning, he was shipped out to HM Prison Wakefield, where, at the time of writing, he continues to reside.

There can be only two reasons why Michael Sams would require such a large sum of money. First, he might have been planning to escape through the seemingly lax security of Full Sutton, which nevertheless houses many of the most dangerous killers in England. Sams might well have pulled it off if the authorities hadn't moved him almost immediately under heavy armed escort to more secure accommodation.

The second scenario is almost too awful to contemplate. Sams himself has alluded to someone whom he wanted 'hit', and during our interview, he made the name known to me. He certainly has a grudge.

NINETEEN

Mr Kipper?

In Britain, the kidnapping of estate agents is an extremely rare event. To date, Michael Sams is the only criminal who has singled them out as victims, and this makes him a unique creature indeed.

We know that he attempted to kidnap two female estate agents in Crewe, and we know he was responsible for abducting Stephanie Slater, so could he also have been responsible for dragging Suzy Lamplugh from the streets of London and killing her?

One of the ingredients that make up any crime is 'opportunity', so did Sams have that opportunity? If it could be proved that he was elsewhere on Monday, 28 July 1986, Michael Sams could not (unless he had an accomplice) have been involved in this estate agent's kidnapping and subsequent murder.

What do the Metropolitan Police, charged with the Lamplugh case, have to say about this? They have made two radically differing statements. A senior detective first told me that he could not rule Sams out of the Lamplugh enquiry. Then the same officer later said that it was impossible for Sams to have killed this woman because he had evidence that showed he couldn't, but he wouldn't specify what it was. On the other hand, the Metropolitan Police press bureau say that the force will look at any material that links Sams with Suzy. In February 1995, the police dug up a well in the garden of 29 New Road, Peterborough, which Sams owned in 1986, but they found nothing. Teena has said that her husband was very secretive about this property. He refused her access to the premises on a number of occasions, and she says that there was a large hole in the garden which Sams started to fill in before subcontracting the work.

As far as Suzy Lamplugh and Sams are concerned, the West Midlands Police continue to sit on the fence, while the West Yorkshire Police – who briefly studied the Lamplugh file – say that they cannot rule Sams out.

Another ingredient would be 'motive', which might be described as the mental mainspring of any criminal act. Proof of motive is never necessary in proving the guilt of a criminal – even the most brilliant jury is helpless in trying to identify the mental processes that might actuate him or her. However, where a motive is proved, it is at least an important factor that needs to be taken into consideration. So would Sams have had any motive for kidnapping Suzy around the time she went missing?

We have already examined Sams and his life, along with his state of mind around 1986. And we have discovered that he was very much involved in buying, renovating and renting out various properties. This would have brought him into frequent contact with estate agents. And in July 1988, as we have seen, Sams was trawling for an estate agent in Worcester – two years after Suzy Lamplugh's disappearance and three years before the abortive kidnap attempts in Crewe. The detailed planning he carried out in 1988 could very well indicate that he had done this before.

Just why he became embroiled in so many property transactions is only known to Michael Sams, but we do know that he was struggling to keep Peterborough Power Tools afloat, while fending off a growing number of irate creditors and being pursued by the Inland Revenue and various building societies. Of course, we must also remember that Sams had planned a kidnapping and ransom bid years beforehand, and now that he'd lost his leg, he was a bitter and twisted character indeed. Teena recalled that, at this time, he'd given her two black eyes, and he exhibited Dr Jekyll and Mr Hyde changes of personality – blowing hot, then cold.

All this is a repeat of the behavioural patterns he would exhibit prior to the attempted kidnaps in Crewe, the attempted kidnap and planned murder of the first Leeds prostitute, the kidnap and murder of Julie Dart, and finally, the kidnap of and successful ransom bid for Stephanie Slater.

There were, therefore, undoubtedly common factors in Sams' life in 1986, 1991 and 1992. Financial pressure could have certainly been the motive for any crime committed in 1986, exactly as it was several years later. No one can argue against that.

Finally, when considering motive, we cannot ignore sexual intent. While studying Sams' life and criminal activities, can one find anything to indicate that he kidnapped and killed for some sexually perverse reason? He had undeniable links to prostitutes, for he used their services, he claims to have had paid sex with Julie Dart before abducting and murdering her, and Stephanie Slater has said that he raped her. However, sex was never part of his original intent, because he kidnapped his victims for one reason only – monetary gain.

Having visited Sams in prison and heard his somewhat disturbing if vague confession about Suzy Lamplugh, I decided to look into this matter more closely. I discussed if with various individuals, and then read closely Andrew Stephen's *The Suzy Lamplugh Story*. I came up with some eight links which tied Sams in with Suzy Lamplugh.

The first and perhaps most obvious link is the similarity between victim types. Lamplugh, Slater and the two women in Crewe were all estate agents who were enticed to escort a prospective male buyer around an empty property – Sams knew all about empty houses. This is an established part of his *modus operandi*. As I have already indicated, kidnapping is a rare offence at the best of times. That two different offenders should select female estate agents as their victims is an even more remote possibility, unless one is dealing with a copycat crime. We will look at this later.

The second link was the alias adopted by Suzy's abductor: the infamous 'Mr Kipper', a name that is echoed in the word 'kidnapper'. Obviously, the criminal would not have used his true name, and we know that Sams used the aliases of 'Bob Southwall' and 'Mr Lettin'. Yet false names originate from somewhere within the criminal's mind, so is it sheer coincidence that 'Lettin' originated from Sams' house-renting activities, while 'Southwall' came from a famous train-spotting haunt frequented by him?

The third link revolves around the description given by a witness who saw a young man and woman talking outside 37

Shorrolds Road. This may or may not have been Suzy's kidnapper, and at first glance, the description of this man seems most unlike Michael Sams, who was not young in 1986 and is far from handsome. Nevertheless, Sams wore a dark business suit on occasion and had dark hair that was swept back, and the witness noticed a stubby upturned nose. This might have fitted Sams, and it might not.

Link four was the fact that the driver's car seat was pushed back from its usual position in Suzy's car. This indicated that someone other than Suzy Lamplugh drove the vehicle, and whoever it was was taller than the missing estate agent. Sams and Suzy were about the same height, so if Sams were the driver, why would he push the seat back? We can look for the answer in Sams' disability. He could drive a manual car like Suzy's Fiesta, but to do so, he would have had to push the seat back to accommodate his locked artificial limb.

This brings us to link number five. This concerns the total lack of forensic evidence found at 37 Shorrolds Road, in the Fiesta and (with the exception of a small splash of blood) at 153 Turnberry Road, where Stephanie escorted Sams on a guided tour. This indicates that whoever overpowered the two young women did so professionally, using controlled threats and force. Sams has a proven track record in this respect.

Link six is the similar *modus operandi* shown by the choice of empty houses with vacant possession in all three estate agent cases. The criminal hunted down this type of property, made appointments with the estate agents involved and, using false names (cryptic at that), lured the women to him.

Link seven is witness Barbara Whitfield's statement that she saw Suzy driving her car. This supports the general police theory that Suzy's kidnapper forced her to drive her car away from Shorrolds Road. However, that theory comes apart with the added knowledge that the driver's seat was pushed back from its normal position. Sams might have wheedled Suzy into letting him drive the car, convincing her that he was merely going to steal it.

Link eight involves the way these women were spirited away. Suzy Lamplugh just vanished into thin air; Julie Dart was spirited away, then killed; and estate agent Stephanie Slater disappeared only to be returned safely home. Therefore, there can be no doubt that this killer was quite able to take Suzy from

37 Shorrolds Road and ensure that she was never seen again.

Of course, all of these links could be so much 'pie in the sky'. But if we cast them to one side – and forget that Sams made a confession of sorts to me at Full Sutton prison and the fact that he is entitling his own book *Mr Kipper* – could there be anything else that might indicate that Sams is the offender responsible for Suzy's kidnapping?

Recently divorced Teena firmly believes that her former husband killed Suzy Lamplugh, for she says he confessed to her while at Winson Green prison. Then he wrote to her:

> *I haven't heard a word from C Berry-Dee. I don't think I can trust him. I gave him one bit of information which no-one knew about (Suzy), and told him how I wanted to use it. The idiot tried to find out if the police knew, and they rumbled what he was on about.*

In a more recent letter to Teena, Sams wrote:

> *He [the author] has omitted to tell you two other things. 1). Suzy Lamplugh's killer had two legs. He was seen running by a taxi driver. I had only one leg in 1986. It was that fact which stopped the West Yorkshire Police investigating it any further. They told me that.*

These remarks from Sams are fascinating when one tries to understand his mind, for on the surface he appears to be denying culpability. However, there isn't a policeman alive who will say that a taxi driver saw Suzy's killer running away because no such person ever made this observation.

Sams also puts in another quite erroneous reference to the West Yorkshire Police by stating that this taxi driver sighting – which is untrue – prevented them investigating him any further. Again, this is quite wrong. The West Yorkshire Police did view the Lamplugh file and, based on that study, cannot say that they have ruled Sams out of the Lamplugh enquiry. So why should Sams create this smokescreen?

The answer lies in the fact that this book should have been published early in 1994, but was delayed as more information came to my attention. Having fallen out with me, Sams then started his own book, which he intends to call *Mr Kipper*. He said in a letter: 'I plan an April or May 94 release of my knowledge as I term it through a National Newspaper. The truth is in them [the case papers].'

The 'knowledge' Sams is referring to is information about Suzy Lamplugh.

By now, the reader will have realised that there is nothing straightforward about Michael Sams. Perhaps that is why he is worthy of such in-depth study. He is the embodiment of contradiction, a pathological liar who is also honest. He continues to confuse the police and society even today. What can we believe and what may we dismiss as a pack of lies? Many of the things he has said and written, which were dismissed by the police as rubbish, have subsequently been found to be completely truthful.

No one believed his story that he'd had sex with Stephanie Slater, but we now know it to be the truth because the victim herself has told us. It seems inconceivable that a one-legged man using a battered moped and an old car could pick up £175,000 in ransom money with the area surrounded by police. Are we not being just a little naïve to dismiss the idea of Sams having an accomplice during several of his crimes? A proportion of the ransom money – £8000 – has never been found. Where has that gone?

It is fact that much of what Sams has said, on and off the record, is correct. So what about Suzy Lamplugh? He has admitted this offence to a number of people, but then denied involvement simply, in my opinion, because he wants his book to be published first. The police, like the rest of us, don't know what to believe. However, the majority of officers will not accept that Sams was trawling for estate agents – as he has also claimed – well before he attempted to abduct two of them in Crewe in July 1991.

Certain parties within the Metropolitan Police have always maintained that Sams never went train-spotting at Paddington – a British Rail station near where Suzy lived and worked – and he, therefore, would not have known the area. Yet when I visited Sams at Full Sutton prison, he made specific reference to Paddington station, and had cryptically told me to get his photographs.

Eventually hundreds of photographs taken by Sams were passed on to me. Several are of Paddington station, and closer inspection reveals that they were taken by Sams using his Praktica MTL5 camera nearer to 1986, when Suzy went missing, than 1991 when Julie Dart was killed.

Of even more significance are the photographs of station signs. Sams stole a number of these signs from platforms at various railway stations, including one from Paddington. We know that Sams brought this one to Peterborough because he went to the trouble of photographing the board in its half-washed state and again when it was sparkling clean. The fully restored Paddington sign was there for all to see in the utility room at Eaves Cottage.

TWENTY

The Mind of Michael Sams

here is irrefutable evidence that Michael Benniman Sams was very unhappy with his lot. And to be fair to him, before he turned to crime he tried hard to make something out of his life, only to come to believe that society had stacked the odds against him.

As a child, he practised hard to become a proficient piano player, and his struggle to achieve academic status is clearly shown by the results of examinations, which he continued to sit until well into his 40s. His running activities as a young man demonstrate mental and physical strengths and a determination to win. This is reinforced when we learn that, after developing tendonitis, he still completed many an arduous race in record time despite the pain. Passing the ordinary driving test was not enough for Sams, who went on to pass the stringent Advanced Motorist exam.

Perhaps he worked too hard for his own good. All those acquainted with him are quick to sing his praises as a hard worker, who spent every hour of the day and night struggling to build up business after business. When one failed, or he lost interest, Sams would start all over again from scratch. Failure never entered his head.

Maybe it was this determination to improve himself at work

and at play that ultimately led to his downfall. His fanatical efforts in every area closed his mind to anything other than success; he had to win at all cost.

The first to suffer were Susan and their two sons. There is no doubt that Sams' dedication to making himself and his family financially secure, linked with Susan's growing maturity and realisation that her husband was losing interest in her, doomed the marriage, and it ended in acrimonious divorce.

Michael could not accept this rejection, and he became bitter. From then on, his relationships with other women took two separate paths. He used the services of prostitutes for sexual gratification while, at the same time, placing advertisements in 'lonely hearts' columns searching for a permanent partner to replace his lost wife. However, he would carry this major rejection – the absent wife, the lost sons, the failed businesses – as so much heavy baggage from relationship to relationship, marriage to marriage.

Sams was on the threshold of criminal activity shortly before Susan divorced him in 1977, and the short prison sentence in 1978, which should have enabled him to mend his ways, only served to wreck his life completely. The loss of his leg was a blow from which he would never recover. Gone was the running, and his ego was devastated. To say he limped painfully to freedom with an even bigger chip on his shoulder would seem a gross understatement. He wrote in his diary: 'By the time my release comes in October, I should be a very bitter person ... society owes me and I will be repaid.'

With all these mental and physical problems, Sams hobbled defiantly into a second marriage, which was over almost before it began. The once fit and immensely proud man was reduced to accepting state benefit. Everything he had worked for and loved dearly had gone down the drain. All those years counted for nothing.

During this period, Sams was swimming against a strong current, and for a disabled person, there was every chance of drowning. However, he eventually found employment with Black & Decker, and this job and the reasonable income it provided should have given him a foundation on which he could attempt to rebuild his shattered life.

However, Sams wanted to run before he could walk. Always there was the compulsive desire to become self-employed, to build his own castle and to make a fortune. But his castles were built on shifting sands.

Peterborough Power Tools was established in 1985 with a substantial sum borrowed from Sams' mother. He also borrowed heavily to purchase various properties. It was as if this buying and selling frenzy was used by the future killer to make up for lost time. Then, the downhill plunge started again – perhaps predictably.

Michael Sams then attempted to improve his standing by returning to crime, and thoughts of Donald Neilson – and his kidnap and murder of Lesley Whittle – gave him sleepless nights. Sams modified the Black Panther's *modus operandi* to incorporate a scheme of his own. He would utilise his knowledge of estate agents and vacant property with the intention of kidnapping and holding someone to ransom.

The first 'someone' may have been Suzy Lamplugh, whom he may have murdered. If so, the ransom bid was abandoned, but where and how did he dispose of the body so that it could not be found? It might be buried next to a disused railway frequented by Sams, or under one of his former houses. The latter theory is not as far-fetched as it might seem, for criminal history is littered with such examples. One has merely to flip back the calendar to the times when Reginald Christie, Dennis Neilsen and, more recently, Frederick West were active to realise that, under floorboards, foundations and the earth of back gardens rests many a corpse. So why should Michael Sams be an exception?

Again, using his experience of estate agents, empty houses and railways, in 1991 Sams prepared himself for the kidnapping of the estate agents in Crewe. From the evidence of Sams' own photographic collection, we can see that he was always trainspotting at that mecca for rail enthusiasts. There is also some indication that he was intending to use a location near Millmeece in Staffordshire for the cash ransom drop. We do know that he did use the bridge at Millmeece in the British Rail extortion bid.

Sams was in terrible financial straits when the bid to kidnap the Crewe estate agents failed. He looked for an easier target and settled on a prostitute in Leeds. This required an adjustment in his *modus operandi*, but just as he had experience of estate agents, he was familiar with hookers and knew only too well where to find them. This particular one escaped by the skin of her teeth. Perhaps she got away because Sams had pulled his trousers down for the sexual act – giving a whole new meaning to the phrase 'caught with your pants down'.

With another failure under his belt, Sams continued to polish his plan and tried again a short time later. He admits that he would have killed any of these young women; he would be 'repaid' regardless of any cost to human life.

We know he kidnapped Julie Dart. Although here we are examining the dysfunctional mind of Michael Sams, it must be emphasised that he was – is – not insane. Callously, he coaxed the terrified young woman to write a letter; then, as she talked to him, he crept up behind her and smashed a ball-pein hammer into her skull no fewer than three times. Still she was not dead, so he took a ligature, wrapped it tightly around her throat and throttled what little life was left to her. A few days later, with the bloodied corpse beginning to create a stench, he disposed of Julie in a remote Lincolnshire field. As might be expected, this 'grave' was near the East Coast Railway and close to a disused railway track.

Sams doesn't know the meaning of failure. Despite the fact that he'd already murdered Julie, he tried to obtain a large ransom for her 'safe return', only giving up when it became obvious that the scam was becoming too dangerous. So he turned to blackmailing British Rail. Again he modified his *modus operandi*, but retained his usual tools of railways, letters, phone boxes and a familiar territory.

However, like the other bids, the British Rail job was doomed to failure. Financially trapped, Sams backtracked along the mental blueprint of his life – one might say his original *modus operandi* – to try once again to kidnap an estate agent. This time it was Stephanie Slater.

This was a polished performance of criminal activity, and he exhibited a remarkable ability to outwit the nation's police and make fools out of them. The only flaw in Sams' otherwise excellent scheme was to become emotionally involved with Stephanie, which led to him dropping her off near her home and being spotted by Pervis Barnaby.

That they had sex is now, somewhat belatedly, a matter of public record. Stephanie Slater has confirmed it and Sams concurs. That a charge of rape will be brought three years after the alleged offence is another issue, for it seems that there is no corroborating evidence, or so the *Daily Mail* informs us.

However, it is patently obvious that there was a lack of consent on the part of Ms Slater. If she did submit to sexual intercourse, then it was submission induced by force, fear or fraud, and that is still rape, however one dresses it up.

Michael Sams became, at times, a mirage. One minute he was there, the next moment he had vanished. One of the many interesting facets of his criminal activity was that he committed his kidnappings and attempted kidnappings within an approximate 70-mile radius of his homes or places of work. At the time of Suzy Lamplugh's disappearance in London, he was living around 70 miles away in Peterborough. The attempted abductions in Crewe proves the same point, for he was living and working around Newark. The attempted kidnapping of the first prostitute and the successful kidnapping of Julie Dart were both carried out in Leeds, about the same distance again. And, finally, we find Stephanie Slater within that evil circle.

There is a distinctive spatial pattern in Sams' behaviour when it comes to kidnap locations. Like a wild animal, this criminal captured his prey, then immediately returned to his lair, where he was comfortable in his own territory. Sams constantly drew on his inherent psychological narrative – the building blocks that formed his day-to-day behaviour.

As the British Rail extortion bid showed the police, the black-mailer was an individual who was clearly familiar with locomotives, tracks and stations. In this environment, Sams was relaxed, and therefore able to function more efficiently. Not unlike the 70-mile radius employed in the initial stages of his kidnappings, the railway network also formed a defined area of his territory. One merely has to check a map to locate the bridges, railway lines – disused or otherwise – and stations, then link these with the letter-posting points, telephone kiosks and ransom drops, to learn quite a bit about the criminal's working territory. All of these locations meant something to Michael Sams.

Looking at those markers on a map, one can readily draw interlacing lines. Newark – his base – was in the centre of a line running from Leeds to Huntingdon. He tried to abduct a prostitute in Leeds, and he kidnapped Julie Dart from the same city. Sams lived at Sutton-on-Trent, and the East Coast Railway passed the bottom of Eaves Cottage's garden. Further south is

Newark, where he worked, and where there was a station that serves that major railway. Travelling south, we pass Grantham where he bought his pet food, and further on is Easton where Julie's body was found, close by a disused railway, too. In the locality is Stoke Summit, where he and perhaps an accomplice buried the ransom money. Peterborough, where he also once lived, fits neatly into this scheme as just up the line was Huntingdon where he posted two letters.

Each of us evolves an inner narrative, and try as we may, we can never entirely escape from it. We might modify our thought patterns through day-today learning, but the basic blueprint will remain fixed until we die. As far as we may roam, we always have the desire to revisit our roots – scanning the photograph album, seeing our places of birth, returning to former schools.

Michael Sams was living, like all of us, a pre-programmed script, and not even a criminal can escape the confines of this psychological net. He used a specific *modus operandi* for his criminal activities, and this was part of the larger *modus operandi* of his daily life.

Sams left a trail of suffering and human destruction in his trail. Maybe he has killed more times than we know or care to imagine; maybe we have become desensitised to the horror of brutal homicide, as long as it doesn't take place on our doorstep. Have we heard the last of this once dangerous individual? There is a growing body of opinion – which includes many police officers and well-known TV journalists – that we have not, for most of the terrible claims made by the cryptic killer are sadly being shown to have been true. And, as I write, the search for a possible accomplice gathers speed.

Of the principal characters involved in the case of *Regina v. Michael Benniman Sams*, the killer languishes in Wakefield Prison where he occupies his time writing his book, to be called *Mr Kipper*. Recently he became infuriated when another inmate took his artificial leg and threw it from a window.

Stephanie Slater has written her book and now lives quietly on the Isle of Wight. Kevin Watts still lives and works in the suburbs of Birmingham. Teena has now divorced Michael Sams but is still very fond of him. When she recently visited him, they kissed and embraced in what was called a 'tearful reunion'. She wore her wedding ring for the meeting.

The Dart family still mourn their lost daughter, while her killer lives on in prison. Michael Benniman Sams – alias 'Bob Southwall', 'Mr Lettin' and, perhaps, 'Mr Kipper' – will not kill again.